Ivo Stourton was born in 1982 and read English at Cambridge. This is his first novel.

THE NIGHT CLIMBERS

Ivo Stourton

BLACK SWAN

TRANSWORLD PUBLISHERS
61–63 Uxbridge Road, London W5 5SA
a division of The Random House Group Ltd
www.booksattransworld.co.uk

THE NIGHT CLIMBERS
A BLACK SWAN BOOK: 9780552773836

First published in Great Britain
in 2007 by Doubleday
an imprint of Transworld Publishers
Black Swan edition published 2008

Addresses for Random House Group Ltd companies outside the UK
can be found at: www.randomhouse.co.uk
The Random House Group Ltd Reg. No. 954009

The Random House Group Limited supports The Forest Stewardship
Council (FSC), the leading international forest certification organisation.
All our titles that are printed on Greenpeace approved FSC certified paper
carry the FSC logo. Our paper procurement policy can be found at
www.rbooks.co.uk/environment

Typeset in 11/16¼pt Giovanni Book by
Kestrel Data, Exeter, Devon.
Printed in the UK by
CPI Cox & Wyman, Reading, RG1 8EX.

2 4 6 8 10 9 7 5 3 1

For Miff Stourton, Clare Wagg and Jessica Lennard,
without whom I would be someone else.

1

There were security barriers in the foyer, thick glass turnstiles that fell open when you stuck the right card in the slot. The receptionists, however, were the real security. Their 'Can I help you?' and bright smiles were the modern equivalent of 'Who goes there?' It was a surprise, therefore, to find Jessica sitting in my black leather chair, waiting for me to return from the basement gym, where I had spent a cathartic lunchbreak pummelling my personal trainer, sweating out the last drops of the previous night's whisky. I knew from the way she looked at me, tilting her head forwards and peering out from under her blonde fringe with a lopsided smile, that she had lied her way in. Her expression was just as I remembered, and pulled me back into the past with the force of a scent. At thirty-two she was already losing her looks. They were not going gracefully, with the haunting quality that briefly heightens doomed beauty. She had bags under her eyes and a spot on her chin where her make-up had formed a beige scab. I took no pleasure in this, but I did take pleasure from the fact that I didn't care. Indifference, not feigned but genuinely felt, was a hard-won victory, and I prized it. I shook her hand and smiled.

She had been playing with the objects on my desk. My pens were scattered over the blotting paper.

'How can I help you?' I asked.

'Don't you want to know how I got in?'

'I pretended to be from London Underground. I read about the deal you're doing, turning public services private. You used to be so left wing. I'm your two-thirty.' She grinned. 'You look nice. And you look rich. Nice and rich.' She leant across the desk and lifted one of the silver balls on my Newton's cradle, letting it go to hit its fellow with a gentle click.

As I looked at her, I tried to gauge her financial situation. It seemed the quickest way to divining what she wanted. Her platinum hair had been recently cut and highlighted. Her fingernails were salon neat and unpainted, but glazed. The jewellery she wore was simple, a scuffed Tiffany's silver pendant. Her black suit could have been tailored, but Jessica had always had a body that made cheap clothes look expensive. In the days when I had known her well, she had practised a policy of sartorial simplicity designed to exhibit her natural gifts, and I think to embarrass the girls who dressed up. I could not tell whether this policy had survived the passing of her beauty. I thought on the whole that choice

8

had given way to necessity. There was no ring on her finger.

Jessica sat back in her chair and met my eye as if to say, 'And what has become of you?'

'So, you're my two-thirty. I bill at two hundred and fifty pounds an hour. What can I do for you?'

'You can give me a discount, for starters.'

We looked at each other with fixed smiles, headlights speeding towards one another in the dark. She relented first. 'I need a place to stay for a few days. I don't want to go to a hotel. I don't want to go to friends. I don't want to be found.'

She rose from my seat. Her movements still had the light accent of childhood ballet. Born of parental ambition, undone by a teenage growth spurt, a graceful precision was the last legacy of repetition and bleeding toes. To my displeasure I noticed that behind the chair sat a briefcase and a piece of fake Louis Vuitton luggage, its beige midriff distended with female packing. Jessica knew the difference that social leverage could make, and it would be that much more awkward to dismiss her if she had all the practical necessities already to hand. I wondered what the receptionists downstairs would think of my attractive female clients arriving prepared for an overnight stay. It was typical of Jessica to cause disruption simply by virtue of her presence. With an air of unimpeachable honesty, she addressed me eye to eye. The air was still filled with the faint metallic click of the toy she had set in motion on my desk.

'Is there somewhere else we can go to talk? I don't mean to be melodramatic, I just haven't seen you in a long time, and if I'm going to get turned down I'd prefer to do it somewhere pretty. Don't you have client hospitality or something? After all, I am a client.' She grinned again.

We stood in the lift, and I watched as the two halves of my image slid together in the metallic panels of the doors. Jessica's appraising look was still fresh in my mind, and I checked myself out discreetly. My dark hair was perfectly slicked; my blue eyes glowed even in the dull surface of the metal. My arms were thick from the gym. The slight bulge of flesh around my collar appeared again today. I raised my chin a little to tighten the skin. Jessica almost caught me in the reflection, and I looked away. The lift deposited us smoothly on the top floor, like riding up in the palm of a giant. The doors slid apart, and my image divided and disappeared. By the time we arrived Jessica was solemn, demonstrating one of those mercurial shifts of mood that had confounded her youthful suitors. The young men at Cambridge could never tell whether to court her as a child, a princess, an executive or a clown. Only the few of us who had become truly close to her had learnt to read her sudden shifts, like sailors at the mercy of an unpredictable sky.

The great glass wall of client reception disclosed a cinematic view of the City, stretching down to the glittering ribbon of the river and the stately dome of St Paul's. On the South Bank the great blocks of culture faced the towers of commerce, the National Theatre hunkered down on the edge of the Thames, its grey concrete balconies camouflaged against the sky. I put on my overcoat and led Jessica past the ranks of black leather sofas and neatly stacked periodicals, and the fresh fruit and orchids quietly dying in their glass vessels.

The Japanese garden on client reception had one of the best views in the City. Old enemies appeared on the eastern horizon: Magic Circle law firms sitting in state by Moorgate. From the balcony you could see St Andrew's Church, a tiny nub of conscience subsisting in the centre of the financial monoliths, so much older than the buildings that blocked it from the sunlight. The leaves of the weeping willow in the churchyard spilled over the wrought-iron railings on to the pavement. The roof garden itself was composed of large obsidian stones and elegant little shrubs arranged on a bed of white sand. The sand was raked into perfect parallel trenches, like a ploughed field in delicate miniature. A slate walkway paved the edges, and formed a bridge over a tiny stream that bubbled up through the rocks. The sky seemed huge so many floors above the skyline, with no other buildings hemming it in. It closed like the lid of a freezer over the cold city. I felt proud to have brought her up here, on top of my impressive building, above my kingdom.

I slid the door closed behind us, and heard the comforting click of the catch, sealing my working world inside like the body of a despot in a vast stone tomb. The wind was strong so high above the street, and carried a film of drizzle that coated the garden with a thin layer of cold moisture. She walked away from me, her heels sounding on the grey slate, and leant on the stainless-steel railings that separated the balcony from the empty air behind.

'I know what you're thinking, James. I'm not on the run from the Mafia or the police, and I don't want money from you or help or anything else really except a couple of showers' worth of hot water. You work during the day. I go out at night. You won't even see me, if you don't want to.'

'I don't know how you are placed financially, Jessica,' I said, slipping into my professional idiom, 'but it seems to me that you could easily budget for a hotel with a higher degree of anonymity than an old university buddy's house.'

She sat on the metal bar that ran around the side of the balcony and put her feet against the large black boulder nearest the edge of the carefully raked white sand, dimpled from the raindrops. Behind her I could see the roof of a building the architects had never intended for public view. It was ten storeys down. I thought how best to guide her back from her perch without showing that it made me uncomfortable.

'You have become pompous. Is that what we are? Old "university buddies"?'

Angry horns bleated down in the street. With her hands clutched around the bar, and her shoulders hunched a little forwards against the chill, she straightened her long legs slightly, leaning her slender torso fractionally backwards into space. I felt the sharp edge of a fledgling concern tapping against the inside of my skull. With a steady voice, I answered: 'I haven't seen you in the best part of a decade. What would you prefer to be called?' She was already drawing me away from a proper examination of her motives.

'Oh, I don't know. Something with a little feeling. Playmate, darling, co-conspirator . . .' This last one she delivered in a theatrical, breathy whisper.

'I think I have company this weekend,' I said.

'She'll understand. Women like to be made to wait. You can't be overly available.'

Not these women, I thought.

She shivered and tugged the thin material of her jacket tight around her thin body and straightened her legs with little jerks, a childish gesture of distraction that pushed her body further and further out over the edge. I clenched my hands behind my back so that she could not see them. There was a light wind, so high above the street, and it carried the loose strands of her blonde hair up and over her cheekbones.

'My place isn't big. I don't have a spare bed, and—'

She pushed suddenly with her feet; the gesture carried her too far and she fell first backwards, then forwards with a spasmodic tightening of her stomach to the floor. A surge of adrenalin manned my chest, and I ran towards her with an inarticulate cry. She was laughing with the exhilaration of her near disaster, and with triumph at the terror in my face. I had started out across the perfect garden, breaking the patterned surface with my feet. The cut of my suit pushed me into an unnatural feminine jog, and I knew that I must have looked ridiculous. I acknowledged her victory with a sheepish smile, and walked over to where she leant laughing against the rail. Her laughter gave way to a coughing fit, and she bent over almost like an old man, clutching her stomach. Somehow the moment seemed vulnerable rather than disgusting.

'So, can I stay or what?' she said when she had regained some measure of control.

'Fuck it. Why not.'

She was lying, but there would be time to uncover her lie. I could not remember when an obligation had been placed on me that was purely human. I did things because of what I had signed, what was expected, what was right, what was paid. This I would do because of who had asked me. I said yes because I would have done anything for her once, and required nothing in return.

14

There were once many people who would have done anything for her, but from me she would have accepted.

'We'll stay up all night. It'll be like old times.' She said, 'You might even have fun.'

My flat, designed to accommodate no one but myself and infrequent visitors whose opinions were irrelevant, was not the most hospitable place. Jessica cast a critical eye around the apartment. She lifted the single crystal tumbler from the surface of the table, sniffed the residue of dirty brown liquid and made an exaggerated moue of surprise and disgust, wrinkling her nose. I did not remember putting the bottle back in the kitchen, but was relieved that I had. She inspected the apartment with the judgemental eye of a mother-in-law.

The bookshelves, painted a cream that was chipped in places to reveal an old, somnolent green, were entirely filled with law books and DVDs. The former were mostly guides to commercial litigation and corporate finance, but there were some, such as my Chambers guide, that were as old as the decision I had taken to study the law. It had been a sudden and arbitrary choice, made in the conflicting currents of idealism and financial necessity that swept me along in the year after graduation. The DVDs were mostly pornography, a relatively expensive habit that had accrued over the years into a whole library of perversion. She began to browse the titles. She spared me the humiliation of reading them out loud.

'I watch a lot of porn. It helps me switch my mind off.'

'How can you find these sexy?' she asked, running her finger over the DVD boxes, turned spine out to reveal slivers of garish nudity.

'I don't find them sexy,' I lied, 'I find them distracting.'

'Why do you have them all on display?'

'I'm not ashamed of what I like.' And no one ever comes here to see. 'Shall we talk about something else?'

'Sure,' she said, casting one last critical glance over the ranks of DVDs.

It occurred to me as her eyes dissected the visible portion of my life that I was seeing her in a curious double perspective. I knew her well, as only a friend can who has seen that final transition from adolescence into adulthood. I had watched her opinions and her priorities lose their plasticity and cool in the mould of complacent maturity. But I did not know the barest details of her life. She was unmarried, or divorced, that much I knew from the lack of a ring. Something in her manner, a certain residual selfishness, precluded the possibility of kids. She did not have the distracted amiability of someone used to factoring others into their decisions, and her stomach still fit snugly into the unforgiving waistband of her suit trousers. I looked at her flat belly with the judgemental eye of a consumer. It was not right to turn this gaze on her, but habit was stronger than morality, and I knew she could watch out for her own interests. I allowed the fingertips of memory to run over the thin white line where the surgeon had slipped his tongs into her belly, the brand of childhood appendicitis. Despite the great blank of her personal narrative, I still knew her by the way she nosed around my flat, peering into confidential files and collecting dust on the tip of her finger in a playful parody of a disapproving woman. It occurred to me how meaningless were the details of someone's biography beyond a certain age, when placed in the balance against an understanding of their nature.

'Do you see anyone at all? From college?' she asked, peering out of the window with a deliberate nonchalance that roused my suspicion.

'No.'

'I've come across them once or twice over the years.'

'How is Michael?'

'Don't you read the papers?'

'I read the Business section.'

'He's dead.'

'Mountaineering? Sailing?'

'Testicular cancer. He has his own foundation now.'

'How about Lisa?'

She smiled. 'I'm sure Lisa's fine.'

She looked around the room, searching for something. 'Do you still paint?' she asked. She had been looking for an easel.

'No. Did you come back to discuss our contemporaries?' I said it more sharply than I had intended.

Jessica cocked her head and scrutinized me, trying to decide whether or not she had been slighted. 'No,' she said in a measured tone, 'I didn't come to see you to reminisce. Or rather I did, but not pointlessly. We've got a problem, and I thought I should warn you. In case there's something you can do to protect yourself.'

There was more than a hint of posturing in this statement, and she larded her motives with altruism to reproach me for my rudeness. Nevertheless, her words induced a brief wave of nausea, of old fear rising like bubbles through a thick liquid. 'What problem?' I asked, keeping my breathing under control.

She popped the catches on her briefcase and removed a folded newspaper from the neat beige interior (the leather was so pristine that I suspected the briefcase was a prop). It was a copy of the *Telegraph*, dated four days previously. 'It took me a little while to track you down,' she said by way of explanation.

I did not have to read the article to get the gist. I felt faint. The headline was enough to release all my fears. My head spun. 'Dire Financial Straits at Oxbridge College' read the banner in thick black type.

I wanted to throw the paper away, as if not being able to read it would make it untrue, but read on compulsively. There was a satisfying finality in seeing my nightmares resolved in black and white. Tudor College, Cambridge, after a series of extremely poor investments, was hoping to cover a five-million-pound black hole in its budget by selling off a couple of pictures from its permanent collection.

Jessica stood silently whilst I read. It occurred to me I should be relatively grateful to her, for bringing the news to me like this. I tried to picture the scene where she, sitting at the breakfast table before work, perhaps with her partner or flatmate, had turned the pages, and come with no warning upon the article. It would have shoved the orbit of her life aside, with the sudden force of the policeman's knock late in the night when your loved one should have been home.

'How long would we get?' she asked, perching on the back of the chair with her long legs lightly crossed and her arms folded across her midriff.

'How long?' I said, unwilling to understand.

'How long. As in sentence.'

'I'm not a criminal solicitor.'

'Oooh . . . evasion. That can't be good.' She smiled. I saw that my discomfort provided her with relief from her own. I could help her by emphasizing my fear, but I wasn't sure I wanted to.

I relented. 'Well, there are all kinds of circumstances that could be mitigating, but if it went wrong . . .'

'Then?'

'Seven years, give or take.'

She was silent as she absorbed the information.

'I'd be thirty-nine,' she said quietly, looking out of the window at the rain.

Too old for children. The thought scuttled out of some mental crevice, and I crushed it quickly underfoot. 'You'd be out in five for good behaviour.'

'What makes you think I'd behave?' she said, and grinned.

This was the kind of response we had always adored in her. Yet now, made in the dingy confines of my living room, with no one to hear her defiance but herself and me, and no one at all to believe in it, it seemed a tired routine. I was surprised to find I remembered how she took her coffee. I went into the kitchen and made her a cup, whilst she sat at my dining table (there was dust on all but two of the seats) and scrutinized the pink pages of my *FT* with the attention of a general studying the maps of his campaign. I topped up my cup with the bottle from the cupboard. We each took advantage of the few minutes we had apart, and when I came back into the room it was to find her calm. She had removed her suit jacket. The blouse underneath was white, and she wore it with the sleeves rolled up. She held her coffee cupped in both her small hands, and leant forwards with her elbows on her knees. It occurred to me how unfair I had been in assuming she wanted money. She needed a different kind of support, and one I was far less willing to give.

'Are we fucked?' she asked, taking just a hint of relish in her own frankness. She seemed invigorated by the danger, or perhaps by being brought back into proximity with the past. She looked alive. She removed a cigarette from her bag and lit up without asking.

My emotions were stiff and weak, like unused muscles, and they protested under the weight of this moment. I was struggling to find the right mixture of feeling, as if trying to speak a foreign language in which I used to be fluent, searching forlornly for the right word to break the spell of incomprehension. 'I don't know. Have you contacted Lisa?'

She looked down at the table and tapped off a length of ash. It lay like a dead insect in the bottom of the glass. 'You're the lawyer. We made a deal with her. You remember.' It was not a question, it was a statement of fact. Neither of us could have forgotten the last time we had seen our silent partner.

She continued, and I felt from the way her eyes shifted that she was looking back into her own head, reading me a prepared speech off the walls of her sockets 'I've forgotten a lot of what happened. I've tried hard to forget, in fact. Before I read this, I had half convinced myself it was all a dream, a year-long dream from which I woke at graduation, and my adult life was my real life, my waking life. Now I need to make a risk assessment. Once I know what the risk is, I can begin to plan. But I've done such a good job of forgetting. I can't . . .' She laughed, apparently in frustration at having to make the admission. 'I can't do this on my own. I need your memories.'

She looked relieved, and I knew she had finally disgorged her real purpose. As the perpetual gloom of London in winter deepened into night proper, I felt a tremendous sense of isolation. The ticking of the pipes in the walls and the rush of water in the metal system sounded like cooling rock, as if the sun had disappeared from the sky, and heat was quietly seeping out of the earth. I felt the walls of my skull had expanded to the size of my room, and the two of us had climbed inside for warmth. It felt good to have someone else to share this loneliness, but terrible also, because she would have access to all the classified files, the old diaries, the scrapbooks and albums my ego had collected with the fervour of a devoted fan, and the extent of my obsession with the past would no longer be a secret. I felt some-times as if my life had stopped at twenty, when Jessica said hers had begun. The subsequent period had been outwardly active; I had acquired all the concrete evidence of a life; the possessions and the CV of a professional man. But no tendrils of affection had grown out from me to embrace another mind. Instead, my thoughts and feelings had continually interrogated that year, trying to guess its purpose. I wanted to tell Jessica these thoughts, to draw comfort from her company, but without the hidden context of my life they would seem like em-barrassing melodrama.

'I'll go through it all with you, if you like,' I said evenly. 'Do you want a drink? It's Friday night, after all.'

Her scarlet lips blossomed suddenly into a broad smile. A minute crack split the make-up over her spot. I smelt her perfume, a delicate citrus scent mixed with the chemical tang of tobacco. The smell bypassed the border controls at the edge of consciousness, slipping right through with its illicit cargo of associations, and I felt a warm stirring in my groin.

'Fine,' she said.

I went back into the kitchen and poured us both a generous whisky. Whisky always tasted like memory to me.

I allowed myself a moment of self-abandon, like an old addict who finally disclaims his abstinence. I lifted my glass. 'To Francis. He fucked us all in the end.'

'To old times,' she said, raising her tumbler. When she drank, she left the print of her mouth on the rim of the glass.

And then I knew the feeling – it was regret

2

When I first arrived at Cambridge at the age of eighteen, my world fell apart into two hemispheres like a neatly halved melon. There were, it appeared to me, those who were talked about and those who were not. All I wanted in life was to be one of the former.

There are two striking things about this judgement, which appeared with the benefit of hindsight. The first is its inaccuracy. I believed fervently that a small group formed the centre of the conversational universe, a hub around which all news and interest must necessarily orbit. The majority continued with their own lives, formed their own relationships, made their own betrayals and alliances, but always lived in the shadow of these others, these elevated beings. In reality, university society was too large to be hierarchical in the same way that school had been, and too small to evolve the hierarchies of power and celebrity that emerge in the real world. The people who organized the parties and wrote the newspapers might have been elevated above the rest of the university, but the other students did not really care about the lives of their social superiors any more than the fish care about the birds. The second is how little it mattered what was being said. I didn't care what the nature of a reputation might be, so long as it was a prominent one.

As to why I made this judgement, it is difficult to recall. I know that it appeared in the guise of a revelation, something so obvious and true that it obviated the need for rational questioning. I had not been a popular boy at Solhurst, a minor Catholic public school in Dorset, and I felt that popularity was the missing ingredient that would turn me from stodgy fare into a delicacy. I was reasonably good-looking, a natural sportsman, academically quick and hard-working, but I could not make friends, could not get laid, and had yet to find my own version of fun.

My father and Evelyn Waugh had warned me against the dangers of making early friends, so I deliberately avoided contact with my fellow freshers in my first weeks, hoping to cultivate a vague air of mystery, which would bring me to the notice of the social elite. Fortune intervened to aid me in my plan, as my rooms on New Court were hidden away up a creaking flight of oaken stairs. Through the lead latticed windows I could observe the courtyard, a neat green oval of grass ringed with paving stones and a mantle of ochre gravel. Around the edges of the drive were parked the cars of various fellows, each one a mechanical version of their personalities. There was the ancient Daimler owned by the Chair of Theology, a man who had come to prominence through sheer familial endowment, the Porsche 911 of the young Computer Sciences supervisor who had made a fortune in the early nineties and wore only black, the muddy bulk of the Range Rover owned by a classicist doing her Ph.D, who was wire thin and always seemed to be engaging in some sport that necessitated tweed. From my vantage point I could see the young men and women, away from home for the first time, stumble home drunk late at night, and rise late in the morning. The medieval masonry had prevented the installation of heated plumbing in several of the staircases, and I would see them emerge at midday, crossing the cold stones barefoot in their dressing gowns to reach the shower block in the eastern corner. At the centre of the lawn stood a great beech tree, its arms sweeping in a magnanimous gesture of inclusion down to the edges of the grass. Its copper-coloured leaves were beginning to fall, and clog the drains that lined the gravel. It was early October at the end of an Indian summer, and it was still warm enough to have the windows open in the midday sunshine, but chilly in the evenings. Early in the morning the court was filled with the crunch of gravel and the brusque chat of sport, as rosy-cheeked girls set out for lacrosse practice on the Backs, their hair in ponytails. Their cries and the clatter of wood on wood floated back on the clear air, like the tumult of a distant battle.

It soon became apparent to me that my plan had some major flaws. Firstly, I was disgruntled to discover that, far from having to avoid the friendly advances of my fellow students like the whiskery kisses of a maiden aunt, I was completely ignored by all the other freshers. My plan to avoid making the wrong sort of friends worked too well, and I made none at all. Soon the artificial events set up by the college to encourage two hundred socially awkward teenagers to integrate had given way to an organic blossoming of social contact, and in the rooms around and below my own, bad guitar music, loud conversation and inexpert sex were all audible late into the night. Work too began in earnest and a stern supervisor, disapproving of undergraduate excess, set me two essays a week, so that I had to spend much of my time in the library. When I began to get friendly nods from the creatures, bespectacled and pallid, who spent more hours in the reference section than they did in the sunlight, I realized my plan to cultivate an aloof persona had gone disastrously awry, and I was in fact someone the socially incompetent workaholics recognized as one of their own. In the college cafeteria I sat alone, but I would try to place myself near to large groups, so that a casual observer would think me a part of them. I bought a second-hand TV and began to customize my routine to fit around soap operas.

From my poor social vantage point I could not see out over the heads of the crowd to where the speakers sat, elevated on their dais of common interest. I did not know whom to approach, could not divine who was popular and who might make a good patron. I had assumed that this division would be so obvious as to negate any need for investigation, but having cut myself off almost completely from my peers I found it impossible to get any measure of the fashions.

When our ingenuity fails us, fate sometimes steps in to take up the slack. It is events like this which, when seen from a distant vantage point, give our lives the shape of purpose, like a face appearing in an outcrop of white cloud. In my case, fate erupted into my life through the window in the early hours of Thursday morning in the third week of term, just after I had finished work, closed my copy of medieval English lyrics on my bureau and turned off my lights. My room was situated at the very top of the staircase. Beyond the window set into the eaves loomed the sandstone squares of the crenellations, the ornamental battlements that ringed the top of New Court. I had climbed up and poked my head out through this window several times whilst observing the comings and goings in the court below, and had discovered between the edge of the sill and the fanciful walls a narrow lead-plated walkway that housed the gutter for the sloping roof. It was almost like a private balcony, elevated and inaccessible, and I had already earmarked it for sunbathing in the summer.

On this particular night I had heard cries and shouting from the middle courtyard, but I had not bothered to look, as there was a strong correspondence between these disturbances and kicking-out time at Cindy's, one of the local nightclubs. I lay in bed and pictured the scene with my eyes closed: a girl sitting in the gutter, dressed in a miniskirt and carrying her shoes, laughing or crying whilst two boys tried to lever her into an upright position. It was then that I heard what sounded like movement in the ceiling, and the branches of a tree tapping at my window. At first I thought I must be imagining the sound, since I could think of no explanation for it, but the knocking grew more insistent, and was joined by a man's voice, a loud stage whisper ordering me to 'Open the fucking window!'

For a few seconds I could not reconcile the presence of the voice with the position of my room: the height of the building and the lateness of the hour combined to make the intrusion so unlikely that I could not quite believe that it was happening. Suddenly another noise jolted me into action. The acoustics of the stone stairwell leading up to my room tended to amplify voices and footsteps, and I heard the slap of patent-leather shoes hitting the bottom flight, and the pant of laboured breath. There were further shouts from the courtyard, and now I could make out the odd word: 'Quick!' and 'Don't let him—'

By this time the knocking on my window had given way to the sound of someone trying to force the catch. The huff and rumble on the stairs grew louder as the intruder rose through the floors. I unhooked the catch and, as if the night had given birth through my window, a swarthy gleaming head, slightly podgy and sweating with exertion, popped through with a gust of cold air and a stream of abuse into my bedroom. A pair of meaty arms followed swiftly and gripped my shoulders, and with my help the man wrestled his cumbersome body through the narrow hatch and landed on my floor like a side of beef on the butcher's slab. It was only when he picked himself up that I realized I recognized him.

'Walker, yes?' he panted, and, attesting to the ludicrously strong hold of manners on the English upper-middle classes, he stuck out his hand in greeting. He was still adjusting his corduroy trousers, which had been pulled down to the tops of his thighs by his passage through the window, revealing his boxer shorts. In the light from my anglepoise lamp I could make out thinning black hair and a rugby top smeared with black grime and lichen from the roof. He finished adjusting his trousers in a last deft heave. He stood with his feet firmly apart and his broad shoulders facing me squarely, taking possession of the room he had just entered through the window. I had been lying in bed without a shirt and, despite the fact that he was the intruder, he made me feel uncomfortably conscious of my bare chest. I resisted the temptation to cross my arms over my stomach and reached out to meet him in open handshake. Our eyes and palms met in unison, and I held his officious blue gaze as he covered my hand with dirt from the tiles. 'Michael Findlay. I was two years above you at school. West House, class of ninety-eight. May I hide?'

His tone expressed both tolerance and mild indignation, as if anyone who knew how to behave would already have offered him a closet. We both cast our eyes around my room, the search given some urgency by the acceleration of the feet on the stairs in response to the thud of Findlay's body on the floorboards. As a result of my relative isolation, I had begun in my first fortnight to dote on my room. As far as my budget would allow, I thought it exceptionally elegant. I had constructed the decor around a recurrent fantasy that had now been honed over many idle hours into a perfect model of desires fulfilled. In my daydream I was bringing a beautiful girl back from a very exclusive party and, as I turned on the lights in my room, a whole new world of insight into this charming stranger was revealed to her. The objects and furniture, carefully chosen and arranged, induced in her a long pre-coital swoon in which every detail raised her estimation of my virtues and abilities, tightening her desire until it shook with tension like a single string of a violin. The dusty prints above my bed (bought from Scope for their antique air and sober sepia colouration) indicated my maturity. I had invested a considerable portion of my student loan in Egyptian cotton sheets from Peter Jones, a fabric I had read about in an airport novel, which I felt had an air of sophisticated experience. The brass art deco lamp, the bottle of good Scotch, the books liberally arranged (and, in some cases, read) to express a whole spectrum of cultural interest, all had their story to tell. The most prized possession, the one most likely in the confines of my imagination to initiate the final swoon into my arms, was the easel complete with fresh canvas standing in the corner, where the light from the window lasted longest. The old mahogany bureau (part of the room's original furnishings) was entirely taken up with a series of drawers, and the fitted cupboard in the corner by the door was quite small. The interior of the room had been tailored, however optimistically, to facilitate a seduction, and it was difficult to see how it could be used to harbour fugitives.

Michael was more resourceful than me. First, he switched on the radio beside my bed. It was tuned in to Radio One, and quiet R and B covered the sound of his breathing. Without waiting for an invitation, he moved with surprising speed, his portly frame bouncing lightly, and hid himself behind the blank canvas on the easel. His arm reached around from behind the white square and pulled a second picture, a landscape that had been turned face out against the wall, against the thin stand to cover his legs. This irritated me greatly, as the picture in question was a pencil sketch for a larger oil, showing the detail of the stone statues above the majestic colonnade of the college library, and I was quite pleased with it. I did not have time to register any dissent, however, as at that moment there was a knocking on the door, a sound that managed to convey polite urgency by its insistence.

I took my dressing gown from the back of the door and slipped it over my naked chest. When I opened it, I found one of the college porters waiting outside. Despite the coolness of the night he was sweating, the beads collecting under the brim of his bowler hat, and he was breathing heavily from the climb up the stairs. The porters were the college security, the gatekeepers and the guards, and I could never quite tell if they were my servants or my masters. They wore black waistcoats and bowler hats that made them seem like the vengeful spirits of a past century.

'Sorry to bother you, sir, but I wondered if I might come in and have a look out of your window?'

'Sure,' I said. Though his words had been couched as a request, they were delivered as an order. I had already resolved not to lie for the man hiding in the corner of my room. If asked point blank whether or not I had seen him, I would say that I had. I had no wish to compromise myself with the college authorities, and I sensed from the porter's grave and pressing manner, and from Michael's bluff desperation, that he was in quite serious trouble. However, I was still too much a schoolboy to grass on a fellow student without good cause, and I saw no reason to volunteer the information. The porter crossed the room, climbed up on the chair by the desk and thrust the upper half of his body through the window. He looked left and right along the line of the roof, and then called down to an invisible colleague in the court below that it was no good, they'd got away again.

He pulled back into my room and apologized for disturbing me. He was about to leave, but I found my curiosity piqued, and saw an opportunity to make my hidden guest squirm a little for his presumption. I asked him whom he had been hunting.

'Oh, a couple of young lads and girls. Been climbing up the buildings and generally making a nuisance of themselves. We'll catch them in the end, and then they'll get sent down, and maybe they'll even learn a lesson from it. I just hope we get them before they get themselves killed.'

I offered him a glass of water, which he took gratefully. He sat down in the chair by the bed, and it occurred to me that he was only a little younger than my own father, and quite old to be made to run up and down flights of stairs after privileged young students. The thought made me even less sympathetic to Michael, and I decided to tease out his purgatory a little more with a few questions.

'Who's doing it?' I asked.

'One group. We think there're three or four of them.'

I was interested to hear that my guest was not alone, that he was part of a larger outfit. I wondered where the others were hiding.

'Is it so bad, climbing the buildings?' I asked him, sitting down on the edge of the bed. 'I mean, do they damage anything?'

'No,' he said, 'not damage exactly. But they do something. It's no good, seeing people like that going all over the college, and everyone knowing about it.'

'Why?'

He shrugged, as if it were obvious. 'Sets a bad example. Can't have things like that going unpunished. We've had more problems this term than we did last year, and that's more than the year before. Most of it's just high jinks, and we don't mind that, high jinks, but there're other things, fights and drugs and cheating and such . . .' He trailed off glumly, as if contemplating an invincible host of evils. I could tell he was the type of man who enjoyed a good portion of doom, and his claims about narcotics and violence seemed ridiculous in the peace of the Cambridge night.

'But you can't put that down to people climbing buildings, surely?' I asked.

'Well, they're a danger to themselves, and a danger to others,' he said, 'but that's not it. A thing like that, it can upset the tone of the whole college, and people who do one kind of wrong will do another.'

I found this statement a little cryptic, and thought it

might be some proverb conscripted to an awkward use. I decided to change the subject. 'Why do they do it? The climbing, I mean?'

'Couldn't rightly say.'

I was beginning to regret having invited the man to stay. I was aware that, though I had not lied to the porter, my silence would look like complicity, and so as he spoke I became more and more uncomfortable. Each passing moment seemed to increase the chances of Michael being found, and my guilt in concealing him grew. At the same time, however, I felt an uneasy fascination as I heard him speak. Each word seemed to open the door a fraction on to a shady world of midnight pursuits. Presently he relieved my dilemma as he rose and thanked me for the drink. He asked me how I was settling in to college, and I could see that his concern was genuine, for when he posed the question the slight fold of tension that had lodged between his eyebrows when discussing the chase smoothed away. He told me that I should come and see him in the porters' lodge if there was anything I needed, and I was surprised to find myself touched by the offer. I realized at that moment how lonely I had become: isolation had worn away my resistance to small acts of kindness. He said he must be getting back to his duties. He explained that the night's chase had begun when he had caught a glimpse of a man on the rooftops whilst patrolling New Court. I said goodbye to him, and wished him better luck in the pursuit of his quarry. He called me 'sir' when he said goodnight.

A few moments after he had gone, a large hand reached around the easel and carefully set the pencil drawing back against the wall, revealing a disembodied pair of legs. My guest appeared before me in a series of limbs, first one arm, then legs, then the other arm, until he stepped out from his hiding place and gravitated to what he clearly regarded as his natural home at the centre of the room.

'What an arse that man is,' he remarked cordially. 'All absolute rubbish. I heard him whispering, and whatever he said you mustn't believe it. He's one of those people who simply cannot reconcile themselves to the fact that someone somewhere may be having a jolly time.'

Beneath his gay bravado I sensed genuine relief, and I realized he must have been very frightened of discovery. He was exaggerating his nonchalance in the aftermath of danger, a male habit I recognized from the older boys at school. I thought his choice of words slightly odd. I was soon to discover that Michael affected a vocabulary which he thought gave him a dense, solid air of tasteful maturity, like the thick carved legs of an oaken dining table in some venerable London club.

'He's been after us all since last year, and the fact that he can't get his grubby little paws on us drives him wild. From the way he puffed up those stairs, I should say he's about due for a coronary infarct.'

I saw that I was expected to laugh a little at the man's expense. I did not want to, as I had found him kind, but I immediately sensed that Michael was the type of person it would be useful to know. I gratified him with the required laugh, feeling guilty as I did so, as if my host at a party had made a vaguely racist joke, and I had let politeness get the better of my distaste. When he saw my reaction his expression shifted from one of pronounced mockery to a kind of genial, avuncular approval.

'You did rather well, I must say. He didn't exactly put on the thumbscrews, but he can be a rather unsettling fellow.'

It irritated me that I felt a brief rush of pride at his praise, as if I had pleased a respected superior with the performance of some trivial task. I decided to sit back down on the bed, and to recline on the cushions in order to repossess my room with a display of my own relaxation. It seemed to work for a moment, as Michael looked down at me unsure of whether he too should sit down. The grand proportions of his torso amplified any moment of physical indecision, and he seemed suddenly bulky and oversized. 'Look,' he said, breaking in on his own paralysis, 'I know it's asking rather a lot, but would you mind if I borrowed some clothes, and washed my hands before I head off? They caught me in their torches from down in the court. I felt rather like a rabbit on the estate.' He paused for a beat to let the social implications of the comparison sink in. 'I'd be in hot water if they recognized me. You look a big enough chap. Perhaps if I could just borrow a jumper and a pair of trousers. Oh, and do you have a baseball cap, or a . . . a sweatshirt, or whatever they're called?' I nodded my assent, and got up to search through my cupboard. Meanwhile Michael went over to the sink, a white enamel block set into the wall with a small mirror screwed into the plaster above it. He had to stoop to see his reflection, and when he was certain his hands were clean he used a palm-full of water to pat down his black hair. Something about the care with which he performed this ritual told me he was not going bald gracefully. I produced a pair of old Gap jeans and a green hooded Nike jumper I seldom wore from my shelves. The cupboard itself had a strong smell of transitional life, the newspaper, disinfectant and dust smell of cheap hotels and railway stations, and it was starting to permeate my wardrobe. His wide nostrils contracted a little as he took the clothes, but if he had any reservations about my choices he was gracious enough to conceal them in silence. I turned away whilst he changed, not wishing to get a flash of his broad flanks or hairy naked chest.

'Bloody good of you,' he said, admiring himself in the mirror after his transformation. 'I'll leave my own things here if I may. You needn't wash them, you can give them back to me next Thursday. I shall take you out to dinner, if that's all right, to say thank you for being such a good sport. I would entertain you this weekend, but I have a

39

rather important debate to prepare for the Union. Let it never be said that Michael Findlay doesn't know how to repay hospitality.' This last comment he turned away from me towards the room at large, an actor soliloquizing to the pit.

We shook hands, and he took a last peek out the window to ensure that the coast was clear before departing. I listened, becalmed in the lonely waters of my room. Before his footfalls died completely in my ears I went to the window to watch him emerge into the courtyard. The court was deserted, illuminated only by the wrought-iron lanterns bolted to the stone walls in New Court, and the occasional oblong of a lit window where students with ground-floor rooms were still awake. The light from the lamps in the neighbouring square cast the shadows of the colonnade on the gravel, so that dark fingers clutched at the oval of grass. The moon was bright, its blue details clear in the black sky. I saw the top of Michael's head emerge beneath me, the moonlight glinting slightly on his wet skull, and I was about to pull back into my room and shut the window when I became aware of three figures emerging from between the sash branches of the copper beech. He lifted his hand to these figures in a silent salute, and they greeted him with words which reached my room as an indistinct murmur. My dressing gown fell open, and the cold air stung my skin into anticipation. I took a deep breath, and tasted the flavour of bonfire smoke. The groundsmen must have been burning leaves on the Backs. I thrilled at being unseen, hovering above them. The moonlight poured into the court, filling up the walls like silver liquid.

I tried to get a clear view of Michael's companions as the four of them fell into formation and walked out of sight behind the tree. There were two girls, one quite short with dark hair, the other tall and blonde. The tall one might be beautiful, I thought, or she thinks she is, or she wouldn't walk like that, her head held up high, going deliberately slowly so that everyone else had to fall in time. Her hair fell down her back. She progressed with a stately grace. The shorter girl walked with a tough little strut and a roll to the shoulders, so that every step seemed like a challenge to the world. There was one boy, tall and black with short curly hair, broad-shouldered in a long blue overcoat that almost brushed his heels.

It seems ridiculous, but I knew the feeling that moment reminded me of; it pressed a specific neurone. I recognized it from childhood, looking down into a well in my father's holiday home in the south of France, when I saw the silver backs of distant creatures flashing in the dark water. I peered down as my father chatted away with the estate agent in a half-known language, asking him questions about the surrounding buildings, the woods, something else I didn't understand. I wanted so much to take off my clothes and sandals, to slip over the warm granite rim, away from the sunlight and the sound of crickets and the rough dry grass which tickled my ankles, to plunge into the cool silent shadows so far down. When my father saw me standing on tiptoes to look over the rim, he shouted at me to come away, and gripped my forearm very tightly, making me promise not to go near the edge. When he finally bought the place, he had men fill it in, and we came back the next summer to find a brown circle of earth in the back garden, burying the beautiful animals deep underground. The year after that, my father's business took a bad turn, and the newly purchased property had to be sold.

3

Of all the things a man can approach with a plan, social conquest is perhaps the most apt to failure. As I was to learn over the course of my first year, even if I had succeeded in identifying and accessing my chosen cabal, the desirable react fiercely against those who desire them, and can sniff out conscious intent as wild animals smell human contact on their brethren, and turn on them. I think I got away with it because I was too inexperienced to be calculating, and therefore too incompetent to be suspected. Even those who make it through such means are tolerated rather than embraced, and treated with a mild scorn that their vanity transmutes into intimacy.

Such a boy it was who eventually introduced me into the circle that was to constitute my world. Michael Findlay, old school acquaintance, had been two years above me, and something of a figure of fun despite his prowess on the rugby pitch. Once he had left the bleak fields of Dorset, however, and come to university, people had discovered in him the redeeming gleam of vast sums of money, which Michael liked to pretend was the natural mineral accretion of hundreds of years of familial nobility, but was really a consequence of a glittering paternal career in the City. Conspicuous consumption had not been possible in a boarding school, as there was nothing to spend money on, and the uniform effaced economic differences between the boys. In Cambridge, however, Michael had blossomed into a conspicuous consumer, and everything from the elegant Rolex on his wrist to the MG he kept parked on Library Road spoke of his financial status.

The night-time encounter took place on a Thursday evening. I left for London on Saturday, as the weekends, lacking the loose structure of morning lectures, soap operas (I did not count the Sunday omnibus editions) and supervisions, gave my isolation an uncomfortable edge. My grandmother was moving out of her Wandsworth flat to go to a home where she could get twenty-four-hour care, and my father, together with several auxiliary aunts and uncles, were packing up her possessions in shifts. The process was frightening and confusing for her, and it helped to have people she knew well around her. I liked to be useful, and spent Saturday and most of Sunday sitting with her, drinking tea in her little kitchen and telling her about college, until I had to leave to catch the evening train from King's Cross.

Thus I did not think much more about my visitor or

about his invitation until Monday morning, when a particularly dense lecture on Eliot's supposed anti-Semitism chased my fugitive attention into a daydream. The weather had begun to turn, and all over Cambridge antiquated heating systems were clunking into life like animals coming out of hibernation, shaking and groaning as warm blood flowed back through their arteries. The wooden benches of the lecture hall were bathed in drowsy warmth. The dread-locked girl next to me began by feverishly taking notes with a furry pink biro, making the bench shake with industry, but by the ten-minute mark she was doodling. As I dreamed, the dinner with Michael took on the same seductive glow of possibility that comes with a date: the gratification of mutual attraction, the promise of fulfilment and the secret hope that it will not come easily enough to lower the value of the prize. The usual fears of rejection were also in attendance, and this was perhaps the first time in my life that I ever remember agonizing over what to wear. Michael was my only link to the shadowy, glamorous world I had glimpsed down in the courtyard, a slender line that I had to gently coax back to the source, or else break in a tug of frustration. In my loneliness, the image of the four receding figures had taken on a peculiar status, and I had already decided that the encounter was down to the hand of fate. Coupled to this, the vague awe of a young schoolboy for the upper years still clung to Michael's image. I wanted to impress him.

By the time Thursday arrived I was quite frantic.

In my first year Cambridge had still to adjust to its status as a wealthy London satellite, and the restaurants and bars that met Michael's elevated standards tended to be of the old and uncomfortable order. Over the next three years expensive gastro-pubs and nightclub-restaurants with names that involved puns and random numbers (O2, 2 Much) sprang up, but that evening we had dinner in Browns. Browns was opposite the Fitzwilliam Museum on Trumpington Street. It was a large open-plan restaurant that looked like a hilltop club from the British Raj, with fluted columns supporting a lofty ceiling of moulded white plaster, wicker chairs around bamboo tables, and palm fronds emerging from bronze pots flanking every doorway. The floor was that of an ornate bathroom, with black and white tiles arranged in a chessboard design. Vast wooden fans paddled the lazy air around the skylights, turning like the wheels of old-fashioned steamers in calm water. The building had been a mental asylum before the Second World War, and there was still a vaguely recuperative air about the cocktail lounge, particularly on a Sunday morning when you could sit for hours with a newspaper mounted on a wooden handle, and a brusqueness to the staff which suggested regular dealings with a mentally deficient clientele. Michael was waiting for me at the bar, and when I came in he handed me my old jeans and green hoodie in a bag of thick card with the legend

'Turnbull & Asser' printed on the side. Later I would come to realize that he had returned the cheap clothes I had lent him, freshly laundered and pressed, in a shopping bag from one of the best bespoke tailors in London, but at the time his slight was too subtle for me, and went over my head.

That night Michael appeared fantastically grown up to me. He ordered his three courses with a certainty and exactness of pronunciation that spoke of generations of Findlays completely unable to prepare their own food, and a cavalier disregard for his own health or the health of his wallet. We talked in a desultory manner about school, about the fates of mutual acquaintances, and the boys in his year who had had brothers in mine. All the time, I was thinking about the four figures in the moonlight, wondering how I could introduce them. Teachers had retired or moved on; there had been a brief scandal over child pornography, delicately handled by the headmaster. Michael said that sports, morals and academics were in decline. At the end of the first course, a generous dollop of foie gras in a tiny ceramic ramekin, we had exhausted the little stash of natural conversation available, and I was able to steer the talk round to the night of our meeting.

He glanced to left and right, as if the college authorities might have tailed him to dinner. On one side was a raucous birthday party of second years arguing with the waiter about the set menu, and the table on the other side was empty, the white napkins standing in rows like a well-ordered campsite. Satisfied, he put his elbows on the table, bringing his chin over the centre of the cloth, and gestured for me to do likewise. Finally, he refilled my glass with the last of the Cabernet, and without looking up gestured to a passing waiter to bring a second bottle.

'So you want to know about the Night Climbers, do you?' he asked.

'The Night Climbers?' I asked, the name sending a little tremor down my spine.

'It's a little club I started some time ago with a couple of friends.'

'And who are your friends?' I asked.

'Just like-minded individuals,' he said, waving the allusion above my head like meat over a starving dog.

'I saw them down in the courtyard,' I said, 'two girls and a guy.'

'Oh,' he said, rather put out, 'well, I suppose if you know who they are by sight there's no harm in me telling you a little bit about them. Discretion is our watchword. I myself plan to be something of a public figure and prefer not to broadcast my exploits, but since you already know, and you're an O.S. . . .'

My fear that he would tell me nothing was unfounded. He was quite willing to trade in his confidences for a moment of importance. When prompted, he gave up an excess of precious information like a geyser spitting pressurized oil up from the ground, and I thought at first that I must already have some special glow about me to warrant such attention. Michael, much mocked and maligned by the friends he sought to emulate, was really taking the opportunity to display his social plumage to an eager and inferior male. Whatever his motivations, this is still my first impression of them all, given a salacious tint by the lens of his gossip. They were sold to me perfectly as creatures of social fantasy. His fondness for his own voice, and mine for free food, meant that his dominance of the conversation was uncontested and total.

'Francis, he has a rather interesting history. I'm sure you'll hear it from someone else, so you might as well get the truth from me as a pack of lies from some dreadful gossip who barely even knows him. Francis's father is Lord Soulford. Yes, that's right. *The* Lord Soulford. I've been lucky enough to do some work with him myself at Conservative Central Office. Yes, another bottle of the Cabernet, please, and will you bring me some Dijon? In the late seventies and early eighties Soulford, or Manley as he was then, was rather a different man, no political ambitions, something of a playboy by all accounts, and of course enormously rich. Imagine, that prodigious intellect devoted entirely to furnishing his own pleasure. Of course he hid as much as he could from old Lord Soulford, who was quite an abstemious gent, but he couldn't keep himself out of the papers for ever. Orgies will out. Well, he went off to New York for some time, ostensibly to do some work managing the family investments, but really to get away from the old man's ire. Out there he behaved just as badly, until eventually he fell in love with this fashion model from Zimbabwe. Utterly unsuitable, utterly beautiful – Francis has photographs of her stalking the catwalks of Milan and Paris, and I defy any red-blooded male not to fall in love with her instantly. They married in secret in Las Vegas, honeymooned at the family villa in St Tropez, and the old man was none the wiser. That's where I suspect Francis was conceived, in the south of France, so you see it really was a love match, and nothing to do with social obligation. Then some awful journalist snapped the two of them having breakfast on the balcony, and the whole story came out in the British press. Lord Soulford read about it on page two of *The Times*. Would you call this rare? I'm not sure I would. Perhaps I should send it back . . . Well, he phoned through to the family lawyers from the breakfast table, and had his only son quite excised from his will, and cut off his allowance completely, as well as having the locks changed on the apartment in New York. The two of them stuck it out for a while, living on the money she made from modelling; Manley sold a couple of the jewels his grandmother had left him, good pieces but not enough to support them for long. They kept on living like a king and queen you see, neither of them could quite acknowledge the change in their circumstances. By the time Francis was born, they were defaulting on the medical bills. I heard they had to smuggle him out of the hospital wrapped in a blanket. Are you enjoying the steak? It looks a little overdone to me, I prefer the blood and jus to seep out when you spear it with the fork. In the end Manley came back to his father. He couldn't survive without money, and he wasn't really fit to make any of his own. A brilliant man of course, but I always think ability of the financial sort the sign of a rather vulgar and debased intelligence. His ideas are infinitely better suited to the political stage, to the structure of the great machine than the workings of the individual cogs. He ran through Francis's mother's cash pretty quickly, and she couldn't work again after the baby. I get the impression the modelling world's rather cruel to those who fall out of fashion, if you'll pardon the pun, and all her friends peeled away. In the end she went back to Harare, and took Francis with her. Manley had the marriage annulled, and married an earl's daughter. Would you like another glass? Francis has two half-brothers by her, they're charming but rather stupid. It's a shame, because the elder one will get the title, and most of the money. Lord Soulford keeps Francis on a pretty tight leash with a generous monthly allowance. The annulment cut him off from the family trust.'

'How did he come back from Harare?'

'What? Oh, his mother was killed in a car crash, and since old Lord Soulford had shuffled off the mortal coil there was no impediment to his being taken back into

51

the family. I think his mother's relatives understandably felt he might have a better life in England. Came back when he was still a toddler. His mother had taken to calling him Nyasha, but his father quite sensibly changed his name back to Francis.'

I listened to this extraordinary biography in silence. I wanted to challenge Michael on its authenticity, just in case he was playing a game with me. I didn't because I was so desperate to meet the man he had described that I wanted to sustain the illusion of truth, if it was an illusion, for as long as possible.

'What about the girls?'

'Which girls?' he asked, reaching for the salt.

'There were two women with you in the courtyard.'

'Oh yes. Jessica and Lisa. Jessica's rather attractive, if your tastes are obvious. Her father used to be something in property, but he went bust and finished up in Ford open prison. Lisa is quite a human dynamo. No background to speak of. A great organizing force around the university, particularly where there's money to be made. Jewish of course. She's always running some scam or other. In fact . . .' He paused and looked at me critically, wanting me to know that I was being measured for some special privilege. I submitted rather awkwardly to the appraisal, shovelling up mashed potato on my fork. 'How are your plans for later this evening?' he said, returning to his plate.

'Oh . . .' I said, unwilling to reveal that my plans for

the evening revolved exclusively around Chaucer, the ten o'clock news and bed. 'Nothing I couldn't cancel. Why?'

'Well, I thought you might like to meet some of my friends, since you're so interested. Do you have black tie?' he asked me.

'Yes. Yes, I have, back in my room,' I said, then mentally censured myself for my eagerness. The suit had been a matriculation present from my father.

'How much money can you get your hands on?'

I baulked a little at this question. I did not wish to reveal how little money I had, but I could not afford the pretence. Michael, who could be quite perceptive when it came to other people's discomfort, dismissed my hesitation with an airy wave. 'But what am I thinking? Tonight was to be a thank you. Just meet me by All Saints' Passage at eleven o'clock. And you might want to take a look at your hair.'

He refused to drop any further hints about our destination. We had dessert and black coffee. I didn't usually drink coffee, but he told me I needed to keep myself awake for the evening's entertainment, that it didn't do to let dinner set in too early. When the bill came he scrutinized it with a heavy frown, as if expecting to be cheated. He pulled out a gold moneyclip, and paid cash, so that I saw four twenties going between the card sides of the folder before he closed it. I steeled myself to avoid an excessive show of thanks, one that would betray how seldom I ate a dinner that expensive. As we rose to leave I asked myself why Michael would want to invite me to something private and special. He had more than discharged any obligation of gratitude with dinner, and we had no history of friendship that might require such a favour. At the time, I could think of nothing but the fact that I intrigued him in some way, and he wanted to know me better. In retrospect, I think he was simply carried away with the joy of total superiority. I think he wanted to show me around his social set like the owner of a stately home issuing an invitation to a penniless relative, leading me down beautiful corridors, pointing out the priceless and the unique, before ejecting me back into the everyday world with a polite wave and an empty promise of future contact. He was not a malicious man, and I do not think for a moment that he was motivated by a desire to hurt; he was simply addicted to the idea of being better than others, and would go to extraordinary lengths to satisfy his need. He was compelled to make others aware of their low status in relation to his own, and in their forced acknowledgement that his life was better than theirs was lodged the kernel of his self-respect. He never foresaw that I might make myself at home in his world, and he never quite forgave me for making his friends my own. He saw it as a betrayal of his hospitality.

4

At the appointed time I waited by All Saints' Passage, standing in the shadow of the trees in the market square. Rival groups of students and townies were prowling the streets after closing time, each laying their claim to the city, and raucous laughter echoed down the cobbled road. I felt vulnerable in my evening wear, as if I had declared my allegiance in disputed territory. The Tudor gatehouse stood as a guardian across the forecourt, and it was a comfort to glimpse the porters moving through the tiny square of light in the red-brick flank. When a group of men strolled by in the deserted street, I turned inwards and pretended to be studying something beyond the railings. The last week had flushed out the remaining traces of summer. The night air was freezing, and my breath came in clouds. There was no wind, allowing the cold to distil the city to a crystal clarity.

Michael arrived late. His bowtie was real and perfectly tied, and his shoes gave off a military gleam. His black hair was slicked backwards, revealing his high forehead.

His cheeks were clean and shining, and I thought he might have shaved since dinner. He had the kind of dark stubble that can never be wholly removed, and leaves a blue-black shadow on the jaw. I asked him where we were going; all he would tell me was that we were visiting his old boys' club, a private set of rooms above a restaurant. I was surprised to hear that such places still existed, particularly in the radical atmosphere of a university town. He led me down the passage on to Bridge Street, which we crossed over, heading towards Jesus Green. Michael would never have compromised his dignity so far as to break into a jog, but I had the feeling we were late for something. We stopped on the pavement outside the walls of Sidney Sussex. There were three doors in the face of a rather grand red-brick building, each divided from the others by thick pillars supporting a white neo-classical portico on the second floor. Flat-headed black spears, linked along the top by a strip of black metal, formed a fence along the front, punctuated by a gate for each door. The middle one was glass, and disclosed the marble lobby of an up-market Pizza Express, with a pianist just visible in the interior. The second door stood open, and was manned by two large Asian men wearing earpieces and tight black T-shirts under their Puffa jackets. Bass emanated from the smoky subterranean darkness, and the occasional flash of disco lighting appeared on the wall. A queue of feral teens had formed outside, and they jeered at us as we made our way to the closed door on the left. Their derision would normally have made me blush and walk quickly past, inspiring hours of self-reproach in the safety of my room, but Michael brushed it aside with a grunt of satisfaction.

We stopped at the unobtrusive black door, and through the panel of glass above it I could see that the room it led on to was unlit. Michael pressed the intercom and stood back from the door to look upwards. I followed his gaze, and saw that he had positioned himself in full view of a security camera hanging on the underside of the pediment. There came a distant crackle from the intercom, and then a startling buzzing sound to indicate that the lock had been opened. Michael held the door for me and ushered me into a darkened corridor. The entrance was equipped with a doormat and a shoe brush. In the corner, lying on its plaque, there was a large stag's head, whose antlers supported a number of designer handbags. The image of the wooden mount was cast in negative on the wall above, a lighter thumbnail shape on the dirty paint showing where it must have hung. The coat rack was laden with expensive overcoats, every brass peg trailing dark blue wool and black cashmere. Michael removed his own and added it to the pile. The passageway was long and narrow, clearly running along the side of the dining room in the restaurant next door. The walls were lined with Spy cartoons, pencil and ink caricatures of sporting, political and academic figures from the late nineteenth century. As we moved into the building thick green carpet deadened our footfalls. The air smelt of polish and dust. I began to hear a noise, a kind of rumbling coming from somewhere above, as of many feet stamping and voices baying in unison. The disembodied voices filled up the abandoned coats in my mind, giving them each a ghostly shape. My guide heard it too, and he turned to me and smiled. Beneath his proprietorial air, his need to seem in control to emphasize his own superiority, I sensed a frisson of excitement. His small eyes glinted in the dim light of the hall. At the end of the corridor there was a flight of steps that twisted back on itself, leading up into the second floor. The rumbling sound grew closer, and I thought I could distinguish individual cries as it came into focus. We came through the doors at the top of the stairs and were confronted by a man of about twenty-five, standing behind a desk in an elegant lobby.

'Hello, Findlay, you fucker,' he said, giving him a friendly slap on the arm. Michael returned it with the same jocular obscenities. Their greeting was curiously stilted, as if someone had told them that this was the way men were supposed to behave to one another, but had omitted to explain why. Beneath the cheerfulness, I sensed that they did not much care for each other.

'Who's this?' the man asked, turning his attention to me. 'I don't think we've met. Is he a new member?'

'No, no, he's a guest,' Michael said, blustering.

'A guest?' The man raised his eyebrows and the signet-ringed hand that had been edging towards me in greeting fell back by his side. 'You know we decided not to allow guests at . . . well, this evening.'

'Come on, Marley,' Michael said, taking his arm to imply they were both men of the world. 'We can hear dinner's over. I'll vouch for him, he's an old school mate. Utterly reliable, quite discreet.'

They discussed me as if I were not there, and so this description gave me a little gift of pleasure, as if I had overheard it from behind a closed door. Marley wavered for a few seconds, and then nodded. 'All right, if you say so, Findlay. But there'll be hell to pay if the Club Secretary finds out. I'll put his ticket on your bill.' He wrote down our names in a large leatherbound ledger on his desk, and we were ushered through into a spacious room with red walls and deep green leather armchairs. Michael stopped to have words with Marley on the threshold. I took advantage of the moment's privacy to examine the room. A pile of newspapers and periodicals was strewn across a central table. There were a few good pieces of heavy furniture, and along the back wall bound copies of *Punch*. Everything had the comfortable, lived-in air of a venerable country house that contains several children. The leather was scuffed and shabby, the bindings on the books were frayed, but they gave the impression of waiting patiently for repair, rather than sloping off towards the dump. The Lincoln-green carpet was pockmarked with a constellation of cigarette burns. A fire burned in the grate beneath a portrait of Pitt the Younger. There were two doors, one leading on to a kitchen at the far end. From behind the second, the roaring and stamping hurled itself like an angry dog against the old wood. A steward in a tailcoat, visibly drunk, emerged from the lighted kitchen. He called me Mr Collingwood, and asked me what I would like to drink. In a spirit of experimentation I told him to bring me a bottle of champagne and a cigar, and to put it on my tab. He turned around in a lazy circle.

By the time Michael had finished his conference, the steward had returned with Mr Collingwood's order. Michael took a swig from the bottle, and made for the closed door. He grasped the handle, ready to release the pent-up sound. 'Come on,' he said, 'it's started. No one will notice you if we come in now. If you want to place a bet, just let me know.'

He swung open the door and released the sound like a wall of water. It rushed over us, and I felt stunned by its volume. Beneath the roar of voices there was the heavy bass beat of hip hop. The air beyond the door was warm and moist, and it held the sweet smell of fresh sweat, of cigar smoke, expensive wine and rich food, and many scents and colognes. I could see the room at the end of the passage. I could see the backs of a number of men jostling for position, crowded around one another and waving fistfuls of money like brokers in the bear pit. They seemed to be surrounding something in a ring. I felt like an explorer penetrating deep into the temple of some forgotten tribe. I came into a room filled with young men and women in evening dress. There were perhaps thirty or forty, the boys heavily outnumbering the girls. It was difficult to tell through the press of bodies, as the only light in the room came from the fire burning in the grate, and the vast silver candelabra growing like some mythical tree out of the centre of a long dining table. Each of its slender silver limbs bore a great ivory candle, which had already burned halfway down, the wax suspended like luminous fungus from the base of each one. The table was still set with the remnants of a sumptuous dinner, and had been pushed up against the far wall to create a space in the centre of the room about fifteen feet in diameter. A ring. The crowd had gathered around the other three sides, and were leaning over as far as they dared, straining to get close like hungry animals about a patch of firelight. The rap came from wall-mounted speakers, with bass so loud the beat hit the air in little percussive bursts. A blackboard had been erected on one end of the table, and a small dark girl was marking the changing odds in chalk and taking bets from the howling boys. Her dark brown hair was pulled back in a severe ponytail that stood out from the back of her skull. She was conspicuous by being the only person in everyday clothes, a singlet and black combats, and had about her an aura of calm efficiency quite out of keeping with the prevailing abandon. She plucked money out of the sea of raised hands and gave out tickets. She moved nimbly between the decanters, the cheese plates and the place mats. Some of the spectators stood on chairs against the walls, which were panelled with oak edged in gilt. They raised their fists. The room was hot, and their wide-open mouths punched black holes in their faces, turning them into thick red rings. The amber firelight burnished them to a passionate glow. Many of the boys seemed very drunk. Some still carried the crystal port glasses they must have picked up from the final course, half full of burgundy liquid.

I lost Michael as soon as we came through the door. He was moving in amongst the crush of bodies, looking for somewhere with a decent view. Pushing and shoving was licensed by the atmosphere of masculine excess, and everybody was enjoying the break from politeness, shouldering one another harder than was necessary, falling and charging with the surge of the crowd. I leant forwards over the broad black backs of the men in front, and stared into the ring. Two boxers were fighting.

I had never seen a boxing match before. It was clear from the level of physical damage that this one had been going on for some time, and was not bound by the usual rules of safety. The man facing me was small and compact, his meaty frame heaving with exhaustion, shaking like an engine housing. He had his gloved fists up in front of his nose, but they dipped from tiredness to disclose a swollen and bleeding face, with brown hair matted by sweat to the forehead. The other fighter was tall and black with short cropped hair. His skin was dark enough to mask the red of the blood, so his face looked slick and wet. His torso was a perfect anatomy of muscle, uncompromised by the slightest hint of fat or bone, and in this atmosphere of carving and sculpture he looked like a piece of art come to life. He was still moving on the balls of his feet, swapping his weight with a neat step from one to the other. He worried his opponent with a flurry of jabs. When one of the fighters was forced back against the edge of the living ring, they would be shielded from further blows and then repelled by a forest of arms. I drank quickly from my bottle of champagne, eager to catch up with the mood. Some of the men in the crowd were crying 'Francis!' and others were shouting 'Jonny!' I guessed that Francis was the tall fighter, Jonny the shorter and more compact. Francis was the subject of my host's story, the other boy I had seen walking away from my rooms. As they danced around one another, their blood fell in small dark spots on the rich green carpet. At first I was indifferent to their fate, happy to enjoy the carnal spectacle. As the fight wore on, however, I became aware of a preference, evolving unprompted from the unconscious ooze and breathing thought: I wanted the black guy to win. The preference grew into empathy. My feelings, my hopes and fears became caught up in the shuffle of his feet. I felt the visceral pain of a blow landed on his fine body, and the bloody pleasure of a strike in return. I let my emotions grow up his fate like a creeper, winding around his thick limbs. I had never cared for sport before, but I began to watch with a fan's commitment. I began to murmur to myself, inarticulate whimpers and cheers at first, which grew louder as I lost my self-consciousness, forming words and then whole sentences, until I was clamouring along with the rest. 'Come on, Francis! You can do it!' I pictured myself leaping on his attacker if he fell. I imagined myself into the drama. I felt as I willed him on that my faith could exert some practical effect on his chances. I thought at the time that I was inspired by the sport, but I was really inspired by the sportsman. Francis's greatest charm was to make everyone, from the waiters who refilled his glass to the girls who wanted him, think: I could be the one to help him. From the moment that thought had struck, to give in to exasperation and leave his side was to betray oneself. As I watched him fight, I was lost.

After a few minutes, the girl standing on the table announced the end of the round by ringing a large bronze bell with a hardwood handle that stood on the table at her side. After that she stopped taking bets. The two fighters struck gloves in a gesture of mutual respect, and backed away into their corners. I was pleased at the sign; the lack of real enmity seemed to excuse my enjoyment of the violence. Jonny was immediately surrounded by two or three men who clenched their fists in excitement, poured words of encouragement into his ears and cleaned the blood from his face with a towel. I could see, however, that he hung his head, and he shook it a couple of times as if in bewilderment. The man who seemed to be his trainer pulled his head back and placed the plastic tip of a bottle in his mouth, squeezing the middle to pump fluid down his throat. The shouting had died down to an uneasy murmur, and the sounds of laughter and greeting could be heard around the ring. Francis sat down on his seat, a high-backed wooden chair that I guessed had come from the head of the dinner table. He spat blood into a silver tureen with sea-shell mouldings that was offered to him by a girl in a simple black cocktail dress. Her blonde hair was held up by a long silver needle, disclosing her high forehead and delicate ears. She was the most beautiful woman I had ever seen, and she leant down to kiss him on the cheek. When she came back up, her own high white cheek was stained with blood. It looked like a smear of lipstick. The sight of her tall, elegant figure poised by the chair and his muscular naked body covered in blood and sweat thrilled me. One of the men broke away from Jonny's camp and went to speak to the dark girl standing on the table. He looked older than the others, and ominously sober. Her brow furrowed. She asked him a question, and he shook his head emphatically, as if driven to reiterate a denial. She shrugged, and stood up straight. Some of the more astute spectators, and those who had handed up particularly large sums of cash, broke away from their conversations to look at her, then the music was turned down and a domino hush spread out through the ranks.

'Ladies and gentlemen, our medic on call has told me Jonny Woods ain't in a fit state to finish the fight.' She opened her mouth to say more, but mouthed inaudibly as a great shout went up from the crowd. She held her hands up, palms down, and stood for a few seconds in the attitude of a Christian martyr, her feet planted firmly apart, her chin high in calm defiance. Though her cheap clothes were out of place, she radiated control. 'I therefore declare Francis Manley the winner!' This time the bellowing was less equivocal, as all the crowd, winners and losers, acknowledged the bravery of the victory. She beckoned Francis over from his corner. He came with the blonde woman holding his hand. The dark girl held up his arm by the wrist, still standing on the table, so that her own hand was only raised to her shoulder. There was something faintly ridiculous about seeing this girl standing with her feet level with Francis's waist, but the heroism of the moment engulfed it and washed it away. The tall blonde girl embraced him. Her dress and hair were pristine, and I loved her disregard for the blood and sweat running off Francis's skin. He went over to congratulate his opponent. He lifted the other man's hand into the air, and that seemed to break the warding spell around the ring. The surface tension broken, the edges poured in to the middle. I wanted to share my joy, the spoils of victory, with somebody else, but I did not know anyone else in the room. I could not see Michael. Unwilling to be visibly alone, I went back through the library to find the toilets.

After the fight, a weekday morning bled the club dry. It was half past midnight. The crowd had eaten and drunk well, and with the momentum of the fight spent they rolled to a dead stop. The losing boxer emerged walking unaided, with an overcoat draped around his shoulders, and a woman I took to be his girlfriend following behind, trying to conceal the tears in her eyes. I could feel pity for him, now that he was no longer a threat to my chosen champion. I thought about going up and congratulating him, but decided against it. To give myself something to do I took out my cigar and attempted to bite off the end as I had seen people do on television, accidentally filling my mouth with foul-tasting tobacco leaves. I spat discreetly into my hand. I sat in one of the deep leather armchairs in the library, and watched the crowd file past, waiting for Michael to come out. In accordance with his intentions I envied him his life, his connection to this strange building and to the people I had seen next door. I was filled with the need to belong.

He came out with his arm around the hero of the hour, leaning in towards him and whispering something in his ear. Francis had put on DJ trousers and a dress shirt, unbuttoned to the waist, stained with blood and wine. His bowtie hung around his neck like misplaced laurels. He was carrying his jacket over his shoulder, and limping slightly on his right leg. But for the bruising on his face I could not have guessed he had just been fighting. He looked like a rakish model emerging from an epic party. The two girls, the beautiful one in the evening dress and the shorter mistress of ceremonies in her tracksuit and vest came out behind them. The latter was holding a small black box of the type used to store money at outside events. She swung her arm with each step, and I could hear the tidal roar of change sliding backwards and forwards as she walked. She set the box down on the table by the fireside and opened it. I felt a little unseemly peeking at the contents, as if through a lit window at a woman changing, but I could not help myself, and was amazed at the mess of notes that sprung up like a pile of autumn leaves from the metal interior. To my unpractised eye it looked like a couple of thousand pounds. Without a flicker of wonder she took a handful of notes, tapped it quickly down to straighten it out in her hands, and began to deal in piles from fives to fifties. Her apparent indifference to the quantity of money awed me more than the money itself. Michael gestured to me, and said some words to the remaining couple, at which the other girl broke off and came over to me.

'Don't get up. I'm Jessica,' she said, taking my hand in a firm shake. I took her hand at the level of her groin. The curve of her hip bones was visible through the black material of her dress, which opened at the side to disclose a sliver of thigh. She had a little dried blood on her shoulder, a rusty stain from where she had embraced Francis, and I could smell his fresh sweat under her perfume.

'My name's James.'

'So you are the hero? The man who saved Falstaff from the porters?' She fell into the chair next to mine. The seats were too low to allow for any dignity in sitting down, and she vaulted the challenge to her self-possession with childish aplomb. She sat side-saddle, with her slim calves lolling over the arm on one side, and her back propped against the other.

'Why do you call him Falstaff?' I asked.

'He thinks it's because he's witty. We know it's because he's fat,' Jessica replied, jabbing him in the buttocks with the pointed toe on her black high-heeled shoe.

'It is because I share with my namesake an irrepressible sense of humour and a shrewd proximity to powerful figures,' Michael said primly.

'You must have a very large room for a first year. Where on earth did you conceal an object this size?' she asked casually. After a dinner of forced inferiority, I laughed gleefully at my host's expense.

'My size is proportional to my intellect,' he said quite seriously.

It was odd to see the way he interacted with these people. The ruder they were to him, the greater his pomposity became, as if he could flood the world with an excess of self-regard. Jessica left their exchange at that and returned her attention to me. As she faced me I felt reilluminated, quite brilliant, as if her beauty could catch the parts of me I liked the best and make them shine with reflected light.

'Did you like the fight?' she asked. 'Wasn't Francis brave?'

'Very brave. I've never seen a fight before, and I was spellbound.'

'Spellbound,' she repeated, as if she had never heard the word before, her blue eyes widening.

Jessica did not yet know me, but she thought it safest to have everyone worship her from the outset. She pulled the silver needle from her hair and the silky blonde bulk uncurled like a muscle down her back. The gesture implied an intimacy between us, as she disrobed in front of me without shame or comment. I wanted to give her something to justify the confidence. Talking to her, I had the genuine impression that whatever view I proffered would henceforth be law to her. The idea that someone like this would value my opinion made me swell with pride. She could instil self-worth in a moment – and excise it with a flash of her scalpel tongue. I did not know it, but I was already eating into my allotted quota of attention. After that everyone always craved more, and very few people ever worked hard enough or played well enough to get it. She was like a drug-dealer, creating need with a free sample, then suddenly escalating her price.

The slight girl with the ponytail had finished counting out money on the table. She gave half the winnings to Francis, and he folded them into two fat wodges and slipped them into the breast pockets of his dinner jacket. They shook hands briskly. She wore no make-up and no jewellery. She was pretty, I thought, with large dark eyes and a small oval face, but her abrupt manner indicated that her appearance was not on the agenda. She took another of the slabs, unzipped a pocket in her combats and slipped it inside. The rest of the notes and the float of coins she returned carefully to the strong box, before locking it and pocketing the key.

'I gotta dump this in the club safe tonight,' she told Michael. 'I told the punters to come get their winnings tomorrow, and I don't want to be lugging it about.'

Michael took the box and went into the lit kitchen. Francis came and sat on the arm of Jessica's chair.

'Did I do well?' he said. His voice was deep and sonorous, possessed of an aristocratic authority that jarred with a desperate need for approval.

She looked up into his eyes. I envied each the other's gaze. 'Darling, you fought like an angel,' she said, half mocking herself in the delivery. 'How much did you make?'

'I made three thousand.'

'But that's perfect! You can pay off all your debts and still survive until the end of the month, and your dad won't know a thing.'

Francis smiled, bathing his wounds in her approbation.

'Now, you won't spend it on anything silly, will you? You must promise me.'

'But if I promise not to spend it on anything silly, how will I spend it on you?'

'I don't want you to spend anything on me.'

'Please, don't make me laugh, my ribs hurt when I laugh.'

'You're cruel!'

'You're cruel, trying to stop me having any fun.'

Lisa came up beside him, and made her own brusque offering. 'I can take it for you. Look after it until you need to hand it over. Might be useful for me, I can think of a few things I could do with it till you need it.' I guessed she was dressing an offer of help as a request for help. She was uniquely equipped to play this trick; she had a way of narrowing her eyes when she was speaking, and a firm unsmiling set to her dark lips that precluded both altruism and sensitivity.

Francis wavered. He turned his handsome face towards the ceiling, as if looking for guidance. Jessica put her hand on his leg, and Lisa tapped his shoulder with her fist. They did not look at one another, but their movements were perfectly synchronized. I could see the two of them gently applying pincer pressure, each in their own particular style. I sensed something, some significance flex under the event like muscle under skin, providing the mechanical force to drive this little tableau, but I could not identify it exactly. The girls seemed to be trying to downplay their tension, their hope that Francis would hand over the money. I felt privileged to be witnessing this private dynamic. If Francis felt he was being manipulated, I knew instinctively that he would bolt.

'OK,' he said, giving up with a graceful shrug. 'You keep hold of the money. I have to pay up on Thursday, and I was planning to make the bastard wait until then anyway.' He said this, but he made no move to hand over the cash. Lisa took his jacket from him and emptied the pockets. She zipped the two bundles away in her combats with her own money, and the slight trace of effort in Jessica's cheerfulness dissolved instantly. It was as if a wilful child had been coaxed down from a high place.

'Everyone seems to have left,' she said to Francis. 'I don't feel quite ready to go to bed, do you? We need to get some ice on that face of yours.'

'There's too much adrenalin still in my system. I could use a drink,' Francis agreed.

'Michael's got the keys,' Lisa said. 'I'll tell him to get us a bottle.'

They were no longer speaking to me, they were addressing their own affairs, but I was content just to share in the warmth of their conversation. They were more vivid for me, more real than almost anyone else I had ever met.

'What about you?' Francis said to me, feeling his swollen eye with his fingers, as if testing a fruit for ripeness. 'Will you accept a drink in thanks for rescuing Falstaff? You really rescued us all, he would have turned us in in a moment to save himself from being sent down.'

Jessica laughed at this, but quietly and to herself, as if gilding the joke with private experience.

'I would love a drink,' I said.

'Do you drink whisky?' he asked.

'No.'

'Well, you must start, you really must. Nothing helps when you've taken a beating like whisky. There's some Laphroaig in the store, I'm sure Falstaff's tab can accommodate a few more rounds.'

We drank together, and I felt bathed in anticipation as I spoke with them. I was filled with the unique sensation of getting what I wanted, and finding it every bit as glamorous as I had imagined. Towards the end of the evening, I found myself talking to Francis. He mentioned that the next day he and Jessica were going hunting, and idly suggested that it would have been lovely if I could have come with them.

'Oh, I could come,' I said, pouncing on the suggestion before he could move on, 'I have no plans for tomorrow. I've never done anything like that before. What time are you leaving?'

Francis's beautiful, swollen face stalled for a moment in mid-expression and a bemused smile parted his split lips. I understood my faux pas immediately. The proper thing to do with such a slight invitation, having landed it, was to toss it back into the conversation and let it slip away. It was a tentative sign of politeness, an acknowledgement of the possibility of future contact, not a practical step towards initiating it. Francis, however, was far too well mannered to register his surprise for more than a moment. His good nature led him to see inexperience in me rather than a conscious attempt to insinuate myself into the event, and I saw him smile inwardly at my eagerness. He leant forwards in his seat, leaving generalities behind as a businesslike tone entered his voice. I was to meet the others at seven o'clock the next morning in Great Court, and the three of us would make our way down to the meet. When I asked what I should bring, he said only myself, and my fabled grace under fire. The compliment drew a blush, before Jessica came over to the two of us and retook her rightful place in his attentions.

By the time we left we had only a few hours before our journey. We stole the morning papers and milk for tea from the delivery van waiting outside Sainsbury's. We staggered back to Michael's rooms on Bridge Street. The birds were singing, and I was happy.

5

When I arrived in Great Court at six-forty-five in the morning, it was clear that Francis had forgotten to tell Jessica that he had invited me. She was waiting on the broad stone steps by the entrance to the chapel, and waved to me and smiled as if at a chance meeting. She told me where she was going for the day. When she asked me what my plans were, I was mortified. I mumbled that Francis had asked me to tag along, as a thank you for rescuing Michael. I could feel this slender excuse fraying: it had held my weight for only a few hours in their company, and I knew it would soon break. Jessica was less disposed to hide her surprise than Francis had been the previous night. She arched her fine eyebrows, and then shrugged, as if to say, 'Then he can take care of you.' I had clearly exhausted my free trial period, and would get no further indulgence from her. Her beauty made her difficult to talk to. It was something that had to be got used to, like the coldness of water. She had at her feet a canvas bag which, I was soon to discover, contained her riding boots, hat and jodhpurs. Before her family had lost their money her parents had had a mania for activities, and at fourteen Jessica had been a champion tennis player, skier, rider and ice skater. The development of all these skills had been arrested at the same time as her father and, without Francis, she lacked the means to indulge them. Unlike the rest of her body, her feet had not grown since her early teens, and the riding boots were a legacy of better times, nursed in a storage cupboard until she came up to Cambridge. The hat was a gift from Francis.

I again felt embarrassed, since it was clear that Jessica had been invited to participate, whereas I would be a mere spectator. It made the previous night's mistake even more gross, and Francis's willingness to make good his offer all the more generous. I would spend the day relying on the good grace of people I had never met to ferry me around, explain what was going on and make conversation. I had only slept two or three hours, and my hangover was nagging at me. Jessica, who had not been drinking, seemed in perfect form. Only the thought of the happiness I had glimpsed at the club allowed me to keep my nerve, and prevented me from making some excuse and leaving.

Francis himself arrived a few minutes later to tell us that his driver was waiting for us in Old Court. He seemed every bit as fresh as Jessica, though his eye, still swollen from the battle, gave him the air of a conquering hero. He looked at my face, and I must have been visibly suffering, for he immediately apologized for the early start. 'This early in the season, you have to go out in the twilight, when the frost's still on the ground, because then it holds the fox's scent,' he explained.

We came under the cold shadows of the colonnade to find a mighty Mercedes, its exhaust breathing heavy white smoke in the freezing air, the engine humming with lazy power. The driver was a uniformed man of about forty-five who Francis cheerfully informed us had been in the special forces. He said this in the man's presence as he loaded Jessica's bag into the boot, and the driver's sad features broke into a brief smile when he heard it. I read into that smile a long and happy history, and Francis later told me that the two of them had shared the drives to and from Eton when he was a young schoolboy (his father being always too busy to take him), and he had told Francis many tales of heroic missions and dead comrades, which were received with open mouth and shining eyes by the teenager bouncing up and down on the passenger seat. On the rare occasions when he travelled with his father, they always sat in the back, and Francis would have to stare at the silent fold in the back of his neck. I wondered at the time why Lord Soulford had hired someone with such specialized skills to be his driver, and when I came to know more of the man I concluded that he had taken him on for just that reason, to make you wonder. The air of manly mystery, and the possibility of loyal muscle trained in the British army suited his idiom. Having ex-military personnel on his staff must have given him a little thrill of officer status, and given his political opponents brief pause for thought.

Francis hopped into the front seat and sat with his knees up against the dashboard. Jessica and I climbed into the back, separated by a wide channel of cream leather. Even the clunk of the smooth belt in the buckle sounded expensive. Francis said casually, 'Papa's still down in London, isn't he?' The driver nodded. As we rolled out of the college gates, Francis slid a silver CD with red handwriting on the front into the player in the walnut console, and the car was filled with the confident rap of Mos Def.

The meet was being held on the land of a farmer in Francis's village. I was disappointed to discover that we would not be seeing his house, which I imagined must be very beautiful. There were perhaps thirty horses and riders, and a churning mass of ninety hounds milling around the legs of the spectators, who drank port and ate sausage rolls in the cold half-light of the autumn morning. The honest stench of the animals filled the clear air. Francis introduced me to a family who were tenants on one of his farms, who kindly offered me a place in their Land-Rover to follow the hunt. When the riders set out, we barrelled along the winding roads, tracing their route as best we could, trying to anticipate the run of the fox.

Initially, it was breathtaking to witness those proud riders on the fields, but the postcard elegance quickly wore thin, and I found myself becoming bored, riding along with the good-natured family, who asked me questions about Cambridge. I was also acutely aware that I might have pawned my last excuse to see Jessica and Francis for a day when I would not be able to speak with either of them, and that at the hunt's end, with politeness satisfied, they might cast me back into loneliness.

At the end of the morning, however, I saw something of the two of them that set their seal upon my heart. We had perfectly guessed the direction of the hunt, and were able to wait at the edge of a field to watch the whole body of riders sweep down a hillside towards us. They were galloping across a green field, their red and blue torsos crouched low in the saddles, their white legs clenched tight around heaving brown flanks. The terracotta smear of the fox streaked under the bars of a high wooden gate, and the squirming mass of the hounds flattened their bodies underneath it, heedless of the master's horn. As the riders came up to the jump, they broke upon it like waves on the rocks and flowed away to either side, seeking for the safe way into the pasture beyond. Francis and Jessica were bringing up the rear. He spurred his brown gelding with a fierce dig in the ribs, and the animal catapulted forwards towards the gate. It was five or six feet high; his stern black face looked well under the bill of his top hat as he trained his eyes on it. The horse leapt over the bars. As it landed its front legs buckled, and it stumbled forward on to its knees, tossing him over its head so that he spun through the air, still holding the brown thongs of the reins in his hands. For a second, it was as if he hung frozen by his own momentum in the air, and the thing had the look of a surrealist painting, with a young black man in a top hat hanging upside down in the cold glory of an English autumn morning. The impression ended when Francis's heavy frame met the turf with a sickening thump.

Jessica, the moment she saw his horse begin to stumble, spurred her own on towards the same jump. She arced gracefully over it, landing perfectly on the soft ground, and reined her mare back in. She gripped the pommel and swung her leg over the saddle before it had even come to a stop, and ran over to where Francis was lying on his back in the grass, twitching but not rising. She sprinted to his body and fell on her knees at his side, staining her long cream legs with grass and cow shit. I too was running across the field, and as I gripped the bar of the gate with my hands, I saw a thing I could not explain. Jessica was still kneeling in front of the fallen body, but she was slapping and beating his chest in fury. It was not until I came closer that I saw the reason Francis could not rise. His whole trunk was shaking with uncontrollable laughter, so much so that it racked him like pain. His horse stood a few yards away from him, unimpressed by his display, cropping the grass, steam wreathing its flanks and back. When they went for the jump, Francis was not thinking of himself, and Jessica was thinking of nothing else.

After Francis had picked himself up they found they had lost the hunt, though the distant echo of the master's horn could still be heard across the valley, and the three of us, two mounted and myself on foot keeping up as best I could, went to a pub that Francis knew in the village for lunch. They left their horses tethered in the car park. He stepped under the low lintel of the pub's doorway into the warm wooden space beyond, and a cheer went up from behind the bar. When the barmaid saw Francis's black eye she cheerfully teased him, asking him how the other guy was looking. The first round was on the landlord, though Francis graciously fought to pay. He and Jessica were so exhilarated from the ride, and from the fear and laughter of the recent tumble, that her coolness towards me melted in the warmth of the hearth.

'So, what do you make of your first hunt?' Francis asked me.

'It was . . . amazing,' I said, 'just incredible.' In my desperation to find something intriguing or insightful to say, I was rendering myself idiotic.

Francis laughed. 'Amazing! Incredible!' He was mocking me, but his eyes included me in the joke, inviting me to laugh at myself, so that I was able to turn to Jessica and give her a hopeless shrug. When I spoke to

83

him again, I tried to make my awkwardness seem like the product of sincerity.

'I mean, when I saw you come off the horse, the cream and scarlet hanging against the deep green fields . . . I don't mean to sound weird, but I wanted to draw you.'

'Do you draw?' Francis asked, leaning forwards in his chair. 'I would love to see your stuff.'

When we left the pub, the horses were already gone. Francis had texted his stable master, who had collected them in a horse box. The sleek silver Mercedes was waiting in the car park to carry us back to Cambridge.

It was just what I needed, Francis's fall and the day that surrounded it. After that, I had a little material I could fashion into jokes and conversation and I knew how to husband the link. Francis had slightly injured his wrist, so I could go around to his room to see how it was healing. I was able to ask him for his father's address, to write to him to thank him for the use of his driver. I could compliment Jessica on her horsemanship, and on the way she had rushed to Francis's aid. I delighted in being the first to tell Michael about the day we had spent together, and in his attempts to hide his irritation by indulging in some territorial spraying on the subject of how well he knew the countryside around Francis's house. He asked me if we had been to this farm or that pond, and said how pretty such a village was in summertime, and restored himself.

Soon I had them nodding to me in the corridors, and if I chanced to see them at mealtimes in the Great Hall I would go and sit with them, though they did not often eat in college, and never dined. I was careful throughout this period to pay as little attention as possible to Jessica, who I sensed believed every newcomer to be wildly in love with her, and thus beneath contempt. It was not their trust which I had to cultivate, but their interest, and I think in being rather curt with Jessica in those first few days I did myself as much good as all my flattery of Michael and my indulgence of Francis put together. When she sensed my indifference, which was wholly artificial but convincingly managed, she began to seek me out. I do not mean to say that she was vain – for me, vanity always implies some measure of delusion, and Jessica was fully justified in her self-assessment. Rather I think that she was used to dealing with people who wanted something from her, whether in the obvious sexual sense or by the reflected glamour of her presence, and she was drawn to those who wanted nothing. A mixture of irritation at my failure to swoon and interest in the reasons drove her, almost against her will, to try and discover me.

It was she, I am sure, who invited me to Francis's birthday party. I found the invitation in my pigeon-hole, an embossed rectangle of thick cream card from Smythson. I kept it in the inside pocket of my coat, and snuck little looks at it during lectures.

When the day arrived, I was to meet the group in Jessica's rooms in Tudor. Lisa was getting ready with Jessica in her set and they had left the door open. I could smell the warm waft of perfume, and hear the beat of house music turned down low. It was common practice among the second years, who would often group their friends together on the same staircase when choosing sets, to leave the doors connecting their living rooms open. It gave the place an air of communal gaiety, and the bare stone steps transmitted conversations, cooking smells, laughter and music between the floors with the ease of friendship. One flight before their room I stopped on the stairs and bent down to do up my shoelace, pretending to myself as much as anyone. I did not wish to think of myself as the kind of person who eavesdropped.

'There'll be a bunch of rich twats at this party?' Lisa was saying.

'Yup. Michael's coming, and Jeremy, and Lily . . .'

'Anyone I know?' Lisa was a little too aggressive in asking the question, betraying, I thought, a hint of social insecurity.

'You remember that boy James? The one from the fight night? Francis invited him.'

'Why?'

'Why does anyone invite anyone?'

'Don't ask me. I'm usually a gatecrasher.'

Jessica laughed at that. I rose, having spent as long as

was plausible on my shoe, and announced my presence on the stairs by coughing. I knocked at the open door, but my modesty was wasted on Jessica, who shouted at me to come in, and appeared in the living room in nothing but jeans and a bra. She was not merely fashionably skinny, but muscled from her leisure. Her smooth flat midriff made me stare at my shoes. 'Make yourself a drink,' she said, indicating a bronze Moroccan tray with her cigarette, 'and you might as well make Francis one while you're there. We'll be out in a sec.'

'Where shall I put this?' I asked, holding up a bottle of champagne, keen that it should be noticed. I had not dared to buy anything cheaper than thirty pounds, though I had agonized over the purchase. It seemed to me that these were the sort of people who would at least recognize expensive alcohol, and appreciate the gesture if not the taste. I was a little perturbed when she indicated the table without so much as a glance at the label, and walked back into her bedroom, closing the door. I looked around the room: it was friendly-filthy like a teenage boy's, with dirty sports shoes, sweat bands, tennis rackets, balled-up jeans, CDs and jewellery, fake and real, covering every surface. Only the smell of the place betrayed the sex of the occupant: the faint citrus scent of her was everywhere. It amazed me that Jessica could conjure up her perfect appearance from this chaos. I lifted a sheaf of notes off an armchair and took a seat.

Francis bounded in a few minutes later to tell us that the party was waiting down by the Mill.

'And would you look at this?' he was saying, waving a letter backwards and forwards. 'My father has remembered my birthday! On Commons headed notepaper, no less.'

The girls came out of the bedroom. Jessica was casually perfect in black jeans and a figure-hugging silk top that looped around the back of her long neck. Lisa seemed a little discordant next to her in a rather ugly, though no doubt expensive, sweat jacket sewn with innumerable beads and scrawled with graffiti. The letter Francis brandished was a single typewritten sheet with a governmental letterhead and a handwritten scrawl at the bottom. He did not seem to expect any present from his father, and I suppose that given the amount of money he received from him weekly it would not have been appropriate. It was touching, the way he tried to conceal his joy from us in parody. You could see that behind his wry smile there was real elation tugging on the corners of his lips, and his eyes sparkled, not with the brilliance of his own fooling, but with excitement.

'What does it say?' Jessica asked.

'Yeah, go on, read it to us, Francis, please,' Lisa said, rolling her eyes, playing up to Francis's pretence of scorn.

'It says, "To my firstborn on the occasion of his twentieth birthday . . ."' His voice deepened, and he rounded and polished his public school vowels into what I guessed must be an imitation of his father.

'At least he knows how old you are,' Jessica interjected. Francis held up the palm of his hand for silence.

' "You are nearing the age of manhood . . ." How kind of him to say so! He's called me many things, but never a man.' He looked more closely at the letter, reading it for the second time, and he seemed suddenly to sag a little, as though the breath had gone out of him. 'So very kind . . .' he repeated quietly.

'Come on, let's hear the great statesman speak,' Jessica said, throwing a Biro from her desk at him.

'It's just the usual stuff,' Francis replied, still scanning the letter. Then he balled it up in his fist and brightened once more. 'Come on then! Let's go, people, my purpose holds to sail beyond the sunset. Carpe P. M. and all that.' I was a little shocked to see him destroy what a moment before had seemed a treasured article.

The girls made a few more calls for the letter, but he waved them away with his eyes down. He popped the bottle of champagne I had bought him as we walked down the stairs and upended the neck as we came into New Court. The effervescence bubbled up out of his mouth and down between the high banks of his pectorals, making wet shadows on his white shirt where the fabric stuck to his flesh. I was piqued when I saw him gulping the precious liquid without registering the quality, but I turned to the others, hoping to offer them a comic shrug to indicate that I was in the know about Francis and his excesses. When I turned, however, it was to see Jessica and Lisa looking with unease at one another.

Tudor had their own boats, but Francis did not want any of the party to have the trouble of punting, so he had hired one of the flat-bottomed barges from Scudamore's, complete with a uniformed gondolier in a white shirt and tartan waistcoat. There were perhaps five guests waiting for us there, all beautifully dressed. I did not know any of them, though I recognized some from around college. The banks of seats for the passengers faced one another across the deck, which was decorated with a sumptuous picnic. Red tartan rugs lay across the seats for the cold, but the night was so still that the flames of the candles lit in the centre were barely troubled. The Cam was quite empty. When we set off from the weir and passed under the Mathematician's Bridge at Queens', the only sound was our quiet chatter reverberating on the stone walls, the clink of toasting flutes, and the splash of the punt pole as it fell into the black water. Mist rose from the fields along the edges of the river, shrouding the ancient buildings, where warm orange squares of the lead-latticed windows glowed in the dark walls. In the shadows on the banks appeared the white bodies of swans, their necks tucked under their wings.

Twenty minutes later we had slid gently through the

body of the city and found ourselves outside Magdalene. Francis had been drinking steadily since our departure, and he chose this moment to rise on shaky legs and give a speech. 'I would like to raise a toast to you all, my friends, for sharing this evening with me, for eating, drinking and being merry.'

An appreciative cheer went up from the audience.

'And one to our guide, whose fingers must be turning blue with the cold water.'

A second cheer went up.

'But, most of all, I think it incumbent upon me to make this speech in the name of my dear old papa. Peace to the nigga!'

At this, he raised his glass higher still, so that his arm was completely straight; his hand holding the brimming glass was directly over his head. When he mentioned his father, I felt a stiffening in the group, a quick gagging at the peculiar smell of a good joke gone bad. There was another cheer, but this one was ragged; it frayed into nervous laughter. The boat wobbled in the river as his weight swapped from one foot to the other, and the puntman, who was standing side on on the back board, had to shift on to his heels, then back to his toes.

'Or rather, not to Papa, but to Rebecca Newman, his private secretary, who has loved me like her own son, and who has gone to the trouble of forging his signature on the birthday card she sent to me from his office, and an excellent effort it is too, though Papa puts a little more oomph into the loops of the ascenders. She should not have tried to put one over on someone who has received as many cheques from him as I have, though I appreciate the effort!' He drained off his glass.

'Francis,' Jessica said, so quietly it was almost to herself.

'But he is no doubt away on important business. Guarding our borders, saving us from ourselves, kicking out the riffraff . . .' he was rambling.

'Francis, old chap, I think you ought to sit down.' Michael rose from his seat and clambered over the shifting deck towards Francis. What began as a steadying hand on his arm quickly became downward pressure.

'Falstaff, unhand me! I have a horror of doing what I ought.'

'Sit down, Francis.'

The two men wrestled for a few seconds, the puntman vainly remonstrating with them both, but unable to abandon his pole. A great whoop went up from the drunken party as the scuffle carried Francis's calves to the wooden sides of the boat, and he dodged, throwing Michael into the cold and murky water. Francis turned to face him and burst into laughter.

'That is the best present a man could hope for,' he said to the spluttering figure that surfaced from the river. 'You are a true friend.'

For a moment, clouds of outrage gathered in Michael's cheeks; he looked like a spoilt child preparing a tantrum.

The water, which was so shallow it only came up to his waist, had undone the careful arrangement of his hair, revealing his bald patch. However, he saw the laughing faces of his friends in the punt and instead of raging he smiled graciously, and gave Francis a playful knock on the shins. Then he gripped the side of the boat and wobbled it as if to tip us all in.

'It's very bracing in here, lads. Why don't you all join me for a dip?' His pride allowed him that much room for manoeuvre. He judged the mood just right, and the laughter was with him now, as people thought him a great sport.

We were on the Backs opposite Trinity, and Michael waded to the bank to go in search of warmth and fresh clothes. The incident seemed to have satisfied Francis's need for drama, and he slowed his drinking as the puntman propelled us with grim and steady pushes back towards the weir. Once we were docked he remonstrated with us about our behaviour, but Francis worked him over with a hundred soothing apologies, all topped with a hefty tip. In the end he bid us goodnight with a friendly wave, and gave Francis his number, telling him to call him personally if he required any such service in future.

On the walk back to Tudor, Jessica seemed in a dark mood. She lagged behind the rest of the group, and I fell back with her, grateful to be spared the other guests. I asked her if anything was wrong, and to my surprise she answered me.

'Did you see how much Francis paid the boatman?' she said.

'No.'

'And that champagne we were drinking . . . it was far too good. I know this sounds crazy, but I think he steamed the labels off some bottles of Louis Roederer Cristal and stuck on some from Sainsbury's, just to keep me and Lisa off his back. We set him a budget for this party, and he's blown it completely. All those parasites, he doesn't even like them . . .'

I could not decide whether this comment was aimed at me, or whether my own social paranoia had nudged me into the firing line. Jessica did not look at me for a reaction; she seemed to be occupied with her own thoughts, so I let it pass unremarked.

Sure enough, when Francis sobered up the next morning, he confessed he had already spent most of the money he had earned on the night of the fight, and with his allowance not due for another week he was back in trouble with the bookies, the tailors, the tobacconists, and a whole host of creditors too numerous to mention.

Here, I would like to say a few words about money, for as my relationship with Francis developed I came to realize how foolish it is to believe that you cannot love someone for their fortune. Of course, in the shallowest sense, this is true, but there is rarely an instance where someone spends a great deal of time with someone else in the pure pursuit of their material wealth. The effort of being with another, and of constantly concealing one's motives, comes to outweigh any enjoyment that might be had from the cash itself. Rather, it is the cause and effect of money that can form the basis of enduring love between people. Francis had been raised all his life in the midst of a fortune the like of which I had only encountered in books and glossy magazines. He had come into it at the age of four from a poverty which, whilst not extreme by the standards of east Africa, was also beyond the realms of my experience, and which he himself remembered only as he remembered his mother: an intellectual fact disconnected from his own memories, and an indelible impression with no specific recollections to act as handholds, a sheer face in his own mind which he could not scale. It left him free to enjoy what he had to the full, without ever forgetting the privilege of doing so. He lived so easily, and with such freedom from the grinding little concerns which informed my day-to-day existence, such as whether I could pay my rent that term, or peering into my wallet the night after a binge and wincing at the empty leather, that it made his soul beautiful. His family's extraordinary fortune, to which he himself had access only by permission, served to elevate him above the world in the same way a monk seeks to free himself through a vow of poverty. When I say we loved Francis for his money, I do not mean for one moment to diminish our friendship, for it was part of the bedrock of his nature.

6

As I gave my account of my memories, night had set in, and there was noise again from Hoxton Square. The ceiling of the living room flashed blue as a police van rolled past, the lights on and the sirens off. A car pulled up outside the restaurant below, and someone jumped out of the passenger side, unleashing a wave of hip hop against the window. The new arrivals were intent on Friday night pleasure. It was a strange crowd, beautiful and loutish, a mixture of models and fashionistas fresh from warehouse shoots, bankers and journalists from Canary Wharf and local boys and girls from the housing estates. The area around my square was composed of a warren of dead ends and one-way streets. The freezing rain drove them quickly on towards 333 and Jaguar Shoes, to live hip hop, eighties electronica and cheap ecstasy. It felt good to have this concrete proof that we were not alone in the city.

At the beginning Jessica made a show of asking me questions about the painting; then, as time went on, she became content just to sit and listen. Certain moments drew smiles from her, and once or twice she sighed or nodded, gently encouraging me to go on like a shy lover. We never forgot the picture, it provided a centre point around which a pattern of reminiscence could be arranged, but I moved into all the corners of those days, rediscovering old treasures, brushing away cobwebs and burnishing dusty scenes until they gleamed like gold. I went and retrieved the Scotch from the kitchen, and spontaneous toasts began to burst from the memories, to Michael, rest in peace, to Francis, to us; they punctuated my monologue with the jolly barrage of tumblers on tabletops. There was, however, something in the memories that I was sure was never present in the original experience, the imposition of my adult eyes on the past. I found myself mentioning money, heard the distant rustle of folded notes in the midnight cloisters. Each recollection seemed to come with a price discreetly attached, like the tags in expensive antique shops, hand-written and stuck to the underside, or hanging out of sight, only visible when you lift an object up or turn it around to inspect it close up. I wanted to purge these fiscal details from my talk, but each time I would catch myself just too late. Jessica did not seem to notice, but the problem began to gnaw at me.

Neither of us had eaten, and I went briefly to the phone to order Chinese takeaway from Deliverance. Jessica had always liked Chinese food. Both of us were wearing our work clothes, with the sleeves rolled up on our shirts and the jackets off. I loosened my yellow silk tie and undid my collar button. The costumes reminded me of a late-night scene at the office, the mixture of coffee and booze and adrenalin in my system, the heightened sense of importance that came with working on the deal after hours, rubbing computer-red eyes with thumb and forefinger.

When the doorbell rang, I thought it must be our takeaway, though they were quicker than the half-hour I had been quoted over the phone. Then there came the sullen clunk of the intercom, and a woman's voice said, 'Hello?' It was a voice I recognized, and it made me wince. Clearly the message of cancellation I had left before leaving the office had not made it through. Jessica looked at me questioningly, and there was a brief and unwelcome bump of reality, like the lights coming on in a darkened cinema halfway through the film. I knew that I had only a few seconds in which to avert disaster. I could not leave the woman in the rain: she would continue to ring the bell. The lights in my living room were visible from the street. I could not dismiss her over the intercom: Jessica would hear everything at normal volume, and nothing would inflame her curiosity like an attempted whisper. The only option would be to go down into the street, to hope Jessica did not look out of the window, and on the way back up to invent some plausible explanation. With this in mind I started for the door, ignoring her quizzical look. I arrived and threw it open, only to find Alysha standing directly behind it, clearly surprised in the act of checking her make-up in a small handheld mirror.

She looked stunningly beautiful, this tall black woman who always seemed to me to have been fashioned deliberately for others' pleasure out of some material more precious than flesh, her hard body encased in a long leather overcoat that framed her broad shoulders, open at the waist to reveal a black evening dress that shimmered slightly in the light falling through the open door. She wore shoes with long heels that stood her feet on the toes in a ballerina's pose, with a thin strip of leather fixed high on each ankle in a tiny gold buckle. In heels she easily matched my six feet two. She regained her poise in a second, folded her compact together with a decisive click, smiled and slipped it back into the tiny evening bag she was carrying. She placed her hand on my shoulder, leant forward and kissed me on the cheek, exhaling slightly, raising the hairs along the back of my neck. Her body brushed lightly against mine as she moved through into my apartment. 'I know I'm not s'posed to see you this weekend,' she was saying as she made her way in, 'but—' She stopped in mid-stride, nonplussed for the second time in as many minutes, and found herself looking at Jessica.

There was the brief pause that always follows the unexpected meeting of two very attractive women, and I could feel them in the silence clicking beads on the abacus of status. The pause gave me a brief respite, and I marshalled the scattered armies of my thoughts for one final push. If I could interject now, and give some sign to Alysha, her natural discretion would handle the rest, and she could be out of my house in ten minutes, the two of us having laid the foundations for some alibi (stopping off to pick something up, a forgotten file from work) that would sustain me through an interrogation with Jessica. She was an intelligent woman and highly socially perceptive; it would not take much to give her the nudge. I had got so far in my calculations when I froze. I could think of nothing to say, inspiration tossed no lifeline phrase to my drowning brain, and I stood there in mute desperation as Alysha, her judgement made, slipped her coat gracefully from her shoulders and folded it over her arm. She put out a slender hand in greeting to Jessica, who took it without getting up. It seemed to me in that blissful moment that she had already taken the measure of the scene, and would save me from both embarrassment and my own incompetence.

'Hi, I'm Alysha.'

'Jessica.'

'I love your pendant. Is that Tiffany's?'

'Yes,' Jessica answered, pleased.

'It's lovely. Real nice. Can I touch it?' Without waiting to be asked she reached out, and with her long glossy nails picked the silver bar from the skin between the tops of Jessica's breasts.

The knot in my gut began to uncoil. I was going to get away with it. She placed the pendant back, and lightly pressed it in place with the palm of her hand. Jessica returned her smile, a little surprised at the intimacy of the contact. Alysha turned towards me. 'James, I don't know what you had fixed up with Laura, yeah? I'm happy to do couples this one time as your girlfriend's a stunner, but I charge six hundred pounds. Is that OK with you?'

There was an awful pause, and I saw the look on Alysha's face shift from one of seductive confidence to abject horror, as she sensed that she had misunderstood the situation. I was mortified for myself, and I could have become angry if I had wanted to, but I felt a rush of sympathy, an odd sensation, since my feelings towards her were usually confined to desire and shame. After a few seconds, Jessica burst out laughing.

She offered Alysha a coffee, and had the grace to slip out into the kitchen, closing the interconnecting door behind her. Alysha apologized profusely, stroking my arm and repeating herself in her confusion. It was the work of a moment to discover the mistake – Laura had gone down with flu, and though I wasn't due to see Alysha until two weeks later Laura had called her and asked her to cover. Laura had not picked up her messages that evening, as she was in bed at her mother's. Someone in my building had left the downstairs door on the latch, and rather than exposing herself to the cold and the whistling of passing bankers she had simply come straight up. She peppered this explanation with further pleas for forgiveness, and begged me not to tell her boss at the agency about the mistake. I assured her I would not, and found myself trying to explain my relationship with Jessica, quite as inarticulate and stumbling in my way as she had been.

'She's not my girlfriend, I mean she's a friend, an old friend from college.'

'I've gone and fucked things up, yeah?' Alysha asked, and the look of panic crept back into her eyes.

'No, no, it's not like that at all. As I said, you know, she's a friend, and she's pretty broad-minded. She won't think too badly of me . . .'

She looked away, and nodded to herself. I was afraid I had insulted her. Then she folded her bare arms over her chest as if cold, though the flat was warm. I could see she suddenly felt ridiculous in her beautiful clothes, not seductive but overdressed and silly. A terrible notion suddenly struck me, that she might think I had meant Jessica did not mind that she was black, rather than that she was a prostitute. Or 'escort'. She reached up with one hand and began unconsciously to finger the lobe of her ear, a gesture I had never seen in her before. Again, I felt compassion like an irritating itch at the back of my skull. To fight the feeling off I summoned an image of her from some weeks before, kneeling naked in my living room with her hands on my buttocks, pressing her face down against my crotch. I pictured the scene from outside myself, from the perspective of a voyeur standing in the far corner. She gave head like the girls in the movies. The image could not hold, and I saw her again standing in front of me, her arms wrapped protectively around her chest, cradling her dignity. I did not want to see her like this, and I did not want either of these people to get a glimpse of the other part of my life.

Jessica returned like the spirit of social nicety with three neat little white cups and a cafetière on a silver tray, together with the dainty little sugar bowl my mother had left me and a tiny jug with cream in it. I was amazed to discover that I owned such a thing. I called Alysha a cab, which was less conspicuous than her waiting outside my house in the square, but proved to be a dreadful mistake. In the twenty minutes before the arrival of the taxi Jessica engaged her in conversation, and began to learn details about her life. Alysha spoke readily and warmly. She was looking to buy a new flat. Her parents were originally from Angola, but had come here before she was born. I knew she was funny and clever, that she did not like champagne, offered everything, smoked and preferred white wine to red, but beyond that I had no wish to go. Jessica was ruining her for me one detail at a time. Throughout the course of the conversation Alysha snuck little looks and conspiratorial nods at me under Jessica's radar. It was clear that she no longer believed that Jessica was just a friend, and had deemed our late-night drinking session a budding romance. I felt the awkwardness of the situation escalate like a pain in the inner ear as a plane climbs away from the runway, building to a maddening climax.

I took my Scotch to the bathroom for five minutes to escape the tension, and sat with my head in my hands on the closed lid of the toilet. The smell of disinfectant, clean and inorganic, soothed my nerves. Even in there, however, I could hear the dull murmur of conversation seeping under the door. Eventually the thought that they might be discussing me and the fear of what details Jessica could divulge about my life drove me back into the living room. I downed the drink before I left, the empty glass making a satisfying clink when I set it down on the black porcelain bowl of the sink. I never really got drunk any more, but I was beginning to feel the companionable hum of alcohol in my system, like turning all the lights on for comfort in an empty building. I flushed the toilet and washed my hands for verisimilitude.

When the doorbell went to signal the arrival of the cab I leapt away like an athlete at the starter's pistol crack, and was holding Alysha's coat for her before she had even risen from her chair. She actually kissed Jessica goodbye on the cheek, and when we came out on to the stairwell she gave me a softer kiss on the mouth; I drew in a deep breath from the warmth of her skin, and placed my hand briefly on the boyish jut of her hip. She pulled away slowly, giving me a look of terrible sexless intimacy, like a big sister whose wayward playboy brother finally brings home the right girl. To ward off the moment I dug my hand in my pocket, pulled out my wallet and thrust a handful of notes between the two of us, twenties in a fan that briefly concealed her décolletage. She shrugged and took the money, folding it away into her neat little purse. She was a practical girl, and she knew better than to argue with money. I had given her two hundred, the standard half-fee for late cancellations, plus an extra fifty for her time. 'Maybe I'll see you next month,' she said, with a pointed optimism on the 'maybe' that made my skin crawl.

I saw her into the cab. One man in a group loitering outside the restaurant noticed her and whistled. His friend shouted, 'All right, darling!' I held the door open for her in redundant chivalry (if any of those men had a spare four hundred pounds, they could call her what they liked), and walked slowly back to my front door. The night air was cold and sharp after the sleepy warmth of the flat. The rain had stopped, and the square was glazed with brilliant droplets. I looked back up at the lighted window, and saw Jessica waiting for me, leaning her shoulder against the wall, a drink in her hand, smiling down on me from behind a protective sheet of glass. I took the stairs slowly.

When I came in she did not speak immediately, but let her advantage simmer. We were alone in our world, boxed inside the four blue walls of my living room, a parcel of history like the ones from children's birthday parties, unwrapped one layer at a time. I went to the table and refilled my glass, before reaching into the plastic ice bucket. It looked naked without the gaudy foil bulb of a champagne bottle leaning out of the top. The ice had sat for too long in the warmth, and I came up with a soaking handful of slivers. The biting cold of the water on my wrist felt right, like a little punishment, and chilled my blood.

'I suppose all that money had to come bursting out somewhere,' she said. 'I like your flat but it hardly befits the two hundred and fifty pounds an hour, and you don't seem to have any other hobbies.'

'If you don't like the flat you can leave.'

'Did you know her name's not really Alysha?' she said. I had a sudden overpowering impulse to put my fingers in my ears and begin chanting.

'I don't want to know what her name is.'

'Mary. I had an aunt called Mary.'

'Stop it,' I said, and I meant it as a command, but it came out as more of a plea.

She eyed me, deciding how far to push, and then relented with a magnanimous shrug. We sat in silence for a few moments, whilst I debated whether or not to tell her a story.

'I tell you something else about that painting,' I said at last, my mind made up. 'I put in a lot of work. I could get the style, I mean I could copy the lines, but I couldn't capture the essence, I couldn't capture that lively, living quality that comes from the direct interpretation of the subject. I don't know if it mattered to anybody else, I'm not even sure such a quality exists any more; reproduction can be exact, and the price people place on authenticity is obscene. But it mattered to me back then. Do you remember, in the first months of the summer, Francis and I used to disappear for whole weekends?'

She squinted, as if trying to pick out a detail of a distant scene. 'Yes,' she said thoughtfully, 'yes, I think I do remember that.'

'You used to pester us for hours to tell you where we went. One time you even hid in the boot of Francis's car, and we had to let you out when you started banging against the back seat on the A14. You must remember that.'

Her lips tightened, and she moved her head back slightly, though whether to indicate 'yes' or 'no' I could not tell.

'Did he ever tell you where we went? He promised me he wouldn't, but, well, Francis and promises . . .'

'Yes, I know. No, he never told me anything.'

'He used to take me to a brothel in Shoreditch, not far from here actually. I drive past the building sometimes, but it's not there any more, the council closed it down. It used to be a strip club on three floors – there was a dance floor on the first, with booths for private dances at the back, and everything done in plush purple felt, with stools that looked and smelt like rings of mushrooms. In the middle there was a large disc of fake black marble with two poles erected in the centre, and a chrome spiral staircase where the girls came down, tottering along on these huge perspex stilettos. It was the kind of place where the girls came round with a cup before their dances, and you dropped in a pound to start them up. Up the staircase there was a second room, the champagne room, with low sofas around these glass cubicles, and the first time he took me up there I had no idea what they were for. Then this poor girl came in and began to dance around in the middle, and somebody switched on a jet of water, so that she was bumping and grinding like something out of a shampoo advert, flinging her hair from left to right and shaking her buttocks. To get to that floor you had to buy champagne, and you chose one or two girls to be your hostesses. Francis was paying, of course, running out the last of that endless fortune. "What does it matter," he used to say to me, "soon we'll all be rich for our whole lives . . ."' At this Jessica frowned in sadness, and I changed tack. 'Then, finally, when we got to know the manager a little bit, there was the locked door that led to the rooms at the top. Bedrooms fitted out in exactly the same material as the ground floor, all purple and red and humid, like the inside of a bruised heart. Each one had a cupboard with pretty much every costume you can imagine, and hundreds of frightening toys.'

Jessica lit a cigarette and passed it to me. I had not smoked in five years, but I took it, and it fitted on to my body like handmade gloves.

'The girls loved Francis. I mean I know it's their job to make every guy think they love him, but they really did. It wasn't just that he was young and good-looking and generous with tips, whilst most of their clientele were tight and ugly, though I'm sure that was part of it. And I know that everyone loved Francis, but these were people who looked like they weren't much used to loving anybody, you know? I think Francis chose that place specifically, I mean it wasn't a dive, but he could have afforded much better. The girls were just beautiful enough for you to fall in love with them, but not so beautiful they wouldn't be interested in you. The place was so seedy it reeked of exploitation, and I think he liked that too, because he came in like a breath of fresh air. All of the girls had accents: Eastern European and African mostly. Anyway, the first time Francis took me upstairs to the brothel, he chose this sweet girl called Misha. She was Polish, but she spoke fluent English. I think she must have been about nineteen. She had only worked there a little while, and she told me the other girls didn't like her very much, because she got a lot more attention and made a lot more money than they did. Francis would go downstairs and pay – it was always payment first – for a couple of hours of her time, and she would take off her clothes. She let me arrange her with her arms behind her head and the cum-stained rug lying loosely over her thigh, just like the girl in the picture, and I would draw her. At first she felt ridiculous, you could see it in her eyes; she would fidget and even try to initiate sex through sheer awkwardness – you know, tug the corner of the cloth away and start touching herself, or put a finger into her mouth, as if that was what she really wanted. After the first few times, though, she started to like it. Francis told her that I was a brilliant artist, that the paintings were going on display in galleries and rich people's drawing rooms, and she began to love the idea of being part of something important. Of being valued, of being essential even, a kind of muse. Francis would stay in the champagne room playing with the other girls, and leave us alone. She used to talk to me while she posed, as we spent more time together, and tell me about herself, and I started to like her. I really felt that some element of her, of her reality, entered the drawings, and made them come alive. By the end, for a couple of hours on a Saturday night, I think the two of us felt genuinely happy. The room smelt like semen and cheap perfume and sweat and champagne, and you couldn't help but wonder what had been done in there, what she had done in there, in that little scarlet box near City Road. But still I forgot why I was drawing, and she forgot where she was, and that was when I created the best version, the version we finally used. I remember I used to wish I could draw her in my own style, paint her in my own way. I promised myself that after the picture was done I would come back and draw her for myself. I used to think about what it would be like to take her out for lunch, how she would look in the daylight without her make-up on.'

'Did you ever see her again?' she asked, her voice softened to a whisper by sentiment.

'No,' I lied. 'After it was finished we never went back. Francis thought it would be too risky.' I did not want to tell Jessica about what had happened the last time I had visited the strip club. I did not want to risk her newly emerging sympathy on an unpalatable truth.

'And do you draw Alysha?'

'No. We fuck.' I told Jessica what I genuinely believed to be true. 'It saves time. I could go out and find a girlfriend, or a wife or a mistress, or even a one-night stand, but why would I, when all I really want is sex? I don't want someone to share my life. I'm courteous, I stay in shape for them – I'm not like some of the other dirty old men they have to see, I stay clean and smart. I want someone to fuck, someone to do the cleaning, someone to do the laundry, so I have prostitutes, maids and dry-cleaners.'

'You're a one-man service industry,' she said bitterly, and stood to leave for the toilet.

When she came back into the room, something in the

mood between us had undergone an irreparable change. Jessica looked tired, her eye shadow lending a bruised darkness to the skin under her eyes. She toyed listlessly with her pendant. I would have suggested that we call it a night, and pulled down the sofa bed for her, but I was still ravenously hungry. I did not want to cheat my stomach out of the takeaway for the sake of a botched reunion. Nor did I know whose fault it was. I had been so long without another opinion on my lifestyle that I could not tell if my behaviour was objectionable in itself, or simply objectionable to her. Did she feel that it was her duty to be outraged, as a woman? I did not feel like apologizing, and I couldn't think what to apologize for. We simply sat for a while in silence, each of us stubbornly refusing to be the first to move for a reconciliation.

When the food arrived, Jessica seemed to revive. She had always been a creature of simple physical pleasures, and the greasy, promising smell from the brown bag filled the gap between us. My mouth was watering as I went to retrieve plates and cutlery from the kitchen. When I came back in she had already broken open the seal on one of the boxes, and was holding half a spring roll. She stopped chewing and looked at me like a guilty child, and the last of the tension melted away. We did not bother with the plates, but ate straight from the cardboard cartons, jousting with our plastic chopsticks for the final dumpling. We sat up and had a midnight feast, like the ones I used to have in my prep school dormitory on the last night of term, each of us feeling as if we were awake later than was good for us, on the verge of that private landscape of reflection that opens up when the whole of the rest of the world has gone to bed.

7

In the next few weeks of Michaelmas term, I stopped
going to the library. I quit all the college teams I had
joined in a last desperate bid for acceptance. I phoned
my father less often, and I no longer went back to
London to see my grandmother. I stopped working, and I
attended my supervisions for the express purpose of not
getting thrown out. Francis introduced me to the system
called essay rotation, devised and run by Lisa. She had a
bank of essays written by first-class students of previous
years, who had sold her their notes at graduation. She
kept a spreadsheet indicating which faculty members had
marked which work. For a small subscription fee, which
Francis paid for me, she guaranteed a weekly essay of
at least mid 2:1 standard on nearly any topic I could
conjure up, distributing the work with gruff efficiency.
She only failed me once, when my medieval supervisor
set a particularly obscure exercise on Christian mysticism,
and that week I simply didn't turn up to class, telling him
I had flu and was vomiting into a plastic bucket. Michael

told me, in strictest confidence, that she was making over five hundred pounds a week.

Whilst the demands of academic work were reduced almost to nothing, my financial situation was vastly improved. We were not technically allowed to have jobs during termtime, but I had applied for the late shift working the bar at Po Na Na, a club in the city centre, to supplement my allowance (my sixty-year-old supervisor did not seem the type suddenly to drop in for a spot of commercial hip hop or hard house, so I was not afraid of detection). In the event I didn't have to do anything. Francis gathered me under the broad wings of his allowance. He was better than anyone I have met, before or since, at giving gifts of money. Cash usually brings with it an entourage of troublesome associations that drive a rift between even the closest friends. Because it has no sentimental value and infinite practical value it is a tough thing both to give and to receive in the right spirit. Francis had a knack of purging any condescension or imposition from his gifts of money, because he presented himself as a mere conduit for wealth rather than a source, a hole in his father's pocket down which the coins tumbled without ever stopping long enough to acquire a new owner. Taking it from him gave me the same feeling as finding a bundle of twenties in the street, having a cursory look around for the owner and then pocketing it. Far from feeling embarrassed, he encouraged me to congratulate myself on my own good fortune at having made friends with him, just as he was fortunate to be his father's son.

With money and work taken care of, we were left with the problem of how to spend our time. When I was alone I painted and sketched, but for the most part we were together. We attended lectures, but seldom on our own subjects. We saw plants, sculptures and plays expertly dissected. I learnt a few words of Japanese. We tended to go to these lectures together so we could discuss them afterwards, and only in the afternoons. We would meet before midday in the Copper Kettle on King's Parade, each of us brandishing a printout of the day's programme, and make a case for our favourite lecture. The five of us, sometimes four if Francis was badly hung-over, would sit down at the table by the window with a stainless-steel teapot on a plastic tray and argue for half an hour. Then the winner would lead the party, all wrapped in thick overcoats and woollen scarves, off towards whichever lecture halls housed their faculty, heading across the icy pavements to take a short cut through King's College, the red rock salt crunching under our feet, or back towards Old School Lane. Lisa's preferences were generally scientific, for Medicine, Chemistry and Law. Francis and Jessica preferred Humanities and Languages, and Michael could be relied upon to launch into a robust defence of whatever was playing in Politics or Classics, which was his own discipline. I liked Art History, and took the derision which usually met my suggestions in good humour. Francis explained to me that the key was to divorce study from its associations with labour, to treat it as a pure pleasure, with no pressure to remember or even to understand what we heard. When I asked him what we would do about exams he laughed, and told me that, so long as I was not set on a starred first, Lisa would sort it out. She had left school at sixteen, had never taken A levels herself (a fact known only to her immediate friends), and the means by which she had secured her place at Christ's was a mystery she refused to elucidate.

There was one occasion which stands out in my memory as one of those experiences that can never be unlearned. It had snowed the night before. The sloping roofs of the windows were thatched with snow, sitting above warm yellow squares of light where the students were awake. When I came to the Copper Kettle at eight-thirty my footprints were among the first in the thick white crystals, scoring the surface like musical notes in an exercise book. I opened the door, and saw Francis sitting alone in a fug of teapot steam at one of the tables opposite the windows. This in itself was a strange beginning to the day – he almost always arrived last, just when the rest of us had given up waiting, and were sorting our scarves and coats from the pile on the bench. When he heard the door open he looked up expectantly, and when he identified me a great smile spread the width of his jaw, and I knew I was just the person he had wanted to see first. I smiled back at him and went to take off my coat.

'No time, we're late for a very important date,' he said, pushing the table away from him and dropping a folded copy of *The Times* on to the bench.

'Where are we going?' I asked him.

'It's a surprise,' he said, and he did not look me in the eye.

'Shouldn't we wait for the others?'

'Not today. I can only take one person, the first one who came through the door. Unless Michael came through the door, of course, in which case I would have distracted him with faultless banter and taken the next person. Now, before we go, you are Austin Willis.'

'What?'

'Just repeat it. Who are you?'

'Austin Willis?'

'Perfect!'

I laughed at this, and I followed him out. We walked back down King's Parade towards Corpus Christi, and turned down Bene't Street. Like everything else about him, Francis was so singular in the way he put one foot in front of the other that you could always recognize him at a great distance, before the broadest detail of his face was visible. His shoulders were wide, and the muscle twisted down like a thick tree root from his neck to his shoulder blade, but you never noticed it unless he was standing still. When he moved, he was so like a child that all the heavy, masculine tissue seemed to melt away. He could not walk past a lamp-post without swinging on it, or a bollard without vaulting. He would sometimes run several feet in front of you, and then turn and walk backwards, still talking and somehow never stumbling into the people and objects behind him. He had the heedless grace of an animal, and like a wild animal he had no sense of social convention to check his movements. He would swoop down on gloves lying in the street, pick newspapers out of bins to read the headlines, and check his appearance in the plate-glass windows of passing shops. The universal curiosity which possesses children, and is generally satisfied by the end of boyhood, as if all surprises have been exhausted, had been sustained in Francis as a constant fascination with the material world. On that morning, however, his playfulness barely concealed an underlying agitation.

The two of us passed into the road opposite the giant grey slabs of the Lion's Yard Parking, stacked four storeys high behind us. Here, the snow was already brown and slushy with morning traffic. We turned right, and walked away from the centre of the town, out where the buildings grew younger, like ripples growing fainter from the centre of a dropped pebble. At the New Downing site, Francis stopped me with a hand on my shoulder. The two of us stood in conference in the middle of the wet tarmac.

'Listen to me, James,' he said, 'you have to do exactly

as I say. And you have to be brave, do you understand? It's halfway through the term. People's stomachs have settled. If you show you're afraid, or disgusted, they'll know we're fraudsters, and then we'll have to run for it, or we'll be arrested.'

'Francis,' I asked, frightened and excited, 'what is it we're going to see?'

It was apparent to me later that he was reckless in not warning me properly. Nor was there any reason for his silence beyond sheer theatricality, although he may have feared that if I had known what we were going to do I would have refused to come with him. It is one of my first clear memories of his preference for drama over safety.

He took my hand and led me through the doors and down the corridor beyond. We went down a small flight of stairs, so that the windows above our heads were at floor level in the courtyard outside the building. We came to a point where ten or so students were waiting, talking to one another in small groups, their bags slung over their shoulders, their shoes and cuffs wet with melting snow. It was then that I became aware of a smell, lying under the institutional atmosphere of floor polish and dust. I caught only isolated breaths of it, which came to me like odd bars of a distant song, staying just beyond the edge of recognition. Those breaths made my nostrils flare with an acrid tang that made me think of strong chemicals. At the same time there was a meaty layer to it that was organic and unwholesome. The smell increased my trepidation. I looked again at the faces of the students crowding around the door, and tuned in to their voices. They were not laughing, or telling one another anecdotes, or asking questions that required answers. They were talking about the snow, about how far they had got with their essays. They were making small talk to fend off silence. From the academic content, I gathered they were first-year medics. The groups were gathered around the wooden swing doors of a lecture theatre, which were inlaid with small windows of safety glass. Without drawing attention to myself, I tried to peek through into the dim interior, but all I could see in the gloom was a series of white sheets, draped around as if over furniture in a house closed for the winter.

A tall woman in a white coat appeared from the other end of the corridor, announced by the business click of her heels on marble floor. She walked straight up to the door and unlocked it. Then she turned to us, and said, 'Professor Lister is ill, I'm afraid. My name is Dr Fitzgerald. I'll be taking today's seminar. I'll try to pick up your names as we go along.'

When she pushed the door open and the lights in the dissection room guttered into neon life, the smell rolled out, and I almost gagged. I looked at the young faces around me. They registered no surprise, but they also showed an attempt to suppress discomfort. These fledgling doctors were already working on their clinical calm, trying to show their peers that the layman's reaction was well behind them. In most cases, the assumed air of professionalism looked ridiculous, like a child tottering downstairs in his father's shoes.

The room was as cold as the day outside. As I stepped out of the warmth of the corridor, I could see my breath in the air. In the light, I made out the unmistakable shape of the forms under the sheets, and I knew where Francis had brought me. The room was filled with steel trolleys. It was a vast space, with perhaps ninety separate mounds spaced at regular intervals on a ceramic floor of square white tiles. These same tiles in orange climbed the walls to a height of about five feet. At the end of each trolley there was a tray of shining steel tools, blades and tongs glittering in the glare of the strip lights. The students paired off, and stood in twos before their veiled mounds. Dr Fitzgerald took up her own position on the podium at the front of the room, and switched on the computer display hidden in the pine rostrum. The projector above us came to life, and an image of the human brain in X-ray appeared on the white screen behind her. She read out names from a clipboard in front of her, and the students answered in turn. Whilst she did so, they took latex gloves from boxes on the tables in front of them, and coaxed them into place. Francis talced his own hands before putting them on, unobtrusively showing me the technique. He answered to the name of Edward King, and it reminded me to listen out for my own alias. When Austin Willis was called out, I replied 'Here' without hesitation. I was amazed when she accepted and ticked me off her list. I did a brief inventory of the other faces in the room. Only one person was looking at us – a small girl with a short brown ponytail; she stared over at us with naked contempt. I could tell, however, from the way that her eyes narrowed into little slits when she saw me looking, that it was the hatred of impotence. She was trying to make me ashamed of myself for want of a more effective reproach. I was not afraid that she would say anything.

When the roll call was completed, the other students around the room pulled back their sheets to reveal the dead faces underneath, that same cold layer of calm lying over their features like the new snow over the city. Francis took our sheet in his hand and pulled it smoothly down to the chest of the man in front of us. I understood that any hesitation or show of emotion would now be fatal to our pretence.

I had never seen a dead body before. The smell came off the flesh, a mixture of the chemical preservative and the dead meat itself. The man under our sheet was old, perhaps in his mid-seventies. His white hair was confined to two thin downy strips above his ears. The skin of his cheeks was grey and rough with stubble. His eyes were closed; the lips of his mouth rested open, showing the yellow edges of his incisors. I tried to bite back the urge to vomit as I looked down at the chest. Work had begun in earnest on the organs. I felt as if I was breaching the old man's privacy, gazing down into the cavity of his stomach. But it was the look on Francis's face that I remember most of all. It jarred so strongly with the assumed impassivity of the scientists around us that I feared it alone might give us away. He gazed at the old man's face with pure compassion, and for the briefest moment placed his hand on the back of his skull, touching the skin through the soft thinning hair, like a priest giving a final hearing to his weaknesses.

'Take up your bone saws, please, and remove the top of the skull, starting on the forehead just below the hairline. I want us to take a look at the outer cortex.'

Francis took up the white-handled instrument with the same look of pity in his eyes, and the serrated blade whizzed into the bone. At the sound of contact I closed my eyes.

The doctor left the podium and stalked the rows, conducting her lesson and asking questions. It meant that for the most part, it was impossible for me to talk to Francis, or to vent my anger or disgust on him. I was forced to play the role of the cold clinician, and delve with tongs when required. The texture of the cold body I recognized from cookery – not the moisture of fresh meat, but the rubbery grey feel of strips boiled too long for school meals. It was the downy feeling of his white hair between my fingers that was strange. It appalled me. Despite my shock, I found myself admiring the dexterity with which Francis's fingers accomplished their grisly business. They danced the way his feet danced when he fought, with instinctive logic. Sounds echoed in that cavernous mortuary. The metallic click of the knives on stainless steel ricocheted off the walls. He risked a whisper only once, when we had peeled back the fibrous protective layers beneath the skull, and broken into the vaults of the brain proper. Dr Fitzgerald had her back to us, and was walking down the opposite row, discoursing on blood flow. When she stopped to answer a question, he leant in to my ear. When he spoke, I felt the warmth of his breath on my cheek, and caught its scent through the harsh reek of formaldehyde.

'Do you see here, in these neat little grey pleats? This is where the fugitive "I" hides. This is where you are, and where I am. When I first saw this, on a young man, I couldn't stop thinking, Where has he gone too? He was right here   '

'What the fuck are you doing, Francis?' I hissed back.

He didn't answer, and the doctor came back towards our table. Even through my fear and confusion, I was impressed by Francis. He knew the anatomy of our subject better than any of the other medics there, and he fielded the doctor's questions with intellectual grace, never giving any more than the perfect answer required. I had no idea where he had accumulated the knowledge, nor the source of the skill and precision with which he took apart the head. When he severed a part, he placed it in a small wooden box slung underneath the trolley. When I later asked him what made people give up their bodies to the students, he said that many of those who did were too poor to pay for their own funerals. The small wooden boxes that housed the bits would be buried by the university at the end of the year, in a modest ceremony that all the students would attend.

The class lasted an hour and a half. At the end of it, we thanked the doctor, who informed us that our regular supervisor would return at the end of the week. We threw away our gloves and passed out into the corridor, the room exhaling us like a long-held breath, the tension of the morning dissipating. Some of the students, exhausted from maintaining their pretence of indifference, laughed and made jokes in their relief. As we were putting on our coats the girl with the brown hair came up to me and whispered, 'Ghoul,' over my shoulder. Then she ran back down the corridor to catch up with her friends.

The two of us were the last to leave the building. Francis said he had to meet some friends for brunch on the other side of town, and did not invite me to join him. Before he left, I demanded an explanation. 'How did we get away with that?' I asked him.

'I pay Willis and King a retainer to tell me when one of their teachers is off sick. They usually know before the lesson, because the teacher will email to cancel that day's supervisions. Then I pay them a flat fee not to turn up. To be honest, I think they're rather grateful. Do you have any idea of the average starting debt of a medical graduate?'

'And what about the other students?'

'What can they do? They may not like it, but since they didn't say anything the first time, they really don't have much choice other than to continue in complicity.'

It seemed odd to me that I had asked him how he had accomplished the morning, and not why, which was the single question turning over and over in my mind throughout the lesson. It was only when I came to actually asking it that I realized I was afraid to hear the answer. I was afraid because, despite my anger and disgust, I had done nothing to stop what had happened. In the lecture hall I had convinced myself that my compliance was forced, that Francis had roped me to the dissection with the threat of discovery. But even now I couldn't find it in me to raise my voice to him, though the two of us were alone in the snow-covered street, with the experience and the danger it entailed left somewhere behind us in the warm corridors. Certainly, I had felt myself compelled to go through with the plan. Compelled, but not forced. Francis was waiting to see if I had finished questioning him, a good-natured smile balanced on his lips. He was tapping his feet in the slush, impatient for the company of his other friends. It was the wish to hold on to him for a few more moments that finally forced me to ask the question.

'Why did you want me to go through that?'

'I wanted to see if you had the stomach for adventure. I wasn't quite sure of you, James . . . you mustn't take that the wrong way, really you mustn't. If I didn't like you I wouldn't have taken the time to check. Also, I wanted to show you something that might help you be a little braver. When I was sixteen I was stepping out with a medic from King's College who brought me into her anatomy classes, just the way I smuggled you into that one. I used to ditch cricket on a Friday afternoon and take the train from Windsor down to London. We would slice on down into their bodies, and I would sit there, wondering who they were, what they did with their lives, whether they were happy, as we peeled back the skin on their upper arms and dissected the bicep. It's funny, but we used to have the most amazing trysts after that. We never even made it out of the teaching hospital, we'd just take the elevator down to the furnace room and beat each other to pieces on the brick walls in the searing heat. There's something about the concrete fact of death that accentuates pleasure. I think it's seeing how sad you are going to look when you can't have fun any more. Anything else?'

'What happened to the medic?' I asked.

'Oh, she found out how old I really was. And now I really must say goodbye. Only deliberate lateness is fashionable.' With that he turned and trotted off through the snow.

I went back to my room alone and climbed out on to

the roof where the snow had collected in a drift by the balustrade. The cold of the metal sheeting burned my fingers. It had begun to snow again, and the white flakes drifted down out of the white sky, falling silently on the sloping roof. I sat with a cigarette unlit between my lips and thought about what Francis had shown me: a man on a slab, without the wit to stop two fraudulent strangers fingering his inmost parts. At the time, the experience was too close to me, and it was only as I pulled away from it in the days and months that followed that I made out the whole shape. By showing me the face of death, Francis had begun to cut me loose from the illusion of immortality that keeps us from doing what we want today by offering the consolation of tomorrow. At the same time, by inveigling me into what should have been a sacred space, he had given me a demonstration of how easily we could slip through the cracks in a system, if only we dared do it. I lit the cigarette and felt the nicotine rushing through my vessels to calm my nerves. By the time I crawled back into my room, my hair was matted to my head with melted flakes, and the icy water was running down my back beneath my shirt.

8

I got to know Michael better during this time, and even
to like him, though I always felt too self-conscious to
adopt the nickname the others had given him. He was
initially stung by the success I had with his friends,
but quickly conceded his monopoly and repositioned
himself as a kind of interpreter – my social patron. I
did not wish to risk alienating him, so I accepted his
advice and interference with good grace, even managing a
show of gratitude. Despite his girth he was immensely
physically fit, and his vitality was part of his charm. He
played every sport. He would tackle and punt, vault,
volley and vie with amazing strength and stamina, and
what he lacked in grace and coordination he made up for
with a dogged unwillingness to lose. The Union shook
with the thunder of his opinions, and from his vantage
point on the podium he eyed the spires of Westminster.
The more I understood of his plans, the more I saw how,
despite all his bluff and bluster, he must have been
genuinely frightened on the night I rescued him from the

porters. Had he been caught, he almost certainly would have been sent down. Such a black mark on his CV might have been fatal to his ambitions.

He had two much older siblings, both in their thirties with families of their own, and Jessica would sometimes mock him for being a mistake. He was well educated, and witty in the erudite fashion more common to literature than to real life. His laughter and joking did not mitigate against the meaner elements of his personality; rather it manifested them in a more acceptable form. His humour was a matter of profit and loss: someone, whether it was a stammering lecturer, an oddly dressed stranger or one of his friends inadvertently mispronouncing a name on a menu, would always pay for the increase in his own status with a little portion of their self-respect. I used to envy him for being able to get away with the things he said and did, but it was perhaps a kind of curse to him to be able to make people cry with laughter at his cruellest exploits. It denied him the public condemnation that might otherwise have curbed his impulses. Rather than criticizing him on the spot, people tended to wait until he was out of the room, to wipe their eyes with their fingers as their laughter subsided into chuckles and then to say, 'No, my God that was funny, but I think Falstaff went a little far that time.' From time to time he would mock me about my painting, when he saw dirt under my nails or spatters on my jeans, using the pieces he had seen around the easel on the night of our meeting as a guide for his derision. These were the moments when I found it hardest to deal with him.

Much of my attention during this time was devoted to working out the relationship between Francis and Jessica. I wanted to ask Michael, but I did not want to pay the price of his condescension. They exerted an easy air of ownership over one another, such as often characterizes the complacent love of beautiful young couples, each aware of the other's desirability as well as their own, but they didn't seem to sleep together. Though they were always touching and stroking in an absent-minded way, there never seemed to be anything definitely sexual in their contact. Nor, however, did I ever see them with anyone else, and I came to think of their physical closeness as a mode of exclusion, a warding spell against a lesser intimacy with someone else. Each in their way was a formidable guardian, and successfully warned off any outside attempts at sexual contact. If Jessica was standing at the long chrome slab of Tudor bar, and one of the college's acknowledged male beauties finally worked up the courage to offer her a drink, Francis would appear, light and playful, and slip his hands over her bright blue eyes from behind, blindfolding her and saying, 'Guess who?' If a young girl sidled up to Francis at a party and asked him for a light or a cigarette, or said she had seen him box against Oxford, trouncing their middleweight champion, Jessica would appear at his shoulder and whisper something in his ear. I felt this exclusivity more keenly the closer we became. It was like a locked room in my own home.

Michael knew no such limits to his appetites, and the women who got too close were pulled into the black hole of his ego, where they would inevitably be squished. He was much further advanced in his seduction techniques than the rest of us, who still thought that sex was in some way linked to mutual affection. He understood that sex, like conversation, could be an interaction expressing any emotional relationship, from love to hate to plain indifference. Armed with this knowledge he would target a woman, insult her in public as often and as strongly as possible and then ask her out for dinner. When she refused he would break into her room and strew floral arrangements across her bed, commission men's choirs to sing outside her windows and leave presents on the steps of her lecture halls until her curiosity got the better of her and she agreed to meet him. Often there would be two or three of these campaigns running simultaneously. The final stage usually took place in a London hotel, the Met or the Mandarin Oriental for choice, and immediately the deed was done he would call Francis from the bathroom, who would put him on speaker-phone, then describe the girl and her sexual preferences until we were all crying with guilty laughter. He had had a number of silver ring pendants made on private commission in Hatton Garden, and in the morning the whole performance would end with the solemn ceremony of placing one of these pendants around the girl's head as a gift. He said it tickled him pink to think of the twenty or so women wandering around Cambridge wearing the same necklace, each believing they were unique, and whenever I caught a glimpse of one lying on the breast of a woman sitting at dinner or walking through the cloisters I felt a little thrill of appalled jealousy, and pictured her sitting astride the pale hirsute bulk of his stomach, still primly dressed. Michael liked classy, self-possessed women, and I was always struck by the contrast between the elegant fronts they presented to the world and the knowledge of how they had allowed themselves to be exploited.

If Lisa had liaisons of her own, I did not know about them. She was an incredibly private person, and never offered her friends more than one perspective on her life. She distributed small slices of knowledge to different social groups, with associates among the students, the staff, local businessmen and regular visitors from London, taking great pains to ensure that none of these people ever met the others. It was part of her power that no one could really say they knew the whole of her, and I'm quite sure she could have concealed nymphomania and celibacy with equal ease. I had never met someone so capable of realizing their own desires, and I liked her, but she frightened me a little. Her rough London background was a constant reproach to the life we were leading, and to the family money that underpinned our leisure, but she never registered any envy or disapproval. She seldom made concessions in her clothes or manner; when she did, on the social occasions that required evening wear or elegant formality, Jessica was her pattern, and the attempts were never wholly successful. Her brown hair stayed scraped backwards in the resolute grip of a scrunchie. Unlike me and Jessica, who were entirely reliant on Francis, or Michael who had his own trust fund, she made her own cash, and probably earned considerably more in that first year in university than I did in my first year of law. Of all the group, she was the one I understood the least.

It was a cold winter that year in Cambridge: ice crystals glistened on the rough sandstone walls, and the trees over the Cam dipped snow-laden branches into the still surface of the frozen river. Every evening there were snowball fights in Market Square, big public battles that involved anyone willing to come out and scoop up a fistful of snow from the cobbles. It was after one of these late-night skirmishes that I first saw Francis's room. My fingers were stinging and patchy red and white, and we were breathless with laughter and the cold. He asked me up quite casually, as he claimed he wanted to fetch a scarf and black shoes before we met the others for dinner, but as the invitation had never been extended before in the month or so of our friendship I could not help but see it as a landmark, a further pledge of trust, like an expensive gift wrapped in newspaper and left without ceremony on the kitchen table.

We went in off Green Street into Blue Boar, the satellite colony where Tudor stashed its second years, and from there along a series of heavily salted walkways to the door of the main lobby. We took the lift up to the fourth floor. Francis had a view out over the walls and towers of Tudor Great Court, and beyond them to the dome of St John's. He was engaged, as he explained to me, in a long-running battle with the Sunday bells from Tudor College Chapel, which called the faithful to morning mass at eight-thirty. He was experimenting with rolls of sound-deadening cloth, and one was pinned to the roof above the window, which ran from floor to ceiling all the way through the building. His room was chaotic, a testament to his tendency to develop sudden and explosive passions, to become quickly proficient in random disciplines and then instantly abandon them. The bed was unmade. Around the frame of the door there hung part of a butterfly collection in glass boxes, the wings pinned back, meticulously labelled in his loopy handwriting. There was a photograph of the Hon. Jeremy Manley, his younger brother and heir to the family throne, standing against a vine-covered stone wall, looking at the camera with an uncertain smile, squinting against the light. There was a trumpet. There were books on diverse subjects, first editions and flimsy paperbacks, hanging like circumflexes over the arms of chairs, or closed and discarded with fragments of paper poking out of the middle to indicate a place. Everywhere I looked there were empty bottles and cans, some of them with dirty, auspicious labels dating back to the seventies, some of them crumpled old tins of Budweiser. He had a penchant for buying expensive things and treating them badly, and there were Versace jackets, Favorbrook waistcoats and D & G T-shirts in piles on the floor. Amongst the general debris only one series of items was properly cared for: he had a large collection of records, bought and traded since he was sixteen, and a set of decks. Francis liked to DJ, the only thing he did with a total lack of skill, a deficiency which was made charming by the contrast with his usual effortlessness. It was perhaps his lack of ability that had sustained his interest so far beyond the usual period of infatuation. As if in acknowledgement of this one shortcoming, the records he used to mix were always wiped clean, carefully boxed and filed away at the end of a session. They lay in ranks against one wall in the belly of an open trunk, lined with professional-looking grey foam. But the most extraordinary object of all hung above Francis's bed. When I saw it I felt a thrill run through my body and pins and needles in my hands that seemed at the time only proof of its genius, but which I have since been tempted to diagnose as the tingle of destiny.

Francis gestured to it without looking whilst he hunted

around on the floor for new shoes, and said, 'Do you like my Picasso?'

First I took it to be a black and white print, housed in an ebony and gilt frame with a brass plaque screwed to the bottom edge. It was a foot and a half high, and one foot wide. I could see at once that it was not a complete picture; it was the preliminary sketch for a larger oil. On the paper a group of angular female nudes clustered around a fruit bowl. The women at the centre had their arms slung up behind their heads in an attitude of posturing allure, the curving lines of the sheet the central figure held over her naked groin contrasting with the sharp, inorganic lines of her torso. The whole composition had the crudeness and the vitality of experimentation. As I looked at the picture, I became aware of a certain yellowness to the cream paper upon which it was drawn, and a grainy quality in the black lines that seemed almost like texture.

'It's beautiful,' I said. 'It almost looks real.'

Francis laughed, and found his shoes. 'It is real! Well . . . It's part of the college's art collection. Scholars can apply to have pieces hung on the walls of their rooms. I had to go in front of the art committee, all these old men with beards, and old women too, bearded women, and tell them why I wanted it. They made me sign the most complicated forms, and if I go out without locking the doors I get sent down, but in the end they let me have it.'

I made it a point of pride with my new friends never to

register how much they surprised and even shocked me. They had an air of expecting and deserving all the benefits that life extended them, and as a result no one ever begrudged or questioned them. They were self-fulfilling prophets, and it was a trick I desperately hoped to emulate. On this occasion, however, I did not have time to bring down the shutters, and my natural reaction escaped me in an incredulous burst. 'Do you know what this is? This is the first study for cubism, an idea of an idea. Nineteen-oh-seven, just after he came back to the rue Ravignan from Spain . . .'

'Really?' Francis said, reaching up and taking the picture down from its nail on the wall. 'How fascinating.'

Looking back it seems incredible that any institution would ever let so casual a relationship exist between a multi-million-pound masterpiece and a student. At the time, however, I was surprised by the picture and not the arrangement. Cambridge University, and Tudor College in particular, had such a surplus of history that it was impossible to sustain a proper reverence. After all, we ran and washed and went to the toilet in the midst of buildings older than the countries of the tourists who came to see them. Daily contact with the treasures of the past inoculated the student body against wonder. Hundreds of generations of the great and good had left their legacy, both material and academic, and the offhand manner in which such things were handled was almost a point of pride among the faculty and staff.

Scarcely a year went by when a dying alumnus did not divvy up his collection between his family and his alma mater. There seemed to be an idea that excessive awe and the fuss that went with it were a barrier to proper appreciation. I once opened a normal loan copy of Pound's cantos in the University Library to find a handwritten dedication from the author to T. S. Eliot, to whom the book had obviously been given as a present. The library card was stuck to the opposite page. This is not to say that artefacts were abused – the university had the best facilities for storage and maintenance, and experts who loved the pieces and treated them accordingly. It did mean, however, that access to extraordinary objects for those lucky enough to be students was almost unprecedented, almost unregulated. It was actively encouraged by the staff, for what better way to inspire young minds than to immerse them directly in the atmosphere of their specialisms. Excessive practical barriers to this were considered to be in bad taste, and the sign of a philistine disposition. The Tudor Art Foundation was merely one symptom of this pervasive condition, and the college had perhaps twenty paintings of near or equivalent worth scattered around its buildings at that time, works by artists ranging from Stubbs to Rothko, each one the gift of a different benefactor. Anyone who marvelled at the fact marked themselves out as new to Cambridge, and quite unsophisticated in their thinking.

Francis laid the frame face up on the middle of his wooden coffee table. It sat slightly askew on a pile of old issues of GQ and an overflowing ashtray. I noticed that what I had first taken for fading of the picture was in fact a series of streaks of creamy residue on the surface of the glass. I thought he must have taken the picture down for me to have a closer look, and I gazed at it in awe. I had only ever seen such a thing before from behind the velvet rope of a museum or country house. I felt a sudden surge of importance as I welcomed it into my private life like a prized guest. As I traced the lines with my fingers Francis turned his attention to his bedside table. He took a small Chinese lacquer box from the bottom drawer and opened it. Inside there were a couple of oblongs of thick colourful paper, each one folded like a little display of origami so that the edges turned back into themselves, making a two-inch packet. Francis took out one of these packets, and it blossomed under his clever fingers into an open square in the centre of which was a mound of white powder. As it lay open I saw it was a part of a page cut from a pornographic magazine, with two girls lying one on top of the other on all fours, their raised buttocks concealed by white crystals, their shoulders and faces cut away at the side. It was not until he poured some of the powder on to the glass of the picture lying upturned on his coffee table that what he was doing connected with a wealth of images plundered from the movies, and I realized it was cocaine. My heart beat hard in anticipation.

'Have you done this before?' he said quite gently as he used a razor to cut it into lines.

'Yes,' I lied.

'Really?'

'Yes.'

'You don't have to do it now, if you don't want to.'

'I do want to.'

'I'll cut two.'

Francis went first. I was shocked by how loud the noise was when he snorted, and how inelegant it looked to have your head pressed down into the table, doubled over on your seat. He came up and shook his head around, blinking at me once or twice as if surprised to find me still there. As I took the rolled note in my hand, my mind filled with a jumble of random warnings, facts and urban legends about the dangers of drug-taking. As I lowered my head to the picture, it felt like walking against the wind, leaning against the forces of years of good advice from parents, politicians and friends. I wondered if I would be the one in a hundred who suffers an allergic reaction. I did my line, trying to copy what Francis had done. When I came up I gripped his shoulder with the strength of a drowning man. I waited for my throat to close, for my eyes to roll back in their sockets. Then I felt a surge of triumph that washed away my fear, and my heart hammered along to keep up with the emotion. He looked into my eyes, laughing, and gripped my shoulder as I was gripping his, so that we turned inwards in symmetry. I thought, Now, I am experiencing things.

'Hey,' I said, suddenly inspired, wanting to seem like I knew what I was doing, 'that's good stuff.'

'Only the best for my friends,' Francis said. He rubbed the surface of the sketch with his finger, and then gummed the residue. He picked it up, and hung it back in place. 'You know, if you ever get caught short, and I'm not around, you can usually scrape a spare line off Picasso.'

We both laughed at this, and he grabbed his scarf. At the time it felt quite unselfconscious, but it was with such acts that Francis crafted his mythos. After that, I felt I had edged a little closer to them all, as we had another thing to share, and another wall between us and the everyday world. The mystery of their bathroom trips, quick elations and unfinished dinners was solved. We never did too much, perhaps once or twice a fortnight, as Jessica said we had to keep it 'special'. If Francis sometimes failed to keep it as special as she would have liked, nothing was said. Lisa never touched drugs. If offered, she would dismiss them with a quick shake of her head, and say, 'Nah, man, I don't do that shit.' Michael too kept his nose clean, anticipating the plush green leather of government. As with everything, Francis paid.

143

*   *   *

In those early days, the only danger I remember was Lord Soulford. Francis had no photographs of him. I picked up his image from the newspapers. The irascible tone of his politics seemed to combine so perfectly with the shots of him in the broadsheets, emerging red-faced and brisk from important meetings or giving a stern smile of approval at a charitable function, that I always pictured him talking, his arm raised in fist-shaking emphasis. I happened to see him once on *Channel 4 News* being interviewed about the government's proposed reforms to A levels, and was impressed by the conviction with which he denounced the plans, the government and, when things became contentious, the interviewer himself. He stood like a colossus astride our expenditure, casting his shadow over the trade and exchange that was the life-blood of our leisure. His relationship with Francis was more like a business arrangement than a familial one: his son consented, for an enormous fee, to be governed by his father, to keep his name out of the papers and to smile at Lord Soulford's side in photographs when required. Though the deal was mutually beneficial, something in Francis's nature compelled him to test his father's tolerance. He would turn up to appointments late, lose a little bit more money than he had to spend at the Peterborough dog track, and write slightly lunatic letters on political subjects to *The Times*, which would invariably be printed with his real name and home address. He liked to keep his father simmering, but never allowed him to come to the boil. Either cowardice or prudence kept him just the right side of the line.

I only challenged him once over this tendency. The two of us were drinking coffee on the second floor of Caffè Nero, sitting under a giant poster of beautiful women drinking espresso in a Roman piazza, whilst outside the windows the rain fell on the traders and tourists doing business in Market Square. It was midday after a binge, and we had the intimacy of mutual discomfort, and the slight disconnection from the rest of the world that makes everyone who shares it feel like brothers. Empowered by this, I confronted him with some of his sins against his father, and asked for reasons.

'Habit, I suppose. When I was younger I used to love finding new ways of infiltrating his calm. He was always so scrupulously polite to me when I was at school, as if I was a guest. I never embarked on irritation deliberately, but if I could do something I wanted and know that it might strike a nerve, it added an extra spice. When I was at Eton I used to steal one of his cars and go drag racing in Epping Forest. There's nothing up there, just miles and miles of abandoned tracks, and the highbeams lacing in and out of the trunks. Red tail-lights glowing like coals in the woods, and the roar of engines. The roads split, then come back together, and you had to make sure that your opponent was looking at your bumper before you swung back on to the track, or you'd side-swipe him and wipe out together. I used to make a bit of money that way, winning races. I'd bring home Papa's MG all bruised and battered in the morning, and I'm pretty sure he knew something was up, but he couldn't say a thing. He was trying for nomination as the local Conservative candidate and he couldn't afford a scandal. He would just sit there at breakfast and pretend not to know, asking me how I was enjoying school and how I planned to spend the rest of my exeat, while I fell asleep in my cornflakes.' Francis smiled to himself and closed his eyes.

'Why did you stop?' I asked.

He shrugged, and blew on his coffee. 'Someone crashed. After that the police started doing patrols. No more fun.'

I remember that story particularly, because it occurred to me for the first time that Francis might be lying. The tale had a cinematic quality about it which suggested it could have been lifted straight from an old American movie. I wavered for a second, then quashed my doubts and stowed the story carefully amongst the other details of his biography, giving it pride of place in my collection. It wasn't that Francis was a good liar, if indeed he did tell lies, but rather that his listeners became good dupes. He had the knack of making you want to suspend your disbelief, of stretching your credulity so you could drink in more and more of his magic. I wanted to believe that there were people like this in the world, people who shed the usual skein of fears and insecurities, bills and tickets, and were free to engage in more elevated dramas. I swallowed the car story, and much else besides over the following weeks.

9

I was also initiated, at Michael's behest, into the Tudor Night Climbers. In the aftermath of his close escape in my room they had called a temporary halt to their operations, waiting until the eye of authority turned back to drugs, vandalism, noise pollution and the 101 other infringements that ate up the fabric of communal discipline. By the time night climbing was back on the agenda, Michael sensed the inevitability of my inclusion and headed it off with a great show of magnanimity, inviting me out for a solitary pint at the Granta and issuing me a solemn invitation, making me swear repeatedly never to divulge anything about the organization or its members. There then followed a speech about the trust that had been placed in me, and an insistence on this remaining a private matter between us until such time as he could 'break it to the others'. I discovered without surprise that it was Francis, rather than he, who had founded the club. From the very beginning, night climbing seemed of a different order to the other ways we occupied our leisure. It was also distinctive among our pastimes as the only one that was free.

Michael and Francis vied with one another in displays of daring. At least Michael vied, and Francis pretended not to notice, which infuriated him. Lisa never baulked at anything attempted by the others, but there was no showmanship in her ascents, just a grim determination to get to the top. Her pride seemed to lie in never questioning, never complaining, and never accepting help. She took pleasure in the fact of conquest. As for Jessica, she told me that in the beginning she had joined the boys not out of desire, but to prevent Francis from doing anything too stupid. She'd left them to do the first few climbs on their own, but could not sleep when she knew they were out together, and spent the small hours smoking and watching television in the Common Room until Francis called her to say he was safely back in his bed. Her first climb had bound her to their rooftop adventures, and when she spoke about it her only regret was her ruined nails, which she would look at and sigh. The pressure of fingerjams and rough grips had left them blunt and ragged, and they made a strange contrast to her smooth skin and perfect hair.

At first I thought Francis was just an adrenalin junkie, and this was certainly part of his motivation. Physical danger had been restricted to brief cameos in my life, and even then only in its reduced capacity on school playing fields and sanitized mountain slopes. Combating those sorts of risks had been like fighting a drugged bull, the odds neatly stacked, the potential harm contained. The first time I looked down from my perch between two fluted columns and discovered that the distance between myself and the ground would generate a fatal fall, I felt a sweet ordering process sweep through my cluttered mind like the perfect secretary, banishing all but the immediately relevant. With adrenalin manning my chest, sending out extra strength to reinforce my limbs and aching fingertips, my thoughts became cold and hard: left foot, right hand, balance. It was a wonderful release from the throng of little demands and insecurities, whose needs, small but insistent, usually filled up my head. It was as if one great voice, the old imperative of survival, rang out over their heads and awed them all into silence. That, for me, was an adrenalin rush, being brought into proximity with my own mortality, and retaining control over my own salvation. I know the others felt this, because the parties we had on the roofs were always a wild kind of thanksgiving, a celebration of still being alive. We would run up and down in the cold darkness, looking out over the rooftops and the huge grey sky, exploring. There was, however, a more fundamental aspect to Francis's climbing that throwing himself out of planes or driving too quickly on the motorway could never have fulfilled.

I had assumed that the limiting factor in my ability to join the others would be either strength or nerve, and at first this was the case. These obstacles, however, were easily overcome. Francis taught me a game for building all the muscles I would need: he rearranged the furniture in my room to leave spaces of several feet between the bulkier pieces, and then challenged me to get around the room on the picture rail, a sturdy wooden ledge hammered into place one foot below the ceiling, designed to carry hooks for framed paintings. The rail stood about one inch out from the wall, and had a slight indent on its upward face into which I could jam my fingertips. Under his tuition I began to learn how to distribute my weight, how to turn my body in the air, how to layback and chimney, the basic skills required by the local architecture. The climbing itself, Francis told me, was simple, and did not make the demands on the body that natural surfaces tend to present. Hand- and footholds were plentiful, and pillars, gutters and drainpipes accounted for most of the pitches, with isolated moments of complex negotiation between them. There were few overhangs or fingerjams, and no equip- ment was needed. When I could do thirty press-ups, fifteen chin-ups and thirty or so squat thrusts without collapsing into a heap of cramps, Francis estimated I was physically ready. As to my fear, I found that if I kept strict order among my impulses for the first twenty feet or so, real physical danger promoted the adrenalin rush that swept fear away with all the other mental debris, leaving my mind clean and efficient.

The real limiting factor, as Francis taught me, was imagination. He argued that the vast majority of people failed to find joy because it never occurred to them to look. It was not only the depth of creative thought, but the direction in which that thought was employed that marked Francis out from the other people I had come across in my life. He was not confined to dreams, to financial or romantic intrigue or even to art – his fantasies were omnivorous. This was the real reason Francis climbed; it was a model of his interaction with the real world. Where the rest of the passing pedestrians saw only a door or a window, Francis saw a fingergrip, a foothold. He thought in different dimensions, and he applied to the buildings a new set of rules in opposition to the strict proportions that dictated the classical façades or the judicious physics that maintained the Gothic fan vaults. His imagination swarmed over them. He had the habit of recognizing possibilities in everyday scenes, so that even as we strolled down the street he would be checking pipes, roofs and railings for possible points of ingress. He was truly unique in this, and it made me feel privileged to be in his presence. I tried to understand the way he saw things, and to incorporate something of his vision into my sketches, so that my work began to grow. My pictures became not merely accurate renderings, but interpretations, and I even made myself thrill with pleasure at my finished pieces, though I showed them to no one. When Francis spoke and plotted, I sometimes felt like a scribe, privileged to follow and record for posterity. In this I was my own audience too, and I would never sleep the morning after a climb, but lie awake as the sun rose and repeat to myself something he had said or done, puzzling out the meaning.

My memory of those climbs is a montage, a blend of similar but distinctive experiences amounting to a kind of advertisement for living passionately. I remember standing with the statues of saints on their pedestals above the Wren Library looking over Tudor Great Court, and clasping my legs around the pinnacle of the lightning conductor on the dome of St John's, spreading my arms in the void as the sun rose. But I know the climbs themselves were authentic – the exhilaration was real, and left no room for self-consciousness. We began on small and distant buildings, climbs that were both simple and removed from the city centre where the streets were never entirely empty, even in the hours before dawn. If I had any doubts that these choices were made with me in mind, they were dispelled by Michael talking of the time when they could 'take off the training wheels', and return to the more interesting haunts near King's Parade. He was in his element on these climbs, and his boisterous success was almost as effective in driving me as Francis's careful tuition; I could not stand to come over a lip of brick at his feet, to find that he had already controlled his breath whilst I panted with exertion. Despite our best efforts we were sometimes spotted on the faces of the buildings, and our night would end with a brief and wild chase like the one that first guided Michael through my window. The porters never won, because they could not match our willingness to take risks.

The climb I remember above all others came near the end of my first term. Francis had found the lightning conductor running along the wall of King's College Chapel, a thin band of green copper spanning 130 feet from the topmost turret to the ground. The chapel, a masterpiece of perpendicular Gothic architecture, had been begun by Henry VI in 1446, and was by far the tallest building in the city. When we stood on the gravel path that led into King's from the Backs and checked Francis's route, I had to crick my neck backwards to take in the grand upward sweep of the sandstone walls. I felt afraid then, contemplating what we intended to conquer, and caught a hint of the awe that religious architecture must inspire in the faithful. The gargoyles designed to frighten off evil spirits at the roof of the outer section would, Francis told us, make perfect handholds to swing ourselves up after the first pitch. From there we could use the angle between the main wall and the terminal buttress to chimney all the way to the roof. The Gothic turrets, rising above the stone spears of the finials at the four corners of the chapel, we could attempt when we got up there. Michael estimated the climb would take almost an hour, so we decided to take up a picnic and sleeping bags, and spend the following day on the roof, climbing down the next night.

We watched a cold grey dawn from the roof of the chapel. The views so high above the ground were magnificent, and the whole city seemed to have been arranged for our benefit. Cambridge opened hundreds of feet beneath us bathed in the watery winter sunshine, from the shining seam of the Cam running under the Bridge of Sighs to the tiny rugs of the picnic parties on Parker's Piece, from the coloured covers of the market stalls to the sandstone bell towers, and there directly below, the heads and hats of the college inhabitants going about their daily business, seen from above like fish in a rock pool, oblivious. Everything appeared in extraordinary detail: I could make out miniature people working through the windows of King's, a man asleep in his bed in the flat above the Photo Shop on the High Street. It was like peering through the portals of an exquisitely detailed doll's house. Beyond the suburbs, wheat fields, playing fields and woods unfurled, not wilderness but friendly countryside shrouded in low mist in the morning, rolling all the way to the horizon. The wind blew hard so high above the street, and we could scream and shout and sing with no risk of discovery. I leaned out from the walls into the deep air, drunk on space and sky. It was a freezing day, but the walls and roof provided shelter. We had drawn up supplies from the ground on a line, and we had a lunch of Coke and sandwiches bought the previous day from Sam Smiley's. We read books and played travel chess. In the evening when the cold really set in we hunkered down in the space between the crenellations and the sloping lead sheeting of the roof, and wrapped ourselves in our sleeping bags. Lisa produced a Thermos of hot chocolate that she had hidden away as a surprise. Gifts from her always touched me particularly, as they were given with a deep frown, a caveat that the present was not a sign of weakness, that next time you would still have to pay. When we had settled into the hollow between the walls, Francis told us a story he had read when researching the climb.

It was about a fellow of Divinity called Matthew Noaks, who, in 1915, had declared himself a conscientious objector. At high table the day after he had officially missed his draft, a single white feather was waiting for him on the leather seat of his high-backed chair, and the maids, who had brothers and husbands in the trenches in France, served him last, after the most junior student in the hall, and pretended not to hear when he asked for wine. His undergraduates, who before had worshipped him, would not look him in the eye at his tutorial, and when he returned to his rooms that night, he found another white feather, slid between the pages of the book on his night stand. The next day the Masters of all colleges received an invitation to lunch on the green outside King's Chapel. Dr Noaks was waiting there, and by one o'clock a great crowd of students, fellows and staff had assembled. In bare feet, in broad daylight, he tied a Union Jack around his waist, and began to climb the north-east tower. He made the 160-foot ascent in just over twenty minutes and, at the pinnacle of the topmost spire, bound the flag to the lightning conductor and watched it unfurl, before coming back down and walking off through the assembled crowd, returning to his lectures. The Master of King's called out marksmen from the barracks at Grantchester to shoot away an 'obstruction' on the chapel spire, but when the men arrived, the Major informed the Master that no enlisted man under his command would fire upon the Union Jack, and he would personally horsewhip any that tried. The Master hired a steeplejack to climb the spire and retrieve the flag, and was told that the ascent was far too dangerous. The Master hired a contractor, and was told that there was not the manpower to build the necessary scaffolding, all the able-bodied young men having gone to France. The flag stayed flying on the top of King's Chapel until Armistice Day, when Dr Noaks, by now the Master of Trinity Hall, climbed the building a second time and brought it down with him. No one ever called him a coward again.

Francis was a magnificent storyteller. He mixed words like an alchemist, turning base metals into gold.

I remember also the last climb we made, or perhaps I cannot forget it. It was the closest we ever came to being caught, and I suppose to dying, though none of us ever spoke of it in that way. We simply met at the Copper Kettle the morning after, each of us nursing our scrapes and hurts, and agreed to lay low for a while to let things settle. By the time the matter arose again, the night climbing season was over.

Francis did much of the research for the climbs we made ourselves, but there were certain things, such as the condition of the stonework on lofty spires, or the presence of handholds invisible from the ground, that he took from the work of our forebears. Night climbing was, I discovered, not our own invention: there had been another group of students in the sixties who had done something similar, and before them generations of young men stretching back into history as far as the buildings themselves. According to Francis there was, on a particular ledge near the topmost spire of King's College Chapel, a line of pennies showing the years of each ascension that dated back to 1630, as proud and incongruous in that lofty place as a line of footprints on the moon.

The most recent group had been caught and sent down, and after their expulsion had published a guide to the rooftops under the pseudonym Herodotus. Ever since its publication the university, acting for the safety of the student body and to protect its own reputation, had tasked its librarians with buying a copy whenever one arose for sale, and destroying it. Only a hundred or so had ever been printed. Even Francis's budget was no match for the acquisitive resources of Cambridge, and whenever one of the books had come to auction, he had found himself outbid. There were now so few left in the world that the ones lingering in private collections were never likely to come back into circulation.

The original Night Climbers themselves, however, had been farsighted. In conversation with a sympathetic fellow, who had as a student joined the young men on their climbs but had stopped some time before they were caught, Francis learnt of the existence of a copy which was hidden in the very shelves of the Wren Library. The book had been torn into its constituent chapters, so that it might never be discovered and thrown away in its entirety. Each chapter detailed a different building, revealing all at once its secrets and pitfalls, together with the story of how it had been conquered. Francis was able to combine this knowledge with his study of the recent additions of motion sensors and CCTV cameras to predict with great certainty the course of our climbs. Much had changed in the forty-odd years since the book was written, but it was still an invaluable guide.

The key to finding each chapter lay in a copy of T. S. Eliot's *The Waste Land*, which was positioned on the shelves in the place where the book itself ought to have stood, lingering amongst the works of the real Herodotus. The poem was high modernist, an arcane maze of literary references, some of which were underlined in pencil. Each marked reference, if properly understood, would lead the reader to a library shelf housing a chapter. So for example the first line, 'April is the cruellest month', which is taken by scholars to refer to the first line of Chaucer's General Prologue, led Francis to *The Canterbury Tales*, where the chapter for St John's College was tucked neatly against the wall behind the reference copy.

Francis always chose routes that allowed us to climb with no equipment. There were several reasons for this: we did not have the skills to employ grapples and crampons; and their use would have scarred the stone and damaged the tiles, something that was anathema to us. Most of all, however, it sullied the purity of the thing if we did not accomplish it with our own bodies, and our own ingenuity.

There was, however, one particular climb which could not be made without a rope. It was the ascent of the Senate House. The building had foiled the original Night Climbers, who had declared it impossible, and when Francis found no chapter describing it his curiosity was inflamed. It was a neo-classical building that made us all grateful for Cambridge's Gothic heritage, with its excesses of carved stone. The straight perpendicular lines and stern proportions of the Senate House presented no handholds and no chimneys, just a barren face of rock. Rumour had it that if any man could get on to the roof they would be able to escape over the Senate House Leap.

This legendary jump would take the climber over Senate House Lane and on to the rooftops of the college opposite, which furnished a paradise of eaves, ladders, arches and gargoyled gutters. Francis spent a long time studying the building, and finally devised a technique which would get one of us on to the roof unassisted. That person would then lower a rope for the others, and we would try the jump for ourselves.

The Senate House lay at the very centre of the city, and so we had to adjust our normal pattern. Firstly, because of its prominence, we would have to wait until the streets were completely dead before attempting the climb. By four o'clock, we thought, the last stragglers from the clubs would have wandered home, and the rowdy queues in front of the fast-food vans in Market Square would be satisfied. The problem with leaving things so late was that by five the city would begin to wake again. This left us less than an hour to scale the building, make the jump and return to the ground in safety. There was no time for mistakes, and no room for second thoughts. Secondly, because of the risk of discovery inherent in scaling a low building of white stone in the middle of the city, we decided to conceal our identity with balaclavas. Francis gave us each one before the day of the climb, and I tried mine on in the privacy of my own rooftop. The black wool was itchy, and the area around the mouth and nose became wet and cold with spit and the moisture in my breath. Despite the discomfort, I was secretly pleased with the half-face that leered at me in my bedroom mirror when I climbed back through the window. The costume, and the fact that it was necessary for our purpose, made me feel like a real outlaw. I spent a little time pantomiming in the mirror, and making demands of imaginary soldiers in a bad Irish accent.

The climb itself went off without incident. Jessica and Lisa kept lookout from behind the cover of the thick wrought-iron railings at either end of the square. Francis found the right place to make the human ladder, and with Michael's help he scaled my back and stood with his feet upon my shoulders. From this height he could grip the ledge at the top of the two-storey window, and lever himself up from fingertips to palms on the thin slice of stone. Squatting on the ledge with his shoulders wedged beneath the overhang he snaked his thick arms around, and disappeared over the lip of the roof. Seconds later a coil of rope slapped the stone steps on the back side of the building. We headed for the sound, and found the line wagging eagerly in the wind. We called the girls back from their posts.

'All clear?' Michael asked as he gave the rope a firm tug.

'I thought I saw . . .' Jessica was peering back into the darkness in the direction of St Mary's Church.

'What?' he asked.

The note of impatience in his voice quashed Jessica's moment of self-doubt. She was not about to display such an emotion in his presence, and shook her head, saying, 'Nothing. Go.'

We all of us climbed the rope, just as Francis had taught us, and paused on the roof to regain our breath. The view was not spectacular, hemmed in as it was on two sides by Caius and the Old Library, but my gaze was still drawn down the length of King's Parade, where the cobbles shone black and slick in the light of the wrought-iron street lamps, with Gothic battlements looming as far as the eye could see. It was a windy night, and my steaming breath streamed away from me after my exertions. There was no sound in the city but the rattle of an empty beer can rolling in the gutter in the street below, echoing off stone walls. Waiting there, I felt the peace and satisfaction that always accompanied the successful completion of one of our climbs. I had come to think of the silent rooftops, always bathed in darkness, as a kind of secret garden from which every waking concern was banished.

It was not until we went to examine the jump that the problem became apparent. Put simply, we had massively underestimated the distance between the buildings. Francis's calculations from the ground had figured on a running jump of about six feet on to a flat roof, with perhaps a six-inch difference in height between one rooftop and the other. For him, the mistake was so uncharacteristic, and the look in his eyes was strange when we saw the truth of the gap. The leap was at least eight feet wide, and though it was possible to sprint at it, the white stone balustrade that decorated the roof of the Senate House would interrupt the run, and widen the gap by a further foot. However, if negotiated properly and at speed, it would also provide another two feet of elevation. For the first person across, there would only be one chance. The leap would mean success or death. Even for those of us following behind with the benefit of the safety rope, a fall would dash our soft heads against the stern walls of Caius.

We debated the point a little, but only Francis had any real enthusiasm for continuing. The rest of us entertained the notion, but did so mostly as a sop to our own sense of pride, so that we would not seem to have given up too easily when we found ourselves warm and safe in our beds.

Then there was the sound of a car pulling up in the street below. We were huddled together in the centre of the roof, and could not see over the edges, but we did not have to glimpse the vehicle to know it was a police car. The sirens were quiet, but the lights swung blue black, blue black, casting an eerie glow on the surrounding brick and stone. For a few seconds we held our breath, hoping they did not know we were there. Then we heard the sturdy clunk of the doors, and a voice called out through a loudhailer: 'You there, on the roof. We know you're up there. The building is surrounded; we're putting a ladder up to you. Please stay where you are until we can get you down safely.'

We looked at one another. Francis silently pulled up the rope at the side of the building. It had been sloppy to leave it there, but no one reproached him. It was not the time.

'This puts a rather different complexion on the matter,' Michael said. At that moment his pompous bravado was rather wonderful. If we could still be ourselves in these circumstances, I thought, they must not be so desperate.

'Do they think we're robbers?' I asked. 'Will they believe us if we tell them the truth?'

It was a childish question, and the others ignored me. Instinctively, they turned to Francis.

'We must do it!' he said, his eyes shining. For a moment, in the madness of adrenalin, it occurred to me that he himself might have summoned the police to provide the final spur to our jump.

'Francis,' Jessica was saying, 'just look at it . . . it's not worth the risk . . .'

'Jessica, we were prepared to do this. It's what we wanted.'

'I was going to do it when I thought it was possible. But just look at that space . . .'

Whilst we talked, I was aware of a second police car arriving from King's Parade. There were more voices in the street around the Senate House. I had hoped that the policeman's claim to have us surrounded was a vain boast designed to coax us down, but I could now see it was not. The beams of torches appeared in the garden by the Old Library; they lanced the shadows, hemming us in. Lisa wandered away from the argument and peered brazenly down at our tormentors. Michael, Francis and Jessica continued to argue.

Then there was the sound of feet hitting the rooftop opposite, and a cry from the street below. Someone shouted, 'Quick, they're going to fall . . .'

Lisa was standing on the opposite side of the gulf. 'Stop pissing about and do it,' she said, and with that moved away across the roof of Caius to clear a space for the next landing.

There was no time for the safety rope now. We looked at one another, and Michael peeled away from the group. He stood for a few seconds at the far edge of the roof, and stared grimly at the balustrade. Then he put his head down like a bull and thundered for the gap. As he hit it, he launched his graceless body through the air, his legs stretched out in front like a pudgy child doing the long jump on sports day, and came down on the other side with such a thud I thought he must have injured himself. He rolled upright with an audible grunt, and turned back to face us across the gulf. Now there was uproar in the street below, and over the city we could hear the wail of the fire engine, bearing the ladder that would seal our fate once and for all. Jessica was breathing hard with fear, but she rose to her feet and shuffled with a gallows walk to the start of her run up. Francis stood in her way. In that instant, I could tell they were alone together, risen above all the danger and the lights and the sirens to a place where only the two of them existed.

'You know I will stay here with you, don't you?' he said. 'If you don't want to do it, I will stay with you when they come.'

'I know,' she said, 'now please move.'

She ran as fast as she could, and jumped. She had judged the distance poorly, and she had to break stride before she hit the balustrade. Her natural agility saved her from tripping, and pitching forwards over the roof into the darkness, with the cobblestones waiting at the bottom. Her jump was a desperate lunge. I felt my heart stop beating as I watched her. She hit the ledge of the roof at Caius, and for a moment she hung there on the edge, her long arms pinwheeling in the wind. Michael and Lisa darted forwards to grab her, and they took her wrists just before gravity bit, and yanked her forwards on to the roof. A gasp laced with screams went up from the crowd below as if at the antics of a tightrope walker.

Francis said he would go last. The fire engine had arrived, and the men were bringing around the mechanical arm of the ladder. I caught up my courage and ran at the leap.

When I jumped, I felt at first that I moved very slowly through the air, accelerating only as I fell. On the opposite bank I could see my friends, their faces hidden under black wool, their eyes and mouths wide with terror and exhilaration. I looked down between my legs. I saw the world from an angle I had never expected. Far below me on the cobbles, beneath my outstretched foot, there were the upturned faces of the police and the porters, staring into the sky like children at a lost balloon. I did not have time to count them, or to see the details of the scene, but I recognized the thought that ruled their features. It was one of pure disbelief. They could not credit that anyone would be so reckless, so brave as to make the leap. They could not believe the figures passing by them in the air above. It made me feel like a god, to inspire that look in another human being. When my feet hit the lead sheeting of Caius' roof, I fell back to the earth.

Francis followed, making easy work of the leap, and we escaped across the roofs of Caius, running along the flat sheet metal, vaulting skylights beneath which were sleeping students, lit rooms and dinner parties. The cold night air was filled with the cries of our pursuers, and with the beams of their torches probing the gutters, swinging up from the streets along the sky like arc lights in an air raid. We shinned down the drainpipe on Trinity Lane, nearly 150 yards from the point where we had made the jump. Francis, Lisa and I removed our disguises and walked casually back around to the Senate House to watch the authorities. The police had cordoned off a section of the road, and we stood at the barriers with a handful of drunken onlookers. A sergeant with a megaphone made sensible appeals to the empty sky for us to come down.

After a while someone arrived with a Thermos of coffee, and Francis got chatting to one of the officers on duty. It appeared that patrols had been put out with a brief to keep an eye on the rooftops, as the university had finally gone to the police with its woes, fearful of its liabilities if anyone were injured. Now that my fear was gone, I was flattered by the resources they had devoted to our capture. As we stood there and quizzed the milling officials, I felt my usual sensation of triumph over the dangers of the climb compounded with one of victory. I felt the visceral pleasure of having got the better of another man.

I say we stopped climbing after this incident, but that is not the whole truth. Some weeks later, I was walking through the main gate of college into Tudor Great Court. The night was clear and cold, and I looked up at the sky to see the stars. It was then I caught a glimpse of a man on the roof of Tudor hall. He was crouched like a black cat on the summit of the building, edging away from the small tower of the lantern at the hall's centre. I did not want to risk signalling his presence by calling out, so I just stood and watched. He padded along the spine between the tiled slopes with perfect steps, and rose upright just before he leapt out of sight on the other side. He stood there, silhouetted against the moon, with his arms outstretched in the darkness, and in his stillness and ecstasy he looked like the stone statue of an angel who had wandered free from his pedestal. Then he disappeared. I never mentioned to Francis, or to anyone else, that I had seen him there. I cherished the vision all to myself.

Climbing together had reinforced the bonds of our friendship. The illegality and the danger both inspired trust, the first through a need for secrecy, the second because we placed our safety in one another's hands. It kept our bodies lean and ready, like a population primed for revolution, and our minds burning with possibility. It was, I see now, a kind of apprenticeship for what followed.

That thought first occurred to me two years later, though I did not then appreciate its full implications. I was sitting in a lecture hall in the Michaelmas term of my final year, long after my friends were gone, listening to a middle-aged woman discourse upon the Athenian tragic festivals, and the image of Francis appeared before me so vividly, it was as if his ghost had walked on to the podium, tall and proud, with the look of easy triumph in his eyes, the way he was in those early days. The lecturer was giving the assembled students her theory on why the young men of Athens danced in the great masques that punctuated the tragic plays of Sophocles and Euripides. The standard line was that the dancing of the chorus was in the spirit of the festival, part of a pattern of art and culture which was to resonate through the millennia. But she told us this was wrong, the misunderstanding of a modern age obsessed with leisure, with no concept of duty. She told us that the male youths may have seemed to dance for joy, but what they were really doing was training their feet for the phalanx. The plays themselves were about the aftermath of battles, of the siege of Troy or the fall of Thebes, and the complicated ballet of young men moving in perfect unison was done in anticipation of battles to come. When the Athenian army fought together, the men went out as one unit, shields closed together, spears raised, feet following specific movements at the command of the officers. What appeared to be the expression of youthful and cultural activity was in fact a drill for the bloody conquests of the empire. I thought of Francis urging us on, driving us to new heights, forcing us to work more closely together and to expand our ideas of what we could accomplish, all under the guise of wild celebration, and then of his final project.

In the phalanx each shield locked with the next, covering not just the warrior holding it, but also the man to his left. Any hoplite who died or fell uncovered his neighbour to the swords and arrows of the enemy. If you lost your footing, you would murder not yourself, but your brother dancing beside you. It was perhaps this last detail that most brought Francis to my mind.

10

When term was over I went back to live with my father in Wandsworth. Jessica, Lisa and Michael all lived in London, though Michael had announced his intention to spend Christmas in Barbados in Sandy Lane, where his parents had a house. Francis would be returning to his father's estate in Northamptonshire, and he warned us not to expect to see too much of him, as his father was unleashing a horde of entertainments on the local community. The mooted ban on fox hunting had given him a good foothold in local sympathy, and he was capitalizing on this by giving over his whole energy to various blood sports. Francis would be expected to look dashing in pink at the local hunt, bring home a brace or two from the weekend shooting parties and make up bridge fours. He had no real taste for any of these activities when they were undertaken in a formal social context, though he was an accomplished rider and an excellent shot. He said that being armed in the proximity of Lord Soulford always gave him a pleasant patricidal buzz. 'It's like climbing and suddenly feeling a powerful urge to throw yourself off,' he told me and Jessica. 'I can feel the barrels twitching towards him of their own accord, like a divining rod.'

I was enchanted by the image of this wholesome world of winter sports, with tweed and wet Labradors, green Range Rovers spattered with mud and the smell of cordite hanging over sodden fields. I thought of the magical day we had spent together after the night of Francis's boxing match. I began to picture his house; a rambling old building with log fires and gloomy portraits, bedrooms with names and historical occupants, and a deep green lawn studded with thick white croquet hoops, ending in a ha-ha that gave on to a valley view. I knew such houses only from the sporadic invitations of a single prep-school friend. When Francis first broached the subject of the holidays I assumed it was his roundabout way of issuing an invitation, and I was excited. Time wore on, and no such invitation materialized. I had got so far ahead of myself in my imagination that this felt like a slight. I finally mentioned the subject to Jessica whilst Francis was buying a round of drinks at the bar of the Eagle, giving the conversation a definite boundary.

'So,' I said, 'have you ever stayed at Francis's house?'

'Yes, once. But not again.'

'Did something happen?'

'Lots of things happened.'

'Don't be tiresome. You know what I mean.'

'I know exactly what you mean. Don't be nosy.'

'I just want to know why none of us are invited!' I blurted out.

Jessica looked at me with gentle condescension.

'I mean, I know it might not exactly be Lisa's scene, but the rest of us—'

Her eyes narrowed. 'Don't be a snob.'

'Look, I'm not being a snob, I'm just trying to see it from his perspective. I would imagine the sort of people Lord Soulford invites shooting are fairly conservative.'

'He's not embarrassed by any of us, if that's what you think. He took me and Lisa last year, and I had a very pleasant weekend, although I did have to bite my tongue when one of the elder guests described me as "peg candy". And I don't think he's particularly embarrassed by his father either. I think the thing he finds most distasteful is himself, or the version of himself he becomes when he's back there. I've seen it. 'Yes, Papa, no, Papa.' It's terrible, you feel helpless and awkward. It's like seeing a friend who was a champion sprinter unable to walk.'

Francis came back from the bar, coughing to announce his return. He set the drinks down, spilling ochre liquid from the broad rim of the pint glass on to the brown wooden tabletop. Jessica, who seldom drank, was having an orange juice. This put a premature end to the conversation, and Francis sensed the lack of closure, a thick anticipation hanging like cooking smells in the air.

174

He had the social grace not to mention it, sensing perhaps that he had been the topic under discussion.

I was surprised, therefore, when three weeks into the Christmas holidays my doorbell rang and I found Francis on my doorstep. He had a bottle of champagne for my father that, despite its château and vintage, had the look of a last-minute airport-bought present, and a small overnight bag. He beamed when I opened the door, and cited a wish to surprise me as his reason for surprising me. His goodwill and humour swept aside all questions like the vanguard of a conquering army, and he had soon subdued any scepticism on my father's part. He greeted everything in my household with a genuine and passionate enthusiasm. He noticed the fishing rod folded away by my father's briefcase and overcoat in the downstairs closet, and when we came back to the kitchen, having first dumped his bag in the guest bedroom, he played my father with a perfectly judged discussion on the merits of a certain river near Dumfries.

It was the day before Christmas Eve. No mention had been made of the timing of his visit, but Francis made it clear from the way in which he spread his meagre possessions across the surfaces of our guest room that he intended to stay for Christmas. On Christmas Day my father and I followed the groove of a well-established tradition. We woke in the morning and opened the stockings that each of us had prepared for the other (I always marvelled at my father's intuitive ability to select presents that would have been appropriate about two years previously), and met the rest of the family at midday mass. We would then process in a series of people carriers to my eldest aunt's house in Wimbledon, where we would have turkey, old feuds would be polished and ceremoniously produced like the family silver, and I would play with my young cousins. The thought of bringing Francis into this was rather like introducing a new letter to the alphabet, so well established and defined were the criteria. I was also terribly embarrassed at the thought of my uncle's smelly feet and cheap whisky, and the fact that my cousins called me 'lame James'. I had never lied to Francis about my private life, but there were details I had tweaked, a little smear of Vaseline on the lens I had used to relay my home and family. I tried to make a mental inventory of the variations between what I had said and what he would see. I was also a little concerned about Francis's tendency towards excess. I wondered how best to inform him politely that I did not want any drugs to be taken in my house. To pre-empt him in this matter ran the risk of insulting him, implying that he could not make it through a week without taking something when he never would have dreamt of doing so. On the other hand if I did not tell him now, I might have to address the issue after the fact, and he would be terribly embarrassed. I had no idea of the right etiquette.

As he unpacked the last of his things, my thoughts

were diverted along these lines, and I was unprepared when he said, 'If you wouldn't mind terribly, I was hoping we might not mention this to the others.'

'Mention what?' I asked.

'My little visit.'

'Why not?' I asked.

'Jessica and Lisa have a tendency to fuss, and Michael to talk. Look, I really don't want to make a big deal out of it. I chose you because I knew I could rely on your discretion.'

This was his checkmate; he cornered my best intentions with a pledge of mutual trust.

'It will be fun,' he said, clapping me on the back, 'we can enjoy a secret holiday. And your father is absolutely charming, I'm so looking forward to getting to know him better. I'm afraid I haven't got you a present, Papa has not been too forthcoming with money this month, but I promise I shall get you something when we get back to university. This isn't a huge imposition, is it? If you can't have me I'll be quite happy moving to a hotel. I just wanted to see a friendly face. It's not good to spend Christmas alone.'

'Of course you're not imposing,' I said. 'I'm pleased to see you.'

It was nothing less than the truth, I realized as I headed downstairs for a private conversation with my dad. I had enjoyed being back at home, and the holiday had felt like a genuine period of relaxation. The charge of termtime had dissipated slowly in a fug of TV and home cooking. My memories of the previous term and the anticipation of the next had kept the border between relaxation and boredom. Francis had been my spice – a little of him every day had kept the meat from tasting bland. With his return there came a return to excitement, and this unannounced entrance was perfectly in keeping with the image I had of him. I spoke to my dad, and we agreed Francis should join us at Christmas lunch; we would tell my aunt that his parents had gone overseas. She had a fondness for the abandoned that made this the perfect cover story, and meant that she would prevent anyone else from 'bothering the wee mite with questions'. In the event, all my preparations were for nothing. The next day Jessica arrived to pick him up.

I saw her neat little Mini pull up in the drive, blocking my father's car and sticking its boot out into the street. When she climbed out I felt an immediate pang of fear for my nascent plans, but I was also struck by how wrong she looked on my street. Her blonde hair was set in a gravity-defying wave, she had on a grey cashmere sweater from which her long white forearms protruded like new shoots, vital and smooth, and her whole air was inappropriate to the cracked and modest suburban pavement, like a peacock wandering among the pigeons at Trafalgar Square. My father was reading in his room, and I was able to intercept her before she rang the bell. I did not want him to witness any kind of scene.

'James,' she said with a tight little smile, 'I hope you're having a festive holiday.'

'Silent nights and cold Christmas mornings. How about you?'

'Well, it was very enjoyable until about six hours ago, when I heard that Francis was in trouble. You haven't seen him, I suppose?'

'Why didn't you just telephone?' I asked.

She ignored me. 'May I come in?'

I saw that my powers of delay were unequal to the task. I could think of no credible reason for keeping her out. I showed her through to the stairs and pointed her in the direction of the guest bedroom. I then went to wait for them in the living room, returning to my TV programme. I was incredibly edgy, fearing for my father's involvement like for a sleeping baby, but the whole conversation was managed without raised voices, and Jessica returned to the living room without his having been roused. She sat in the seat next to mine. The three armchairs in our living room were huddled in a crescent around the television, and I could not easily observe her without obviously turning my head.

'What happened?' I asked at length.

'Oh, nothing to concern you.'

'How did you guess he was here?'

'His brother called me and asked me where he'd got to. Lord Soulford had his account frozen, so he couldn't go to a hotel. Jeremy told me he left with the change in his

179

pocket and whatever he could shove in his bag. I must say, James, I'm a little surprised you didn't call me. Surprised and shocked.'

Jessica was in magisterial mode. She was neither surprised nor shocked, and I resented the imposition of unwarranted guilt. I actually thought she might be a little jealous. Clearly she was too cosy with the family Manley to provide the disinterested support that Francis had felt he needed. I was also hurt that his choice of my house had been, at least in part, one of financial necessity.

'He asked me specifically not to tell you,' I said. I was on the point of adding that I could see why when there was a noise on the stairs. Francis came back in with his bag packed, but when Jessica rose from her seat he dropped it in the frayed lap of an armchair and went over to the drinks cabinet. There was nothing in his manner to suggest any conflict or concern. In fact, he seemed quite cheerful.

'Would you like a drink? James, can I make you something?'

'We don't have time for a drink, Francis,' Jessica said carefully. 'Why don't we have one later, back at my place.'

'If you don't want to drink I can make a virgin.'

'I don't think anyone else wants one.'

'I'd like an aperitif,' he said.

'We're not staying for lunch.'

'We have enough food for everyone. It would be no

trouble,' I said. I was still angry with Jessica. She ignored me, which was the best retort available.

'Francis, we have to get going.'

He turned around to look at her. Behind him, the drinks cabinet had its replica-walnut doors thrown open in welcome, its crystal contents tinkling lightly with the tread of my father in the upstairs bedroom. They looked at one another, and I was once again acutely aware of the understanding between the two of them that was like pig-Latin between children: a code of exclusion, a means of communicating the forbidden. He turned back to the cabinet and gently shut the doors, dipping his head for a moment and collecting himself before he came away.

'Yes, we do. James, it was wonderful of you to have me, I'm only sorry it turned out to be such a brief stay. Will you please communicate my thanks to your papa. I shall write him a letter, of course, but I think for the moment explanations are best kept to a minimum.'

'Goodbye.'

'Goodbye, James,' Jessica said, her face a deliberate blank. 'I guess I'll see you in a fortnight, if not before.'

I explained to my dad that Lord Soulford had telephoned Francis and applied the balm of Christmas cheer. I knew the restoration of sympathy between father and son would appeal to his sense of right. Fortunately we had not yet contacted my aunt. I treated this brief interlude as a dramatic appetizer, a kind of masque before the main show. It did not occur to me to wonder what had happened after the players had left my little set, or to ask what had driven Francis away from his home, or if it did it was only in the easy terms of melodrama, of beautiful vases thrown across drawing rooms and the spinning of tyres on a gravelled drive. I thought only of how much I was looking forward to my return to Cambridge, where events seemed to be important, where the friends I had obtained gave my life weight and substance. After Francis's departure from my house, the whole of Christmas was to me a favour undertaken on my family's behalf, and it was all I could do to conceal from them my impatience.

11

The night that Lord Soulford was due to speak at the Union I was working. It was the first full week of the Lent term. He was to be the proposer in a debate entitled 'This House Believes that Britain is Full', to which Michael, in his role as Union president, had invited him. I was unused to sitting at my desk, but my tutor had set me a practical criticism exercise on a Wyatt sonnet, and the question was so specific it precluded the possibility of a fake. I was not a member of the Union and I had not been asked to the talk, but Francis had requested I come to the dinner afterwards as his guest. At eight-thirty Jessica phoned me.

'Where the fuck is Francis?'

I heard the sound of a car going past. 'I don't know. Where are you?'

'I'm outside the Union. His father's about to start speaking and he's not fucking here. If he fucks this, we're finished.' I baulked a little at the 'we're'. I knew we benefited from Francis's father's money, but it was not something I liked to hear said out loud.

'I'm afraid I have no idea where he is,' I said a little coldly.

'Well, find him and get him to the dinner. That's where the press are going to be, that's what matters.' Her tone changed suddenly. 'Can I trust you to do that, James? He listens to you, you're the only one I can trust to help me.'

I knew I was being manipulated, she was deliberately signalling as much with the speed of her turn around from commands to entreaties, but in my mind's eye I saw her standing on Bridge Street in the cold, talking on her mobile phone in a shimmering evening dress, on the verge of spoiling her make-up with tears. 'Sure,' I said, a little disgusted with myself, 'I'll do it.'

She hung up.

I shut the book of sixteenth-century poetry, and quickly got dressed. I put on my black tie, leaving the bowtie in my pocket and the collar of my dress shirt open. I threw an overcoat on top so that it looked like I was simply wearing a white shirt and black trousers, and went to Francis's room. No one answered my knock. I went to the Eagle, then checked the Mill and the Anchor. I called Lisa, but got no response. Michael I knew would be at the talk. I took off my shirt and jacket and climbed the drainpipe opposite Magdalene where he sometimes came to sit on the roof and watch the river. I came back down and cleaned my hands in the water. I telephoned his club, but the steward said he hadn't seen him all evening. I went to Market Square and checked the reading room at Borders where he sometimes went to sit when he was high, writing random things in the books and putting them back on the shelves, and then down to the basement of the Red Cow where he went to get out of his mind, because he thought none of the rest of us knew he used it. It was nine-forty-five. The talk was nearly over. Soon the privileged few would be heading over to the Senior Common Room in Corpus for dinner, where the cameras organized by Lord Soulford's press agent would be waiting.

With a great sense of dread I walked back towards the college up Bene't Street. I fixed my bowtie in a dark shop window, and put in my cufflinks. I was shown by the porters through into Old Court, and directed up the staircase to the Senior Common Room. I was standing outside the door, deliberating over a wide range of possible excuses, when Francis appeared at the bottom of the stairs. He was sweating despite the cold. His bowtie dangled around his neck.

'Francis, where the fuck have you been?'

'I've . . . I went out, out to see some friends,' he slurred.

'Jesus . . . are you drunk?'

He came up the stairs leaning heavily against the wall. All the lightness was gone from his step. He dragged his feet as if through water. 'You see . . . you see, I'm such a coward. So I made certain to fuck it up. I made it certain this time, you see, there's no going back, I couldn't behave tonight in a million years, not in all the millions of years.'

'Francis, what have you taken?'

He reached the landing at the top and stood in front of me. I held his face in my hands and looked into his eyes. His skin was soft and warm. I tried to remember what chemicals he currently had stashed in his bedside cabinet. I guessed maybe ecstasy and ketamine, or lithium. His pupils were wide, the brilliant whites cloudy and opaque. Deep in the chestnut shade, his sober self was standing, afraid of what he was about to do, afraid to come out of the shadows and take responsibility, or lazy maybe, like a worker lounging in siesta, dodging the midday moment. Inside, his father was waiting with the members of the press, and the men and women in evening wear, and the cameras. I tied his bowtie for him the way he had taught me. I knew that this was the time, the time that would seal me forever in the golden light of his affections like an insect trapped in amber, if only I could think of some way of averting disaster. But I could not. With an inexorable logic, Francis moved towards the door. He stumbled a little, and had to catch on to the handle to steady himself. I moved with despair into the candlelit interior. Lord Soulford saw us and stood up, roaring with hearty delight (and considerable relief), 'My son! Come and sit beside me!' Francis wandered into the barrage of greetings like a shell-shocked soldier. Several camera bulbs flashed as he hugged his father, and he screwed up his eyes to blink them away. On Lord Soulford's part it was a perfect display of masculine affection. When he clapped his son's back I was afraid Francis was going to vomit like a baby over the shoulder of his dinner jacket, so I broke in to say my own hellos.

Francis and I were seated on Lord Soulford's right. On his left was an attractive female journalist from *The Times*. Jeremy, Francis's half-brother, was sitting near the head of the table. At eighteen he looked like a child who had been invited to dine with the grown-ups, and he kept fiddling with his collar, which was too tight and made a little ring of flesh well up around his neck, sealing his torso inside his dress shirt. Jessica was opposite, across the broad mahogany leaves and an intimidating array of gleaming cutlery, and Lisa was sat one down from her.

I barely recognized her when I first saw her; she had on a sheath dress of blue silk, and she wore her hair down, with all the grease washed out of it. Jessica had branded her for the evening with her own advice and direction. It softened her pretty face, and neat lipstick and eye shadow changed her completely. It was not that make-up made her seem more feminine, though this was certainly true; it was the idea that she wanted people to think her pretty. Only her quick brown eyes told tales on her, and because I knew where to look I saw the tactician watching through them, camouflaged in that innocent beauty like a big cat watching from the cover of the sun-dappled jungle. When the wine waiter came around I put my hand lightly over Francis's glass. No one noticed but Jessica, and she laughed at me. I understood the joke. She had clocked Francis's state as soon as he came through the door. Putting my hand over the glass was like raising an umbrella over the sea.

Right the way through the starter and the main course, Francis was mercifully silent. This suited Lord Soulford, who wished to be seen in his company but not necessarily to share in it. Silver service was in force, so he did not even have to pass food to the other guests. From the shaking hands that held his knife and fork I doubted whether he could have managed it. I could barely eat, as diplomatic pressure bore down on me. I had to maintain not only the relationship, but also the appearance of the relationship between father and son. The photographers had mercifully left after the embrace, but several other people around the table appeared to be conducting impromptu interviews. Lisa and Jessica valiantly distracted their neighbours, mobilizing their most charming selves, protecting Francis from anything like an attempt at conversation, but no one could reach the woman on his father's left. As the disembodied arms of the staff deftly lifted away the chicken in a mushroom sauce, she leant over her host to ask Francis what he had thought of the debate.

'It was unmissable,' he replied earnestly.

Lord Soulford toyed uncomfortably with his napkin.

'Unmissable?' she asked.

'I mean it was excellent.'

When she went to the toilet, Lord Soulford turned to his son and hissed, 'Why the hell weren't you at the debate?'

'I'm sorry, Papa,' Francis said with great dignity. 'I was sick.'

'You look it. Pull yourself together.'

When the lady returned from the toilet she picked up where she had left off. 'Do you think the subject of immigration has any relevance to your son or his friends? Don't you worry that ideas of national identity are the sole preserve of the old?'

'I think the younger generation are even more willing to address this issue than we are,' Lord Soulford said, turning to face the three of us, 'as they're not bound by the fetters of prejudice. This terrible paranoia that grips the government when discussing these issues, the fear that they will be labelled racist or xenophobic, these boys and girls don't feel it, and it leaves them free to address the real issues behind the rhetoric, the pressure on our health-care system, on education, on the police—'

'"You don't have to put on the red light . . ."' Francis sang quietly.

Lord Soulford looked at him with barely concealed rage.

'What was that?' said the journalist quickly.

'You know,' Francis said. 'The Police. "Rooooxanne".'

Jessica kicked me under the table.

'I think the real issue for politics and the young,' I said, 'is apathy. I think the point Francis is satirically trying to make is that we'd rather listen to pop music than discuss current issues.'

Jessica had to put her hand over her mouth to conceal a spontaneous fit of giggles, and managed to convert the gesture into a smoothing of her long blonde hair. Lisa cast a glance in our direction, though she did not risk turning towards us. Her main aim was to hold the attention of the people further down the table, damming their gaze. Lord Soulford turned in his chair, partially concealing a semi-lucid Francis from the reporter, and resumed the trajectory of his monologue, making minor adjustments for the interruption.

'Apathy is a real issue. And if we can get just a few more people interested in the debate by offering the public less anodyne opinions and solutions on immigration, rather than the bland lies this government feeds the British people—'

'Who are these British people?' Francis demanded loudly.

'You and me, dear boy.'

'Not me,' Francis said, 'I'm from Zimbabwe. You are only resident, not normally resident, I had a peek at your accounts and saw your tax declaration. Jessica over there is a starchild, and Lisa is Jewish, and James, he's terribly

British but he doesn't want to be. How about you, miss, are you British?'

It was horribly funny. I could not make the seriousness of what was at stake correspond to the farcical situation. The journalist gazed at him, then dropped her chin and smiled from under her brows. I realized with relief that she thought she was being mocked. She took Francis's drugs-induced babble as a challenge to her intelligence. She raised her glass to her lips, and took a long draught of white wine to show that she wasn't fazed. How wonderfully lucky we are, I thought, to have got such an egotist, someone who assumes the joke must be for their benefit.

'I'm Brixtonian,' she said with the sarcastic air of some-one who gets the gag.

When Lord Soulford spoke, his voice was quiet. 'Francis, may I speak with you in private?'

'No, no, I don't think so,' he replied gaily. 'But if my friends can come we can speak outside.'

'Very well,' he said. 'Shall we?' He let the ladies go first, and we all trooped out into an ante-room at the side. The mass exodus drew some looks, but conversations were in full swing and the wine was flowing, so no one paid much attention. The waiters had begun to serve profiteroles. Jeremy, who seemed utterly lost when not standing next to his father, saw us leaving and followed without invitation.

The room we had entered was a snug little space where

coats were stored during dinner. There was a row of brass hooks along one wall, and an oil on panel portrait of Sir William Butler by the door. In the centre of the room there was a small table upon which stood a brass lamp with a green glass shade. When the door closed behind us, Lord Soulford stood thoughtfully in front of his eldest son for a few seconds. The silence was broken by the vague murmur of conversation and laughter from the dining room. Then he hit him in the face as hard as he could.

I was astonished. Francis's head snapped round with the force of the punch, and he stepped back to keep his balance. For a moment, I thought he would hit his father back. Violent potential suddenly radiated from his broad shoulders, and his usual dancer's grace switched to the boxer's shuffle as he reclaimed his balance and squared up to Lord Soulford, his torso swaying with tight vigilance that would not brook another blow. Francis was tall and broad, and more frightening in his rage than anyone I had ever seen, as the emotion simply did not belong in his repertoire. It distorted his features, turning him into someone else. He seemed suddenly massive, as if standing for the first time at his full height. It was strange to see his honed black frame and think that he had grown out of a splinter of the red-faced, portly man in front of him. The sense of impending danger penetrated even Lord Soulford's smug hide, and he took a step away from his son, the mottled blood in his cheeks draining to reveal a queasy yellow. As was his habit, he sought to reassert his authority by speaking in a loud voice, barking out orders even as he was retreating behind the table.

'Look here, boy, you deserved that, you bloody know you did. Take it like a gentleman.'

Francis teetered on the brink, his whole strong body poised on the delicate pivot of his emotions. I held my breath to see if he would close the circuit to let the present incident connect with years of stored resentment and surge forwards in anger. Everyone watched him with their own secret hopes. Nothing happened. In the end the old prohibition was too much for him; he could not strike his father. The force flowed out of him suddenly, the tension disappearing into the earth like electricity. His arms slumped, the fingers uncurled from their fists, and the weight of his intoxication fell across his shoulders, almost carrying him down to the ground.

An ugly look of triumph planted its banner in Lord Soulford's eyes, as if he and not his son's better nature had won the day. 'You parasites. You live off me, you live off my taxes, and you think the world owes you a living. Well, not any more, Francis, you ungrateful little swine. From this moment on, you can take care of yourself. If you can't do the smallest thing for me, I shan't lift a finger to help you, not even if you come crawling from the gutter. I disinherit you.'

This final utterance was pronounced with a theatrical

flourish of the hand. Lord Soulford was one of those who was driven by danger on to the high ground of self-dramatization. The hamminess of his delivery created a jarring contrast with the pain I saw in Francis's eyes. I looked at his father with loathing. It was liberating to feel it on someone else's behalf; I felt none of the mollifying influence of conscience. It was my first taste of adult hatred, and I relished it. I abandoned myself to hating him.

Without speaking people began to arrange themselves in a stately declaration of alliances. Lisa and Jessica stood on either side of Francis, and each of them took one of his hands. The quiet pride of the two women in their evening dresses was a more potent reproach to Lord Soulford than any words could have been. I was standing behind the trio, the four of us facing him. The table was between us, and together with the bronze and gilt fixtures of the room it gave the occasion a feeling of political weight, as if we were at some emergency conference, and it was breaking up in disarray. Jeremy hovered in the middle, clearly uncomfortable with his father's behaviour but lacking the imagination to face him down. Michael, who had been silent for some time, came over to me, and whispered, 'Look, why don't you take him home, he's clearly out of his skull. Nothing can be resolved tonight. I'll see if I can calm the old man down.' And with that he walked over to Lord Soulford, and put his hand on his shoulder, a gesture of frank and manly solidarity. 'Come on, old boy,' he said to him. 'Let's get you out of here before the press get a whiff.'

The mention of the press jerked Francis's father out of his performance, and he looked around him quickly as if he had just woken up. 'Quite right, absolutely right,' he said. 'Now, the rest of you, go and put him to bed, and get a steak on that eye. And not a word of this to anyone, do you understand, or I'll set my lawyers on the lot of you. You can take the back stairs.'

Michael indicated to Jeremy that he should open the door. He received the order gratefully and ran over to the end of the room to hold it open. The sound of the dinner party briefly swelled again, and candlelight fell in through the space. Michael turned his back on us and guided his patron out of the room. Jeremy closed the door behind the three of them, and his last look back at Francis was one of abject shame. The handle clicked as the door shut.

The four of us stood still. The moment one of us moved, we would all have to admit the reality of what had just happened. Then Jessica turned to Francis. I was afraid she was going to reproach him, to shout at him for losing his money, our money. She was dressed in expensive clothes and jewellery she had not bought herself. But she cupped the back of his skull in the palm of her hand and kissed him on the forehead. A look of blissful relief spread over his face.

'James, would you take him home and see he's all

right?' she said. 'I know Lisa has another engagement she can't miss, and I quite want to get out of this dress and take a shower. It's been rather a long evening. The debate was fucking awful, Francis, you didn't miss much. I'll be in to check on you later.'

We all of us went our separate ways. I helped Francis over the side gate to avoid the photographers by the porters' lodge.

I moved Francis through his door with my shoulder beneath his, holding him up. The support was not physically necessary, but I felt him trembling and wanted an excuse we could both live with for being close to him. His breath had the sweet reek of booze. The room was in partial darkness, the only light coming from the dim bulb in the standing lamp by the sink. I helped him negotiate the piles of possessions on his floor, finding the bare spaces between the expensive leather shoes that never seemed to be in pairs, the wooden coat hangers imprinted with the names of London tailors, the stacks of books, the silk cushions and the miniature colour-glass tower of the hookah, and then finally, in a drunken stumble, to the unmade bed. He let me lift up his legs by the calves, tilting him gently back on to the pillows, and as I looked at him lying there in a stupor I felt a brief pang of resentment. How dare he deliberately jeopardize our material comfort, the foundations of our fun, by alienating his father? With his eyes closed and his features slack it was as if the lights had gone out in a beautiful building, revealing it to be nothing more than bricks and mortar. I thought what best to do next. The kitchen on his floor was directly opposite on the landing, and Francis had installed a small freezer for the sole purpose of storing cocktail ingredients. It was an ugly little white breeze-block that squatted under the counter. The contents, decadent and expensive, made an odd counterpoint to the functional bareness of the communal kitchen, the stainless steel sink that sounded like a drum when water fell from the taps, the stained and peeling yellow walls flecked with fat from the grill. I went and opened it, and behind a bottle of Angels' Tears vodka, chilled to a sluggish white syrup, and the ranks of smoky shot glasses there was a plastic sack of ice. I thought about taking through the bottle, but I was afraid he might drink. I tore open the sack of ice and tipped a quarter of the contents into the filthy gingham tea towel. I wound the corners up into a knot, fixed it with a rubber band and brought the whole thing through in a plastic salad bowl, so he would have somewhere to drop it when it began to melt. Francis took the ice pack from me with a total lack of surprise or gratitude, and held it to his rapidly expanding cheek. This practised gesture reminded me that he must be quite used to being hit. With his free hand he groped around on his dressing table until his fingers found a small blue leather cufflink box. It rattled ominously when he picked it up. He flipped the lid to reveal several round speckled pills of unknown vintage, and about ten plain white tablets. Valium.

He shook out two. A third fell to the floor and ran for cover among the discarded clothes. He popped them into his mouth and washed them down with a swig from an old glass of water on the windowsill. I considered taking one myself, but decided against it. I did not want to slip away into oblivion before I had digested the evening's events. He settled himself against the pillows, and after a few moments' meditative silence he began to speak.

'He was right, though. I mean, he rather undermined the force of his logic by punching me (so like Papa, that), but he was right.' He was beginning to sober up, to enter the quiet, oddly lucid period that always came with him after the drugs and before the come-down. The Valium would take about fifteen minutes to work their soothing magic, massaging out the mental knots and cramps that kept Francis awake.

'Right about what?' I said, smoothing his forehead with my hand. I felt the rough texture of his curly hair against my palm. He let me do it. It made me wince to see the swelling already starting in his fine features; I felt as if a schoolyard bully had knocked down my younger brother.

'I do think the world owes me a living. How could it be otherwise? The birds, the lilies, they don't do any work. No one hassles them.'

'I think you're taking that parable a little out of context,' I said, smiling down at him like a nurse at a recovering patient. 'Lilies don't have gambling debts.'

'You see this picture on my wall?' He propped himself up on his elbows and cocked his head so that he was looking at the picture upside down.

I looked up at the Tudor Picasso. I was, as ever, amazed and a little disappointed at its blunt reality. To my mind this kind of treasure belonged in museums, or the houses of the incredibly wealthy, and only such locations could provide appropriate context. I preferred to keep the idea of genius as abstract and remote as possible; it gave me something to aspire to whilst alleviating the anxiety of competition with its untouchable nature. The effect of seeing it hanging in partial darkness among the detritus of Francis's room, with his cracked mirror on one side and a framed *Thunderball* poster on the other, was like meeting a favourite movie star and discovering that they are much shorter than you had imagined.

'How much do you think it's worth?'

I blew out through my lips, and conjured a figure out of the air. 'Ten million?'

'Twelve. We must sell it.' He smiled at his own brilliance and lay back on the pillow. I thought he was joking and smiled back. The two of us grinned at one another in mutual incomprehension. Eventually he seemed to realize, and repeated, 'We sell it,' his tone now one of careful explanation.

'Francis, we don't own it,' I said.

'Oh James, sometimes you can be so obtuse,' he said crossly. 'Of course we don't own it. Firstly it belongs to the college, and secondly as a committed Marxist it would be quite against my principles.'

His flippancy irritated me. I decided to end the conversation by briefly humouring him. I wanted to make sure he was all right, to see him happily off into a deep sleep. I needed to get away, to see the others, to discuss what had happened. 'But, Francis, you can't possibly sell something like this, even if you stole it. I mean you'd be a pretty obvious suspect if the thing went missing, and then it's such a famous picture I think that even Sotheby's might have something to say if it wound up in their catalogue.'

'Yes, yes, of course. That's why we make a nice new copy of the picture, change it for the grubby old one here, and sell the original on the black market in London.'

Francis had just been punched in the face and disowned by his father, yet he seemed oddly elated. It was as if the crack on his cheek had broken the chrysalis of this plan, releasing it into the air. I was torn between dismissing the idea and changing the subject, and attempting to argue him out of it. I felt afraid of the latter, however, since it seemed that taking the time to address his ideas seriously might give them currency, promoting them from fantasy to proposition. My own feelings were still strongly flavoured with shock, and I was wary of this atmosphere – Lord Soulford's blow had been so improbable as to create a sense of limitless possibility. If such a thing could happen, why not a multi-million-pound fraud? The logic was childishly flimsy, but it bore down on me with all the force of reason.

'You think it's impossible, but it's only really one tiny step of the imagination,' Francis said to me. 'Remember, no rules but the ones we make. It suits the art world to give the impression that faking a master is impossible, but it is really incredibly easy. The difficult thing is faking a provenance, a history to authenticate your forgery, and even that is not impossible – John Drewe passed off paintings done in household emulsion and KY jelly as genuine Giacomettis after a few hours' work with ink and scissors in the archives of the V and A. He just rewrote history, then stitched the new pages back into the old catalogues. During his tenure as head of the Metropolitan Museum of Modern Art, Thomas Hoving said that forty per cent of the pictures he considered for purchase were fakes. Ten per cent of all works from the French Impressionist period on the market were painted in the nineteen eighties. Salvador Dali, lying beyond under-standing on his death bed, was forced to sign hundreds of blank sheets that were later turned into fake lithographs. Chagall's widow was accused of flogging off certificates of authentication for a couple of thousand a pop. Giorgio de Chirico, sad and broke at the end of his career, forged paintings to appear to be by his younger self, the darling of the art world two decades past. And those are the tiny fraction which are ever discovered. Just consider it: hundreds of paintings hanging on the walls of the world's most prestigious museums are no more authentic than the picture you will concoct.'

It did not seem strange to me at the time that Francis had all this information at his nimble fingertips. The truth was that he must have arrived at the idea weeks, even months before, and spent time researching its viability in preparation for this day. During the whole speech he gesticulated wildly, but kept the dripping bundle of ice in the tea towel pressed firmly against his swelling eye, so that he seemed like a pirate revealing the location of buried treasure from his deathbed. He had an answer for each of my objections, and so the usual tide of his enthusiasm, quite strong enough on its own to pull me out of the shallow waters of my own intentions and into the blue deeps, was aided by reasoned argument.

'But . . . but they have chemical analysis, to date these pictures, they know the pigments and the composition of the materials . . .' I protested.

'Yes, yes they do,' he replied, nodding as if he had been waiting for me to raise just that point, 'but consider this: firstly, with a watertight provenance, no one would ever bother to check. Chemical analysis is a last recourse to settle questions of doubtful authenticity. Secondly, if we sell the picture illegally, we buy ourselves a certain amount of security. The buyer resigns themselves to never being able to sell the picture on the legitimate market, where any such fraud might be detected, and will never be able to raise the alarm. The picture will never be gone, and there will never be two in circulation. Why would they check?'

The truth of it began to dawn on me, warming the skin of my face. My hands started to tingle. I opened my mouth to speak, and closed it again. I was paralysed by the ridiculousness of his proposition. The impossibility of his scheme seemed so self-evident that I could not frame the terms to disprove it. It was like being asked to prove that the sky was blue: all I could think to do was to point and say, 'But look.'

At last I said, 'What about the style? I mean I like to think I'm a good draughtsman, and I'm flattered you think I'm up to Picasso, but really—'

'That is the simplest part of all,' Francis said, and clapped his hands in front of my face as if summoning a genie. The bundle stayed balanced in his left orbit. 'The picture is exquisite, certainly, but composed of no more than fifty continuous pencil lines. It is a sketch, without the complexity of brushstrokes or texture. All you have to do is practise, copy, trace, copy, until you have the movements stored in your brain, until you could reproduce it blindfold. Imagine the kind of people who actually get to see this painting: students in dingy rooms, with no more sense of a picture's authenticity than you or I have. Do you really think some eighteen-year-old student will have such an intimate knowledge of Picasso's pencil strokes as to be able to detect the difference? Or is it the bedders you're worried about?'

'But . . . but we can't,' I said. 'If we were caught, well, we'd go to prison, I mean real prison.'

'Yes, that is true,' Francis nodded judiciously. 'But what are the real chances of being caught? This picture has hung undisturbed in student rooms since it was bequeathed to the college in nineteen forty-four. That is over half a century of uninterrupted peace. On the open market, I have had it valued at twelve million. In our present circumstances, we could expect to make about a third of that. A million each. Work, to me, to work for a living, that would be a prison, a life sentence. Papa wouldn't have paid for me for ever, even without this evening, and I won't inherit any money. To work and sweat, and answer to others, and watch your waist eat up the space between your chair and the lip of your desk, so that every day you find yourself a little further from your computer screen. Can you imagine me as . . . as . . .' He searched desperately for a job that would sufficiently convey his contempt for life's practicalities. '. . . as a lawyer? I would rather die or go hungry. Everything in life is a risk, and I would say this is a risk worth taking.'

'But, but . . .' I said feebly, my body already caught in the riptide, swept out to sea on the current of dreams, 'is

204

it right? It would be stealing, taking something precious from the nation and putting it for ever in some private vault. And I mean, to fake someone else's work, I would feel wrong.' I hated myself for using such childish terms, but I could think of no other way to express myself. 'I want to paint my own pictures, to make money that way.'

'In nineteen forty-seven, when Van Meegeren was convicted of forging a Vermeer, he said: "Yesterday this picture was worth millions of guilders, and experts and art lovers would come from all over the world and pay money to see it. Today, it is worth nothing, and nobody would cross the street to see it for free. But the picture has not changed. What has?" It will still be your picture, it will still be a work of art. You will just be getting better rewards. Never let them convince you that something is impossible, James. That is how they con everybody, how they keep everyone in line. The hard bit will be admitting to yourself that it can be done, because to do that, you will have to acknowledge that the system by which everybody else lives is a chimera. You have to bid goodbye to your father's dream of a good career, forget your good degree. Cut your ties, float away. Unlearn your . . . expectations. After that, it's easy. Easy-peasy.'

His speech became less lucid as the Valium wound its sinuous coils around his body, lifting him and turning him over into the fetal position, squeezing the sense out of him. I told him quietly that I needed to be alone, that I needed time to consider what he had said, but I think he knew already what my answer would be. He wanted to buy his freedom, to pay off responsibility, and he had shown me a glimpse of a future in which we could be young for ever. He had planted a seed in my mind, a new species that had no business in that ordered and domestic setting, that would grow up around every native thought, strangling it, stealing its sustenance and blocking it from the light. The drugs began to assert their authority more strongly. He became sleepy, a long feline yawn shuddering through his strong body, making him arch his back on the bed, parting the bottom of his shirt and the waistband of his trousers to show his dark muscular stomach. I removed his shoes, and set them down by the bed.

'Michael left me, didn't he? He went with my father,' he said in a small voice.

'You need to get some sleep,' I said to him. His face crumpled for a moment, and I thought he might be about to cry, but the Valium smoothed the wrinkles away. I picked a tartan picnic blanket up off the floor and laid it carefully down over his body.

'I wonder where I'll live in the holidays,' he said sleepily, his eyes closed.

'Maybe you, me and Jessica can get a place,' I said gently. It was my fondest hope.

'I'd like that.'

I left him lying on his side, cradling his broken face with the sodden tea towel, smiling.

12

Our Chinese takeaway was finished. I dumped the greasy remnants into the bin, a chrome cylinder just inside the kitchen door. I went over to the new stereo in the corner, and put on Orbital without consulting Jessica. The weird music was turned down low. We had crossed over midnight as if it were a dangerous border, and were now in the wide empty desert of the small hours. I began to feel the jetlag of my working routine assert itself, telling me I should have been in bed. With Jessica's hunger satisfied, her appetite for the past returned. The incident with Alysha, or Mary, seemed to have plunged us into a deeper intimacy. What was the point of pretending with someone who knew that about you? This imbalance of knowledge might have made me feel vulnerable, but where I had lost my advantage through the confession of a taste for prostitutes, Jessica was rapidly losing hers to whisky. I did not know many people who could drink as much as I did without becoming drunk, and certainly none who would admit to it. Jessica, tall and powerful though she was, was still a slight woman, with several stones fewer of flesh to cushion the blow of the booze, and far less practice. More than half the bottle had disappeared down our throats. Her eyes had taken on a merry gleam that was not entirely under her control.

'I remember the first time we met.'

'The night of the fight.'

'You couldn't stop staring at my tits.'

I bridled. 'That's not quite how I remember it . . .'

'Of course it's not,' she said, displaying a private smile. She turned to playing with her shot glass, spinning it around on its rim in mesmerizing circles. 'You'll have some romantic version all of your own, and the only tits will be in the paintings on the walls. Am I right?'

'No. Some of the sculptures have tits too.'

'Ah. Well, that's good.' She meditated for a few moments, then said, 'Did you know that fight was a fix?'

'Seriously?'

'Yeah. Jamie, Francis, Lisa and that doctor guy. Fuck they made a lot of money. Lisa's idea. I miss her.'

'But why? Francis was an amazing fighter!'

'I think just for the hell of it.'

'I never knew that. Francis never told me.'

'Poor James. So innocent.'

I preferred to think of myself as experienced, so I didn't reply. The music covered the silence. Jessica was nodding along with it, and making occasional taps on the table with the neat crescent of her nail to simulate the beat. Something had been bothering me since she had first shown me the article, a low mental buzz that had seemed too vague to mention. I decided to take advantage of her receptive mood, and articulate my worries. 'Jessica, did it ever occur to you . . . did you ever think we might not just be in trouble with the police?'

She cocked her head on one side, and a frown furrowed her brow. The glass fell over. I caught it before it rolled off the table. 'How do you mean?'

'Well, let's take a worst-case scenario. If the police do cast doubts on the picture's authenticity, and they manage to discover that someone sold the original . . .' I pulled up short. I wanted to test my logic, to see if she would reach the same conclusion without prompting.

'Yeah?' Jessica was impatient of her own ignorance and it whetted her tone. I waited a few more seconds, but saw nothing beyond mounting irritation.

'Don't you think we might want to watch out for the buyer? I mean, the first thing you did when you found out was to see what steps you could take to cover yourself. Don't you think it's possible he might have taken the same course of action?'

'Who, Augustus White? That fat old fool we met in the club? Christ, he must be about sixty by now. A bit too old to go breaking out the crowbars, don't you think?'

'You know, I never told you guys this, but he threatened me. Told me if we ever told anyone what we had done, he'd kill us.'

'What did you expect him to say? "Rat me out and I'll give you a biscuit?"'

This made me laugh despite myself, and though I still wasn't convinced I decided to leave the matter. There was no point in forcing her to feel more worried than she already was. Jessica dipped her chin and looked at the table, proud that she had made me laugh against my will.

'You know the really sad thing?' I asked her.

She smiled. 'Which one is the saddest?'

'It wasn't even that much money. I mean, I know that sounds spoilt, it sounds awful, but the senior partners at my firm make twice that much in a year. We gave up our lives for that.'

'Don't be melodramatic,' she said. 'We didn't give up our lives. Well, I mean, at least you and I . . . Do you want to leave here?'

'What?' I asked.

'Do you want to go somewhere? We've been in your flat all night, and I'm not going to get to sleep. We could go on a field trip.'

'Where do you want to go?'

'I don't know . . .'

'Pick somewhere.'

'We could go and visit Francis.'

I could tell by the way she asked that she was terrified

of rejection. She tried to make it sound off-hand, but I saw her throat flex with anxiety when she swallowed. She looked into my eyes, pleading with me. I had no wish to leave the flat. It was cold and wet outside, and I was cocooned with half a bottle, my old friend and my memories. I had no wish to visit Francis. I did not want to confront him on a cold wet night. In our conversation he was vivid, a smiling, beautiful ghost conjured by the love of old friends. I did not want to put his image back into the drawer, wrapped up in paper and mothballs, and go and see the real him. But I could not abandon Jessica. I felt my selfishness thaw suddenly, leaving me green and unprotected.

'We might have trouble getting a cab. And we'll have to break in. But let's go, if it's what you want.'

'I want it to be what you want.'

'Fine. It is.'

Fine. It had been one of the words that in the days of our friendship had formed the backbone of our private vocabulary, and it did not have quite the same texture for anyone else that it did for us. It had meant something slightly different from the vague indifference or mild annoyance it conveyed when normally spoken. It was more strongly supportive, it meant: 'I'm with you, all the way,' or: 'That is how I feel.' I surprised myself when I used it, I was surprised to be reminded that language could act like this, could help to make little tribes of three or four where much time was spent together.

As a lawyer, I used language to lock out ambiguity, to delineate exactly the respective obligations of two parties. Words were not private in my professional world, they were public property, with universal meanings that allowed people who had never met to reach agreement. Publicly, words could provide solid foundations. Privately, they became nuanced, and were prone to slip . . . It felt good to use them privately, but it made me feel uneasy too.

Jessica smiled at the old reference, or maybe at my support, and I thought she was about to cry. The whisky had made her maudlin. She was prone to sudden shifts of mood, as girls are who have drunk too much. She wrapped her arms around me, putting them under mine so that my own arms encircled her shoulder blades. I tried to remind myself that weakness was a weapon in her hands. I had seen her weep at ticket inspectors, but I held her anyway. I realized we had both been waiting for this, the moment we broke the barrier of physical contact, and I was relieved that it had happened naturally. Alcohol and cigarettes were on her breath, and her hair smelt of synthetic fruit. I watched myself being embraced over her shoulder in the black mirror of the windowpane. We hung, the two of us hugging, in the freezing darkness suspended over the empty square. I told her it was too cold for her to go out with her suit jacket and coat, and she silently acquiesced. I turned away when she changed into her jeans, but again I saw her shadow unclothed for a moment in the glass. I asked her if she had anything more suitable in her bag, and she shook her head. I lent her an old jumper, a huge rough woollen thing with sleeves that hung down past the end of her fingertips. She put her coat on over the top. I found her a tartan scarf from the hall, and she let me wrap it around her throat, taking the ends away from me to tuck them down the front of her coat. I poured some of the whisky into a silver bottle for the trip. It was a silver hip flask with my father's initials engraved on the front. They were the same as mine: J.W. We prepared slowly, unhurriedly, and dressing took on a ritual significance. I took off my black shoes and put on boots. I left my suit jacket and tie on my bed and put on a sweatshirt under my overcoat. Jessica went to her bag for a pair of trainers. She grabbed a handful of change from her purse and shoved it into her pocket. I felt better protected going into the London night in clothes that looked inexpensive. It was not the idea of looking like I might have money that worried me, it was looking lucky that attracted trouble. On our way out I double-locked the flat, something I never remembered to do. When we came out of the front door I felt like a bird emerging from the safety of an egg. It was one-thirty, and there was no one sober left on the streets. The gutter outside my house was filled with half-eaten kebabs and styrofoam cartons of chips. The queue for the trance club stretched around the corner despite the cold. We didn't speak as we waited for a cab, but Jessica held my hand like a child waiting to cross the road. Her breath hung in the air.

The first few black cabs we stopped refused to take us so far out of London. In the end a scuffed unlicensed Audi pulled over, the driver peering up at us out of the dark interior. He agreed to take us for sixty. He sensed too late that we weren't really interested in money, only in getting where we were going, and as soon as we had fixed the price he bit his lip, as if trying to decide whether he should have asked for more. I took the initiative and climbed into the back before he could say anything. He was a friendly guy from Ghana who wanted to talk. We didn't. I asked him politely to put the radio on, and he tuned in to Radio One, a mixture of trip hop and chilled house designed to ease people into their come-downs. He had a palm-leaf cross hanging from the rearview mirror. I turned my gaze outside. I loved looking at the city so late at night, when all the working people and families were in bed. With our private soundtrack playing it seemed as if every pedestrian, every red pair of brake-lights reflected in a black puddle, every silhouette in a window still lit must have its own private narrative to be moving so late at night. I watched the city run past the window with a weird mixture of ownership and alienation, like returning to somewhere you ruled as a child. Once we'd moved out of the centre, we spent time stranded at deserted intersections, waiting for nothing but the lights. We followed brown and white signs for Chessington World of Adventures. The white rims and writing flared up in the beams of the headlights, then turned black again just as we passed. The streets were empty, and lined with bare trees. The cemetery was on a long blank of highway where the city petered out into the suburbs of Kingston. There have been civilizations where the dead are laid to rest in the centre of the metropolis, but we tuck ours away at the edges, out of mind but not so far off that you can't pay a visit when you feel guilty. No one lived there.

We pulled off the road at the gatehouse. Our driver was visibly unsettled by the location and the dark moonless night. Ordered ranks of tombstones appeared as black squares through the thick iron spears of the cemetery fence.

'Why you want to come here anyway?' he said. 'The whole place is locked up.'

'Let us worry about that,' I said to him, leaning forward over the shoulder of his seat to look him in the eye. 'Now, here's sixty for your trouble. I'll give you another twenty now, and if you wait for us there's another sixty for the home trip. Does that sound fair?'

'Yeah, yeah, my friend, that's good,' he said, momentarily distracted from his fear by the money.

As I handed him the cash I realized I had spent almost four hundred pounds since leaving the office. He stashed the money under the driver's side sun visor. It was turning out to be an expensive evening.

We opened the door and stepped out on to the wet tarmac. After the warm interior of the taxi, pulsing with music and the throb of the engine, I gasped at the cold and silence, like plunging into freezing water. The lights in the gatehouse were out. If there was a night watchman, he was asleep. We made our way over to the gatehouse, and having identified a likely drainpipe I hitched myself up, found a foothold in the brick and stepped over the metal spikes, turning gingerly in the air and slithering down the other side to land in a heap on the grass. Jessica followed, and her long lithe body swarmed over the fence without the huffing and wobbling that had characterized my climb. It felt right to come and see Francis in this transgressive fashion. We were ghouls; we were vampires. We were breaking in to visit our friend; this was not some empty daylight pilgrimage with a handful of lilies but a proper eulogy to our time together. The thumping of my heart and the breathless chuckle that escaped me as we looked at each other on the ground made me think of how I had felt with him. We turned around and looked at the graveyard stretching out before us. It was not an old churchyard scene stocked with yew trees and suggestive shadows, but many acres of sanitized plots arranged like a military memorial at the site of some great massacre. The headstones were not uniform – some glittered slightly in the light of the street as the yellow rays caught mineral flecks in brown marble; some were solid white stained with birdshit; some had flat tops and some rounded; there were crosses and angels and stars of David in a square by the right-hand wall – but all occupied the same size plot. The cemetery had been conceived on a grand scale, and was meant to service the city's needs for generations. It covered many acres.

'Can you remember where he's . . . where we can find him?'

'I'm not sure, I think I might be able to,' I said. I knew exactly where he was, but I still wanted to hide from her the full extent of my knowledge, the detail in which I remembered the past.

I led us on to the broad tarmac road that stretched down the centre away from the gatehouse. The surface was perfectly even, having only ever known the stately roll of a hearse. The verge was neatly kept. The path led up a slight incline and, after several minutes' walking, we came to a memorial garden arranged at the top of the hill. Trees rose up around the path – they had been planted as an aid to sadness, arranged in a hollow semi-circle. They were evergreen trees and, though they did not look as desolate as the bare trunks lining the highway, their foliage blocked out the sky. As we moved away from the lights of the street, the darkness began to change. Beyond the trees it was no longer the comforting city shadow that bleached the colour from objects, leaving them a grimy yellow but with their shapes intact. It was real blackness, an obstacle to movement. I was afraid suddenly that I might not find the way after all. Jessica drew closer to me, or perhaps I drew closer to her. We closed ranks in the face of the night. I noticed that despite the difference in the length of our strides our footsteps had begun to fall in time. The only sound was the tread of our shoes on the tarmac and the wind in the trees. A large swath of cloud appeared between the trunks. I got my bearings, and knew that when we came through it we would be very close to Francis's grave.

'This is it,' she said, whispering so as not to disturb the silence. I was surprised that she knew.

'Are you ready?' I asked to delay.

'Yup.'

We walked out of the garden and on to the next section. Francis's plot was three rows in from the edge of the path. The grass here needed cutting, and soaked the cuffs of my trousers with rainwater and mud when I left the road. I found myself wishing that I had put on jeans. My suit would need dry cleaning. Francis's grave was marked by an extravagantly expensive monument of pink Florentine marble. The large square block was carved on three sides with a relief showing what looked like art-deco angels gazing into the invisible interior, their muscular backs and wings on display, whilst the fourth side bore detail chosen by a virtual stranger, the dates of his life, his full name (excluding Nyasha) and the suspect epitaph of 'beloved son and brother'. They were cut into the marble and picked out in gold. I remembered at the wake overhearing Lord Soulford telling a mourner that it had cost him the best part of twenty thousand, that he had commissioned an up-and-coming young artist. All things considered, his beloved son proved considerably less expensive in death than he had done in life.

The turf had been neglected. I remembered the grave as a gaping hole in the earth with straight surgical edges, but the wound had healed over with grass and grown a little wild. The other plots stretched away in all directions. Standing at the intersection of the rows the geometry of the pattern revealed itself, and the headstones looked like pieces set out on a giant board. A generous bunch of white roses lay on the grave. There were droplets and tiny pools of rainwater on their plastic sheath. I looked for a card but could not see one. The moisture and the cold must have helped to keep them fresh, but I guessed they could not be much more than two or three weeks old. I felt deeply cheated. It was as if we had climbed to a distant, uninhabited peak, and found the place strewn with discarded Coke cans. I would have liked to pick them up, shake the heads off them and fling them away. As I felt this surge of emotion, I could not help but analyse its source. I realized how possessive I had become over my isolation. I hated the thought that I was not mourning alone, it chipped away at the sombre statue I had made in my image. In death,

219

Francis was my virgin bride. I could not stand the thought of sharing him with this unknown other. I tried to think of what Jessica must be feeling, looking at the grave of our friend, to invite her into my sadness. She exhaled, and I realized she had been holding her breath.

'I wonder who still puts flowers here,' she said. She sounded a little ashamed. She sniffed. The cold was making her nose run.

'Maybe Lisa,' I said.

'Maybe it's his father. Lord Soulford.'

'If Lord Soulford had done it, you'd have read about it in the papers,' I said bitterly.

'We should have stopped at a petrol station or something and picked some up.'

'I think cheap flowers would be worse than no flowers.'

'Well I don't,' she said.

'They'd be garish and ugly,' I said, suddenly wanting to make her cry, 'they pick up the smell of petrol from the forecourt. Hideous, nasty. Francis would have hated ugly flowers; I would have thought any friend of his would know that.' I found I hated her for snivelling, and thought that one great heave with my aggression would be enough to get her over the lip of a breakdown – after that the weight of her own problems would carry her down like stones in her pockets. But she didn't cry. She rubbed my back with a flat palm and otherwise ignored me, looking straight ahead at Francis's headstone.

'Francis killed Francis,' she said, her arm coming to rest on my shoulder. I felt the weight of it even through the thick wool and cashmere husk of my overcoat. 'I wish there was someone to blame, I even wish I could blame myself sometimes. But I can't. He fucked up, and I hate him for it.' She sounded as if she was thinking about something else. She patted me absent-mindedly and repeated, 'He fucked up,' under her breath like a mantra. Tears crept up on me and took me by surprise, springing out of my eyes before I could take steps to contain them. Then she said, 'Christ, those angels are camp, they look like something on a flyer for a gay nightclub,' and we both started to laugh, and held on to each other. I didn't want to turn my back on Francis's grave, but I found that when I did I walked away without looking back.

On the walk back to the gate, we began to speak to one another again. It was easy and frank, and we might have been sitting over coffee after dinner in a nice restaurant rather than trudging through a cemetery. I asked Jessica some questions about her life. Both her sisters had produced nephews and nieces and huge houses in Surrey. She was her father's disappointment. We came back towards the sound of traffic, and light from the street coruscated again on the gravestones. Her mother was dead, and I said I was sorry and was relieved that I meant it. I thought about her as I had known her: a slim middle-aged woman with a voice like gravel in a country-house driveway, holding on to beauty with

221

whitened knuckles, who outraged everybody but always seemed to be invited to all the parties. It didn't seem fair that she had died when so many less interesting people were still alive. I asked if Jessica was seeing anybody, and she told me that she had a boyfriend; 'But it's nothing serious.' He was a banker and took her on expensive foreign weekends at a day's notice. The thought that he made more money than me made me mildly uncomfortable. Money was usually on my side, it was a useful measure of my worth against others, and I felt a little betrayed. She always kept her passport and the contraceptive pill in her handbag, just in case. She told me a story about picking up the wrong bag at the airport in Valencia and finding it full of sex toys. I had pretty much exhausted my store of autobiography with prostitutes and law, but I traded her my father's death for her confidences. She did not have to tell me she was sorry. She asked me if I had a girlfriend. No, there hadn't really been anyone serious since university. She absorbed this information in silence. We did not speak about Francis, but we did not speak around him either, describing his shape as a blank in the middle of our conversation. We had made our offering. For the moment, he was appeased. I felt young as we came to the gate. I breathed deeply and felt my body invigorated as I swung myself up and over the cruel tips of the railings. The wetness made everything gleam. I felt my senses heightened; I could hear small and distant noises in the night. Grit from the wall got on my trousers and pitted the palms of my hands like the skin of an orange, but I didn't care. My movements and my thoughts were light and inconsequential.

When we got back to the road and climbed over the fence, there was no one on the crescent forecourt. I didn't immediately get the significance of this fact, and Jessica had to tell me that the cab driver had disappeared with my twenty. I was pleased; I didn't mind about being cheated, I wanted to make use of this new sensation by walking. The two of us walked arm in arm up the highway for about half an hour, until we came to an intersection with a bus stop. Time and the cold had sobered us up, leaving behind only the protective varnish of the drink that I hoped would last until we went to sleep. I could still hear the dull slop of whisky in my hip flask, but I did not want to chance my mood on another swig. We waited for a night bus back into town, and all the time I felt freshly bathed like the city after the rain, lithe and happy. After a while, Jessica came under my arm for warmth. Her make-up was smudged and she looked white and tired. The chemical light of the street was unkind to her. Normally I liked women to be perfectly made up, but I preferred her like this.

13

Francis did not approach the others with the plan; he had no need. The slow shift in our circumstances was more persuasive than any verbal argument. At the beginning we were all defiant. Our way of life suddenly seemed all the more precious for being under threat. We wanted to prove to ourselves and each other that the money was nothing, a toy that had amused us for a while, but which, had circumstances not overtaken us, we would in the end have discarded of our own accord. In recognition of services rendered, or perhaps out of simple affection, Lisa picked up some of the slack for Francis himself. She discreetly paid his bill at Haver and Sons, who had been importing illegal, unpasteurized Reblochon for him from France under the counter. She paid for a box of Romeo y Julietas at the tobacconist's on Bridge Street, and dealt with his fine when the police caught him urinating on the new scale bronze sculpture of the city erected opposite the Senate House. The arresting officers knew and liked Francis, and they would probably have let him go, but his insistence that he was expressing a critical judgement antagonized them. But as the spring collections began to bud in the window displays around Market Square, an event that would normally have caused the seasonal migration of Francis and Jessica south to Bond Street, the two of them pulled last year's clothes from the wardrobe with heavy hearts. Hemlines had climbed, patterns had shifted, and whilst such changes were all but meaningless to me, they felt them as keenly as the wind. We had a little trouble with the bookie at the dog track, who had been used to making Francis small extensions of credit, knowing his allowance was paid in monthly instalments. Again Lisa stepped in, but on this occasion she did not give so freely. She went for a private talk in Francis's room, and though there was no acrimony when they emerged, I felt that an understanding had been reached between them that this was to be the last time. Having to be answerable to Lisa for his keep stung Francis; he had never before placed the burden of his habits on anyone but his father, and had perceived his allowance as no more than his due. To realize suddenly that he was the receiver of gifts and not the giver made him ashamed, and conscious for perhaps the first time of the seriousness of his position. After the incident with the bookie he avoided Lisa and all of us for some days. When he saw us his cheeks would become a darker black with a flush of embarrassment, and the wonderful innocence with which he had always regarded money began to crumble. This was particularly painful for us, as we saw that he did not regard his past generosity as any kind of mitigation against his current need to borrow money.

We were not by any means poor, we were simply no longer rich, and we stopped one another from acclimatizing to our new reality. We had food and we had rooms, but our ideas of what constituted essential had been changed. Every time our raw expectations began to heal over it only took a brief reminiscence to pick the scab. Alone, we would all have got used to our new conditions quite quickly; together, we reinforced for each other the idea that we had somehow been cheated, and that no one had the right to tell us to make do. To try to keep my income above the level of my student loan I took the job at Po Na Na, and spent several nights a week mixing cocktails for marines from the American airbase at Lakenheath. They were tall handsome men, mostly black and heavily muscled with short-cropped hair and tight white T-shirts, and the local girls loved them. The job was fun, the Americans joked with me and pushed me around like a bunch of older brothers, and they had imported their own culture of generous tipping. Still I found myself stung by service, used as I had become to being served. I even took a little pride in this sensation, as I felt it marked me out as someone like Francis or Jessica, someone designed to be on the other side of the bar. We stopped dining out and Jessica and I took pains to develop a mania for cooking, so that Francis would not mind eating the food we had prepared, and we could all pretend that it was a matter of choice and not necessity.

At the same time that the money began to run dry, the advent of warmer weather changed the shape of the day. Tables spread out from the cafés. On the bright days tourists would appear, and any journey through the city was punctuated by snatches of the tour guides' monologues, giving out history like goody bags as the assembled group took photographs or filmed on camcorders. Red and blue flowers appeared in the wrought-iron hanging baskets outside the Bun Shop, which had swung empty in the winter wind of Michaelmas with the menace of miniature gibbets. The long nights were disappearing, and with them the freezing air and darkness that had given us cover for our climbing expeditions. The bodies of our fellow students began to emerge from the protective layers of clothing, like rolling fields from under thick drifts of snow, and the coughs and colds that plagued the overworked receded, making everyone seem fresh and new. It was as if they were gaining on us, their spirits accelerating as ours began to flag. Spring brought with it rain that made getting around the city a series of dashes from doorway to Gothic arch. The ancient pavements collected puddles. I felt not only had our former pleasures died, but the new crop that should have supplied us in this new season had been stunted. Several times, I heard the others bring up memories from the previous year, of the kind of things that they had done together then. They talked of ordering a hamper from Fortnum & Mason, of hiring one of the Tudor boats on the first day of real heat and punting all the way up to Grantchester, hanging on under the willow tree by St John's and drinking in the shade, putting their bare wrists in the pale green water to keep cool. One weekend Francis had taken them all to Cambridge airport and whisked them away on a cheap flight to Budapest for a stay in an ancient spa. Later in the term it had been the Eurostar and a night at Maison Blanche, returning the next morning first class without having slept. Jessica had stolen the silver salt and pepper shakers as a souvenir. These recollections were tinged with a mellow sadness, as if one of the participants had died in the intervening year, but we all knew it was the money that was dead. The others raised them in a spirit of nostalgia, but they pierced me with regret for something I had never experienced, but should rightly have been mine. I felt like the son of a noble family whose father has squandered his inheritance, and watches as his estates are sold one by one to pay off another's debts.

None of us talked to Michael after the night of the debate, and he made no attempt to contact us. Although we did not actually speak to him, we still moved in the same social circles, and for a while there was a kind of unacknowledged scramble for turf. Michael took the Pitt Club in the end, as Francis could no longer afford to pay his bill, and we took several of our favourite bars and pubs around the city centre, as Francis was better liked by the barmen, who rightly considered Michael a snob. A similar process of division took place among our peripheral friends. Michael made a good focus for the general feelings of anger and indignation that our deteriorating circumstances had created. We would relish any gossip over his new follies and failures, such as the time a button popped off his waistcoat during his after-dinner address to a politician who had come to speak at the Union, or the time that his tutor caught him copying one of his weekly essays off the internet and fined him fifty pounds. Lisa had cut him off from her service out of support for Francis, and he had been unable either to find another creditable supply or to begin doing the work himself. All the times we had spoken badly of him behind his back, which had previously made us feel guilty for betraying our friend, we now wore as badges of honour, and cited as proof of the fact that we had never really liked him, and that he was not really missed. Francis heard through Jeremy that Lord Soulford had given him a summer job at Conservative Central Office.

I could not go into Francis's room now without staring at the picture. It had been transformed from a thing of beauty and genius into an asset. I regarded it as a starving man in the street might view a groaning table through the dining-room window. It seemed so obviously unfair that this dry and lifeless sheet of paper should contain the wealth it did. The practical problems with the project remained, as did fear of prison and public shame, but as time went on I began to understand the truth of Francis's assertion that the biggest barrier was in the imagination. As we found ourselves more and more restricted the pressure of disappointment increased; my attitude slid slowly from one side to the other, and as it tilted on the pivot all the objections that had been weighing it down on the side of caution slid neatly to the other end. I would catch myself thinking not that we might get caught, but that we might get away with it. If we were caught after the fact I pictured us not in prison, but using the money to effect a very comfortable exile, perhaps somewhere with a beach.

Francis never spoke of what he had said to me. This silence was consistent with the notion in our group that the events of his father's visit had become a kind of taboo. It was considered bad taste to mention Lord Soulford at all, not only because we wished to avoid talking about the source of our misfortune, but also perhaps because we feared it would lead us on to unfair recriminations, to arguing over who had done what and blaming each other bitterly for our current state. Without any communication with him I could not puzzle out my growing fantasies and my confusion increased until I even began to doubt whether he remembered what he had said to me at all. He had been drunk, heavily drugged and suffering from mild shock. It was horrible to think that his idea, which had begun to take hold of me so strongly, had coalesced momentarily from the vapours of his intoxication, then blown apart like a shape in the clouds. I actually became frustrated with Francis for not bringing it up. I wanted to be seduced into crime, and the idea lost much of its attraction if I was to be the one to propose it, or even to mention it first. I did not want to bear the responsibility, either legally or morally, if things went wrong.

He caught me at the peak of my silent need. I could not tell if this was chance, or perfect management. It was the last week of the Lent term, and Francis had actually won some money at the dog track. Even at the height of his munificence, this event would have been so rare as to occasion a celebration, and in our current state it had the communal air of a public festival. Jessica got dressed up, and gave one of her rare displays of make-up. Even Lisa shed her trainers in favour of a pair of black kitten heels, and for once released her features from the perennial frown of scrutiny. I think we all looked beautiful to each other when we met at the bar in Tudor Vaults for cocktails. The girls offset one another, Jessica's paleness and blonde hair being the perfect foil to Lisa's olive tone and almond eyes, and I hope Francis and I were like that too, both of us towering over the bouncer, his brilliant smile inlaid in his dark jaw like a new moon.

The maître d' greeted us as old friends. 'Francis! We've missed you, huh? Where have you been?'

The question made me stiffen slightly, but Francis took it in his stride.

'I've been away for a little while,' he said. 'But I'm back.'

'Ha. We thought you had maybe found another favourite place. You made Christophe cry.'

Christophe was the chef. This made us all smile, and he showed us to our usual table. It was at the back of the restaurant, a glass circular disc mounted on legs like metal bones. Seeing that we were four, not our usual five, the waiter removed one of the heavy metal chairs without comment. We pretended not to notice, and I realized that we were willing to do almost anything to preserve our fragile happiness against the sudden buffets of a happier past. The Vaults got its name from the low-hanging ceilings that curved upwards into little domes above the bar and dining room. The designer had embraced the dungeon theme with low menacing lighting and a series of unsettling paintings and photographs around the walls. In each of the rooms there stood a man-sized sculpture in black wrought iron, skeletal figures in attitudes of pain or supplication. These had a tendency to snag your clothing, and I think Jessica found them a little frightening, because the way she hung her coat and handbag on the crouching demon nearest our table always seemed a little too deliberate, as if she was trying to laugh at a joke that was painfully true. The table at the back was the best in the house, as the restaurant was badly laid out and almost every other seat ran the risk of bumps from waiters heading to the kitchen, or patrons heading for the toilets. Francis ordered enough food for an army, and for the duration of dinner our forgetfulness became effortless, and we genuinely escaped our problems. We found a doorway back into the past, and slipped through.

'I miss this,' Jessica said, as we sat smoking before a heap of ruined puddings. 'I miss this so much. I miss us being together, and not worrying.'

'We're still together,' Francis said, and put his hand on her shoulder, his thumb stroking her clavicle. Although there was genuine affection in his voice, there was something else looking out from his eyes, as if part of him was making a dispassionate assessment of his friend.

'I know we are, but . . . how much was dinner?'

'Two hundred or so. We drank quite a lot.'

'And how much do you have left?'

'Oh, I don't know.'

'Yes you do.'

'Four-fifty. A little over.'

'And have you paid your rent yet?'

Francis was silent. Jessica leant back in her chair, putting herself out of reach of his hand, and tilted her head back, exposing her white throat to the table.

'I'm gonna cover half of dinner,' Lisa said, and it made me laugh.

'There is another way,' Francis said carefully, and Jessica brought her head back down, levelling her gaze at him. As soon as he had spoken I felt an unbearable rush of impatience. I was on the point of interrupting his sly look and adumbrating the scheme myself, but Jessica interjected.

'What do you mean?' she asked.

'A way we could be rich. And not just me. I mean all of us. So rich we'd never have to work again.'

Then he told them his idea, in much the same way he had told it to me.

By the time he had finished, the last of the patrons had left the restaurant and the bar had shut. They would not ask us to leave until they were locking the doors for the night. The spotlights had been turned off, and we occupied a little oasis of candlelight in the corner of the deserted room. The flickering glow made the ribs of the sculpture cast weird cage-like shadows on the wall above. We were smoking and drinking the last of our fourth bottle of red. Francis had chosen good wines, and we had relished not so much the taste of them as the fact of having them on the table. The regular sound of the broom on the flagstones of the floor next door indicated that we had about twenty minutes left.

'We can't do that,' Jessica said, putting her hand up to her mouth to stifle a giggle. 'I mean, can we? That's crazy!' She giggled again, and the red liquid shook in her glass. She was not used to the drink and was quite tipsy.

Lisa began to speak thoughtfully. She was staring into the candle flame.

'I left school young. They weren't teaching me much, and my mum needed money. So I got a job with a mate of my brother's, running prozzies off this internet site. He couldn't tell a database from his own arsehole, so I handled the tech. It was very classy, we did boys and girls all the way through London, Kent and up into Peterborough. I was the smile, my boss was the muscle. And these were tarts you could take out to dinner if you needed, educated escorts, that was our angle. Not too educated, obviously. We had one punter who used to get a little discount for writing reviews of the girls and some of the boys on the site. He wrote well, like a food critic. He made you want to order everything on the menu, you know what I mean? One day one of the girls belled me, and told me she had left some stuff at his place, a necklace and earrings. We never let them call the punters direct, that was a quick way to lose your commission, so she asked me how to arrange a pick up. I looked into the guy's details. Turned out he was a fellow at one of the colleges. I applied the next summer, and I got my place.'

Lisa delivered this little monologue impassively. Her dark almond eyes picked each of us up for a moment between the thumb and forefinger of her gaze, dangling us in front of her, challenging us to question her. At the

235

same time her neat brown features were perfectly set and motionless, as if she had just finished reading out the side of a cornflakes packet. The occasional glimpses she allowed us of her life always appeared suddenly like this, plain and monumental, like an outcrop of rock seen through dense trees. Francis looked at her with frank admiration. I felt a part of my morality baulk at the mention of prostitution and the intimations of black-mail, but it did not hold me back. Rather it left me, as if two old ladies had risen from their seats soon after the opening credits, and with grumbling protest left the rest of the audience to enjoy a lubricious movie.

'I never told anyone that, but I'm telling you. What I'm saying is that there're two sets of rules. There're the ones you follow, and the ones you make. Now, anyone might succeed by the first set, if they work hard and keep their head down. And I mean "might". You could work for ever, do nothing wrong and never make it because your boss secretly wants to fuck you, or you once stood on the chairman's toe at the company picnic. But the second set . . . get them right, and you can really win big.'

'I don't know . . .' Jessica said, but it was the token resistance of a woman who has already made up her mind to sleep with you, and wants to protect her reputa-tion.

'Are we agreed?' Francis asked.

'We're agreed,' I said, and was surprised by the sound of my own voice.

'Fine. Then I'll find a buyer,' Lisa said, and extinguished her cigarette, as if placing a hot wax seal on a decree.

It was simple. The preceding weeks had eroded our resistance, and so the collapse came all at once. Soon after that, we said our goodbyes. I think each of us wanted to get away, to consider alone the implications of what we had decided. I could not sleep for my excitement. The pressure that had been building inside me, the pressure of confining this idea to my head as it swelled and expanded, had been released in a glorious burst.

The next several months were devoted to the accomplishment of our plan, and it filled the void left by money. The four of us drew close to one another in our secrecy, and we felt what men who fight together in the army must feel: the bond of constant danger, and the simple fact of having to trust another with your own welfare. We stopped discussing Michael, and lost our taste for his affectations. The purpose that took hold of our lives drove us forwards, and we shook off our self-pity like a period of hibernation.

When the holidays arrived, we all headed down to London. This was the time that Francis first introduced me to the East End strip club where I met Misha, the girl who became my model. He was living in a flat on Old Street that Lisa had rented for him on a two-month lease over the Easter break. Lisa lived in Docklands, and Jessica's parents had a house in Fulham. I saw one or other of them almost every day. We each developed our own areas of responsibility, in accordance with our natural skills, and we had weekly progress meetings, more out of excitement than with a genuine purpose of coordinating our efforts. We met in a greasy spoon café near the Embankment, an ancient place with curling linoleum floors and Formica tables edged with brown stripes where cigarettes had been left balanced on the side. The place had been chosen because it was roughly equidistant from our homes, and Jessica joked that it was better than the pub next door because it gave Francis no excuse to drink during the day. It was an oasis of neglect among the tall, sterile shops and offices, and the streams of efficient lawyers and bankers walked by the door without ever looking in. It was perfect, as the other patrons, dirty and curling like the linoleum, pretended we did not exist. They all seemed to be in their own worlds of private grievance, and we never felt self-conscious about either the plan or Francis's occasional bursts of heartfelt pretension.

I was responsible for the physical act of reproducing the drawing. Francis, who had taken several photographs of the picture from all angles, was charged with finding someone who could make a copy of the frame, and with trying to develop a method of ageing the paper. He found an antique framers down in Parsons Green who would do specific commissions, and got the idea for treating the paper from a section on producing fake treasure maps on the *Blue Peter* website. We were all amazed by the effectiveness of his simple techniques, and he began to mass produce sheets for me to work on. Jessica was in charge of the logistics of the swap, the actual exchange and transport of the painting down to London. She assumed this responsibility by default, as it was the last thing that needed doing. Lisa was looking for a buyer for us, and figuring out a way of stashing the money. Her style when she filled us in on the week's events was clipped and precise, and she reeled off enormous figures and sketched frightening characters with seeming indifference. Francis's estimate of four million had begun to look reasonable, but required much haggling. Her calmness breathed confidence through us all. With her at our side, we felt as we walked the edges of the criminal underworld like a party of tourists in the company of a local guide. She understood the legalese of high finance and the slang of low money. She was the only person who could bridge the two worlds our intentions spanned.

Sometimes at these weekly meetings the discussion would move from the practical to the moral, and here Francis would come into his own. Lisa would lean back in her plastic chair and drift off into thought, indicating that the conversation had passed beyond her specialist field, and thus beyond her interest. Jessica and I would lean forwards in our chairs, seeking absolution. Francis would tell us about the vanity of art critics, the absurdity of the sums paid for original works, and the fact that if two objects looked exactly the same, and their aesthetic value was based entirely on how they looked, then there was no moral difference between a copy and the original. He would bang his fist on the scarred plastic table-cloth, which was patterned with fading strawberries and cigarette craters, and declare that the only difference lay in the financial value, in the painting as artefact rather than art. This laid bare the hypocrisy at the heart of the art world, which claimed to value genius but only really valued the price tag which genius attracted. For a while after Francis delivered one of his sermons, I would sip my sweet tea in contentment. The small voice of dissent that attended my ambitions would be silent, and I would feel that we were not only going to make a great deal of money, but were also engaged in a fight against an untruth.

There is only one truly negative association that I have with our preparations, for it was during this period, this lengthy process of haggling and negotiation, coupled with the scientific reproduction of the masterpiece, that my relationship with my own drawing began to sour. I became increasingly frustrated that I could not render Misha in my own way. The whole crime was a passionate enterprise, with many bouts of fear, doubt and joy. I wanted to express these things in my own way through the medium of my art, but Francis saw to it that all my energies were devoted towards the reproduction. I spent hours studying Picasso's harlequin period, both in books and in galleries. I stood until my back became sore at the National. I read Gertrude Stein. I saturated myself so thoroughly with his work that it obliterated the nascent style that I had begun to develop at Cambridge, my own pencil strokes disappearing like fresh ink on a letter dropped into water. I traced the same lines again and again until they were deeply carved into my brain, and they had lost all meaning, like a phrase repeated to absurdity.

In the Easter term, Cambridge was busy and bright. Coaches bearing tourists were backed up on the B roads. The swans hatched their eggs and ceased their territorial prowling around their nests on the Backs, so that the Cam and the Mill Pond were full of cygnets. People drank their pints in the sunshine by the river. The leaves returned to the trees, so the views through skeletal branches that had been daunting and spectacular in the winter were closed down, leaving a leafy privacy on sun-dappled walkways. Huge white boards appeared beside the playing fields as the white lines of football and rugby pitches disappeared under the calm authority of cricket. The lawns in the courts were perfectly clipped and dry, like the green on a golf course, and groups of students began to sit on the grass beside the beech tree outside my window. Glass lifted and curtains were pulled back, and the private sounds of music, laughter and conversation echoed on the warm stone of the courts.

Walking along the paving beside a line of rooms, I would pick up a whole sequence of fragments, some snatches of academic debate, weed smoke, stifled gasps and television. At the same time that the sun became a reliable friend, the third years disappeared. They retreated to the University Library and holed up for revision. Finals began in May. We all of us had exams ourselves, but none of us paid them any attention. The academic world was fading away with the rest of our former concerns. We kept handing in fake essays, and went to enough supervisions to avoid being sent to the dean, but these were essential maintenance, like eating and sleeping. In the evenings we climbed out through the window that Michael had used to crash into my life the previous autumn, and drank cocktails in highball glasses, watching the sun go down over the Backs. On storm nights I would shelter under the protective spike of the lightning conductor and close my eyes in the warm rain and thunder. The summer seemed the accomplishment of the whole year, and in this atmosphere our plan neared fruition in a way that seemed bound by seasonal logic. Lisa found a buyer, a businessman named Augustus White, and fixed the price at four million, exactly Francis's original estimate. My visits to Misha had maintained my flagging interest in the actual act of drawing, and I was producing a whole series of viable pieces from which we could choose our replacement. Francis had a frame and mount made up and hidden under Jessica's bed. She had hired a car to drive the painting a little way out of the city to a hotel in Peterborough, where an expert, a private restorer who did a very profitable sideline in no-questions-asked chemical and stylistic analysis, would verify its authenticity on behalf of the buyer before its onward journey to London. Francis had volunteered to be the driver. At the time, I wondered at his eagerness to perform this chore.

As the plan fell into place, I began to feel that we were different from everyone else in the world. We looked the same, and we acted the same so as not to arouse suspicion, but in reality, the secret we held between us elevated us above them, as if the knowledge we carried made us immortal. This, I realized, was the feeling I had coveted when I first arrived at Cambridge, which I had been wrongly seeking in the idea of a social elite. I did not merely want to ascend to the top of the social order – I wanted to step outside it, to leave it behind entirely. I felt the way I had on the roof of King's Chapel, looking down on the tiny people going about their business in the streets. They seemed stupid to me for never knowing that someone hovered above them, and I felt free.

14

We took the train down to London that evening, and arrived at King's Cross at about six o'clock. My prelim exams had finished that day, and I knew I had done badly. For some reason the thought left me oddly elated. Unlike all the other students, I would never need good results to get a good job, to support myself through a good life. We stopped for a drink in one of the platform bars, its transitory population helping to steady our nerves. We sat outside at plastic tables under the great Victorian canopy of steel girders and filthy glass, and kicked at the pigeons who wandered around our feet with idiot persistence. I think we all began to get into character, to prepare ourselves for our secret meeting by slipping into anonymity. We turned what we were doing into a game. We speculated about what Augustus White would look like, we concocted elaborate strategies to be used if things went wrong, and developed secret signals. Lisa, who had spent the day organizing things for us, called and arranged to meet us in the station. She arrived and asserted her authority like the teacher on a school trip, telling us to behave ourselves and giving us details of our reservations. She had taken out a suite in our name at the Baglioni. She checked that each of us had an outfit for the evening, something cool and classy to wear in the club. On Francis's advice I had packed a blue blazer, my only pair of expensive jeans and a T-shirt he had bought for me with a punk print on the front and swatches of fabric stitched haphazardly over the chest. Lisa was going to stay the night at her mother's place in Docklands. The air was bitter with diesel fumes and cigarette smoke. I felt excited to be back in London, my body soaked up the undercurrent of tense purpose that ran through the station. I could tell the others felt the same. Our moods were synchronizing, our emotions falling in step, and each of us amplified the other's anticipation.

I wanted to take the Underground to St James's Park as I had already spent fifteen pounds on my train ticket, but the others insisted we were millionaires now and made me hop in the back of a cab. The hotel was new and compulsively trendy, and we were given a frightening bouquet of orchids at reception to take up to our suite. The suite itself was divided into three rooms: two bedrooms and a drawing room overlooking the street and beyond it the green reach of Hyde Park. Each of the bedrooms contained a king-sized bed, and had an en-suite bathroom. Scented candles burned on the dressing tables. Summer twilight came in discreetly like room service from the park. The expensive hotel confirmed us in our roles as secret agents, master criminals, forgers extraordinaires. 'You take one bedroom,' Francis said to Jessica, 'James and I will share the other bed.'

Francis produced a plain white T-shirt that hugged his torso and a heavy damask coat embroidered with a rich tapestry of black roses.

'I got it at auction last week,' he said, displaying the back to us, 'I was bidding against the V and A. It's eighteenth century. Can you believe they wanted to put it into a glass cabinet? I told the director they could have it when I die.'

'How did you pay for it?' Jessica asked, a little warily.

'I got credit,' Francis said, and disappeared into the bathroom.

We changed, and before we left at ten-thirty we each did a line of coke and downed vodka from the mini-bar. Jessica was wearing black leather trousers and an elegant pink corset. Her hair was up, and she had black smudges on the lids of her sockets that made her blue eyes gleam. After a brief debate we left the coke in the hotel. I walked out of the lobby into the waiting taxi feeling like a god.

It was in the gilt belly of Vagabond that we were to meet our business partner for the first time. Lisa met us at the door and ushered us past the courteous bouncer and the laminated women running the cloakroom. The actual exchange of the picture and subsequent money transfer had gone off without a hitch, and she had presented the meeting to us as a mere formality, a courtesy requested by our buyer to mark the completion of the deal. It should perhaps have occurred to me that it was odd for him to waive his anonymity in this way, but I was too excited to be suspicious. We came down the stairs and waited for guidance in the crowded foyer. The main dance floor looked to me like the drawing room of a country house, with extensive carving in the oaken panelling on the walls, which were hung with oils depicting drab hunting scenes. In the most impressive painting a group of hounds brought down a stag before a wooded hillside. A splash of scarlet on the stag's flank was the only discordant point of colour in a tawny landscape, and it produced a sense of shocking violence. A great fireplace flanked by sturdy fluted columns and a tumbling brigade of pudgy putti dominated the wall opposite the doorway, and vied for attention with the DJ booth, which jutted out into the dance floor like a rich mahogany pulpit. The sober elegance of the decor contrasted strongly with the clientele, who appeared to be neither sober nor elegant, but aggressively high and attractive.

A waiter darted out of the crowd. He was neat and uniformed in black, and he moved through the stumbling throng with quick precision. He seemed to recognize Francis, and embraced him like a brother. I thought how typical it was of Francis to know someone in every corner of the earth, to have been everywhere and never mention it until after you had arrived. The waiter led us away from the dance floor and the lobby into the dining room.

Augustus White sat in state in the corner booth at the furthest end of the restaurant. He was flanked on one side by a young female escort in a silk gilet, and on the other by a man who, judging by his physical similarity, was either a son or nephew. There were several other young women and older men sitting at the table, but they all seemed to be arranged around Augustus White like the apostles around Jesus in a Last Supper tableau. Lisa began to make introductions, and was the perfect hostess, dropping unobtrusive quips to relieve tension, leaving each pair with a point of social contact or shared interest from which to start a conversation before moving on to the next. The music and the hubbub would take care of any awkward silences, but she clearly felt it was important for everyone to get on as well as possible.

'Ray, this is Francis. Francis is a boxing blue at Cambridge. Ray used to run a sports promotion company, didn't you, Ray?'

'Jessica, this is John. John has a daughter at St Paul's, isn't that where you went to school?'

And finally.

'James, I'd like you to meet Augustus White.'

Augustus White was a huge man in both width and height, and he was dressed like a fashion designer. Some expensive Harley Street surgeon was in the process of correcting his receding hairline, and a forest of sapling plugs appeared in regimented rows above the line of his forehead. It seemed to me that some much younger and very beautiful mistress, finally resigned to the fact that she would occasionally have to be seen with him to gain subsidiary benefits, had taken his appearance firmly in hand. He wore a Hugo Boss suit which, Francis confidently informed me in the bathroom, did not come in a size large enough to accommodate his worldly girth and must have been specially tailored. The deep blue material held a faint lustre in the spinning beams of light, gleaming like something glimpsed in deep water, a flash of teeth seen from the edge of a summer raft. He had short fat fingers covered in rings, which he habitually interlaced in front of him on the table like an old man at prayer. He was clearly not yet settled in his finery, and it occasioned endless fidgeting: touching his hand to his plugs; tugging at the sleeves of his suit; checking his platinum watch. He was surrounded by a mist of heavy eastern cologne, so much so that he seemed to exude the spicy smell like a musk. He inspired an odd combination of fear and ridicule. He was like a hippo on safari, fat and ungainly and more lethal than all the lions and snakes and spiders combined.

Lisa manoeuvred me into the seat next to him. At first I was saved from making conversation by the girl on his other side – he spread his attention thickly over her ears and mouth, and she laughed at his jokes and gazed at him admiringly when he let slip the smallest personal confidence. The man I had displaced joined Ray and Francis in a conversation about the chances of a bantam-weight fighter I had never heard of called Sean Drummer. They slipped quickly into a technical patois that excluded the uninitiated. This arrangement left me free to watch the people who whirled around our table like colourful specimens in a tank full of tropical fish. I felt detached from their world, as much an observer as the child with his face pressed up against the glass of the aquarium, quite unaware of which ones were poisonous, of who was food for whom, seeing only an exotic and cold-blooded world of primal intrigue. Ray had his hand on Francis's shoulder, testing his muscles with an air of masculine detachment. He asked him if he'd ever fought for money. Jessica had entranced the man called John, a lean and handsome Londoner in his sixties, who looked to me more like an ageing rock star than a businessman, with long grey hair slicked back to his collar. She was being masterful with him, telling him which shares to invest in, which part of Majorca to search for a villa, where to buy his shoes. She had assumed the tone that made every one of her opinions a statement of fact, and she paused only to listen or smoke. It must have been a long time since anyone had told him what to do. He expressed his delight in her company by tending to her every need – waiters were sent off in search of fresh fruit and clove cigarettes, and one returned with a tray bearing a mini bottle of Veuve Clicquot with a fluorescent straw poking out of the top. Jessica took it in her hand and sucked daintily on the end, looking up at him from under her fine brows as she did so, an incredibly alluring mixture of innocence and sophistication. I thought how much more beautiful she was than all these other girls, whose living was their looks. I caught myself staring, and shifted my gaze.

My luck did not last. The girl eventually excused herself to head to the toilets to take more cocaine (the line we had done in the hotel had worn off) leaving me alone, and Augustus turned his attention to me, partially rotating his great torso slowly in the narrow confines of the seat. He smiled broadly and put his arm around my shoulder. 'So what do you think of the club? Nice, innit?'

'It's amazing,' I said. 'It makes me think of one of Gatsby's parties.'

'Who's Gatsby?' Augustus asked, his great brow creasing into mountainous ridges.

I realized my mistake, and tried to make my explanation a partial apology for bringing up something so pretentious. 'Oh, he's nothing, he's just a character, a character from a book by someone called F. Scott Fitzgerald?' My voice went up at the end, making the statement sound like a query.

'I know,' he said. 'I saw the film. I like Robert Redford. You must think we're all pretty ignorant, huh? I mean,

251

we don't have your brains, do we?' The meaty hand on my shoulder began to massage the muscle slowly as he looked into my eyes. The whites of his eyes were slightly yellow, and a roadmap of tiny capillaries spread out from the corners, threatening to engulf the green iris.

'No, no, not at all,' I said, conscious of my own insincerity, 'I don't think you have to study to have brains.'

'So, you think that what you've been doing, all that studying, you think that's for nothing?'

'No, no,' I said carefully, 'for me it's fantastic. But for other people . . .'

He stared at me intently. 'Other people? You was saying.'

'Well, you know. Horses for courses . . .' I trailed off lamely.

'D'you know how I got the cash to buy that pretty picture?' His voice had dropped dangerously low.

'Excuse me?'

'I said, d'you know how I got the cash to buy your fucking picture?'

'I don't think I want to know, do I?' I said, smiling, desperately trying to sound like one of the lads, going along with the joke.

'I'll tell you, shall I? I got it by being a businessman. Not a thug – a businessman. Do you get what I'm saying?'

'Yes,' I said, still grinning, though my smile was frozen

in place now, a fossil of the old organic one. 'I think I do. Shall we get some more drinks in?'

The arm around my neck tightened. His huge body pulled on me as if possessed of its own gravitational field. I thought of my tenth birthday party when my father had hired me a petting zoo. The arm in its designer sheath reminded me of the smooth, lethal, muscular weight of the python my father had draped around my neck, with the flashes of cameras in my eyes. The club, with its noisy beauty and graceful racket, had receded from my thoughts and, despite the crowds, despite the presence of my friends laughing on the other side of the table, I felt completely alone with this man. The melody of the music disappeared and only the bass was left, thudding up through the floor and into my trunk, combining with the savage beat of my heart.

'If you or your faggot friends ever trace this back to me, I'll make it my business to find you. Don't ever fuck with me, son. Even if I didn't think you were a poncy tossrag, I'd still cut your fucking throat soon as look at you.' This last sentence he whispered into my ear, and I felt his hot boozy breath down my collar as his spittle flecked my cheek.

All of a sudden White released his hold and clapped me on the back. The room, the lights, the music and the dancing rushed back into my head like air into a vacuum. 'Look at his face,' he shouted to his associate, the young man who had moved up to let me sit down, 'isn't that a fucking picture? You can tell he's a smart kid, he scares easy.'

His companion laughed uproariously. Lisa laughed too, but I felt her eyes on me, checking me over like a mechanic appraising a working part under particular pressure. I felt humiliated. I was not used to being threatened by anyone, and righteous indignation swelled up in my chest. Then, quite suddenly, I realized I had no protection. It was not that he was stronger than me – I was close enough to my schooldays to recognize the tactics of the playground bully even through the jewellery and paunch. It was that I had cut myself off from my usual recourse to higher authority. The freedom from threat that every law-abiding citizen takes as his due was no longer due to me. I had contracted with this man by a different set of rules, a system of which I had no knowledge, a culture where the customs and language were mysteries to me, and the slightest faux pas could be lethal. I understood now why he had insisted on meeting us. It was not simply to deliver this stark warning, but to make us grip the concrete fact of what we had done. Francis had convinced me that illegal in this case did not mean immoral – that if no one could tell the difference between the picture we had created and the original it had replaced, the fault lay not with us but with a hypocritical society that claimed to value art but in truth valued the wealth art objects conferred. In the dingy pocket of the club, this fine intellectual distinction melted away, and I saw only that I was bound for life to the whims of the violent man at my side. Francis had presented the deal to me as freedom from the bonds of law, and of social expectation, but I felt now as if I had substituted one yoke for another. This was my first taste of the creeping vulnerability which was to inform the rest of my life, but I brushed it away as a pang of conscience, like the man who mistakes the first headaches of a brain tumour for over-tiredness.

We took a cab from the club as soon as was deemed polite, and arrived back at the hotel at about twelve-thirty. Francis seemed genuinely to have enjoyed talking to the man Lisa had introduced as Ray, and the two swapped cards and shook hands before we left. John kissed Jessica's hand, and said to her fondly that he hoped his own daughter would grow up to be like her. The compliment raised one of her rare grins, and she kissed him on the cheek. Lisa decided to stay on, and we left her talking earnestly to our buyer, who evidently did not extend to her the disdain with which he regarded the rest of us. The others had not shared my unpleasant experience, and I had already decided not to tell them – they did not feel my need to escape, they desired only to be alone to revel in our triumph. I took pleasure in the way we must have looked to the concierge working the midnight shift, young and drunk, black and white, rich and free as our smart heels tapped on the marble floor of the foyer. As soon as we were inside I began to feel invincible again, the air-conditioned ambience of the hotel washed the fear and sweat from my skin. We picked up our keys, and ordered champagne at reception. The whole place was geared to my needs, and the atmosphere of service restored my self-confidence. We took the lift to the first floor. Fashion TV was playing on a large flat screen console by the brass panel of buttons. This season would be our season.

We stumbled down the corridor towards our suite. The carpet and the walls were decorated in nausea-inducing geometric patterns, and the floor sloped suddenly downwards like a wheelchair ramp. The walls were lined with blank canvases, each illuminated by a stately picture lamp fixed above them. It was the wilful tastelessness of real money, money that did not have to hide its nature behind sense or aesthetics, but was its own justification. The suite cost £1,500 a night. We slipped our keycard into the electronic lock and headed into our room.

Francis cast his antique jacket aside in a mock dance move, plucking one sleeve off and then the other before whirling it around in the air, and fell gracefully backwards on to the cream sofa in the centre of the drawing room. He lay on his back, his legs encased in fine black material hanging over the arm. He took a handful of strawberries from the crystal bowl on the central table, a carved slab of black wood that had slender segmented legs, curving inwards under its belly like an insect's. He fed himself in an exaggerated fashion, lowering the fleshy tips slowly into his mouth and then snatching at the whole thing, almost catching his fingers. Jessica went over to the stereo and started flicking through the CD collection provided by the hotel. She settled on something, placed the silver disc in the player, and melodic hip hop of the Roots, 'Things Fall Apart', swelled from the speakers hidden in the walls. She shuffled a backward step in time to the beat as she came to join us in front of the black marble fireplace. I looked up into the great mirror that dominated the room, and saw her and Francis as if through the eyes of a painter looking down from a stepladder. She laughed as she flopped into the soft cushions at my side, and Francis laughed too, and so did I, as the enormity of what we had achieved began to dawn on us, like a new day full of promise and resolution. Francis pumped his fists in the air in a compulsive release of energy, and Jessica howled I cast my eyes in a delighted circle around the room, a brief inventory of its splendour, at the things we could now afford. The last of the fear and the vulnerability I had felt in the presence of Augustus White evaporated to leave a sweet residue of recklessness dried to the base of my brain, and I was the first one to hunt out the wrap of coke from Francis's wash bag. The colourful little packet was swollen with two grams, bulging in the middle like a moist seedpod, and it burst over the glossy magazine sitting on the table, spreading a little drift of white powder over the advert (for a watch, I realized in heady joy, that I could now afford). It felt like the last day of school, the happiness that comes after exams, when a long grinding build-up of pressure dissipates in a moment, and the kids converge on the grassy banks outside the hall to lounge in the sunshine. We had climbed up a steep and unforgiving path, and the future opened up before us, a fertile and sunny valley we had reached by our own cleverness and labour. I loved them both, just for being there with me.

The suite was decorated to give an impression of imperialism: the drapes were heavy red velvet, the wallpaper was patterned with broad stripes of red and gold, the furniture was commodious and heavily padded. Yet the sealed test-tubes of mineral water, the leafy projections of bulbs that emerged from the wall on slender stems of iron, the bank of remote controls that governed sound, heat, lighting and refreshment, making almost any small desire simultaneous with its fulfilment, were all impeccably modern. The room made us feel the weight of our wallets, and we began to spread out, to throw glasses, to tap ash on the carpets, phone room service for more champagne. The suite demanded such behaviour, and its opulence helped us to slip the last tethers of frugality. We indulged in the lawlessness of the rich, leaving the coke out on the table when the bellboy came, refusing to tip him, and shouting at passersby from our balcony above Kensington Gardens. At last, I felt we had been returned to the paradise of my first term, where money was freedom. I began to allow myself to believe that it was true, that from now on all would be as it had been, when we were happy. The night was perfect in its isolation from consequence, brief and beautiful like an advert for something expensive. At first some element of my intellect detached itself, to savour the fact of what I was doing as well as the sensations. I wanted to be us even though I was: I felt the same aspirational pang I used to feel seeing the perfect bodies on TV. I wanted to sustain every second, but each one shrunk like cooling metal at the touch of the next.

'What will you do?' I asked Francis as he sat with his arms spread out across the back of the sofa at three o'clock, with half the cocaine gone. 'With your share.'

Jessica looked at me with a little shock, and then grinned broadly, putting her white teeth on display. I was breaking the last taboo. In the months of preparation, the idea of success had seemed so remote that the four of us had never dared to mention the possible future, afraid of scaring off our wildest dreams with eagerness even as they drew closer to where we lay in wait.

'I will go back to Harare,' Francis said, gazing at the ceiling as if he could see the stars through the white plaster, through the other floors and the clouds and the ambient light of London. 'I will spread wealth through all my mother's family. I will take several wives, and grow old and fat surrounded by children, who will make the best marriages, and have grandchildren who will come and cling to my knees. I will take a huge old colonial house, something that used to be owned by the governor. I will have gardeners in white trousers, and a balcony from which to survey my gardens, always filled with the delightful chatter of sprinklers, so that the grass is green and soft. I will greet foreign dignitaries from Europe, entertain them in my house, and they will say, "Do you know, this is the son that disowned Lord Soulford. How generous, what a cultured soul, how unlike his father." The girls will wear pink dresses, and the boys will be dressed in sailor suits. I will build an opera, a theatre, a hospital with gleaming corridors. I will hire a tutor, and read prodigiously in many languages. I will have aunts and uncles, brothers and sisters, and everyone will depend on me, and the day I slip quietly away, an ancient and happy man in tartan pyjamas, they will declare a national day of mourning, and all the policemen will wear black cotton gloves, and my beautiful granddaughters will weep over my coffin.' Francis seemed to visualize the scene in every detail, and tears stood out in his red-rimmed eyes. Cocaine had touched him with honesty, and where the vision strayed into the ridiculous it was an overflow of sincerity rather than deliberate irony. Jessica and I received our cue from him, and each of us lay back, enjoying our due, the right to describe our spending dreams.

'I will make sure that I never have to rely on anyone

else,' Jessica said. 'I will invest it, live quietly for a little while at university. Build a portfolio. Some property, some stocks.'

'But you can't,' Francis exploded, 'you have to spend it all now! What would happen to all that money if you were hit by a bus tomorrow? All that opportunity mouldering away in some distant bank account and a big ornate tombstone.'

'Oh shut up, Francis,' Jessica retorted, her sharp tone tearing the delicate mood. 'You have no idea what it's like not to have money. What you have to do.'

'I have!' Francis said, a tremble in his voice.

'These last five months, you haven't had as much as usual. But you had options, you had your food and fees paid, you lived in beautiful rooms. When my father went to prison . . . we spent two years trying to make things work, with no friends to help us. I'm pretty now, but when I'm forty I don't want to be alone.'

'I'm sorry,' Francis said quickly, with a look of genuine sorrow, 'I'm so sorry.' He got up and came over to where we were sitting on the largest sofa. It was terrible to see him cut off from the steady flow of her approval. Like an embolism in the blood, an air bubble in the sap of a tree, the interruption of this vital life-giving force was more fundamental than any threat, more effective than any punishment. We were very close now, the three of us. Physically close. Francis put his arm around Jessica, and the hand rested lightly on my shoulder. I wondered if he knew he was touching me, or whether he thought his fingers were brushing the inanimate bulk of the sofa. I felt a tiny shiver, like a premonition.

'What about you, James?' Jessica asked. Her arm lay along the length of my thigh.

'I don't really know. I want to spend mine on . . . pleasure.'

'Pleasure?' Jessica said, amused.

'Yes,' I said, 'but I must discover what it is. I'll find something that makes me happy, and then I'll pour my money into that.'

Jessica rubbed her cheek against my hand like a cat. Perhaps it was the sleazy brilliance of the hotel suite. Perhaps it was the sense that we had beaten everyone and everything, or a simple desire to indulge in every possible excess. It was context, the same force that allows us to watch a man in tights at the ballet and think it elegant, that enables a sane and rational man to stab another in the stomach when their two countries are at war. It seemed reasonable, natural, inevitable for me to break the film, the thin membrane between the physically intimate and the sexual, and slide my hands around her face from behind, gently penetrating her mouth with one of my fingers. I felt my fear of rejection dissolve in her mouth as I sensed a fledgling pressure; she sucked the tip, a slight instinctual pull like a baby's lips around a nipple. As I touched her, I caught Francis's eyes. He slid off the sofa so that he was kneeling in front of her, a supplicant asking for forgiveness for what he had said and for what we were about to do. She leant her head back exposing her throat, a gesture of willing vulnerability. She slid smoothly into submissiveness, but kept one tiny measure of veto, like a woman lowering her tanned body into warm clear water down the swimming-pool ladder, keeping her neat hair above the surface, her neck prim and straight. Her yielding to every pressure had a strange logic; it was the natural compensation for her daylight dominance. Francis took off his shirt, sliding his shoulders out one at a time. I put my hand on his body. He gave me a smile of licence. His flesh felt different to hers, he was composed entirely of skin and lean meat, his shoulder muscles rising like healthy swelling on the bone. His body felt like silk wrapped around sun-warmed stone. Hers was soft and yielding and strangely cool to the touch, contoured like a landscape under snow. I put my hand inside her corset and held one perfect breast. I pinched suddenly, and heard her gasp in a way that made me rip the fabric open.

We moved from the sofa to the bedroom. Francis lifted Jessica off the sofa and carried her through as if she were a sleeping child. We made objects of our own bodies, and consumed them. We turned cannibal on our own conventions, because they were the last rules we had left to break. The three of us had been adrift for too long on a featureless ocean, starved of all limits, until we fell upon our own and devoured them. I never again in my life felt a pleasure so great that the physical present eclipsed everything: the past, the future, the personal, the moral, like the moon coming across the sun at midday, cloaking all the drab details of the city for a few moments in a delicate, sensuous half-night. After it was over we lay, the three of us a muscular knot of intertwined limbs, wound together like a length of rope, with Francis and me flanking Jessica. I saw in the candlelight how his black skin stood out against her white smooth body, and my own brown limbs, lightly covered in hair, interposed between them like the child of their two colours. Birdsong and morning traffic filtered through from the street, and the heavy curtains were mounted on a frame of sunlight. Her head was turned in towards his shoulder, and he looked into my eyes through the blonde veil of her hair, which shifted slowly with the pattern of his breath like seaweed underwater. The chemicals in my bloodstream imparted a goodbye kiss to the system, and I sank in the blissful warmth of living flesh. I knew then, as I know now, that perfection is the first point of decline.

15

We left the hotel separately. Jessica had a day planned
with her family, and I woke to find her gone. Francis was
sleeping naked in the bed next to me. I hoped she might
have left a note, some kind of clue to how she had felt
about the previous night against which I could calibrate
my own reaction, but there was nothing except the
absence of her cosmetics in the bathroom and the space
where her trousers had been discarded on the floor.
Embarrassed by Francis's nudity, I stayed out of the
master bedroom. He was sprawled over the bed on his
front, the sheet lying over his thighs, a pillow clasped
under his cheek. The pale soles of his feet were turned up
towards the ceiling. The smooth flesh I had so relished
the night before I now found vaguely unsettling, like a
succulent piece of steak I had taken into my mouth,
chewed and then removed, placing it back on the edge
of the plate. I put it down to the fact that my bloodstream was saturated with minor poisons, which made
the beautiful summer day seem like a sun-faded

photograph, dull and flat. I had a two o'clock meeting with my tutor in Cambridge to explain my recent absences from college. It was a requirement of the course that I spent a certain number of days a term in my room, and the porters had notified the authorities of my frequent trips to London. The previous day the obligation had felt absurd – I imagined myself as a general, returning in triumph to his home city to find his car had been clamped. That morning as I wandered around the suite collecting my scattered things I was almost grateful for the appointment, for a chore to anchor me back in normality. I did not wake Francis to say goodbye. We did not call each other that night, and as I lay awake in bed in my rooms in Tudor, my tutor's condemnation still fresh in my ears, I realized it had been months since a whole day had gone by without the three of us speaking. When I closed my eyes I kept seeing the two of them moving together, her pale body straddling the taut cradle of his hips as I pinned her slender wrists behind her back, like a bright light burned into my retinas. I had to open my eyes again in the darkness to stop seeing them.

There were two weeks before the end of term. Exams were over, and the exhausted student body was gearing itself up for one last burst of hedonism, for the college balls and Suicide Sunday, the weekend of endless garden parties that marked the end of work and the beginning of play. Lisa was running her inevitable scam, trading tickets at inflated prices. The fact that her activities continued unabated following our deal, and that she poured almost as much energy into making a couple of hundred pounds as she had into making a million, confirmed something I had suspected about her character. Her goal was the accumulation, not the owning, of money or the advantages money could provide. She had a computer sciences postgraduate, with whom she had periodic arrangements, trying to see if he could forge the barcodes and hologram seals on the Tudor tickets, which were already changing hands at a hundred pounds a go. I sold her my own tickets. White plastic marquees with chipboard dance floors began to appear on the sacred grass of the courts, springing up overnight like crops of giant fungi.

That summer, Francis said we should not see each other. He said we shouldn't spend any of the money either. With his irresistible mixture of logic and fantasy he convinced us all it would be suspicious. We had to remain inconspicuous; we could not draw attention to ourselves. He conjured bogeymen, police and the Inland Revenue, college officials and Mafiosi, who patrolled the borders of our desire to spend. Lisa was his silent partner in this enterprise, and her sober nodding provided the perfect counterpoint to his impassioned pleas for self-control. This galled me a little, as I was sure that Francis would begin to fritter and Lisa to invest the moment term ended, but as the principle instigators and facilitators of the deal they seemed above reproach. In fact he was spending it already – every night he went out clubbing in a blizzard of coke, flooding his quickly assembled entourage with cheap champagne. When I asked him about these evenings, he would become evasive. I dodged and resisted, and they had to extract the promise not to touch the cash from my mouth like a rotten tooth. For the next few days I made gentle inquiries as to where Francis planned to spend the summer, and hinted as strongly as my pride would allow that he would be welcome at my house, that we could even spend just a little of our money on a place of our own if he wanted, or go on a holiday together. All my hints were lost in a fog of vague allusions – he said he was planning on going abroad, maybe to Ibiza where his friend was managing the V.I.P. at Pacha, maybe Mexico or to friends who were making an independent film in LA, but when I pushed for details he would just wave his hand and grin. Eventually, after a particularly embarrassing session sitting on the benches by the river at King's, watching bare-chested men wrestling punts between the narrow walls of the Cam, his evasiveness threatened to turn into an awkward silence, and I stopped mentioning it altogether.

In the event, we had nothing to fear from the money. Lisa had had our respective millions paid into a series of accounts so secure and secluded that it took me three years of city law to unravel what she had done. A complex series of holding companies, all purpose-built and based in Jersey, acted as a mutual trust and paid the cash back as dividends from the shares into other overseas accounts. The money was not only untraceable, it would have been legally untaxable until the Inland Revenue busted a Premiership football club pulling a similar stunt for its players and closed the loophole.

I wanted a solid goodbye to support me through a whole summer of social hibernation, a summer away from the light of my friends. I had envisaged long, crushing hugs, meaningful eye contact and waving from the windows of receding cars until they cornered out of sight, but in the end I was denied. Francis left suddenly, and I found a note under my door saying he was not taking his phone with him as he didn't want his father to be able to contact him. The note was written on the back of a scrap of cardboard torn from a cornflakes packet. I felt sure I would find a corresponding mauled box in the kitchen cupboard across the landing. He didn't mention how we could reach him. I searched the note for some sign of the loss I felt at the suspension of our friendship, and I found it in the lack of emotional detail, as if any reference to the four of us might make it impossible for him to leave. I thought I detected the echo of my own sense of isolation, and perhaps even a wobble in the usually solid loops of his descenders. Lisa simply disappeared off the radar: one afternoon she was there, and the next she was not. Her exit was nothing like Francis's puff-of-smoke showmanship, and there was no gasp from the assembled crowd – she simply slipped away, like a tired guest from a party, and it took me a while to realize she was gone. Her success at sectioning off bits of her life was such that I could not imagine her on summer holidays, could not imagine her doing anything except slinking around Cambridge or Docklands in combat pants and trainers, doing deals. When I tried to picture her jumping off a rock into clear blue water she was still wearing a singlet and tracksuit bottoms and carrying her laptop case. The previous holiday she had spent with us to keep an eye on her investment. I knew that this time I would not see her until the start of Michaelmas, when the natural currents of our lives caused us to drift past each other again, on the way to different places.

Only Jessica threatened the satisfaction of a decent farewell. On the last full day of term, she came to see me, and sat smoking by the window of my room in the armchair. The summer suited her; her fair skin was dusted with a light tan. It brought out the brilliance of her eyes, which glittered like sunshine on deep water. She drew up her knees to her chest and leant with her head propped on her elbow, looking out into the warm day. She had on a shirt of white diaphanous material tied off at the midriff that kept threatening to disclose one of her small nipples, and torn blue jeans. She was wearing baby-pink lip salve that coloured the filter of her cigarette. This was the look I associated with her, an outfit just on the edge of indecency, so that no one could quite pin down a specific transgression for which to upbraid her, try as they might. I never fully shared the delight she took in antagonizing the moral majority, a group, I thought, that existed more in her imagination than in the real world. I busied myself with packing, fearful that if I looked at her I would not be able to find the appropriate response to her beauty. Since the night in the hotel I had forfeited my camouflage of disinterest, but I could not let her know how distracting I found her presence. The college authorities had informed me that I could keep the same room next year, but the whole building was to be invaded by American high school students over the summer, and anything personal or precious had to be removed. She had ostensibly come to help me sort out my things, but tended to regard her mere presence as ample help in any enterprise.

'You're not packing up your easel?' she asked.

'To be honest, I've had enough of the thing for the moment.'

'I know what you mean.'

I was folding my clothes. A pall of silence had descended over the events of the night of the deal. I did not know how I had expected things to change, but that they would change I had felt certain. Nothing had prepared me for the atmosphere that had unfolded in the aftermath, an abject refusal to discuss things, a bland sheen of scar tissue that had grown over the incident, leaving the bullet still in the flesh. In the days immediately following our return to Cambridge I had been able to ascribe our listlessness to a prolonged comedown, and by the time I was forced to admit that something more fundamental was responsible the moment for addressing it had passed. I had been used to talking about anything with them, things I had never spoken of before, and I was sad to think that we had formed our own taboo.

'What are you planning over the holidays?' I asked her to staunch the flow of silence.

'I thought I might go on an Italian course in Florence. I've always wanted to learn Italian. I've got the clothes and the gestures, I just need the language.' She twirled her free hand in the air as if summoning a waiter across a crowded piazza, and shouted, '*Ma che cosa fai?!*'

'And, of course, you can afford it now.' I snuck a sideways glance at her to see if she had registered the implicit sedition, but she either didn't hear or chose to ignore me.

'Also I'm going to Croatia with the family. Since he started working again Daddy likes to take a villa for three weeks, on the coast by Dubrovnik. It practically bankrupts him, but I think he'd rather look rich and be poor than live comfortably.'

'Will you get bored?'

'No,' she said. 'Irritated maybe. All the sisters and steady boyfriends will be in attendance. They play tennis with Daddy and make rude jokes about my bikinis. And I'm taking friends.' Then, quickly, 'More friends of the family, you know? I've known them all since prep school, they still call my father "Mr Katz".'

I packed more intently, trying not to let her see how much it pained me to think of her having something I did not: another life. I did not want there to be anyone who could lay claim to knowing her better than I did.

'What are your plans?' she asked. In terms of intimacy the conversation was on a level with the exchanges I had with my barber, a woman on Silver Street who always smelt of bubble gum. I decided to punish her for her insensitivity with a barrage of glamorous lies.

'Me and some friends are going to St Tropez,' I said recklessly. She didn't bite, just nodded her head and breathed smoke. She trumped me with a lack of surprise. For most of her acquaintance, I realized, this might be nothing less than the truth. For me it was an obvious fantasy. I had processed the clothes and was down to the knick-knacks. Confronting the meagre collection of cufflinks and collar studs in my bedside drawer I thought how sparse my lifestyle would be without Francis to provide. The money in the Jersey account did not feel like mine, and even if it had not been officially out of bounds I would never in truth have thought to touch it. I pulled the drawer out and upended it on top of the neatly folded shirts in my overnight bag.

'Has it occurred to you . . .' she said after a while, 'that it may not have been the best thing to send Francis off with all that cash?'

I could not muster the energy for this conversation. It irritated me that we could not spend half an hour in one another's company without the subject of Francis bobbing to the surface. It made me feel like half of a couple staying together for the sake of the children. The packing accentuated the impression of weary domesticity.

'He's twenty,' I said. I picked my anglepoise lamp up off the bureau and turned it over in my hand, pretending to wonder whether to pack it.

A flicker of annoyance passed over her face at this rebuff. She took a last furious pull on her cigarette, a deep drag as if she was leaving the smoking lounge for a transatlantic flight. She flicked the butt out of the window. This was deliberately antagonistic, as I had confided to her my obsessive fear that a stray butt in the gutter would ignite dry leaves and set the building on fire, obliterating hundreds of years' worth of history. The rental agreement on my room stipulated no smoking.

'I'm off,' she said abruptly, unfolding her legs from the armchair and stretching.

'Thanks for all your help with the packing.'

'My pleasure,' she said without a trace of irony.

'Have a good summer.'

'And you.'

She walked over to the door. I thought that she would pause at the threshold and turn around, try to make

274

things up between us, but she left without even the concession of a slam for effect. I waited until I heard her footsteps recede down the stairs, but when her feet hit the flat stone of the hall I buckled. I scrambled to the window and leant over the balustrade. Preparations for the Tudor Ball were in full swing. Outside I could hear the metallic tap of hammer on tent peg coming from Nevile's Court. The cigarette was still smouldering on the lead sheet.

'Jessica?' I shouted.

She turned around and looked up at me, shielding her eyes and squinting in the afternoon sunshine.

'Yeah?' she shouted back.

'. . . Nothing.'

She grinned. 'Nothing yourself.'

She waved, and skipped once as she went back to walking. One of my neighbours had come into the court from the Backs, a girl in her second year who always wore one of the red Christian Union hoodies with a verse from Matthew printed on the back, and she looked up, startled by the shouting. Her disapproval set the seal on my happiness. I still felt the thrill of being observed with my beautiful friends, like driving around in an expensive car with the top down, attracting a mixture of envy and tutting. I watched Jessica disappear out of sight under the sandstone colonnade with a resurgence of affection, then stubbed the cigarette and crawled back into the cool of my bedroom.

I rushed to finish my packing as my father had agreed to pick me up at three. At ten to three I was sunbathing on the roof. The grubby hood of our Volvo nosed out of the shadows of the archway forty feet below, peeking into the court like a reef fish checking the open waters: Dad making sure he had the right place, fearful of straying off limits into an academic sanctuary. After a few seconds he made up his mind, and advanced with a crunch of gravel. Looking down at the car I read in each of its heavy movements the extension of my father's own familiar manner, his hesitations and sudden, bullish decisions. He was slightly awed by Cambridge, and openly rebellious against his awe, so that he could not discuss my education without a certain reverence mixed with bursts of anti-intellectualism: 'James's teacher is the world expert on Chaucer. They have some of the original illuminated manuscripts in the library. Beautiful, they are. It's all bollocks, of course, I don't know who's going to give him a job for knowing medieval poetry!' He parked aggressively in compensation for his former trepidation, jamming himself in against the ivy-covered wall and partially blocking the Porsche in the corner, jumping out of the driver's seat before he could change his mind. He walked a few feet away from the Volvo towards my staircase with his long, confident stride, then stopped and turned around. He ran back, got in and straightened the car to release the 911. I had a love-lurch watching this little performance, and I wanted to call out to him and wave, but something held me back.

The next two months were, I think, the worst of my life. My terraced house seemed mean and depressing after New Court, and the knowledge that the comparison was unfair did nothing to lessen its effect. A few days after my return Dad told me that he could not afford to pay my allowance out of termtime. I strongly suspected that the real motivations behind his cutting me off were not financial, and that he was acting out of some sense of parental obligation to teach me about the value of money. Given that I was sitting on a stolen million the lesson seemed a little late, but even without my promise not to touch it there would have been no way of integrating the cash into my life without arousing his suspicions. He encouraged me to get a job.

I took the late shift at Movie Time Video, which started at six and finished at one in the morning, and paid £5.30 an hour. I found myself treating the work as a penance: the video store was my own personal neon-pink purgatory, but no matter how many hours I did, no matter how many times I took the insults of manager and customers, I still had no relief from the crushing weight of the money sitting in its offshore haven. I had begun to imagine it as a physical entity, a block of notes bobbing like a swollen body off a pebble beach, waiting to wash ashore and be discovered. The drip drip of what I had done kept my conscience awake at night. What I had undertaken as a gesture of freedom had begun to look like recklessness. It was not the theft itself that troubled me, though Francis's logic of innocence was beginning to crumble without the maintenance of his rhetoric. Rather it was imagining what my father would think of me if I was discovered. The idea that I had put myself in a position where I could cause him so much shame and pain made me nauseous with guilt, until I felt panic rising in my gorge and thought I would have to blurt it out. Later such worries would give way to more prosaic fears, such as a terror of prison, but for me fear was no match for guilt. These sporadic attacks were like the waves of fever brought on by a tropical malaise, and when they were at their peak I would have to take long walks on Wandsworth Common, or lie in my room with my door shut, desperate to avoid any kind of human contact. Movie Time Video allowed me to take home two videos a night (excluding new releases) for free, and after I had finished my shift I would watch old films until the city began to glow with a muggy dawn, breaking like a sheen of sweat over the Common. I started to take out pornography too, and when I had exhausted the store's meagre collection of soft core I made morning jaunts into Soho on the tube in search of something harder. I would lie towels along the crack under the door and keep the sound turned down low, for fear the grunts and cries might wake my father. That summer, London was afflicted with a superfluous heatwave, and with no clean air or open water to bring relief the slightest task was horrible. My guilt was compounded by a physical dirtiness. Within moments of a shower, my hair was matted, my eyes and throat stung with fumes and my shirt was stuck to my back.

My job granted one small mercy: the shifts, which most young men and women would have found punitive, helped to eat up the nighttime when I was most vulnerable to loneliness. The after-work movies took care of the small hours, which insomnia and isolation had taught me to dread. Sometimes I thought about the others, tried to imagine them distant and happy and imagining me. As the weeks went by with no contact, however, I reasoned they could not miss me as much as I missed them, and stopped. My father caught sight of Francis in the *Daily Mail*'s gossip column heading into Asprey's with a blonde on his arm, the daughter of a shipping millionaire, and he left the paper by my door with a note that read: 'Isn't that your friend!? Very glamorous . . .' He was spending the money, as I had known he would. This sense of abandonment poisoned the way I perceived our time together; even my happiest memories smacked of inauthenticity. It also added an extra flare of guilt to what I now saw had been a total neglect of my dad. I had simply taken our love for granted, and had barely spoken to him once during termtime. Grief had proved a great leveller for us; the support we had given each other in the months following my mother's death had made us equals when I was still a child. At the age of twelve, when other boys were receiving orders and prohibitions from their fathers, I was getting advice and counsel. Away from the intoxicating influence of my Cambridge associates I realized how much I had abused this most important of friendships, but the fact of what I had done made it impossible to put right. If I'd tried to talk to him, to rekindle our intimacy, he would have immediately begun to ask me what was wrong, and I would either have had to confess, which was impossible, or lie, which would have made the effort insincere. Our respective work schedules kept us mercifully separate. Physical division foiled most of his attempts to reconnect with his son. At six o'clock after a night of cinema and porn I would be heading to bed as he woke for work, and I would already be out before he came home for supper. I tiptoed when I got in, and hid under the covers when he peeked blear-eyed into my room in the early morning to see if I was still awake. It was at these moments, when I hid away from his concern, that the temptation to tell him everything was almost unbearable. When I came home I would tidy his mess, and I would leave the breakfast things ready for him before going to bed. I moved around him in my twilight world like a ghost around a living loved one, equally unable to make contact or to let go entirely. That holiday laid the foundations for a creeping estrangement, a continental drift that continued for years, and which I failed to heal before his death.

It was, I believe, this acute lack of human contact that precipitated one of the most shameful episodes of my life. One night after work I took my dad's car keys from the wooden rack in the kitchen and went for a drive. It was late on a Saturday. To ensure that I would not be around when my dad was at home I had asked specifically for the weekend shifts, which unfortunately finished several hours earlier than their weekday counterparts. The streets were full of young men and women drinking and clubbing. Most of the bars and pubs had large crowds spilling out of their doors, hanging into the street like bellies over tight waistlines. I was filled with a mixture of envy and disgust. I desperately wanted to talk to someone, but everyone I saw in the convivial summer darkness looked somehow grotesque. I drove over Wandsworth Bridge, and up the Wandsworth Bridge Road into Fulham, not thinking about where I was going. I don't know when I decided to do what I did, I hope the decision was never consciously made, but I stopped off at the cashpoint at the garage on the King's Road and withdrew two hundred pounds, about forty hours' worth of video-shop time. After three-quarters of an hour behind the wheel I found myself in Shoreditch. I parked the car.

'Hey, all right, James,' the friendly Irish bouncer said to

me on my way in, 'we've missed you.' The taste of familiarity revived me for a moment, but his next question ran me through. 'Where's yer pal?'

'You tell me, Justin,' I said to him with a queasy smile.

'Ah, he'll find his way back,' Justin said. 'Misha's on tonight, do you want her sent upstairs?'

'Yes,' I said.

Our credit was perfect, and they didn't ask me to pay anything up front. I walked up the first flight of stairs. There was a group of drunk men with their ties loosened in the shower room, watching a wet girl I didn't recognize with stocky legs gyrating in the perspex box, and they cheered, 'Get in, son!' as Justin showed me through the door to the private area upstairs. I thought, I'm not like them.

'Quieten down, you lot, or I'll belt the lot of yer,' Justin said. He had an amiable way of making threats that came from the mixture of a good nature and a fearsome reputation. Justin could afford to be affable when he threatened, because everybody seemed to know that if they stepped out of line the promised damage would magically materialize.

I waited for Misha in our private room. Her eyes lit up when she came in. Obviously Justin had not told her who had requested the pleasure of her company, knowing she enjoyed our time together and keen to give her a lift. It was exquisite, watching the pre-prepared smile of seduction transform into one of genuine joy.

She ran over and hugged me, and kissed me on the cheek. She had been dancing downstairs, and she was cool but sweaty and was wearing nothing but a black thong. She treated her nakedness with professional indifference – no need to pretend to be sexual around a friend. The feel of her body pressing against mine made me happy for the first time in weeks. Her neat shoulder blades were slippery with perspiration. I leant my head into hers and took a deep breath from her bottle-blonde hair. I could have drawn her from memory, had done once or twice, but she looked fresh in the flesh. I had forgotten how her broad smile disclosed too many of her uneven white teeth, a chink in her prettiness that made me want to protect her from the world, to cover the gap in her armour where insults might get in.

'James! It is wonderful to see you, I had been thinking you had found another girl for your pictures.' She pushed me playfully. 'Is Francis here? I know the girls will love to see him.'

'No, Misha,' I said, holding on to her for perhaps half a second longer than was natural, 'I'm here alone.'

'Oh well, no matter. I would want to see you more anyway.' She sat down on the bed, pulling me down with her. 'Where is your funny bag? Oh, I'm sorry, your friend's funny bag?'

This was a private joke, a reference to the crocodile skin holdall in which I had transported my easel, pencils and paper. It was a casual heirloom lent to me by Francis,

283

and I had loved him all the more for seeing nothing exceptional in its appearance. Misha had teased me for it when she had begun to relax, and laughed at my insistence that it wasn't mine. I ignored the question, quickly asking her one of my own. 'How are things here?'

Misha pulled a face. 'Terrible, especially now you don't come. But I have saved a lot of money. I will be quite rich soon, I think, though nothing like a famous artist! I am thinking next year I may be a student, like you.'

'What will you study?' I asked.

She looked down and shook her head.

'What?' I said, delighted at her shyness. I put my hand on her bare shoulder. She had put on some kind of body make-up to make her skin glitter in the light.

'No, you will laugh.'

'I won't laugh!'

'Well . . . I thought I might study Art History.'

I felt so happy at this that I was almost ready to leave. I felt replenished, and knew that there was one good thing I had done for another human being I liked, who liked me. I was about to get up and hug her goodbye when she asked me, 'So, James, did you ever sell your pictures? Did you sell your pictures of me?'

The question returned me to my purpose.

'James,' she said, laughing nervously and ducking away from me, 'what are you doing?' I ignored her, willing myself to believe that it was just the first shock that made her resist, and tried to kiss her neck again. She stood up, and instinctively pulled the sheet with her to cover her breasts.

'Where are your painting things?' she repeated. 'You have left them downstairs?'

I did not answer her, but we looked at one another, and came to an understanding.

I think if you killed an animal that would have given its life for you, the look in its eyes would be like that. The comparison with an animal flashed into my mind, creating an impression I am still trying to destroy. After that, all emotion left her face. She told me how much it would cost, and asked me exactly what I wanted, telling me she didn't do anal. I don't know if she spoke like this to hurt me, or whether all emotion had simply shut down for her, and she was navigating on automatic. This was not how I had imagined it, how I had pictured it in my dreams.

She was not still and compliant, as I had feared, but grotesquely animated, which was somehow worse. It was over quickly. Afterwards, she got up and went through to the adjoining bathroom, and did not come back out. I waited for her, even knocked on the door, but the only reply was the sound of running water.

Downstairs I went to the desk to pay. I knew the woman working behind the till, and she gave me a friendly smile. I couldn't remember how much Misha had said that full sex would cost.

The girl said, 'Sixty for the naughty modelling is it,

James?' The details of our arrangement had become well known around the club. It had required the negotiation of a new tariff with the manager, and had been much discussed as the other girls had been curious and Misha proud. I thought now of how they would punish her for her pride, for her faith in human nature.

'More than sixty,' I managed.

'Did you have a few drinks?' she asked. 'You tell me what you had, I'll tell you what it cost.'

'No drinks.'

'Well, what then?' she said in a friendly tone, and a second later understanding illuminated her features with surprise.

I threw the two hundred down on the desk and ran out of the doors. Justin shouted, 'Bye, pal, don't leave it so long.' I made it around the corner and slowed to a walk. When I got back to my father's Volvo I sat behind the wheel and stared into the halogen glow of the streetlights, feeling nothing.

16

We waited half an hour for the bus. My elation seeped away from me as we sat stranded on the highway. I had no change, so Jessica bought my ticket. We had been sitting in the cold for so long that her fingers fumbled the coins as she took them out of her pocket, spilling a couple of them on to the floor. The driver looked into the distance, and sighed with infinite patience as we both stooped to pick them up, bumping into each other in the process. No one else on the bus seemed to notice. They had no time for other people's lives. There were only a couple of other passengers, a washed-out white junkie with dreadlocks and a patterned hoodie, an old woman and a couple of uniformed security guards coming back from a night shift. No one spoke. I remembered a story I had read the previous week, about a man being fatally stabbed on the night bus for taking issue with a drunk throwing food at his girlfriend. The story recalled the real function of night in the city, to demonize strangers. We were all exiles from the daytime, but we were united in mistrust. I led Jessica up to the upper deck and sat on the orange seats nearest the front window. The heaters were on, and the glass was fogged up. We took the places either side of the aisle, as my legs were too long to fit comfortably in a single seat. We were alone on the top deck, which made my heart beat more easily. When we pulled away from the stop the bare branches of the trees clawed the roof, as if trying to get in. There were no other cars on the road. The bus bore the human driftwood of the city back into the centre like a midnight tide.

Jessica spoke first. 'I'm sorry I've left you alone for so long. When this thing came up, I have to tell you, I was almost grateful, because it meant that I could see you again.'

'Why couldn't you just see me anyway?'

'Why couldn't you call me?'

I could not give her an answer. She shifted in her seat.

'Look, there are still some things I need to know about the painting. For my own peace of mind.'

'Just ask. I'll tell you whatever I know.'

'Would it bear up under chemical analysis?'

'No. I drew those sketches with modern pencils on thick cream paper we stained with cold tea and flecked with brown ink. Any kind of technical investigation would immediately reveal them as fakes. As to the style, I don't want to congratulate myself too much, but I think it will hold up under close examination. I followed the lines of the original exactly, but I didn't trace them, so that the picture has accuracy and spontaneity in just the right proportions. The hardest part of any picture to fake is the provenance, and the Picasso has a flawless and accurate history. As you know it's not in the interest of the auction houses to prove it a fake – their cut relies on getting a good price for it. Besides, the sheer volume of pictures they sell precludes proper safeguards. The sellers don't want to know because it would make their goods worthless, and the buyers don't want to know because it would invalidate the objects of their desire. It's a wonderful conspiracy of ignorance. I don't foresee any dangers in the sale, unless the new owners decide to have it cleaned or restored. If that happens, we're fucked.'

'So even if the sale goes through without a hitch, it will just hang over us, like before. We'll never be quite safe.'

'Man knows not the hour.' I surprised myself when I said it. It seemed to come out as an automated response.

Jessica shivered. 'What do you think we did?' she asked.

'We committed a crime.'

'Don't be obtuse.'

'Actually, we committed crimes. Law school was a real eye-opener for me. Theft, breach of fiduciary duty, tax evasion. You have no idea what it's like to sit on the front bench of the lecture hall and realize your life basically constitutes a case study.' My tone was flippant, I was trying to restore some sense of levity after my previous comment, but I knew even as I spoke that I had misjudged the mood.

'Shut up, James. Of course I know what we did,' she said, irritated, 'but what did it mean, to be so wrong that we should always be punished like this, never knowing peace for one minute, always waiting for the police car to pull up outside?'

I paused to let her know I was thinking about the question seriously. When I spoke, all the forced lightness was gone from my voice.

'I don't know. Sometimes I think we're punished for our greed. I mean we weren't starving, we weren't cold or living on the streets, but somehow it still seemed so desperate. I think maybe that's what real greed is, a blindness to proportion. And we were selfish. Christ, we were selfish, and worse than that we were selfish when we pretended to be thinking about each other. We insisted on handling what was happening to Francis on our own, we drove away all the offers of help, and I think that part of that was because deep down we were afraid of getting caught.'

'I don't think we were selfish. Look at what we gave up.'

'I did that for my own conscience. I guess . . . I guess we went through with it in the first place because we wanted to be young for ever. I don't mean that in a trite way, no one wants to get old, I mean we tried to achieve it by disclaiming all responsibility. We tried to step outside of time, never to work, never to worry. And it worked, in a way. I don't feel I've ever moved on, I still feel the same inside as I did when we were together, the years haven't touched me. Only it's not the same. It's like the difference between a warm, living body and a perfectly preserved corpse, frozen in ice.'

It was a dialogue punctuated with the sound of the bus rattling and the wind. I felt frustrated. This was the conversation I had been waiting for. This was my specialist topic, I knew it intimately; but somehow the ideas I had rehearsed through insomnia in the darkened theatre of my bedroom had lost their fluency, they were coming out all wrong.

'Things were like that though, even when we were there. Frozen in time.' When Jessica said this, I became wary. She had not finished speaking, something else was coming, but she paused. I felt a kind of trap had been set. I would either have to dispute this statement and suffer the stigma of being the one to start a confrontation, or else let it pass, and thus allow her to found her next statement upon it as solid ground. I decided to stall.

'What do you mean?'

'I mean it was an odd kind of life, even at its best. An old-fashioned way of living, preserved beyond its sell-by date. All those picnics and tailors and titles and silver and candles. I don't think I ate dinner by electric light once in twelve months. It was theatre, a kind of role-play. I think Francis had read a lot, spent a long time gazing at all those splendid portraits in his gallery, and had formed an idea of what aristocratic life was supposed to be. Then we all set about recreating it with him, like those people on TV who go and live on an Elizabethan-era plantation for six months, then come back and talk about their experiences. I think we did a pretty good impression of a golden past, but it was still just an impression.'

'Your memories must be different to mine,' I said at last.

Jessica was silent for a while. When she spoke again, it was in the small, insistent voice of someone determined to forge on with a disagreeable topic. 'Do you ever wonder why Francis made us go through with it?'

'We chose to do it.'

'Don't delude yourself, James,' she said to me gently. 'You would have robbed a bank if he'd asked you. I think I would too.'

I let this pass without comment. 'I suppose that Francis wanted to do it because he was wild, and didn't want to work for money. He liked the idea of securing his own future and cheating the system into the bargain.'

'I used to think that,' she said.

I felt uneasy. The material of my trousers was sticking between my thighs and the orange seat, making the skin itch. I shifted to loosen it. In that moment, I became consciously aware of something I had always known, but which had slipped from my mind in the years since I had last seen Jessica. There is in every serious friendship a trove of confidences. Secrets is too mean a word, because it is not merely the facts that require proper handling. It is the way those facts relate to the friend, the emotional context in which they are buried, the moment in which they were told. We think we will be weakened by giving away each one, but with every trade we feel stronger, knowing that a burden has passed out of our keeping and into the hands of someone we trust. I had forgotten this, until Jessica's return that afternoon. I had re-discovered the stored treasure, like a chest of childhood toys found in the attic; I had blown the dust away, wiped the grime with my palm and read her name on the wood. Now I had a terrible premonition. I could tell that Jessica was on the point of taking something I had traded her and using it against me. If she did that, I would begin to worry about each and every point of ingress into my heart. I would have to go around boarding them up to make sure I was safe. Things between us would be for ever colder. I wanted another drink.

'And what do you think now?' I asked.

'Did you know that many forgeries take place as a kind of revenge? The primary motive's usually economic, but a lot of artists who feel their talents have been overlooked by the art world forge the works of other, well-respected painters to demonstrate what they perceive as the stupidity of critics. The arbitrary apportioning of fame and fortune.'

'So?'

'So sometimes I think we were part of Francis's revenge on the world.'

'That's not true.'

'Sometimes I think Francis deliberately caused the rift with his father. That he got us hooked on a lifestyle we couldn't afford, then cut us off to soften us up for his grand design.'

'That's not fair,' I said. 'He's not here to defend himself.'

'That's right,' Jessica said. 'He's not here.'

There was a silence.

'Did you know that Francis and Lisa used to deal drugs?' she said. 'She imported the stuff from London; he would send her a steady stream of clients.'

'Don't be melodramatic. They sorted things out for friends. If you wanted to party they would help you. That's hardly the same as pushing outside playgrounds. And anyway, I don't seem to remember you complaining too much at the time.'

'No, no, I didn't. One of the many things I have to live with.'

We took Putney Bridge over the river. I had not been paying attention to where we were, and the sudden expanse of water surprised me with its mobile beauty. The Thames glittered black and cold. It rumpled like a precious fabric in the wind, giving silver reflections of the moon as we mounted the bridge's curving back.

'And you . . .' she said.

'What about me?'

'Did you ever wonder why Francis took to you so quickly? Why he told you about his plan first, before anyone else?'

'We were friends.'

'I know that, but I mean, maybe he was drawn to you on some level because . . . he could feel you were suggestible. Willing to do almost anything to be a part of us.'

I turned away from her and looked out of the window. I leant my forehead against the cool glass. We had come down past the public gardens on the bank of the Thames and paused at the lights.

'Do you ever wish we had kept the money?' she asked.

'No. Not for a second.'

'Me neither.'

The conversation was over; we were nearing our stop. I pushed the red button on the handrail and the light came on. The critical moment had passed. I breathed a sigh of relief, for I felt she had pulled up short of bedrock truth. What was it I had feared from her? It was her shaking my love for Francis. It was my unquestioning devotion to his memory that needed protection, because it was all that could justify my failure in life. She was

295

casting doubt on whether he had ever been worthy of this kind of worship, chipping away at my graven image. I knew that if she succeeded, she would not free me, as she thought, but injure me horribly. A true tragedy was a kind of excuse for having no family or friends to speak of. I had always held Francis's death and the events surrounding it as reason enough for never seeking out new loved ones. But if Francis was not the heroic figure he had seemed, then devotion to him was not tragic sacrifice, but mere foolishness and vanity. In short, my life so far would have been a waste. I would do anything to resist this idea.

We climbed off the bus at Putney Bridge tube station, the last stop before it headed back towards Hammersmith. A tall Rastafarian in a fluorescent orange waistcoat was undoing the padlock on the metal gate over the station doors. He sang quietly to himself. A delivery of flowers still wet with artificial mist to keep them fresh was being unloaded from a white van at the shop across the road. I caught their scent on the cold air, not merely the fragrance of roses mixed in with diesel fumes from the bus but also the clean, organic smell of the freshly cut and weeping stems. There was still no natural light, the streetlamps dyed the world a dirty orange, but as the girl from the shop signed the delivery man's register I felt that we had lost our monopoly on London. It was no longer a place to play out our private drama; the scenery was coming to life again with business and commerce, the extras were waking up to be leads in their own days. There would be no more climbing over walls, no more deserted highways. I felt sadness at this, as the isolation that had been the lifeblood of our magical night ebbed away, but also some relief. There were things you could not say in daylight, there were rules, and more importantly it would be much easier to find a cab. Out of habit, I looked at my watch. It was almost six in the morning. I had been awake for nearly twenty-four hours. The fact itself seemed to make me feel tired.

'I think that place will be open soon,' she said, indicating a light that had come on behind the metal grill covering the Putney Bridge Café. 'Do you want to get a coffee before we get the tube?'

I looked over at the café. I pictured last night's pastries lying stiffly under the grimy glass counter. The roses had been taken inside the flower shop, and the diesel fumes were making me nauseous. 'Do you mind if we don't?' I said. 'I suddenly feel quite exhausted. I just want to get home.'

'Fine,' she said, and quite unexpectedly reached out to stroke my hair. I flinched away slightly on a reflex, then relaxed and allowed her to touch me. We walked away up the New King's Road, and the first little drops of life began to gather pace in the early morning, as milk and papers appeared on doorsteps and the Saturday commuters stepped out of their warm homes into the freezing morning, seeing their breath and locking their doors. Joggers swept by in their self-important exertions, and a group of kids on bicycles appeared from the estates on the Munster Road. By the time we hit Parsons Green the city was shaking off the night with the vigour of a dog flinging droplets of water off its coat. We passed the framing shop where Francis had found a mount for the picture. The spot ambushed us both, but the place had closed down and metamorphosed into a clothes shop. The world reminding us that things had moved on. Neither of us said anything, but I thought I heard Jessica catch her breath. We finally found a cab along the green shoulder of Eelbrook Common, a peaceful-looking expanse of grass guarded by neon-yellow signs requesting information on a serious sexual assault. The streetlights were still on in the dim twilight, and I could make out a woman walking her dog on the distant path. I opened the door for Jessica, running on courteous autopilot. I felt secure within the familiar interior of a black cab. I gave the driver my address through the sliding panel of glass. He looked at us as we collapsed on the back seat, and said, 'Good night, was it?' He chuckled, congratulating himself on his own perspicacity, and turned back to the road.

When we got back to Hoxton Square, the last of the Friday-night revellers were wandering home bewildered in the morning, shambling across the streets like extras in a zombie movie. The cold had deepened, and the chill of the wind was replaced by the bone-deep freeze of winter. The man who took our taxi was white as a sheet, his jaw moving as if to chew up his teeth, and he looked so grateful for finding a cab that I thought he was going to cry when he gave the driver his home address. I felt sympathy for him. The waters of the party had receded and left him stranded at the high-tide line, quite exposed and alone. His T-shirt and tracksuit top, perfect for the warmth of the dance floor, were pitifully inadequate against London in January. I paused in front of my flat. I pretended to be checking my pockets for the keys, but I was preparing myself for the plunge back into domestic space. We had been gone for about five hours, but as I looked up at my windows, still lit to simulate life, I felt like we had been away for years.

I unfolded the sofa bed for Jessica. It was not made up, having never been used, and the springs squeaked with surprise. I had to move some of my stacks of files to pull the mattress all the way down. Undone work reproached me from the grey boxes. I heard the mournful wail of a siren in the distance. I smiled at the sound. It was not merely a portent of disaster, but the sound of someone taking responsibility, taking the first steps towards making something right. I retrieved fresh bedclothes from the cupboard, and I was happy to have someone else to tuck in the other side of the sheet. She unzipped her holdall and took out her washbag. I showed her to my bathroom. I kept an extra stash of toiletries, toothbrushes, toothpaste, combs and conditioner for my female guests, and I told her she could take anything she needed whilst I finished off the pillow cases. I was unused to having a woman in my flat who was not entirely sexually accessible, and it made me perform every action with an exaggerated formality. I gave her a wide berth when she came in from the bathroom, pressing myself against the bookcase to allow her to walk around the bed. She sensed my awkwardness. I offered her a T-shirt to sleep in, and she took it. She pulled off my jumper in front of me, possessing the centre of the room with the challenge of her bare white stomach. She stripped down to her bra, two simple cream cups holding her breasts. She lowered her trousers with no shame, kicking them off with the freedom of a woman preparing to dive into the sea. I did not want to notice it, but I found myself thinking how well she had kept her figure. She lifted the duvet up at the corner and slid between the sheets. I heard the sound her skin made against the material, a whisper like wind in long grass.

'Was there something else you wanted?' she asked me, her eyebrows raised in mock innocence.

I grinned at her and gave her the finger. Before I left the room, I turned back on the threshold and asked her a question. 'Jessica,' I said, 'how much money do you have?'

'Oh, I don't know. About fifty. Why?'

'That's not what I meant. How much money do you have total? You know, savings, current account, credit card, any shares?'

She looked at me with an uneasy smile and propped herself up on her elbow under the covers. 'Why do you want to know? Are you going to give me some investment tips?'

'Humour me.'

She shrugged. 'I don't know. Maybe a little over sixty thousand. I was saving for the deposit on a house, but I never really seemed to find anything I liked. Ditto car. Why, how much have you got, big-shot lawyer?'

I did not need to think about it. I knew exactly. 'Seven hundred and sixty-five thousand.'

She whistled. Despite myself, my chest puffed a little with pride, like a sail in the wind of her whistle.

'Tell me you asked that for some reason other than my humiliation,' she said. She was trying to curb the hope in her voice.

'I need to think about something.'

'We can't buy the picture back,' she said, dropping back on to the pillow in disappointment. 'I thought about that too, back when I first read the article. Even if we could find Augustus White, and even if he still had it, and even if we could convince him to sell it back to us, even at the original price, we still wouldn't be able to raise half the capital.'

'You're right,' I said, but I hadn't been considering anything like that. I needed time to puzzle out a different option, and so I let her think she had settled the matter. I said goodnight to her and flicked off the living-room light. After a second's thought, I left the door between our two rooms slightly ajar. I let my clothes lie where they fell, and dropped into my bed. I had changed the sheets that morning in anticipation of my prostitute's arrival, and the linen felt crisp and clean, and smelt of citrus. I found I did not recognize the person I had been twenty-four hours previously, preparing methodically to fuck a stranger. I knew this distancing was an illusion, that there was no real change in me for the better, but it felt good nonetheless to disown my past from the cosy confines of the present. I knew myself too well to say 'never again'. The warmth of the duvet soothed me, and the soft mattress supported my tired limbs. Not wanting to waste the next day, I set an alarm for eleven o'clock. I pictured Jessica's smile when I woke her up at lunchtime with croissants from the bakery on New Street. I had a quick nightcap, a single slug from the bottle in my bedside cabinet. I screwed the cap on and replaced the bottle at the back of the drawer under a sheaf of papers. I touched my hand to the light twice, and the bulb dimmed and then went out. There was still no sign of real daylight. The sun would not rise until about eight o'clock.

Jessica called out, 'I've thought about you a lot, James. I'm so glad that we're here, whatever the reason.'

I smiled in the darkness. Her happiness was important to me. I was happy she was happy. I could not say that about anyone else on earth. I listened for her breathing through the gap in the door, and when I heard it level out into easy repetitions, I fell asleep in peace.

17

As the start of the new academic year approached, I began to construct elaborate fantasies of the same type with which I had peopled up my room with blondes and redheads in the solitude of the beginning of my first year. Inspired by loneliness, they were gaudy, crude tableaux of wish fulfilment. They involved Francis crying tears of regret, Jessica sitting on the floor outside my room begging to be let back in, heading to the bursary to find my rent and fees already paid by Lisa. All three of them would prostrate themselves in apology, and slowly I would become merciful and allow them to do things for me. Eventually I would tell them what I had done over the summer, and they would absolve me by acknowledging that it was their fault. I knew how pathetic these daydreams were, but they gave me pleasure nonetheless, and I had shed the inhibitions of self-respect that might otherwise have curbed them. I came back to Cambridge armed with an arsenal of grievance. I resolved not to talk to any of them, and to ignore their first attempts at getting in contact with me, so they would gradually realize that something was wrong. I wanted my anger coaxed out of me.

As it turned out there had been a rapid inflation of trouble over the months since I had seen the others, and the currency of recriminations I had hoarded over the summer were almost worthless in the new climate.

When I unlocked the door to my room and flicked on the lights, I was confronted with the bare bones of my easel crouched in the corner. The sight of it filled me with revulsion, a reaction so strong that it frightened me. I folded it up as quickly as I could and shoved it violently to the back of my closet. I had returned on the train, unable to bear the thought of a silent journey with my father, and so I had been able to bring only the bare minimum, two bags full of clothes and sheets. The room smelt of the girl who had used it over the summer, a faint cosmetic odour like a residue of foundation powder over all the surfaces, and so it no longer felt like my space. I dropped my luggage and climbed out on to the roof, up to the scene of so much happiness over the summer. I smoked a cigarette, and stayed out there for as long as I could. I bathed my face in the late September sunshine.

In order to let the others stand a chance of realizing how angry I was with them, and how much work they would have to do to gain admittance to my goodwill, I decided to pay Francis a brief visit later that evening. I would drop heavy hints, and be elusive when he asked when we could meet for a proper catch-up. I had no idea when he was due to return, but I had come back on the last possible day before the beginning of full term. To come up any later would be to miss the registration date, and it was his policy to minimize confrontation with the college wherever possible. I went to the porters' lodge to get the address of his new rooms. As a third year with good academic results (thanks to Lisa's administrative alchemy) he had a great set, a bedroom and living room with en suite situated on one of the staircases under the colonnade of Nevile's Court. With his change of address, Tudor had absorbed the fake Picasso back into its collection, swallowing it without comment. I walked out under the stone gaze of the saints above the library, and saw that the light was on in his window. As I came to the bottom of the staircase, I was surprised by the sight of Jessica rounding the bend at the top. She was tanned and skinny, and had on ripped jeans, flip-flops and an entirely superfluous set of sunglasses.

I felt cheated of my control of our first meeting. Surprised like this, I was cowed into civility, and my carefully crafted coldness was forgotten. 'Hey, Jessica.'

'Oh, James. It's good to see you.'

'How's Francis?' I asked, trying not to show how much the question meant to me.

'He's lost all his money,' she said. It was a bald statement of fact, unseasoned by emotion. As she came closer

I saw that she wore her tan like a mask, and underneath looked deathly pale.

'How could he? You know Francis, it's deliberate melo-drama.'

'No, no, he's telling the truth. I was there, at least for the end of things. Not that he would let me help him. I think he just wanted a witness.'

'How can you lose a million pounds in three months?' I asked, still unwilling to believe her.

'Oh James,' she said, with a tired smile showing a brief flash of amusement at my naivety, 'believe me, it's easy if you know the right people.'

I baulked at her condescension, but kept my focus. 'Where did you pick him up? What people?'

'What does it matter?' she said, and closed her eyes.

In that moment, I perceived a terrible thing. She had invested too much of herself in the risky enterprise of Francis Manley, and now that the creditors were clamouring at the door she had no exit strategy. She must have realized it some time before, as her lack of resistance spoke of resignation. There was not even hope to leaven her love, for something in her manner showed that the delicate strings that had kept her image of Francis afloat, performing his charming antics for her with the promise of redemption inherent to all life, had been cut one at a time by disappointment, until the body lay wooden and motionless on the floor, revealing the vital movement to have been an illusion all along.

I had felt the same bitter disappointment at the way he had abandoned me to my normal life. Caring for him had become an empty ritual – she was like a priestess lighting candles for a god she knew to be dead, performing a service that had lost the excuse of purpose. But at least she had the excuse of time; she had come to know and love him when he was at his zenith, before his true nature had begun to protrude, a hard seam of self-destruction that endured long after the passion and zest through which it ran had worn away. I had bound myself to him in his failing moments. I had wilfully entered a falling building, blinded by the beauty of the architecture. I felt the double pain of having my friendship abused, and having sanctioned the abuse.

I dismissed these thoughts with a shake of the head. They were mostly born out of anger for the way I had been ignored over the summer. Jessica was no more in despair than I was a fool, or Francis a doomed soul. Her resignation was just tiredness. This was the melodrama of unsatisfied grievance. I was sure that Jessica was exaggerating.

'Do you know how he was living when I got there? Every day he would go down to the Monaco Beach Club. His father has had a cabana there for years, and he rang up personally to say that if Francis appeared, he should be denied admittance. Their beach hut smells of that pipe he smokes, so it's like he's always there, disapproving while we sunbathed. The porters love Francis though, they've known him since he was six years old, so they let him in as long as he promised not to sign for anything on his father's account. He would walk down to the club with a snorkel and flippers, and swim along the pebbles by the promenade hunting for jewellery. The women down there, they're old European princesses, dolls for the Russian mafia, black girls who come down with the big hip-hop stars on their yachts. They wear their day-pieces whilst they sunbathe, and sometimes they forget to take them off when they go swimming. Francis would find pearls, gold earrings, wedding rings, all glittering in the sun shining down through the clear water. One afternoon by the pier he found a pear-cut diamond necklace with a stone as big as the nail on my pinkie, resting down between the huge flat rocks. It's three yards deep there, and he made his ears bleed diving down for it, but it kept him in the casino for almost a fortnight. I couldn't stop him, no matter what I said. Every morning he'd promise me he was going to stop, and every night he would go back. Every night he was drunk and high. It was like he was doing it on purpose. I can't tell you what it was like, James. At first it was just his usual thing, stuffing every minute with life, going his own glorious road and all that crap – that's how he presented it to me. Then things started to go downhill, and just before the end something changed completely. I don't know what happened to him, but the last few days I was really frightened. We were staying in the Hotel du Cap, and sometimes he would come back and climb on to the balcony, and stand astride the railing, just looking out into the sea. I'd pretend to be asleep, but I'd watch him. Sometimes, I felt he was thinking about just spreading his arms and diving away from the building into the air.' She slumped against the wall and slid slowly down until she was sitting on the step. She put her head in her hands. I was still angry enough with her to take a little pleasure in her suffering. She too had left me, but I put my hand on the back of her neck to comfort her.

'Why didn't you contact me?'

She laughed, a short horsey snort. 'Why, what would you have done?'

'How did you drag him back here?'

'I didn't. He wanted to come himself. One morning he just packed up his things and told me that term was about to start. I had almost forgotten Cambridge completely, I was so used to worrying about him. He said he wanted to see you and Lisa. Kept saying he had to see you, had to get everyone back together again. He started saying that a lot when things suddenly fell apart at the end. I bought him his plane ticket home. We came straight from the airport. He still hasn't paid last term's rent.'

I was deeply touched by the fact that he had come back for us. For a moment, all was forgiven. Later, when things became clear, remembering it was like swigging from a bottle of wine in the full anticipation of pleasure, and finding the bitter, ruinous taste of vinegar.

'Did he really say that? That he needed us? At least now we can pay for him.'

'Yes,' she said, 'at least we can keep him. Keep him safe.'

'I mean, we're still rich.'

She did not say anything, but nodded.

'I want to see him,' I said.

'Be my guest. I'm going to get some sleep.' She rose from her sitting position on the steps, slumping forwards to get going down the stairs. Worry had worn her edges smooth – and made her unbearably sexy. It gave her an air of desperation, as if she was ripe for exploitation, and it would be the man's choice whether to protect or abuse her. At the same time she had the armature of her will bearing her up. She possessed all the heroism of the doomed altruist.

I knocked on Francis's door as I opened it. He was unpacking his things. His room looked tidy, and for some reason that made me afraid for him. He had a whole new wardrobe and a set of matching luggage I had never seen before, slightly scuffed and battered. He turned around as I came in and smiled at me as if I had gone out for something five minutes previously, and we were about to resume a conversation. I tried to see if there was anything noticeably different in his face, any-thing that would suggest the same sort of emotional

311

journey that I had been through over the summer. He looked perfectly happy, quite at ease, but I thought there was something manic about his happiness. If what Jessica had told me was even halfway true, his mood was dislocated from the socket of his circumstances. He had lost some weight, and his eyes were tired. All the resentment I had fostered towards him in my solitude and all my own unhappiness dispersed at the sight of him, or rather they did not disperse, but wearily took their place at the back of the queue behind my concern for him. It was simply not appropriate to make Francis responsible for those feelings. It would be like charging a child for the value of an antique vase he had broken whilst playing.

'Hello, James. You have to buy it second hand,' he said, indicating the trunks and bags, 'it looks so vulgar new, and none of the hotel staff will take care of you. New luggage means new money, you see. Papa taught me that.'

'Francis, Jessica tells me you're broke. What will you do for clothes next season?'

'Ah, but this time around I've been clever. I made classic choices when I still had the cash, you see? Wellcut suits in neutral colours, summer and winter, handmade shoes, wool and cashmere. Nothing faddy, it should last me for years.' He picked up items from the bag in a distracted fashion, and allowed them to fall back in.

'And after that?'

'I'm not really thinking that far ahead. Something will

312

come up. I'm going to be doing a bit more fighting. Do you remember that man we met in Vagabond? The friend of Augustus White? He's found me one or two matches in London.'

'Where will that be, Francis?'

He shrugged. 'He said it's mostly in private places.'

'Private like pubs or what?'

'Just private.'

He kept folding his clothes and piling them up on the bed. I wanted to catch his wrist to make him stop and look at me.

'How was your summer?' he asked.

Shame made my cheeks burn as I said, 'It was OK. I didn't do much.'

'Oh, you should have come out to Monaco. I'd have asked you if I'd known you were free.'

'That was silly,' I said.

'Why didn't you tell me you were around?'

'I didn't have your number, remember?'

'Oh well. Next year.'

'Yes.'

After that I made my excuses and walked back to my own room. I lay in my bed, racked with alternating currents of rage and concern.

The next few weeks were mostly taken up with a kind of mutual illusion, the maintenance of which was exhausting. The purpose of the game was to pretend that Francis was fine, and that we were having fun in his company. Jessica and I formed the supporting cast; Francis was the star. Lisa was not much in evidence, citing a major business deal in London as the reason for her absence. Looking back, I saw how neatly she managed the task of distancing herself from us. It was a difficult part for me to play, but made easier by the fact that I genuinely could not believe or understand how much Francis had changed in such a short period. Even when he was forced to tell us the truth several weeks later, even with this key I still could not quite unlock the mysteries of his transformation. He was fighting on the weekends down in London, and though he would come back with money he would spend it compulsively during the week. He returned from these weekends in the city with bruises and cuts, and would not let us come down to see him box. It was not just his face and body, but his knuckles that were bloody, and Jessica told me she feared he was being paid to fight without gloves. During the week we spent every day together as before, we went out and partied, took drugs and drank, but there was no pleasure in it any more. The evenings began to follow a set course: we would meet at about six for cocktails in the Vaults or Browns, and Francis would be in a good humour, already slightly slurring his words. Listening to him tell his jokes was like listening to a man with a stutter give a speech. Even the parts that were fluent and funny were marred by an excruciating anticipation of the next blunder. We would then move on to a bar or a club, where Francis would try to pick up girls. Sometimes he would succeed, as he was still possessed of his beauty and the rubble of his charm, and sometimes he would be too offensive or visibly drunk. I would sit with Jessica, watching him with other women. She would sip her drink in silence. She mourned their chaste companionship like a stillbirth, deeply and with a sense that she had no right. The more she suffered, the more attractive she became to me. I found myself at the end of the night lying in my bed, raiding the store of images of her naked body I had from the night at the hotel, the neat white scar on her belly, her little white teeth sinking into my shoulder as I pushed inside her and Francis held her legs open. I would masturbate thinking of her voice telling us to come.

If Francis could not find a girl, he would start a fight, and one by one we were barred from old haunts where the landlords and owners had often stood us a drink, or the bouncers let us slip to the front of the queue. Something within him was terribly different – the spark that had ignited the dry scrubland of Cambridge dinners and clubs had gone out, and so we were just killing time. The expression came to life: we were murdering time, drowning it in alcohol and choking it on smoke. Everything we did seemed like a washed-out version of something we had done before. The horrible thing was that at times he would really be just like his old self, fun would threaten to break through like a sneeze, a giant, socially awkward release. It was like catching sight just for a moment of someone you know to be dead, from behind or with their face turned away in a crowded shop, before realizing it is just a stranger.

It was on one such occasion that I made my only attempt to broach the cause of the change in his behaviour. It may seem strange that I did not approach him more than once, but Francis was no longer open to discussions on the subject of himself, his erstwhile favourite topic. He was always intoxicated or hung over, and both states had their own particular dangers. He would meet such sallies first with affectionate requests to lighten up, to stop being so serious, and then, if pushed, would become sullen and uncommunicative. To go so far as to suggest there had been a change in him was to shatter the suspension of disbelief, to admit that we were no longer happy, and such admissions invariably enraged him, or left him morose. It was the beginning of the evening, and he was on the up, clutching a glass in a steady hand and humming to himself, gazing out over the diners in the restaurant where I had been for my first dinner with Michael. Jessica had gone to the toilet, and I took advantage of her absence to get off one question at point blank range.

'Francis, did something happen to you? Is there something wrong? You know I would do anything for you.'

He looked down. He could not bear my gaze. He swallowed twice, as if something uncomfortable were trying to make its way up his throat. In the end he gulped it back down, and came up with a smile. 'Nothing whatever, James. Honestly, you're like Jessica, you've developed such a taste for worrying. You don't know what a strain it puts on me, always coming up with new things for the two of you to worry about. What on earth would you do with your time if I wasn't here?'

As the term progressed, the old Francis showed himself less and less, and was replaced by a man with glassy eyes and unpredictable moods. Our problems grew as even Lisa's faultless management of the Cambridge system showed the strain of his behaviour. She took care not to see him, but would do whatever we asked of her on his behalf. He was breaking windows, vomiting in courts, swearing at the porters, fucking girls in the shadows of the colonnade by his staircase. Lisa kept supplying him with essays, but he simply did not bother to hand them in, and if he went to supervisions at all he turned up drunk. He was coming close to being sent down.

In the midst of this disintegration I received a surprise and entirely unwelcome visit from an old friend. Returning home one morning from breakfast I opened the door to find Michael sitting in the armchair by my bed. I had left the room locked, but I always put the key on top of one of the cabinets in the kitchenette across the landing, and he had not forgotten. I was irritated by his invasion, as the room was in a state of squalor. I had taken to eating meals alone, buying food from the supermarket and consuming it in my room. The unmade bed was surrounded by empty Coke cans and plastic sandwich packs. I had not seen Michael in six months. He was wearing a checked shirt, black penny loafers and a pair of smart blue jeans. He had put on more weight, and he looked unbearably vital. The girth of his trunk looked like the result of growth, not inactivity, like a young tree staking a hundred-year claim to the space under its canopy. The blue shadow of his stubble looked like the mark of maturity. He was coursing with dynamism, and it exhausted me to look at him. I felt envious of his luck, of the difference between us, as if we had taken drugs from the same needle and I had been infected whilst he had gone straight.

'I hope you don't mind, old chap, but I let myself in.'

'I don't have anything to say to you, Michael. Please leave.'

'I will in a moment, but first I have something I need to say to you.'

I felt tired. I turned away from him and hung up my coat on the back of the door. 'Did Lord Soulford send you to spy?'

'He asked me to, yes, but I declined. I'm here entirely on my own behalf, and of course on Francis's.'

'I think you've already made your choices, Michael.'

Michael shifted in his chair, and nodded without looking at me. That nod was the closest thing we ever received by way of an apology. It was over so quickly, and his confidence reasserted itself so smoothly, that I immediately doubted whether I had seen it at all. He said, 'I didn't just stop thinking about the four of you, if that's what you're implying. Frankly I've known Francis a lot longer than you have, and I still consider him a friend, despite your best efforts.'

I hated the fact that even in this extremity, Michael could not resist the temptation to assert his social dominance, and in the face of such overwhelming evidence to the contrary. It filled me with a sudden fury that made everything quite clear, like the cleansing fear I had felt during our climbs. All my tiredness and confusion fell away. I made a conscious decision to take the social muzzle off my mouth and speak freely. 'With all due respect, Michael, fuck you. Francis's real friends will look after him.'

It did not have the effect I had hoped for. What I had said was such a direct contravention of the respect Michael demanded from the world that I fully expected him to launch himself out of his seat, cheeks scarlet and thinning black hair in disarray, bearing me to the ground under his flailing weight. Instead he smiled, a tight little grimace that held back inside whatever reaction he might have had, and after a moment quietly replied, 'It was not easy for me to come and see you, James. I am fully aware that, unlike the others, you never really liked me. I thought, however, that you might be the most likely to listen to reason, despite your personal feelings. Talk gets around, and if even half of it is accurate then Francis needs help. Help that neither you nor I are qualified to offer. You would not be serving his best interests by denying him the support that I can afford. Furthermore I might provide a bridge back to his father and family, something you are hardly well placed to accomplish. This ridiculous estrangement is damaging them both. I think that if you would allow yourself to calm down for one moment, you would see that I am right.'

As he spoke he chopped the air with the flat of his hand, a trick he deployed from the debating podium. He let his sentences flow and expand, until they acquired an inexorable rhythm. If anyone else had said this to me, or if it had been put in a different way, perhaps my reason would have broken through the roiling, irrational anger that clouded my mind, shedding light. Perhaps if I had just been less tired, or less in the mood for a fight. But it seemed to me that Michael had deliberately couched this in such terms that to do the right thing, I would have to accept a humiliating defeat at his hands. He had asked me to suspend my petty jealousies, and was trying to score points in the process. The hypocrisy of it was unbearable. I simply could not allow him to be right.

'What authority do you have to talk about his best interests? The only interests you know anything about are your own. If you came here to make yourself feel better about what you did, don't bother. I hear you're doing well for yourself – enjoy it. I hope it lasts, I hope you don't get fucked over the way you fucked us over. But don't you dare come back to me and tell me about how to be a good friend. You sold that right a long time ago. Fuck you, fuck you, fuck YOU!'

He raised his hands, palms out towards me like buffers. I rolled to a halt against them and stood panting. He stood up and took his coat off the arm of the chair. At his full height he was even more impressive. He looked older than when I had last seen him, and calmer. Success was starting to take the edge off his insecurity. 'I'm sorry you feel like that, James, for Francis's sake and for mine. If you need anything, let me know. You seem to be doing all right for yourselves these days. Some scheme of Lisa's no doubt, but if you need any money it was a good summer for me too. You don't need to speak to me about it personally if that would be a barrier, I've instructed Coutts that they're to give you any sum up to two thousand. If you want more I'm afraid we'll have to consult, however briefly. The number of my private banker is on the desk. Whatever you may think of me, I trust you not to steal. I think you're a decent chap, so please don't disappoint me the way I seem to have disappointed you.'

'Believe me, we don't need your money.'

He nodded again, thoughtfully. 'I was trying to offer my help, not my money. Excuse me.'

I moved aside to let him leave my room. I had a

sudden urge to run over to the roof and spit on him as he came out into the courtyard, but instead I ran to my bureau. I pulled my lighter out of my pocket and set fire to the business card I found on the blotting paper. I threw it out on to the lead sheeting. I watched the expensive card burn and crisp, a blue-green flame playing over the surface as some chemical ignited in the ink, the black ash curling up into the sky on the thermals.

I could not say for certain when I admitted to myself that there were reasons for my anxiety beyond Francis's welfare. It was probably around this time, and the catalyst was refusing Michael's offer. Until then, I had maintained a vision of Jessica and myself as stoics, going alone with Francis through thick and thin, spurning the rest of the world out of loyalty to him and to the ideal of friendship. After Michael's visit, however, I was forced to admit to myself another motive far less laudable. My vision of Jessica on his staircase had been a kind of premonition, fostering a growing unease that lasted the whole term, and came into bloom as I watched the ash sail over the parapet. The abstract guilt I had felt over the summer matured into fear, and took up permanent residence. We were bound to Francis by more than our loyalty: if he cracked, or talked to someone else, there was a good chance we would all get caught. I did not think I would survive in prison.

18

Later that week, Lord Soulford made an attempt to contact his son. He used Jeremy as an intermediary, and had him call up Jessica to try to arrange a time to see him. I believe that Jessica had reached the same conclusion as I had about our need to preserve Francis from a possible confession, because although we never spoke about our motives openly, at one point we discussed not telling Francis about the visit at all. The excuse we used to ourselves was that he was too emotionally fragile to deal with the issues raised by his father, but the real reason was far more sinister, a selfish need to keep him isolated. We came up with the notion of inviting Jeremy down without Francis's knowledge on the false promise of an interview, and then telling him when he arrived that his half-brother had changed his mind and did not want to see him. In the end, we both of us contemplated this option, and turned away from it in revulsion, a fact for which I am eternally grateful. It was dangerous to let them meet, but Francis could not continue to live the way he was indefinitely, and it was just possible that seeing Jeremy might be the first step towards a reconciliation with his father, and a return to stability. Besides, if we could arrange the meeting on our own terms we could control to a certain extent what was said. If we lost our place as middlemen, all control was gone.

Having established that they should meet, we discussed when would be the best time to broach the subject gently with Francis. If we talked to him in the morning we risked one of his petulant rages, as he would certainly be either hung-over or coming down. If we talked to him at lunch or in the evening we could count on a better mood, but he might claim not to remember the conversation the next day, and his claim might be nothing less than the truth. In the end we decided that Jessica would raise it with him at the last possible minute, just after lunch on the day in question, capitalizing on the faded bonhomie that still characterized his early afternoons without risking the conversation to the next day's oblivion. Whilst she marshalled him, I was to pick up his half-brother, and the four of us were to rendezvous at the Eagle.

I waited to meet Jeremy's train at Cambridge station, and greeted him awkwardly when he arrived. I had not known how to clarify the situation for him, to tell him that though Francis was to be informed of his visit, I could not guarantee that he would come to meet him. In the end I decided that there was no point in telling him at all; if Francis decided to come I did not want the fact that he might have stayed away hanging over them, and if he didn't then it didn't matter anyway. I would simply explain after the fact.

I took him to the Eagle. It was a ten-minute walk from the station, and we ran out of small talk early on and travelled in an uncomfortable silence. The sky swelled with clouds, and I had brought an umbrella from my room.

The meeting was scheduled for three o'clock. I knew they would be late, so I bought Jeremy a gin and tonic despite his polite insistence that he be allowed to pay, and settled down to wait with him on the wooden benches by the snug. He was deeply anxious, though I suspected the source of his discomfort was as much the thought of disappointing his father in a crucial mission as the prospect of seeing Francis. I could imagine his father, who so often passed him over in matters of importance, calling him into an oak-panelled study and laying weight across his shoulders one word at a time, until he stumbled out under the pressure. I sensed that the drink was not his first of the afternoon, and he drained it quickly, then sat staring at the empty glass. When I at last asked him if Lord Soulford's attitude towards his son had softened, the worry, the alcohol and the English imperative to fill an awkward silence all conspired to make him talk with a frankness I had not expected.

'The truth is that, for so many years, I think Francis was an embarrassment to our father. He was a constant, living reminder of the kind of indiscretions the other party members were able to tuck away in closets and drawers. He began to attribute all his failures to having him as a son; Francis was the great impediment to his progress into parliament. He's not a bad sort, and I know he never consciously took it out on him, but I don't think he could quite forget it either. Then things began to change and I think Francis became, well, useful, I suppose, in some horrible way. Papa's politics strayed further and further to the right, particularly on issues like immigration, and he kept a lot of the Little England voters for the Conservatives who might otherwise have been snaffled up by something more extremist. No one else in the party could get away with it, but I remember every time he made some outrageous speech or comment, he'd go down to Farleigh, and the next day there'd be a picture in the *Telegraph* of Francis and him having scones with cream and jam at the tea rooms in Red Rice, and you wouldn't hear a peep against him after that. It made him . . . valuable – to the party, I mean. He was their double champion, invincible against accusations of prejudice, a living embodiment of Conservative commitment to multi-cultural Britain, but still rooting for England, England. I've never been as clever as Francis, but I can live with that. Cleverness isn't everything; in fact I think it can put the kibosh on many a promising career. But I do wish he couldn't do that for Papa. I can't, you see. I can't be useful to him like that. It makes me quite angry, because I don't think my brother appreciates it at all. To tell you the truth, I think he rather resents it. If I could do it, I would be thrilled. I'd love to be an asset to him instead of a worry.'

It occurred to me as I listened to him that our arrangement had in it something of the confessional. We both sat on the wooden pew, staring forward and away from one another towards our drinks, and the upright of the carved oaken arm between us served as a divide. It made me wonder if Jeremy had ever had the courage to articulate these thoughts before, or whether the presence of a stranger asking questions had acted as the catalyst to years of unformed guilt, veiled from his consciousness by a lack of immediacy. I felt, as a priest must feel, sympathy and disgust in equal measure. Sympathy for his pain, for his not being Francis, a pain that I could empathize with all too well, and which must be greatly exaggerated by their genetic proximity. His lack of intelligence was something of a mercy, as he would never fully appreciate how cruel the hand of nature had been. But there was disgust too, for his passive part in this conspiracy, for his stupidity, and most of all for the aspects of myself I saw in him.

It became apparent as the minutes wore on that Francis would not come. I was afflicted by the deeper certainty that, even if he did, Jeremy's ingenuity was not up to the task of making him take the first step towards a reconciliation. Only a resurgence of the natural love between brothers could have achieved that, and Francis was becoming impermeable to love. At about four o'clock I walked him back to the station through the grey drizzle. I held up my black umbrella over the two of us as we went, tilted forwards against the wind. We walked in silence.

At the station we shook hands, and I asked him, 'What will you tell your father?'

'I'll tell him that Francis is safe and well, but that he isn't ready to speak to him yet.'

This made me so sad that I wanted to hug him. I wished with all my heart that it could be true. I put out my hand and shook his firmly before showing him to his train.

Later, I guessed that this half-hearted attempt at contact must have been worth more to Lord Soulford than all the money and trouble his son had cost him in the past. He could say to himself, and to others (once even to an interviewer in *The Times*), that he had tried to bring Francis back into the fold, that others had lied to him about the true state of his son's welfare, and that he had been cheated of his chance to save him. He thus neatly laid a blame at Jeremy's door which the poor boy was not equipped to handle. I am inclined to believe that Lord Soulford's ignorance was rather more constructive than he cared to admit. He never deigned to call or visit in person.

When I asked Jessica what had happened, she said she had found Francis in an excellent mood that morning, and he had readily agreed to come to the meeting. Then, on the walk to the pub, he had simply bolted, running away down Green Street and across Market Square. She had called after him, even chased him a little way, but he was a quick runner. I asked her where he had gone, and she shrugged and said he hadn't come home.

We might have spent more time trying to make Francis see his half-brother, but very soon after that, everything became irrelevant, because he told us what was wrong. It was then I learnt why he had been so desperate to see us again, and the true value he placed on our friendship.

19

It had been decided that I would speak to Lisa. Jessica said she was too tired, and besides someone needed to be with Francis almost all the time now. He had abdicated all responsibility, and keeping him out of trouble was a full-time job. I called Lisa up and asked her to meet me at the Slug and Lettuce. It was a pub we never went to, an anonymous franchised space with standard chrome and pine fittings and uniformed bar staff. I chose it because it was neutral turf. I had not seen her in three weeks, and I knew there was something to be feared from her conspicuous absence, as she did nothing by chance. I had planned to make small talk, to remind her of our personal relationship, perhaps even to try to draw her into a little nostalgia, but she turned up in an elegant charcoal-grey suit, which threw me instantly, and was so brisk and efficient in her bearing that all my little spring of gossip dried in my throat. She bought me a coffee from the bar, banishing my attempts to pay with a wave of her hand. I was outmanoeuvred, as even a gift of coffee might have provided me with a little emotional leverage with which to shift her. When she sat back down and asked me what I wanted, I just came right out with it.

'Francis didn't just lose a million in Monaco. He lost four million. If he doesn't come up with it, they say they're going to kill him.'

Despite myself, I relished the melodrama of my revelation. I sat back proudly, waiting for her reaction. For a while she stayed silent, leaving the conversation ajar, and background jazz from the wall-mounted speakers drifted across our table. It did not seem like the silence of shock. She seemed to be weighing her options calmly. She stirred sugar into her black coffee with a neat, deliberate motion, tapped the teaspoon twice on the porcelain rim and set it down on the saucer.

'I know.'

For a moment, I was too astonished to speak. 'What do you mean you know? Did he tell you about this?'

'Nah. But a debt that size doesn't stay private for very long. It's already been auctioned, haggled over, sold on. When Francis started acting loopy, I started asking questions in London.'

'How long have you known?' I asked.

'About a week.'

'And who has the debt now?'

'I can't tell you that.'

'Why not?'

'All right, I won't. What would the name mean to you anyway?'

'I don't know. Maybe I could . . . How did he get that much credit?'

She took a sip of her coffee. 'These people aren't like fucking Barclays, James. They don't take a look at your credit history and see if you can make the monthly payments. They look at your friends, they look at your family and they say, "How much can they all afford to lose?" because, as fucked up as the world can be, at the end of the day most people won't choose a nice house over a dead son.'

'I'm not sure that's true of Lord Soulford,' I said.

'Me neither. I don't think it is,' she replied. 'I think we were Francis's security. I think he put us up, they checked us out and gave him the money. You should have a good hard think about that when you're writing out your cheque.'

'They'll really kill him?' I asked.

'It's a strong possibility. He's made the debt public now, it has to be payment or punishment. And let's face it, James, I love Francis, but someone was going to.'

'What do you mean by that?'

She shrugged, her matter-of-fact shrug, an urban gesture that I imagined must come from repeated confrontations with an aggressive reality. It was unanswerable. 'Look at him. He looks doomed. Always has. You can just tell he's going to get knocked off, sooner or later. Suppose he speeches you. You give him this money today. What you going to give him tomorrow? Because he'll come knocking.'

This speech was only partly authentic. She had betrayed herself in the slight slide into rude-girl patois. I had heard her use that voice too many times when trying to front a taxi driver or forge a discount. But her words connected, I could not fend them off. Despite myself, I attacked her.

'You set us up with these people. You introduced them. You have to help him. This is your fault as much as it is his.'

'Sure,' she said, and got up to go. She threw her phone and wallet back in her bag like a merchant shutting up shop, bored by the buyer's haggling. This was Lisa's great strength – she had the veto of walking away. Her separate lives, her many friends, her own fortune; if you fell out with her, she could just cut her losses. She could become one of her other selves, and I was painfully aware that these friends were all I had.

'Please, please, that was unfair, I'm strung out.'

'You know what?' she said. 'I think part of you is enjoying this. Part of you wants to play the hero, because then he'll owe you, and then . . . what? What will he do to pay the debt to you?'

I did not answer this, and lowered my head.

'James, you can't win,' she said, and her voice had dropped its air of implacable realism. She almost sounded kind. 'Take your cash. Go have fun. Leave Francis to sort out his own mess. Take care.' She put her hand on my shoulder, then patted it twice in quick succession. I grabbed her hand through her coat as she turned away, and pulled her close to me. For perhaps the first time since I had met her, surprise filled her dark eyes. A group of students drinking at a neighbouring table looked over to us in mild curiosity, sensing the ripple in the sterile peace of the bar.

I spoke quickly, in a low voice. The words were ugly, and I wanted them out of my mouth and away from me as quickly as possible. 'Francis has three choices: pay up, die or go to the police. If he can't choose the first one, what do you think he'll do?'

Lisa shook her hand free. She did not look at me, but walked unhurriedly across the pub. She paused in the doorway as she felt the wind, and lit a cigarette before stepping out into the cobbled street.

I sat there and thought about Francis. I considered the possibility of taking out a loan and putting it on a dog. I sized up Lord Soulford, dropping a stone into the well of his hatred for his son and listening for the 'plink' that would mark the bottom. I even thought about trying to find these people myself, to go and speak to them on Francis's behalf. I thought of getting him out of the country, or into a secure place. Even through my fear and sadness, I was aware of the gift that he was giving me. As ever, he made me feel important, he elevated my concerns to the plane of life and death. I went back to my room and lay on my back looking at the ceiling, smoking. I wondered how I was going to break it to him that Lisa had abandoned us, that he might be about to die after all. I pictured his acquiescence, his gentle nod and rueful smile.

Later that night, I went out to get a sandwich from Marks & Spencer. When I got back I found a note from Lisa slid under my door. It said: 'Meet me in Ha Ha's at ten. Don't call, I've changed my number.'

I put on my overcoat against the wind. The storm drains were clogged with dead leaves and water pooled by the kerb. The wet cobblestones glistened dark and slick in the light of the lamps. When I pushed open the heavy glass door of the bar, Lisa was sitting reading the papers just inside the entrance. She was no longer wearing the suit, but had changed back into a velour tracksuit top and baggy pale blue trousers, her Puffa jacket slung over the back of the chair. I did not dare read this as a good omen, but I found her less intimidating. She had a backpack at her feet. She did not have a drink in front of her. I wasn't quite sure where we stood following our earlier meeting, but I thought it was better to decide we were still friends.

'Would you like something?' I said, indicating the bar with my hand.

'No thanks. Sit down, this won't take long.'

I sat down beside her, and she tossed the paper back

on the chrome rack. The door opened behind me, engulfing me in a blast of freezing air.

'You can have the money,' she said. She was looking me straight in the eyes, and I was aware that some kind of response was required. I rose awkwardly to try and thank her, mumbling my gratitude, not really feeling anything beyond surprise. She waved me back into my seat, a look of impatience stealing across her face. 'You can have the money, but I ain't doing you a favour. I want something for my million. I don't ever want to see you, or Francis, or Jessica again. I never want to speak to any of you again. I've changed my phone, and I'm moving rooms. If you accept this deal, and take the money, I'll take a nod in the street as a breach of contract. If you breach, I will get the money back from you personally. That's a fact, not a threat. I've had a chat with Augustus White. He's been keeping one eye on you, and we've come up with a story you can tell the police if you get unlucky. I'm not in it, and neither's he. He's taken a personal interest in my future, and if you break this deal he'll make it his business.'

She removed a black file from her bag and slid it across the table, her palm and fingers flat against the binding. 'It's got dates, times, where you put the money etc. You sold the picture anonymously over the internet; you never met the buyer. Learn it and burn it. You get me?'

Part of me could not believe that Lisa was serious. Part of me knew she was. Her face was completely blank, her tone neutral, but I could see that her fingertips and knuckles had gone white with pressure where she pinned the file down on the chrome tabletop. In the throng of alien emotions, I caught sight of a familiar one – I recognized admiration for her. She was doing what Jessica and I could not, and doing it well. She was cutting her losses. Then I lost sight of it, and the whole crowd overwhelmed me, trampling me underfoot. I felt exhaustion engulf me in a wave of indifference.

'Fine,' I said. 'Where do I find the money?'

'Wire transfer. It'll be in your numbered account on Monday. You tell the others exactly what the deal is. You were always handy with words, I'm making that your responsibility.'

Before she got up to leave, she took my hand. The contact was so surprising it ran through me like an electric shock. I could not remember ever feeling Lisa's skin before. It was smooth and cool

'I'm sorry, James, I like you, I like all of you. I want to help you all. But I can't afford this no more.'

When she left, I felt another cold blast of wind on the back of my neck. I picked up the file, and before I left I went to the bar and ordered a single whisky.

Parting with the money was, for me, the easiest part of the process. Jessica treated it like pulling off a plaster, a painful experience best dealt with quickly, but it was almost a relief to me, since with the money went my

337

capacity to take responsibility for Francis, to pay his bills and keep him out of trouble. I had spent barely a penny of it myself; all it had done in the four months it had spent in my account was to accrue a healthy portion of interest. With it gone I felt the blissful release of someone who disclaims any hand in their own fate.

We no longer trusted Francis to hold the cash for so much as a day, and he no longer disputed our right to distrust him. This saddened me in a way I had not foreseen, for though I had feared an argument with him his meek acquiescence was worse. He had lost the will to pretend. He had taken Lisa's withdrawal harder than either Jessica or me. I think that somewhere in his imagination there survived a peaceful corner reserved for our mutual happiness, and neither money nor parties nor drink nor drugs were part of the vision. But with the loss of one of his friends, one of the pillars supporting this private space collapsed, and the dream was finally gone from him completely. Now at last the mania that had possessed him during the first weeks of term abruptly vanished, leaving him alone to face its consequences.

He had an account number into which we were supposed to transfer the three million. The debt had gathered speed faster than the interest being paid into our accounts, but his creditors indicated they were willing to take what we had and write off the remaining thousands. We knew Francis too well to believe that the account number was real, so there was a delay of two days whilst they sent a letter of confirmation to Jessica. The message came on a piece of paper with a letterhead, a property company with a London business address, and it was coded as a request for payment on building supplies. It bore the legend 'Final demand' in red at the top. With this confirmation, we made the transfer of funds. We skimmed off five grand to last us the rest of the term. We considered taking more, but decided against it. The bankers asked no questions, just as Lisa had said in her notes. After we had completed the transaction, we waited for some signal that the money had been received, but nothing happened. The three of us were holed up in Francis's room watching movies on Jessica's laptop. Whenever we ran out of films, one of us would walk to Borders and buy a couple more disks. We watched thrillers, horrors, comedies and teen flicks, but no gangster movies and no romantic comedies. We binged on entertainment for seventy-two hours, trying to keep the lights in the cinema down, and in all that time I successfully thought about nothing. By the end of the first week, we took our creditors' silence for acceptance. Lisa had at last cut us off from her services in accordance with the terms of our deal, and as the danger cleared I realized I had the first draft of a seven-thousand-word dissertation on A. E. Housman, an author whom I had never read, to hand in before the end of term, and no idea where to start. I had effectively skipped a whole year

of study, and I was missing basic skills that my contemporaries had mastered. For Jessica, who had entered
her final year, the problems were even greater. I took care
not to ask Francis about the future of his studies. I
returned to the college library, which was only a hundred
yards from his room, and prepared to start working. I
eased my mind down into this simple disaster like a
battered body into a bath of warm, scented water. The
librarian smiled at me and asked me if I had been away
on exchange. My old life, the one that predated Michael's
entrance through my window, was waiting to enfold me
in thick obscurity. The battle seemed to be over.

We continued to see each other almost every day as the
Michaelmas term drew to a close; Jessica and I met
for lunch at the University Library, and Francis would
come and have coffee with us in the afternoons. These
conversations were cordial, and that fact alone should
have frightened us – the things that needed to be said,
the apologies and pledges, were too large, and so rather
than take them on we fell back on empty civility. The
canteen at the library was full of students and research
fellows servicing their bodies after hours of solitary study,
cracking their backs and blinking with surprise to find
themselves back in the twenty-first century, and I liked
the restful air. One tutor was there every day in a pair of
cords held up with baler twine and sporting a wild beard,
and he set the tone for the place; total abandonment of
the self was sanctioned in the pursuit of knowledge. I

wanted to lose myself, and Jessica and I talked mostly about our work. Both of us, I think, sensed that the exhausted peace we were experiencing was not shared by Francis, but we had no energy to investigate further.

His behaviour in the first part of term had left serious problems in its wake, and he spent much of his time shuffling between tutor, dean and bank manager in an effort to avoid being sent down. He looked awful, and the receding waters of the drugs had sucked away the last of his charm. It became apparent that the things that had been making him ill had also been sustaining his wit, and so his efforts to arrest his descent seemed like a pyrrhic victory. His boxer's body seemed to have become both loose and small at the same time. He no longer walked the way he used to, bounding backwards and forwards to every point of interest, covering two miles for every one we actually travelled, but took slow, methodical steps with his gaze fixed on the pavement. His grace was all used up, and at mealtimes he fumbled his cutlery with a regular clatter that made other diners tut. His eyes were round and red around the dark centres, bloodshot like a Bedouin's from the desert. He had begun to see Michael again, and he had not mentioned the fact to us. Jessica had seen them drinking together at our old table through the fish-tank window of the Copper Kettle.

In the penultimate week of term he came to see us in the early evening, and told us that he had been for a consultation with a psychiatrist, and the college had agreed to allow him to write off his debts and repeat the year in return for a stint in rehab, and commitment to a programme of random drug-testing. The deal was a good one, and a testament to his residual ability to inspire affection. He spoke to us at the University Library. It was only six o'clock, but a bitterly cold night had already settled on the internal courtyard where we went to smoke and chat during breaks. My head was full of quotes and the thread of arguments, and his startling words formed an odd cocktail with the rarefied concerns of my dissertation.

'Michael has booked me into the Priory. He's paying for everything. I asked him if Papa was behind it, but he says not. I believe him.' He smoked as he said this, the cigarette mingling with the steam of his breath. Jessica had finished her fag and blew into her cupped hands, looking at Francis over the tops of her white fingers. I leant back against the cold brick wall and tried to give proper consideration to what he had said. The cigarette in my hand was one of his. Since we had signed over the money he was always trying to do little things for us, despite his penury.

'I guess that's good,' I said at last, 'if it's really what you need.'

'That's really great, Francis,' Jessica said. 'Will you excuse me? It's too cold for me out here.'

She broke away from us a little faster than seemed

natural, and strode with her head down towards the heavy glass door that led back into the warm hive of book-lined corridors. She was so thin now that she had to lean back on her heels and use her whole body to pull it open. I had not noticed how thin she had become under the jeans and jumpers.

'I think she feels like she failed you,' I said to Francis. I said it without inflection, a simple slender shard of information designed to pierce him to his core. After weeks of his impenetrable intoxication, I found myself relishing the novelty of being able to cause him hurt with the sacrifices we had made. It was easy work, and satisfying, like biting down on a wobbly tooth. 'She felt it was her job to protect you. Now you've given that job to someone else, she knows she failed.'

Francis winced, and looked at his feet. I felt his pain, hated myself for being the cause, but I felt I was getting back some control over myself by hurting him.

'I know I messed up, James, but there's something you don't know. I did something, something that was just for you and Jessica. I hope that one day it will be enough for you to forgive me.'

All the lordly authority was gone from that voice. The whining strains, the need for approval had grown, swelling out of the other tones with cancerous strength. I decided to ignore his coded reference; I knew him too well to fall for a hint of intrigue.

'I can't forgive you, Francis,' I said, 'I'd have to be angry

343

with you for that. The truth is I don't feel much of anything right now. I used to think feeling was infinite, that if things kept happening you kept reacting to them. But now I know different. It's too tiring, sooner or later you have to let it go or die of exhaustion. I've let it go. I don't care what you did or didn't do. It's better than forgiveness, it's obliteration, as if nothing ever happened. Take it as a gift. I have.'

That was the last day I saw Francis. I went back inside. When I left the library at seven I walked down the corridor that ran along the courtyard. He was still sitting there, a black figure perched like a raven on the wooden bench, his overcoat hanging down like wings at his skinny flanks.

Francis hanged himself five days later in rehab. He used a tie that he had bought from Thomas Pink with Jessica from the shop on Sloane Street. It was one of the few personal items he was allowed to take in with him. I found out because one of the people in his therapy group took a photograph of him before the authorities discovered the body, and it wound up on the internet.

It was Jessica who broke the news to me. Jeremy had phoned her from home. Post-mortem logic leaves no room for the subtleties of relationships, and the doctors first called Francis's father, and then Michael, who had been paying the bills. We found out indirectly. I noticed that morning that Jessica was not at the library, but thought little of it. I took our morning cigarette break promptly at eleven-fifteen expecting to find her in the courtyard, but she wasn't there. She came and met me at my desk in the main reading room, a long even pine surface with a green leather top and enough space for twenty crouched bodies. The light in the room came from huge plate-glass windows high up in the vault that showed regular slabs of slate-grey sky, and the warm glow of hooded reading lamps bouncing off books on the tabletops. In this odd mixture of warm and flat light, of multiple shadows from above and below, her face appeared gaunt, her eyes swollen and red. Her blonde hair was tied up, but several strands had escaped to form a dingy halo around her forehead. She asked me to come outside with her, and when I headed for the corridor that led to our smoking hangout she took my arm and pulled me gently in the other direction, towards the huge art-deco doors of the foyer. We walked out into the lifeless day. The wind was up, and it carried the voices of girls from the hockey pitch, crying to one another like gulls. Jessica led me around the back of the library, and presently we were walking away from Cambridge, through the gates of the playing fields and on to the flat, unbroken grass. Her bones felt as brittle as a bird's through the thick layer of her coat. As we trudged across the dull green reach of turf she told me what had happened, and the tears she had feared in public rolled down her cheeks. My eyes were watering from the wind.

At first, I could not think of anything to say. In the end I patted her on the shoulder and said, 'At least now no one will know.'

'What do you mean?' she asked, knowing already but unwilling to believe.

'I mean that now he can't tell anyone what we did. We're in the clear. I'm just trying to find some good in this . . .'

Jessica looked at me, with the wind blowing the stray strands of her hair around her face, and her ears and the rims of her nostrils chilled a coral pink. She studied me for a moment in disbelief, and then slumped, almost falling. I tried to hold her to support her, but she shook me off. We walked back to the library in silence. On the steps outside she kissed my cheek, and smiled at me, finding kindness, a sole survivor thrown from the wreckage. 'I'm sorry, James. You're obviously in shock. Come and see me tonight, OK? Just call if you need anything before then. It's not our fault. We did everything we could.'

She walked back towards the town, passing under Clare's memorial arch that stood like a bridge over a river of wind. It was then that I realized the truth of the curse I had called down upon myself. I found I truly did not feel the pain and the anger that were my right. I downloaded the picture of Francis from the internet and stared at it for hours, trying. I went to the funeral and cried along with everyone else, but I cried for myself. Francis was to be buried in London, ostensibly because his father wished his many friends to be able to visit him easily. People nodded in approval at this convenient explanation, but I guessed that the same reasons that had excluded him from the family trust kept him from the burial plot in the churchyard of the family's Northamptonshire estate. Even with his history and genes hidden under the soil, his headstone would strike a wrong note amongst so many venerable English ancestors. It was a miserable day, black and stormy, and the congregation huddled under dark umbrellas. I saw Lord Soulford across the grave and scowled at him, but even the sight of him weeping tears over his abandoned son did nothing. I felt no anger at his hypocrisy, no pity at his grief. We had not been invited, had in fact been conspicuously not invited, but I knew Lord Soulford would not risk the unsightly incident that would arise if he tried to eject us. Lisa was there, and in accordance with our agreement we said nothing to her. Her black suit was Gucci, the veil and hat handmade. She looked sexy. She came over and hugged us wordlessly before returning to her car, the driver holding open the door for her to climb back in. Jessica and I took the bus back from the cemetery into central London, and then the train from King's Cross. We were wearing black suits, and Jessica would from time to time start crying silently, dabbing at her tears with a wodge of tissues we picked up from McDonald's. The crowds of busy people parted for us, half in respect and half in fear, as if death were a disease that could be caught. I thought that the well of my soul had run dry.

Jessica and I saw less and less of each other over the course of the year. There was no argument, no waystone to mark the end of our friendship, just a drift that was too comfortable to arrest. I began to avoid the U.L., as the Wren Library was quite sufficient for my needs and close to my room. I continued my habit of buying films, and progressed from buying the movies to buying books about the movies and attending the special cinema nights held around the city. Most of the money I had left went to fund my habit, and the quiet darkness of the cinema became my retreat. I pulled it over my head like a blanket.

Jessica worked hard, and on the day her results were posted on the Senate House I watched from a vantage point in the Cambridge Bookshop for her to come and go, so I could see what she had got for myself. The results were due to be posted at four o'clock on a sunny afternoon in June. I stood by the door so I could see through the black iron railings that fenced off the stately enclosure from the street. Groups of students in shorts and T-shirts, trying to make small talk and drinking Coke, hung around the bright green lawn or leant against the warm white walls of the Senate House, where once the police had cornered us. The stones were cut from some kind of sedimentary rock, and when you looked up close you could see tiny white fossils trapped in the surface. Jessica was there with two girls I had never seen before, and a guy I recognized as a rowing blue from college. Her usual elegant pallor had been replaced by a healthy tan. I had seen the team sheets posted around college, and I knew she had taken up lacrosse. She looked happy. The man was huge, with amiable good looks. He had an aura of goodwill such as surrounds someone who has missed the point, and bases their contentment on a misunderstanding. We had laughed at him in the past. He would never have dared approach her when Francis was her guardian. When the results finally arrived, borne by a black-clad official, a hush spread over the group. Jessica hung back from the first wave of people crowding around the board, practising her trademark nonchalance, until the man began to laugh and pushed her playfully towards the steps. When she read the paper pinned to the wall she turned, threw her arms around his neck and kissed him. I waited until she had gone, walked out and found that she had taken a first, as had Lisa, though by what means I could not tell. I arranged with the college authorities to change my room. I did not go to the graduation balls, and by the time I returned for my final year the last human traces of what had happened, Jessica, Michael, Lisa and Francis, had all been washed away, with a new set of young men and women arrived to take their places. As the few other students who had known them intimately left, they took their names with them.

Some time later, I tried to write about Francis, to summon him up on the page and stop him slipping away from me, but I gave up after a few fruitless weeks. There is a version of *Hamlet* called the bad quarto, which was the first to be printed, in 1603. It is a pirated edition, designed by an unknown bookseller to cheat Shakespeare of his royalties. To make it, the pirate hired one of the minor actors, the man who played Marcellus, to write out what he could remember of the play. In the Globe Theatre, where Shakespeare's plays were first performed, the actors were only given pieces of paper holding their own lines. They never possessed a complete copy of the script. As a consequence Marcellus's largely irrelevant words are perfectly rendered, the speeches of other characters he shares scenes with are competent, and the rest of the play when he was not on stage is a garbled mess. It is a pointless jumble, the work of the finest mind in English literature filtered through the memory of a bit-part player, catching snatches in the wings, then scribbling them down months later in a scam by a venal London merchant. His ineptitude is funny only because we have the original to compare it to. In Marcellus's version, Hamlet's famous soliloquy begins: 'To be, or not to be, Aye, there's the point.'

When I studied the pirated version, I laughed at the men who wrote and printed it, at their greed and the unimaginable arrogance of paraphrasing Shakespeare. When I tried in my last year at Cambridge to write about

Francis, I felt like Marcellus. I was not a leading man. I was not on stage when the major events occurred. Much of what went on was wholly unknown to me. With the exception of the one memorable night at Corpus, I never saw Francis with his father. I missed him over the summer. I was not there when he, Jessica, Lisa and Michael were at the height of their friendship, and I was not there at his death. My own little lines, which I could remember with perfect accuracy, amounted to little more than exposition. I found that, in trying to capture his voice and the effortless grace of his presence, my attempts were as silly and inadequate as the bit-part player's, though in my case there was no authoritative text to do him justice.

20

When I woke, I felt the burden of the day press down on my chest. Just for a moment, I forgot the weekend and my guest. When I remembered, it was like the first day of the school holidays, when for a split second you think you have to get dressed into your uniform, and then suddenly realize you can lie in bed for as long as you like. I stretched and smiled. I could still hear Jessica's breathing through the doorway. It was eleven-thirty – I had outpaced my alarm. Suddenly afraid that my office might try to reach me, I switched off my phone. It gave me a shock to see the dead face of the screen where there usually sat the bright little graphic of blue sky and the grey bars of the signal. Looking through the window into the square, I was amazed to see that the rain had turned to snow. I piled the duvet on top of my shoulders and swung my legs out of bed. I hadn't really had a hangover in years, but I could feel the mess the whisky had left in my blood. I walked over to the window to look down into the road, and gazed out at the snow. A fine layer of powder had been reduced to slush in the streets, but was bravely settling on the scarred grass and the thin fingers of the trees. A group of children, their bodies puffed out like fat little men in layers of garishly coloured ski clothes, were having a fight with snowballs scraped off the hoods of the cars parked along the edge of the square. I could hear them shrieking with delight. A woman in black clothes was directing a small entourage of young men in the construction of an avant-garde snowman outside the White Cube gallery. The flat was warm and cosy, and as I stood above the heat streaming off the cast-iron radiator my breath misted the window. The sky was no longer grey but a brilliant, textureless white, a layer of cotton wool packing London up like a precious thing. I looked forward to sharing this day with Jessica. I decided we should wrap ourselves up like the children and head down to the South Bank, then spend the evening catching up properly in the warm belly of a pub I knew in Belgravia before an expensive dinner in the West End.

I threw on some clothes, an old jumper and some jeans, and edged quietly past Jessica's still sleeping body. She sensed me in the room, turning and mumbling at me, but did not wake. Perhaps she thought I was her boyfriend, but I entertained the idea that she knew it was me and trusted me enough to remain asleep. I was going to cook her breakfast in bed, but there was nothing in my fridge except champagne and ice cream, so I needed to make a run to the shops. I swung open the door of my apartment building. The smell of the snow filled the air, a clean mineral tang. I took a deep breath and the cold chased away the last remnants of sleep. Invigorated, I closed and locked the door. I heard the engine of a motorcycle gunning behind me, and when I turned back to the street it was to find an outrider in black leathers pulling up at the kerb and springing his kickstand. I nodded to him, and he nodded back. The effect was a little unsettling, as his features remained hidden behind a layer of black glass. I waited on the doorstep to let him pass on the pavement, but instead he walked straight up to me and stood there as if expecting to come into my building. As I looked at my reflection in the dark curve of the visor, I began to feel uneasy.

'Can I help you?' I said.

The man, to my great relief, lifted his helmet to reveal a squat bald head. 'You live here?' he said, politely despite the abruptness.

'Yes.'

'You know a James? James Walker?' He looked at me expectantly.

'What if I do? Who wants to know?' I said, and immediately wished I hadn't. The words sounded ridiculous in my plummy lawyer's accent, like a bad impression of a gangster movie. The biker laughed in surprise.

'I've got an offer he can't refuse. Look, mate, I'm just here with a package for him; do you know him or what?'

I looked at the man's bike again and saw the case over the back wheel with a laminated list of addresses strapped to the top. 'Oh Jesus, look, I'm sorry, I'm him, I'm James Walker.'

He went around to the back of the bike and produced a slim brown envelope from the interior. He snapped the elastic strings up and pulled out his list of addresses. 'Allright, Dirty Harry, sign here,' he said, spinning the clipboard towards me in a practised motion. I was so relieved that I let the joke slide.

'Is it something from the office?' I asked. He didn't look like one of our couriers, but I couldn't be sure.

'You a lawyer?' he asked.

'That's right.'

'You look like a lawyer. Yeah, it's from your office. Cheers, mate, have a good one.'

He fixed his helmet back on and swung his leg over the saddle. He kicked the engine into life with a galvanic spasm that made rider and bike bounce on the suspension, and pulled away from the kerb with a roar. I slid the package under my arm and walked to the shops. I usually relished the intrusion of work on the weekends, a fact that had seen me rise faster in the firm than many of my contemporaries, who had wives, husbands or children. Today though, whatever it was, it would have to wait.

Back at the flat I set the envelope down on top of the morning papers on the coffee table by Jessica's bed.

She had pulled up the covers over her head – only the blonde fan of her hair was visible spread out across the pillow. I closed the door between the kitchen and the living room and set about making breakfast. It had been a long time since I had cooked anything at all, and I had to chase a spider out of the pot I used to heat the beans. I made coffee and warmed croissants in the oven, and when I opened the door to the living room I expected a rich reward for my efforts in smiles. I had no idea whether or not Jessica ate such things, whether she had become a vegetarian or loathed carbs or preferred tea in the morning, but her tastes were irrelevant. It was my gesture that mattered, and I was as pleased with my efforts as a cat bringing its owner a dead mouse. I had looked forward to waking her myself, and catching that moment when her face changed from a startled surprise to a smile of pleasure as she realized where she was, but when I opened the door I found her already up and sitting at the table, wearing the T-shirt I had lent her the previous night. She had taken off her bra, and I could make out the shapes of her breasts under the thin cotton. She was staring at a piece of paper in her hand with a frown of concentration. It took me a few seconds to realize that she had opened the letter from my office.

'What are you doing?' I asked.

'Did you look at the envelope?' she asked without looking up. Something in her manner made me prepare for trouble, and I placed the tray down on the coffee table.

'Jessica, I don't want to spoil the mood, but you really shouldn't open my work things. They're confidential—'

'Just read it,' she said, holding out two letters to me, one in faded handwriting, the other on new paper, typed and signed.

'I'll read it when I'm ready, thank you. Now, would you like coffee?' I picked up the cafetière and cocked my head at her with a fixed smile.

'Please, James. Trust me. Just take a look.'

I snatched it from her to show my impatience, and fixed it with my most critical squint.

The top letter was indeed from a solicitor's office, but it was not a firm I recognized. It seemed to be a family firm, expensive and old judging by the watermark and the tasteful weight of the paper. Their business address was near Bond Street. I turned a professional eye on the document, easily slicing through the customary formalities to the kernel of intention. They were passing on a letter entrusted to them by a client, in accordance with his wishes. I looked at the sheet, its edges yellowing with age. The letter was dated 18 June, about two weeks after we had made the exchange and passed the night at the Baglioni. I knew the smooth, assured hand instantly. It was Francis's writing.

For a moment, I was too astonished to take in more information. The porous parts of my brain sealed over, and the words on the page simply bounced off the surface. I looked to Jessica for help, but her eyebrows were arched over wide blue eyes stunned into staring. I sat down on one of the old green leather chairs and laid the letter flat on the table in front of me, where it stuck on the waxy surface.

Dear James,

If you get this letter it means that we are no longer in contact. Perhaps you have finally grown tired of my fickleness, and cut yourself off from me completely. Perhaps I have set off for distant, monkey-infested shores in search of infamy and fortune (well, another fortune anyway), and am even now sipping a vulgarly named cocktail on a deserted stretch of volcanic sand. Perhaps you have caught me seducing your wife. Perhaps I have taken some sort of mortal oath, and ensconced myself in meditative silence at the peak of Everest. Whatever the reason, I do so hope that I remain in your thoughts.

I have placed this letter in my lawyer's keeping, so that it shall never be at the mercy of my own better judgement. There are any number of circumstances that might trigger delivery, but I don't want to spoil it by telling you what they all are: whatever has happened to you over the last few days should act as an explanation. Suffice it to say, James, that I have done something a little naughty, or else painfully good, and I wanted to warn you before others realized first. I wanted to tell you that I swapped the paintings. I couldn't help thinking that the whole thing would be so much better if we really got something for nothing – and so much more exciting, don't you think? When I drove the real picture down to be verified by the 'expert' I took the fake one with me, and after he had checked it over I swapped it in the car park. It was the easiest thing in the world. I simply left the real one in the room, then after he had gone took the fake one out of the boot and handed it to his heavies. I could barely contain myself, I was bursting with my own cleverness at the thought of how we stitched up that brute White, but I knew that if I told you lot then you would give the game away, and Lisa would try and make me give it back.

I sincerely hope you are pleased to discover yourself an artist whose works sell for millions. Please forgive me if you are not. Either way, you are now free to amend your plans as you see fit in the light of the truth. Jessica and Lisa will currently be reading letters to the same effect, allowing a few days to track them down. I always thought they would fall a little further from the tree than you and that, despite my best efforts, you would wind up being contactable. It is a terrible sign if this letter has found you quickly – it can only mean that you are leading a predictable life. I hope it reaches you months from now, stained with tea and coffee rings from mugs set down by foreign officials, covered with a hundred countries' stamps in sheaves as thick as autumn leaves, opened and read and reread by censors looking for a private code, with random words excised in black pen, finally arriving under your eyes on a silver tray, borne by a slave-girl, beside your morning glass of ambrosia in the warmth of a tropical sunrise. I hope above all that you are happy. Regards to your lovely father.

Francis Nyasha Manley

I reread the letter twice, then carefully folded it and returned it to the envelope.

'Is this another joke?' Jessica said, her voice cracking.

'I don't think so. Francis said something to me, just before . . . just before he went into rehab. He said he'd done something for us. I didn't really think about it at the time, he couldn't have said anything I would have believed.'

Jessica massaged her temples with the tips of her fingers. 'What does this mean?'

'We're safe,' I said, and then, 'We always have been.' The thought brought a tough bark of laughter up from my chest, as I thought about the years of surplus fear, stockpiled against a disaster that could never have happened. It was typical of Francis, I thought, to make death no barrier to his disruptive influence. The idea brought a smile to my lips.

'Safe from the police,' she said, 'but Augustus White . . . if Lisa gets this letter . . . do you think she'd tell him? Even if she doesn't, if they sell the painting and nothing happens he might get suspicious. He'd come after us if he knew we'd cheated him, wouldn't he?'

'I would,' I said, 'if I was him. Imagine spending a decade showing select guests your most prized possession, only to discover it's a fake. Those kind of people are at their most dangerous when they feel humiliated.'

'Since when do you know anything about people like Augustus White?'

'You don't work in commercial law for ten years without meeting a few gangsters.' I couldn't resist the opportunity to give my job a gloss of danger.

'But . . . but . . .' Jessica was close to crying. She had let her guard down whilst she had been with me, and this latest revelation caught her unprotected; she had lain her weapons aside, set down her sarcasm and her self-control, and was now ambushed waking from sleep. I felt the implications of the letter shiver through me like a heavy blow, but I found myself uninjured. It was a blow against the tethers holding me down, and it severed them utterly.

'I know what we should do,' I said.

'What?' she said, looking to me in hope. 'What should we do?'

I tried to let my feelings flow through me, without trying to control my words. 'I want to take the good part of what Francis taught us, the part before everything else happened. I want to be free. I don't have anything to live for here. I want to leave, to get away with the one person I still care for. It's what we always dreamed of, only this time we've earned it. This time it won't be stolen freedom, it will be ours by right. We'll put our money together. What's mine is yours. Eight hundred and twenty-five thousand. Do you realize how far that will take you in some parts of the world? We can leave, and we'll never work again. I want to see South America, China, Australia . . . We can start new lives, start to breathe again.'

As I spoke the name of each country, I felt its breath on the back of my neck, the peculiar scent and pressure in the air that hits you when the plane door opens on the runway. I could feel my words were coming up short, that what I was saying risked sounding trite, but I knew as she looked into my eyes that she could see the truth of it.

'James!' She laughed, though the tears were still threatening. 'James, that's crazy. I mean, my family are here, my job, my work, my flat. My boyfriend.'

'Yes?' I said. 'So what? You don't love them, any of them. Augustus White will be looking for us. Maybe Lisa too. I want to run away, but I want to run to something, not just from something. I believe we can do it. You have your passport, right? You said you always carried it in your bag.'

'Yes, I have it.'

'You see? It's perfect. It's the right thing to do.'

'And what about us, James?' she asked, turning her eyes away and shaking her head. Her voice dropped lower, the edge of incredulity gone. 'I mean, when we stop off in Cancún or Bangkok or wherever the hell you have us going, do you see us renting a double room or a twin bed? Be honest, because—'

'Don't say it,' I said, knowing that if she spoke her words could not be called back. 'Leave it. Whatever it is, we'll figure it out. I remember what Francis taught me. He showed me that most people use their imaginations and their intelligence to construct arguments against doing what scares them. Now, that's fine if what scares you is the wrong thing, but when it's the right thing . . . you and I are clever people, Jessica. We can sit here for hours and think up reasons, good, strong, reasonable reasons why we should stay here and face this out. And every second we sit here, we'll be binding ourselves in place, putting down roots, strengthening the ties. We only get this one chance. I won't risk waiting. I'm going, and I want you with me, as a friend, a lover, a sister, I don't care and I won't guess. Let your imagination fight on the other side. Picture us away from the rain, starting again. Free.'

I waited, kneeling in front of her like a man waiting to

become a groom. I had played my last card. I held my breath. I willed my conviction into her. I was already gone, I felt as if I was in a stranger's apartment, a stranger with whom I had conducted a decade-long affair, finally ready to leave. The files in the corner, the ballast of my life, were light and insubstantial, just the pages they had always been, a paper golem bereft of its magical life. The keys were a cold burden in my pocket, and I longed to cast them back through the letterbox, out of reach on the mat. The clothes in the wardrobe did not fit me, the bottle in the drawer could sit there and rot. My landlord could have my porn and TV in lieu of notice. I would go out into the street with my credit card and passport and the clothes I was wearing, and I would leave before my nerve failed me. On Monday the office would call, and my phone would ring and flash and vibrate in fury in the quiet darkness of my bedroom until the battery ran out. In time, I might even make it into firm legend, the young partner-to-be who couldn't take the pressure, and disappeared one snowy Saturday without a trace.

I thought of all the things that had happened to us, not with my usual cold and maudlin detachment, but with the new vigour I had inherited from the previous night. I thought of the parties and the fights, the gambling and drinking and glory and disaster. All this time, I had been mourning not Francis, but the idea of Francis, and the death of the search for a good life. The happiness we had felt together had been like the happiness of a cult, based on exclusion and the promise of final rewards. Francis had never recovered from his disappointment. It had destroyed him. I was stronger. It had taken me nearly a decade, but I was ready to let it go. All my adult choices had been made by default; I had flowed down the path of least resistance, waiting for some obstacle to present itself, a dam against which I could collect my resolve. Now I felt the strength to make a choice for myself. Happiness was so close to me, I thought my heart would break if I was denied.

When she finally spoke, she startled me as if from a dream.

'OK,' she said, smiling down at me. 'Let's go.'

'Then let's run!' I shouted, scrambling to my feet in delight, gripping her wrist before she could change her mind. 'We must go quickly. Don't stop to pack. Let's get out of here before it's too late.'

She picked up her handbag and threw a jumper on over the T-shirt; I took my wallet and passport from my dresser. All the fear and sadness that I had borne for years I was leaving behind me in my dark little flat. It had been with me for so long, I had forgotten that it was not my natural state, and I was almost afraid to be without it. I felt like a lifelong cripple who had been cured by a miracle, so sweet and sudden was the lifting of the burden from my shoulders. When Jessica passed me in the flat, both of us running and bumping into the furniture, our hands would meet, and lag in slow parting behind our bodies, making our arms stretch out straight. We threw together the essential fragments of our belongings, and were ready to run. Already, I could hear the jingle and thump of the keys as I put them back through the letterbox. Then the intercom buzzed.

21

'Hello? James Walker?' for a few seconds, I was able to entertain the fantasy that the courier had returned. Then the voice said, 'Jessica Katz?' and our infant happiness was dashed. There was only one person who could be looking for the two of us here.

The feeling that swept through me was like the calm that possessed my thoughts during our night climbs: the simplicity of survival. I looked through the slat blinds of the living-room window into the street below. There, sitting in the midst of the children's snowfight, was a white Ford Transit van. I could see a piece of the man at the passenger's side, a hairy forearm sporting a tattoo in blue ink too faded to make out the design, ending in a cigarette clasped in thick ringed fingers. The man pressing the buzzer was beyond my line of sight. The intercom buzzed again. 'Look, mate, we need to have a chat. I know you're in, I just watched you walk through the front door.'

I went to Jessica; I gathered up her bag and I pushed

her into the cupboard in my bedroom. She protested silently, pushing against me with her hands, but I did it so gently and so firmly that she could not resist. The intercom sounded again. Nothing was said this time, just the sound of the microphone crackling.

I checked the room, to make sure there was no visible sign of Jessica's presence. I pushed the foldaway bed back into place, covering the used sheets with the sofa cushions. Then I pushed the key symbol on the intercom and opened the door. The tread on the stairs was so heavy it seemed to make the glasses tinkle in the kitchen cabinets. I thought about the throwaway boast I had made moments earlier, about having met gangsters in my business. I had never in my life been in physical danger since the days of our midnight ascensions, and I was terrified at the prospect. When he reached the landing, he fulfilled the promise of his footsteps; he was perhaps six feet four, and his body rolled like a boulder across the frame of the doorway, blocking out the light from the hall. He came into the room and slowly shut the door behind him. He turned his massive back to me for several moments when he did so, and it was a show of strength. Exposing the blind length of his spine to me, knowing I would do nothing, established his dominance absolutely. He lingered over the moment when the latch caught, pushing so gently and precisely that the sound of the deadbolt falling into place was barely audible.

'Mr Walker?' he said, and put out his hand. I took it,

not knowing what else to do. His fingers were cold from the street. He did not tell me his own name, just looked silently into my eyes as he worked my arm slowly up and down. I felt the easy strength in his grip. 'Where's Miss Katz?' he asked, letting my hand fall back to my side.

'She's not here,' I said, and then briskly, 'Can I get you something to drink?' I thought that by showing I had not lost my manners, I would regain some of my power.

He ignored the offer, and nodded heavily, as if what I had said merely confirmed his sad suspicions. His eyes scanned the room. They came to rest on the table, and he walked over to it. I could feel the reverberation of his tread through the floorboards. 'Transvestite, are you, Mr Walker? I know you lawyers are a funny bunch.' He dipped two fingers into the ashtray, then held one of the butts up to the light. The end was smeared with gloss lipstick. He picked up another. The coal still glowed with heat. Jessica must have been smoking immediately before I returned with breakfast.

I was amazed that, despite the cold terror in my guts, my ego still felt piqued that this brute had outsmarted me. I made no pretensions to physical superiority, and if he had beaten down the door with his fists I would have felt the pious victim. But to beat me like this, by noticing a detail I had missed in my initial shock, that was galling as well as frightening. I considered facing him down, concocting some story about a female visitor, but decided there was no point. It was important to me to maintain the illusion of cooperation. If he searched the flat and dragged Jessica into the open by force, that would become impossible. I was used to tough negotiation, but if the encounter progressed to physical violence it would pass entirely beyond my experience and control. I went into my room, opened my cupboard doors and waited for her to emerge, keeping my eyes fixed on the carpet for fear of meeting hers.

'Expecting me then, were you?' he said as Jessica came out of my bedroom.

'Yes. You're here on behalf of Augustus White?' I asked.

'Who the fuck's Augustus White? No, mate, we're here to take you to see Miss Lisa. Would you mind following me down to the van?'

We came down into the street, and I saw that there were two men in the front of the Transit. The side was covered in orange dirt, and someone had written a football slogan with their finger on the side panel. Neither Jessica nor I had taken our coats, and the cold bit in to me. The back of the van was twenty feet from my front door, and so I had perhaps fifteen seconds in which to decide whether to run, to make it clear in public that something was wrong. The children and the young men and women milling happily around the square appeared to me as distant from myself and Jessica as the living must appear to the dead. If I shouted, or ran, it would mean relinquishing the last fragment of social normality. I was surprised by how fiercely I clung to it. I realized that the man behind us, massive and casual as a hill, had managed to leave me with no clue as to what to expect from Lisa. She might be calling us to consult with her, or she might have sent her goons to take us out to a patch of wasteland on the outskirts of London, never to return. If there was one thing I had come to remember over the last twenty-four hours, it was the thinness of the membrane between fantasy and reality. I felt the opportunity to act slipping away even as I made my deliberations. By the time we reached the van, I found myself still marvelling at my own indecision. It was almost a relief when the man swung the heavy door behind us with a thick clunk, as it settled the question.

We climbed into the back of the van, which contained four seats facing each other across the floor. The men sitting in the front seats did not look around. Jessica sat behind the front passenger seat, settling into the rough brown cushion and fastening her seatbelt. There was no fear discernible in her face. I sat opposite her and she smiled at me. Her smile righted me, and helped me to think more clearly. Whatever was about to happen to me, she would be with me. When our escort followed, the load of his body rocked the suspension backwards. He swung the door closed behind us, and the man in front started the engine.

There were no windows in the back of the van, and to look out of the front I had to turn my head ninety degrees to crane past the bald head of the driver.

Not knowing where I was going disturbed me, since I thought the direction would be the best guide to our ultimate fate. If I found us driving out of the city, or heading for less populous areas, it might be necessary to make some drastic plan. We headed north, passing out of London into the suburbs, but not into the countryside. In Totteridge, where the houses made the perceptible shift into mansions, we turned off the arterial roads into the long wide streets of private developments.

Eventually we pulled into the driveway of a large modern house with red-brick walls and shining white-trimmed windows. It was mounted on a small hill of rich brown earth, ornamental boulders and topiary, all fenced by hardwood pikes driven in around the base. Next to these domestic fortifications there was a wide drive at the level of the street. There was another white van parked in front of the triple-door garage, and a BMW 5 series next to it. Sitting between the two huge hunks of metal on the snow-sprinkled tarmac was a child's tricycle, the seat and handlebars dusted with white flakes. This last detail appeared so incongruous to me that I could not square it away with my fearful fantasies.

The large man waited for one of his companions to get out and open the door from outside. He ushered us up to the front door of the house and rang the bell. On the doorstep I smelt a whiff of chlorine. Through a window at the level of my ankles, I made out a peaceful oblong of blue tiles, lit from above with bright orange spots. A basement pool explained the building's odd elevation. My mind was reeling. I could not imagine why they had brought us to such a place. Through the hall window I could see a pot holding black umbrellas. The driver and his side passenger stood just behind the two of us, so close I could smell tobacco on the former, and feel the warmth of his breath in the still cold air. With the odd combination of the menacing and the mundane, and the heightened state of my emotions, the trip had begun to seem like a dream. The intercom buzzed, and he said no word of greeting, just his name like a password: 'Joe.' I wondered if we were safer or doomed, knowing his name. The house had an open-plan interior, and the lounge gave directly on to the hall. On the living-room sofa a large man in a cheap suit sat reading the *Sun*. An espresso steamed on the table in front of him. The floor was strewn with building blocks, and at the centre was a small boy of about five, wearing red dungarees. He was mixed race, a handsome little heartbreaker with huge almond eyes, a king enthroned in his own little heap of chaos. He looked up as we entered, but quickly judged us irrelevant, turning back to his bricks. Then the door at the end of the room opened and Lisa came out. She had another much younger white child balanced on her hip. The baby's sex was only discernible from the pink nappy. Lisa was rocking it and making short, professional shushing sounds as it grizzled away quietly with ambient discomfort. The sight of the child calmed me.

'Here, take this off my hands will you, Joe? Needs a change.'

She handed the baby to the enormous man, who sniffed its hindquarters, making the wrinkles and scars on his mug deepen with disgust. 'Phew! Fucking hell. Come on then, little monster, let's get you sorted.'

He carried the child through the doors into the kitchen, holding it at arms' length like an unexploded piece of ordnance. The volume of the crying increased with the distance from Lisa. You could tell it was a second child from the ease with which she ignored it.

'All right, James, Jessica. It's been time. Why don't you two come into my office?'

I was amazed by how much and how little she had changed. Her neat little body had spread comfortably into motherhood, but the quickness of her movements, the tough strut and the clipped speech of her youth had all remained, had even been intensified by the contrast with her round breasts and padded hips. Her face had not softened, though; there were lines around her mouth, from smiling or frowning. She was wearing a pair of grey tracksuit bottoms and a white T-shirt. As with everything in her life, she seemed to be handling the change in her circumstances by inhabiting her new role with aggressive openness. There was something about the crèche-like atmosphere of the living room, the sloppiness of her dress, and the way she had handed the baby to the thug who had escorted us that challenged the visitor to dare question or criticize. Nevertheless, the presence of the children helped ease away the last of my fears. From the way she had handled the baby I had the impression that Lisa was a good mother, and would have a policy of keeping the less pleasant aspects of her business out of sight of her children. We had nothing to fear, I surmised, at least whilst we were in the house.

Lisa ushered us into her office and closed the door behind us. The room held the smells of warm milk and bileless vomit. I checked the walls and shelves for any evidence of the fathers of the children, but there was nothing, no masculine presence in the room and no photographs on Lisa's impeccably tasteful desk, a carved slab of pine with elegantly curved edges. She walked around to the padded leather chair in front of windows that gave on to a snow-covered garden. Jessica and I sat in a more spartan pair of seats facing the desk.

'How can we help you, Lisa?' Jessica asked. She was impossible to read, her expression had not varied since the moment she had come out of my closet.

'I'm sorry for dragging the two of you out of bed.' Lisa spoke with a hint of amusement.

'Can I smoke?' Jessica asked.

'Nah. The kid's got asthma.'

'I didn't know that Francis faked the swap,' Jessica said. 'Nor did James. We got the letter this morning.'

Lisa laughed. 'I'm not pissed off about the fucking picture. I kept tabs on it for a few years. It got flogged on three or four times, then I lost track of it. Now it's somewhere in India, fuck knows where exactly. It's on someone's wall, making them feel big. I don't know if Francis was telling the truth in that letter, but I know it doesn't make a blind bit of difference if James drew it or Picasso. I could never tell the fucking difference anyway.'

'Are you working for Augustus White?' When Jessica asked her that, Lisa's usual impassivity parted for a moment to reveal a look somewhere between exasperation and tenderness. In that moment, I understood that the dynamic I had always ascribed to the two girls had been entirely wrong. When we were younger Jessica had seemed the driving force in their relationship, as I had read into her superior desirability a general dominance. Lisa had always seemed the satellite girl, caught up in the glamour, borrowing her shoes and dresses for big nights out, trusting Jessica's social identity over her own, at least when she was with us in our world. Here, away from the validating gaze of hundreds of young men and women whom Lisa had hardly noticed, but whom the rest of us had regarded as the final arbiters, the truth of their relationship was revealed. The look said: 'How little you understand of the world.'

'Augustus White was a mate of mine from London. He's a businessman, into mobile phones mostly, with a bit of dodgy stuff on the side, but I knew that's what you lot would think a gangster looked like. I would never have actually let any of you meet the buyer. I needed to put the shits up you enough to keep you all in check, especially Francis. There never was a big bad guy, not really. The bloke who bought it in the end was some poncy prick from Hampstead who fancied himself as a bit of a Bohemian hero. Doesn't matter now, anyway. At the end of the day it didn't work, did it?'

I let this little speech burrow into me in silence. Augustus White had been a fraud. I gazed out at the snow-laden garden. I could not blame Lisa for her deception. My first reaction was not anger, but a deep sense of shame at my foolishness. It told me that she was not culpable. She had been trying to protect her own interests, and trying to shield us all from ourselves in the process. Perhaps we had needed the mechanism of control as much as she had. In choosing the East End wide boy she had done no more than expose my ignorance of the world and my prejudice, like a hacker working into a computer through the programmer's own back door. Her trick was not really a betrayal, any more than a parent telling their child to behave for Father Christmas is a betrayal, but there was something more that made me afraid. Another thought had occurred to me, and I felt nauseous with the wondering.

'Did you really get four million for it, or did you get more?' I asked.

Her eyes narrowed. 'Now you're getting the idea, James. No, I didn't fuck you over. I could have, but I didn't. I had a good time with you guys. You were my friends.'

'Then why did you bring us here?' Jessica asked.

'Wanted to check you weren't going to do anything stupid, like freak out and go to the police, or go looking for the old painting. But you won't. You've both got too much to lose. That's what I like about the Oxbridge crowd. So many vested interests.'

'We're going to run away,' I said.

'No, you're not,' Lisa said calmly. 'Rich people suddenly disappearing makes waves. You're going to go to work at Lennard and Mavor on Monday, just the same as always.'

She did not deliver this as an order, but as a self-evident truth, like a mother telling her young son he was not going to become an astronaut. By making our plans seem ridiculous, she immediately cut me off from my little stash of defiance. Any words of resistance dried in my throat.

'You'll keep an eye on him for me, won't you, Jessica?'

'I will,' Jessica said.

Her answer was a blade and a balm at once. She was siding with Lisa, and any chance I might have had of setting my will against her evaporated instantly without Jessica's assistance. She was implicitly discarding our plans together, that had so recently been the foundation of my fondest wish. But she was also promising to see me again, to stay close enough to me to monitor me, and to take responsibility for my life.

Lisa looked at us both, and then clapped her knees,

pushing herself forward and out of her seat. 'Well, this was a treat. We got to do this every decade.'

'Your kids are beautiful,' Jessica said as she showed us out.

'Yeah,' she said, smiling for the first time, 'they are. Joe'll drop you wherever you want to go. No need to be a stranger. See you round, then.'

She closed the door on us and left us on the doorstep, where a few moments before I had stood in fear of my life.

'Where to?' Joe said, settling into the seat of the van like an affable cabbie. 'Back to Hoxton?'

'Yes, yes, take us back.' I jumped on his question, not wanting Jessica to have time to give her own address. I did not want us to part company before we had had a chance to talk over the morning's events. She did not protest, and sat with her eyes unfocused, her gaze bobbing away on an ocean of thought.

As the suspension bounced us back through the sleeping policemen of the suburbs, I thought of how many things I had misunderstood, and how those mis-impressions had been the mould in which I cast my life. I wondered how I would live without my fears to guide me.

What would Francis have thought? I could see him in my mind's eye, clapping his hands with delight at the deception, smiling as Lisa confirmed the esteem in which he had always held her. It was a habit of mine, to imagine his reactions to the things that happened to me, and though in this case it seemed appropriate to bring him to mind, I decided that in future I would try to suspend my internal critic. In plays and stories, the ghost always returns to see the conclusion of unfinished business, to see their murderer punished or their fate discovered. I wondered if Francis might be ready to quit the long corridors of my thoughts, now that the events which he had set in motion had finally rolled to a halt, a decade later in the snowy streets of suburban London. He had lived long for a personal ghost, his young clothes were starting to seem old-fashioned in photographs, the music he had liked no longer played on the radio. Even his youth and beauty themselves were becoming out of date for me, a charming irrelevance in the midst of adult business. It occurred to me that there was nothing in my world that would casually call him back, if I could stop invoking him myself. I could lay him to rest.

Joe dropped us on the pavement outside my apartment, and waved goodbye as he drove off, his meaty hand flapping behind the filthy windscreen. I waved back to my imagined assassin as he cornered out of sight, driving down towards Liverpool Street.

Jessica pulled out a cigarette, and I cupped my hands around her lighter to keep the flame. I spoke to her as she took the first deep drag, making the coal glow.

'You know, before we got the letter, I had a whole day planned for us. I was going to take us to a pub for lunch, then maybe go to Hyde Park and do something stupid like take a buggy ride or something . . .'

She exhaled smoke. 'Fine. I'd like that.'

'Do you need to call anyone? To tell them where you are, I mean?' I asked. She saw through my clumsy attempt to mask an enquiry about her boyfriend, and smiled.

'Not now. Later.'

The two of us set out together from Hoxton Square. Before we left, I went back up to my flat to get coats and jumpers. When I switched on my phone there were two missed calls from the office, and I ignored them. I fetched my hip flask out of my bedside drawer and brought it up for a pull. I thought better of it and, indulging my taste for the symbolic, I went into the bathroom and poured it down the sink. The loss was not great, as the kitchen still held a half-bottle, but it still gave me a little thrill. Jessica was waiting for me on the stairs; she looked up with a smile on her face. The snow had settled on the ground, and each second swelled with soft additions. We walked down the pavement, arm in arm, past the plate-glass windows of the restaurant on my corner. As a couple, we drew glances. I thought of how we must look to people eating lunch in the warm belly of the dining room: two lovers, or two friends, stepping out together to enjoy the weekend.

THE END

Author's Note

The events in this book are fictional. The characters are fictional. The places and the climbing, however, are based firmly in reality. I first encountered night climbing in the form of photographs shown to me by a friend in the quiet corridors of the Wren Library. They showed young men in old-fashioned clothes hundreds of feet in the air, clinging to the stonework. The photographs reminded me of drawings of comic book superheroes I had seen as a child, of Batman perched in silhouette on Gothic outcrops of masonry. I was amazed by how the activity seemed to prefigure urban free running, as well as stunts by such figures as the 'French Spiderman' Alain Roberts, who illegally scales the tallest buildings around the world.

In the time of relative political apathy at Cambridge, when few people seemed to feel passionately enough about any particular issue to make the kinds of protests or statements that characterized earlier generations of students, I loved the fact that the night climbers of the past had been guerrilla compaigners. In 1936, climbers mounted King's College Chapel and attached Ethiopian flags in support of the Emperor Haile Selassie's war with Mussolini. In the 1960s another generation risked their lives to install a Peace in Vietnam banner between the

Chapel's pinnacles, the highest points in the city. The climbers themselves went on to extraordinary things after graduation, sometimes tragic, sometimes heroic, but always somehow a little larger than life, stretching the world at the seams.

Excited by what I had seen, I began to look into the history of night climbing more deeply. In 1898, *The Roof Climber's Guide to Trinity* was published. This was the first manual which attempted to document the physical environment of the Cambridge rooftops. It was also intended as a satire on the pompous tone of the Alpine climbing manuals available to the Victorian climber. This was followed by Whipplesnaith's *The Night Climbers of Cambridge* in 1937, and Hederatus's *Cambridge Night Climbing* in 1970. All these books contained stories of each ascent, together with technical information on the routes and photographs of the climbers taken in the dead of night, or as dawn broke over the city. As the subjects of the photographs and the photographers would be on adjacent buildings, some of the pictures show extraordinary action scenes, such as a climber stranded on the bare face of a wall as policemen wait for him at the bottom, or captured in motion flying through the air between two vertiginous ledges.

College authorities used the earlier guides to help them defeat the climbers. Concerned for the safety of their young charges they sealed the routes up their buildings, installing spikes, moving lightning conductors and cementing hand holds. As a result the latest instalment, *Cambridge Nightclimbing*, is deliberately reticent when it comes to some of the more precise details – if there is only one way up a building, they will relate how to get to the bottom of it, and leave the rest up to imagination and ingenuity.

I made only one attempt at night climbing myself, but

I couldn't get further than a chimney pot about three feet from my point of embarkation. Most people say that fear recedes into the background the second you actually start on the climb. In my experience it intensifies. It took me half an hour to get both legs out of my friend's bedroom window on Neville's Court, and once it took another two hours to coax me back in by mobile phone.

Modern life is encroaching on the delicate ecosystem of the midnight climber. The Fitzwilliam Museum, which was long recommended as a good novice climb, was lost to would-be adventurers in a recent renovation, which covered the building with alarm systems. Clubs and pubs in the city stay open later, which means that the silent and empty hours in which nightclimbing thrives have been cut back. The first inspiration of young climbers, the need to get into their colleges at night after the doors had been locked, has also been removed; the curfews that until the mid 1970s ruled the lives of all undergraduates are a thing of the past in Cambridge.

Nevertheless, the night climbers are still going strong. They have always been an anonymous bunch (all their stories are written under pseudonyms, and discovery means being expelled from the University), but they love to tell stories. In a recent investigation by *The Times*, one ex-climber told that, when he went up to the roofs on a particularly fine night, he met two other parties of men on a similar expedition, and they wound up having a spontaneous party in the air above the streets. So if you visit Cambridge, and find yourself wandering through the streets in the evening, it might be worth having a look at the sky. If you're lucky, you might see one of the gargoyles move . . .